CORRUPT OBSESSION

POSSESSING VIOLET
BOOK 0.5

DINAH HARPER

COPYRIGHT

CONTENT WARNING

This is an erotic novel that depicts a toxic relationship between step-siblings. This book has been banned from numerous retailers so read at your own discretion.

For a full list of triggers, you can visit my website:

https://www.dinahharper.com/corrupt-obsession-content-warning

CHAPTER 1
JESSE

"Please keep an open mind," Mom pleaded.

Jesse stared out the car window without taking in the scenery. This was the fourth guy Mom dated that she had introduced him to. The others hadn't lasted, and he didn't have high hopes for Isaac either. The men seemed nice enough, but no one could measure up to his dad. He knew it and so did Mom, but that didn't stop her from trying to find someone. She waited a year after Dad died before she started dating. He thought it was too soon, but late at night he heard her sobbing and knew she hated being alone. That didn't mean he had to like these guys, though.

"Isaac's a firefighter," Mom said.

He glanced at her, interested despite himself. Firefighters were bad asses. Not as cool as his dad being in the Air Force, but at least Isaac's job was more interesting than Tom, the store manager or Brian, who worked the front desk at a dentist's office. Mom briefly dated another teacher, Mr. Harding. He taught History, spoke in a monotone, and had awful coffee breath. They'd all been duds.

"Isaac can take you to the station and show you the firetrucks."

His lip curled, but Mom didn't see, since he'd turned back to the window. He wasn't a kid. He wasn't going to be bribed into liking this guy by a trip to the station... Though, it would be cool to sit in the driver's seat of a firetruck or slide down a pole.

"How did his wife die?" he asked.

Mom hesitated long enough for him to glance at her.

"Mom?"

"She walked out."

"Walked out?" he repeated, unsure what that meant.

"He woke up and she was gone. She packed a bag and left him with their two-year-old daughter. That was eleven years ago."

He jerked forward, making his seatbelt lock. *"Daughter?"*

Mom gave him an innocent look. "What's wrong, son?"

"You can't date a guy who has a daughter!"

Mom's lips twitched. "Why not?"

"Girls are annoying! They're always giggling, talking, crying..." He glared as Mom snickered. "Find a guy with boys or no kids at all."

"Sorry, honey, that's not how this works."

"A girl," he said in disgust. So far, none of the men Mom dated had kids, so it hadn't even occurred to him that he could have a step sibling.

"Her name's Violet."

"What kind of name is that?"

"Violet's a lovely name. It's a beautiful color, flower, and a candy I'm quite fond of."

"Have you met her?"

"No, we're going to meet her for the first time together,"

Mom said as she turned into the park. "I'm sure she's sweet. You two are just a year apart. You should have a lot in common."

"She's a girl," he growled. "We won't have anything in common."

Mom pulled into a stall and killed the engine before she turned to him, her expression unusually grave. She reached out and cupped his chin. "It's been hard since your dad died."

Her eyes watered, but she smiled anyway, pushing through as she always did.

"That's an understatement. Losing your father is the hardest thing that's ever happened to us, and it's been rough. Some days I wasn't sure I could get out of bed, but you helped me pull through. You're your father's son, all right. Strong, brave, wise beyond your years. I'm not sure I would be intact without you, but..." She stroked his cheek. "I don't want you to shoulder more adult responsibilities than you already have. You shouldn't worry over things I need to take on. I want you to have a childhood and enjoy life, even though the world seems a little less bright without your dad in it."

He swallowed hard as his eyes stung with tears.

"We need to let people in." She tipped her head to the side. "I think Isaac's a good man and if you give him a chance, I think you'll see that for yourself. Isaac and I enjoy each other, and we want to see how you and Violet get along. If it doesn't work..." She shrugged. "Then it isn't meant to be. But Violet may surprise you. From the stories Isaac's told me, his daughter isn't like the girls you're used to."

He frowned. "What does that mean?"

"You'll have to see for yourself." Mom scanned the park and then lit up. "There they are."

He followed her gaze and saw a tall, burly man kicking a soccer ball across the grass to a girl who looked tiny from this distance.

"Ready?" Mom asked.

"Sure," he said with a shrug, and pushed open his door.

He put his hands in his pockets as they approached the pair. The girl darted forward with a speed that made him blink. He was impressed with her control of the ball, but Isaac was no slouch and blocked her attempt to score a goal. Isaac was nimble for such a large man. When he darted toward Violet's abandoned goal, she let out a banshee scream before she launched herself at her father's legs in an illegal tackle attempt. Isaac's laughter rang out as his daughter fought like her life depended on it.

"Oh, my," Mom murmured, clearly taken aback by what they were witnessing.

Isaac grabbed his daughter who had both arms wrapped around his right leg to prevent him from kicking and tucked her under his arm as he scored. Violet's angry bellow made several people who had been watching their antics chuckle.

"You *cheated*!" Violet shouted.

"So did you."

"I'm allowed because you're ten times bigger than me!"

Isaac was about to reply when he spotted them. He strode over, casually toting his daughter under one arm like she weighed no more than a toddler.

"Lynne," Isaac acknowledged with a smile before he extended his hand. "And you must be Jesse."

He nodded and shook Isaac's massive leathery hand.

"Dad!"

Violet's impatient tone made Isaac grin before he set his daughter on her feet. She flung back a mane of tangled black hair. Her eyes were a striking hazel that sparkled with enthusiasm. She had pale skin, rosy cheeks, and her lips were a deep red he would have suspected was lipstick if she wasn't dressed like a boy in long khaki shorts and a striped, green shirt that was two sizes too big. The girls he knew wouldn't be caught dead in such an outfit, but Violet didn't seem to care about her appearance. He hadn't decided what to make of her when she smiled at him. His lips curved in response, his bad mood and the reason they were here in the first place, forgotten.

Violet switched her attention to his mom. "You're Lynne?"

"It's great to finally meet you."

Violet didn't shake hands. Instead, she gave Mom an exuberant hug and exclaimed, "I've never met one of Dad's girlfriends before!"

Jesse blanched at that label. He knew Mom dated, but he'd never thought about the men she dated as her boyfriend. He resisted the urge to stick out his tongue and looked at Isaac, who was staring up at the sky with an embarrassed expression that made Jesse feel better.

"Is that so?" Mom said, clearly pleased with this information. "He didn't tell me that I'm the first woman he's introduced you to."

Isaac removed his hat to run his fingers through his hair. "I didn't think there was any need to mention..."

"I've been trying to set him up with these women from church *forever*," Violet interjected. "But he's so..."

"That's enough." Isaac clapped a hand over his daughter's mouth and asked, "Are you two hungry? There's a food truck nearby."

"That sounds great." Mom nudged Jesse to get his attention. "Son? Would you like something to eat?"

"Sure."

He was disconcerted when Violet broke away from her father and grasped Mom's hand as if they'd known each other for years instead of two minutes.

"Dad says you're a teacher," Violet said.

"Yes," Mom murmured. "I alternate between kindergarten and second grade."

"Why?"

"I don't like to teach the same thing every year, so I bounce back and forth. Do you like school?"

"Yes, I love English and History the most."

"What do you love about those subjects?"

Walking behind them, he could see their profiles. The raptness with which they stared at one another told him more was happening beneath their surface level conversation. Mom and Violet were engrossed in one another, while he and Isaac hadn't exchanged a word. Violet was clearly of his mother's ilk, a free spirit, while he was more like his father— disciplined, rigid, and preferred routines.

He glanced at Isaac, who strolled beside him. He was watching his mom and Violet's exchange with great interest. He expected Isaac to butter him up like the others had, but Isaac didn't ask him what he wanted to be when he grew up or who his favorite sports team was. Isaac didn't attempt to make any small talk, which simultaneously annoyed and eased his nerves over this uncomfortable meet up.

They ordered tacos and settled on a picnic table. Violet was more interested in watching their parents than eating.

She propped her chin on her hand and gazed at them with rapt attention. It was clear that as far as she was concerned, Isaac and his mother were meant for each other, but he wasn't so sure. He should be assessing Isaac, but his eyes kept returning to Violet's animated face. The way she looked at his mom with such longing made his stomach tighten.

"Jesse's a great soccer player," Mom shared.

Violet turned to him and sized him up. "You are?"

He shrugged, unsure why having her full attention made him feel funny. He talked to girls all the time. What made her different from all the rest?

"Let's play," Violet said, swinging her legs over the bench seat and leaping to her feet.

He glanced at Mom, who gave him an encouraging smile. By the time he started after her, Violet had crossed the field to retrieve the soccer ball and was making her way back to him. As she neared, he stopped and then braced when he realized she wasn't going to slow down. He grunted as she collided into him. He got a whiff of her hair, which smelled like strawberries.

"What do you think?" she whispered breathlessly, even though there was no one around.

"About what?"

She gave him an impatient look and jerked her chin in the direction of their parents. Was it his imagination, or had they moved closer to one another?

"Your mom's so nice."

Violet sounded awed.

"So ladylike and pretty." Violet cocked her head to the side as she watched them. "Dad's so happy. I've never seen him like this."

When he didn't comment, she looked up. Again, he felt

that odd stirring in his stomach. Had he eaten something bad from the taco truck? No, it was the way she was looking at him. Something about her made him nervous, which didn't make sense. Girls flocked to him. They passed him notes in class, asked him to be their boyfriend, and did a lot of annoying things to get his attention. That didn't make him uneasy, but the way Violet looked at him, dead on, without the coy, flirtatious shyness he'd come to expect made him sweat. She treated him like they'd grown up together, instead of being introduced half an hour ago.

"How are your eyes green?" he muttered. "They were brown a minute ago."

"They do that," she said dismissively and dropped the ball at their feet as she said, "What do you think about my dad?"

"I don't know anything about him," he said truthfully.

"He's a good guy." She pursed her lips before she admitted, "Though he can be strict."

"My dad was in the military. I doubt your dad is as strict as mine was."

"Oh." Her expression softened before she reached out and rubbed his arm. "I heard your dad died. That must have been hard."

It was the worst that ever happened to him, but Violet's presence made the pain ebb for the first time since it happened. "I'm okay."

She nodded, taking him at his word, and stepped away. He let out the breath he'd been holding and watched her impressive dribble. When she tried to kick the ball past him, he instinctively stopped it and saw her eyes narrow.

"That was a practice shot," she said quietly.

"Sorry," he said, and stepped back to give her a clear shot. "You want to try again?"

"No. Let's get straight to it."

That had an ominous ring to it. He got a preview of how she played and believed she wouldn't use the same tactics on him that she had on her father. He was wrong. She had some skill, but she was a casual player, unlike him. He scored three times and was about to shoot his fourth goal when she kicked him in the shin.

As he dropped to his knee, Violet made her first goal and let out a triumphant shout. Across the field, Mom was on her feet with a hand over her mouth. He wasn't sure, but he thought Isaac was grinning. He gritted his teeth as he got to his feet. He couldn't fight dirty like her, but he was stronger and quicker. If he was unable to best a girl a year younger than him, then he didn't deserve a spot on the team this year.

He skillfully avoided Violet's fouls and scored goal after goal. He was having the time of his life, while she became steadily more aggravated. When she lost her temper and swore at him, he was so shocked, he stopped in his tracks. Violet seized the opportunity to take the ball, but she didn't get more than two paces before he stole it back. Violet lost her temper and tried to punch him. He bobbed and weaved, slipping every one of her wild swings.

"Okay, I'm sorry," he said with a laugh and held his hands up in surrender.

"You're such a jerk face!" she shouted.

"It's not my fault you suck," he said, and instantly regretted his taunt when she lunged at him.

They tussled, rolling on the grass before he landed on his back with her on top of him. She planted her tiny fists on either side of his head as she loomed over him.

"You take that back!" she roared in his face.

Her face, filled with wrath, was just inches from his. Her

wild hair blocked out the rest of the world. Clumps of it brushed across his forehead and cheek. It was soft and smelled awesome. He should be trying to gain control of the situation before she slapped him, but he was too enthralled to defend himself. She was the wildest, most beautiful thing he had ever seen. Something inside of him stirred, roused by the girl warrior straddling him.

His life had been filled with so much death and loss. He had no other family aside from his mother. He thought it was them against the world, but he had a sudden image of Violet at his side. She was so vivid and filled with fire and fight. Life with her would be an adventure. The tight ball of dread in his stomach that had been there since he lost both grandfathers at the age of six suddenly disappeared.

Violet was shouting, but he couldn't hear anything over the sound of his heartbeat. When she was suddenly lifted off him, he reached out to pull her back before he came to his senses and realized Isaac had a hold of her.

"Damn it, Violet! That's too far," Isaac snapped before he strode away with her once again tucked under one arm.

Mom knelt beside him. "Are you all right?"

A little lightheaded, he stayed put and folded his hands on his stomach as he looked up at her. "Yeah."

She brushed back his sweaty hair. "You held your own against her for a time."

He heard the amusement in her tone. Under other circumstances, he would have been irritated, but he was too busy sifting through the odd feelings and ideas Violet had evoked.

"You did the right thing, taking the high road and not retaliating when she kicked you in the shin."

"It's not a big deal," he said and sat up.

Isaac had taken Violet far enough away that they couldn't hear what was being said. He cupped her chin as he spoke to her. His face was stern and very unhappy. Violet's bravado was gone, as if it had never been. As her father lectured her, she deflated and began to blink rapidly. He got to his feet, dusting grass off his clothes, and started toward them.

"Jesse," Mom said in warning, but that didn't stop him.

Isaac broke off as he approached and faced him, while Violet stayed as she was with her head bowed.

"I apologize for Violet's behavior. She has a hard time controlling her temper. We're working on it."

"She didn't hurt me."

"She tackled you."

"I play football."

Isaac's severe expression eased slightly, but he said, "Thank you for letting her off the hook, but she owes you an apology."

Before he could say that wasn't necessary, Violet pivoted to face him. The sight of her eyes filled with tears made his heart stutter. He'd seen many girls cry, but none of them made him want to drop to his knees and beg her not to.

"I'm sorry," Violet said, rubbing her eyes with the back of her hand. "I didn't mean to hurt you."

"You didn't," he said and reached for her without knowing what he wanted to do. Desperately uncomfortable and aware that Isaac and his mom were watching, he tugged on his shirt before he turned his hat backwards. "I'm sorry I said you sucked. You're better than some of the guys on my team."

Violet's mouth kicked up on one side, even as a tear slid

down her cheek. "Thanks." Her eyes flicked to Lynne. "When I play, I lose my head."

"She's competitive," Isaac said apologetically as he put an arm around Violet's slumped shoulders. "Since she's usually going up against grown men, we let her take any advantage she can get. I didn't know she wouldn't hold back when she's playing with kids her age."

"It doesn't bother me," Jesse said.

Isaac didn't smile, but the flash of approval in his eyes made him straighten a little, even though he didn't know how he felt about him just yet. He hadn't embarrassed Violet, as his father used to when teaching him a lesson. That told him a lot about the man. Though they hadn't had a one-on-one conversation, he found himself leaning toward Mom's opinion that Isaac was a good guy.

"I'm really sorry," Violet said, breath hitching suspiciously.

Jesse stiffened as more tears poured down her face. "It's fine," he said and would have stepped forward, but Mom moved first.

"It's okay, honey. Everything's fine," Mom soothed as she gave Violet a hug.

"I wanted everything to be perfect and I..." Violet hiccupped. "I ruined..."

"You didn't ruin a thing," Mom admonished. "Being passionate is a gift, we just need to know how to channel it and accept defeat gracefully." When Violet began to sob, Mom patted her back. "There's no reason to be upset. You didn't give Jesse a bloody nose or a black eye, which he's gotten from playing sports."

Violet raised her face from his mother's chest and looked at him with puffy eyes. "You're not mad?"

He shook his head.

Violet looked up at Lynne. "You aren't going to break up with my dad?"

"No, I'm not going to break up with your father," Mom said with a broad smile. "In fact, after meeting you, I think I like him even more than I already did."

Violet's eyes widened. Jesse was disconcerted to see that she'd somehow cried the green out of her eyes, and they were now brown again.

"Do you love him?" Violet asked.

"Violet!" Isaac said sharply and reached for his daughter, but Mom's response made Isaac freeze.

"I do."

Jesse's heart slammed against his ribcage. Mom hadn't told him she loved Isaac and from the look on his face, this was his first time hearing it as well. Violet looked like Christmas had come early. All of them were in various states of shock, while his mother calmly stroked Violet's hair.

"Love is a strange thing. It creeps up on you when you least expect it," Mom murmured.

"Are y'all getting married?"

"Violet."

Isaac's voice had lost all power. It was more of a croak.

"I don't know if your dad's in the same place as I am," Lynne said before she put her arm around Violet's shoulders. "I think you and I have given Jesse and your dad enough shocks for the day."

And with that, Mom and Violet strolled away, leaving him with Isaac. He waited until they were out of earshot before he spoke.

"Do you love her?" Jesse asked bluntly.

Isaac closed his eyes, tipped his head back, and stared up at the cloudless sky. His Adam's apple bobbed as he said,

"From the moment I laid eyes on her." He took a deep breath before he looked back at Jesse. "The only other woman I loved like this walked away."

"Mom won't walk. She's a military wife. She'll stick with you till death."

Isaac nodded, but he looked troubled rather than thrilled. They both knew their lives had been set on a different course. He matched Isaac's pace as they followed in Mom and Violet's wake.

"You did well with Violet. I think she scares most boys," Isaac said.

"I don't scare easy."

"I can see that." A pause and then, "I'm not trying to replace your dad or rush things with your mom. We can take this as slow as you need. You let me know if it's too much."

Though Isaac could be saying this to win brownie points, he suspected the man was as honest as his daughter. If he wasn't comfortable with the speed of everything, Isaac would give him time. Since his father died, it seemed that days inched along. There was nothing to look forward to. Nothing piqued his interest like before. Now, everything was moving at the speed of light. He'd come here to meet a guy his mom was dating, and within the hour, he was ninety-nine percent certain this guy would soon be his stepfather.

When they joined Violet and his mother in the parking lot, Mom gave him a searching look and touched his shoulder before she went to Isaac. When she lifted her face for a kiss, Jesse turned away and found Violet in front of him, her gaze fixed over his shoulder. He knew the moment they kissed, not because he heard anything, but because Violet jumped up and down and silently clapped.

He wasn't prepared for her to fling her arms around him. She hugged him the way Mom had when she got the news that Dad died. It was tight enough to hurt, but coming from her, he found he didn't mind.

"We have to keep them together," Violet said fervently.

When he didn't respond, she looked up. The tears were gone, and her warrior spirit was back, making her eyes shine.

"You want us to be together, don't you? A real family?" Violet asked, hands twisting in his shirt.

When he didn't answer, Violet's expression fell. When Isaac called her name, she stepped back. The loss of her body against his made that ball of dread come back. As she started toward her father, he couldn't help himself.

"Violet!"

She looked back.

"I do want that," he said.

She gave him a megawatt smile that made his chest flood with warmth. She ran to her dad, who tucked her against his side. Isaac climbed into a white pickup truck and held up his hand in farewell as they drove away.

"I'm sorry," Mom said as he dropped onto the passenger seat. "I wasn't planning to say that. It just came out. You must be overwhelmed. I know it's too soon, but—"

"It's okay."

"It is?"

"Yeah." He reclined his seat a little and tossed his arm over his eyes, which were burning. He wasn't sure why. "I get it."

Mom clutched his arm. "You do?"

"Isaac's exactly what you said he was, and Violet..."

"She's never had a mother," Mom said quickly. "She's been raised mostly by her father's friends and families from church, since Isaac has long work hours. She just needs some guidance—"

"She's perfect just the way she is."

"Aww, that's sweet of you to say." Mom lightly punched his arm. "Especially when you said girls are annoying, and you didn't think you'd have anything in common."

"You're right. She isn't like the girls I know, though she did cry at the end." He grimaced. "I hope she doesn't do that often."

Mom laughed as she started the engine and rolled down the windows. "Tears aren't always a bad thing. Sometimes, there are no words to express how you feel. The only thing you can do is cry."

He heard her sniffling and extended his free hand while the other arm stayed draped over his eyes. Mom grasped his hand and squeezed.

"I never thought I would feel like this again," Mom whispered.

He knew exactly how she felt because he felt the same. For the first time since Dad died, he was looking forward to something, and that something was seeing Violet again. Something about the way she'd looked at them, as if they were the answer to prayer, and they possessed something she desperately wanted, made him want to be everything for her that she would ever need.

With his father in the military, being an only child, and constantly on the move, loneliness was something he was very familiar with, and it was stamped all over Violet as well. The way she talked to him like they were on a team made his mouth curve. That hug she'd given him, he wished it had lasted longer. He wasn't sure what it was about her that had captivated him, but he wasn't going to examine it too closely. He was grateful for the break from the monotony, for something unexpected and intriguing to turn his life right-side up and bring color back to his world. He'd been trudging through life, but today he'd been offered an opportunity to rejoin the living, and he was going to take it.

CHAPTER 2
JESSE

5 MONTHS LATER

Isaac gripped Jesse's shoulder. "Are you ready?"

He looked up at Isaac and noticed that he had beads of sweat at his temple. He grinned and raised a brow. "Are you?"

"Of course," Isaac said gruffly as he smoothed a hand down the front of his suit. "I just wish we could have gotten hitched at the courthouse and avoided all this."

Isaac gestured to the church where their guests were taking their seats.

"Mom already did that with my dad. She wanted an official wedding this time around," Jesse reminded him, even though they'd heard her say it countless since Isaac proposed.

Isaac scanned the road. "They're late."

"Mom says women are supposed to be."

Isaac gave him an appraising look. "No nerves?"

"About what?"

"You aren't worried things will change once we're married?"

"No."

"What about the adoption?"

Mom and Isaac introduced the idea several days ago. Since they had no other relatives, Mom wanted to ensure he had family if anything happened to her. He didn't need Isaac to adopt him to know his stepfather would be there for him. Isaac was a man of his word, but they both knew it would give Mom peace of mind.

"Once you marry Mom, you'll become my dad. The adoption is just a formality," he said.

Isaac visibly relaxed. "I'm glad to hear that."

"But I'd like to keep my dad's name."

He was his father's legacy, the only insurance that the Sampson family name would continue.

Isaac nodded. "I expected that. You don't have to change your name. You're family whether you carry the Carr name or not."

He'd suspected Isaac wouldn't mind, but he was relieved to hear it, nonetheless. In five short months, he and Isaac developed a bond that rivaled the one he'd had with his father. The fact that he'd been given another strong father figure to guide him through life was a blessing.

"The only one who may fight you about keeping your name is Violet. She was set on all of us being Carr's," Isaac said with a grin. "But I know you can handle her."

"I'll talk to her."

Isaac gave him a considering look. "This has been a whirlwind and you two have taken everything in stride."

If only Isaac knew how much he and Violet had schemed to hurry along their nuptials. Mom didn't need to be convinced. She was in love with Isaac and, after losing his father, didn't want to waste any time. It was Isaac who needed to be prodded and coaxed. With the three of them on board, Isaac had no choice but to surrender, which he did by proposing two months ago.

Mom and Violet had taken over after that, resulting in this hasty wedding. Mom was happier than he'd ever seen her. It was patently clear that his mother hadn't loved his father the same way she did Isaac. Was it meant to be that his father passed so he and Mom could find Isaac and Violet? The four of them fit together like they were meant to be. Life, for the first time in a long time, felt right.

Isaac straightened. "There they are," he said as a minivan turned into the parking lot.

Isaac hurried forward. Jesse followed in his wake, adjusting his tie. The first suit he'd worn was for his dad's funeral. He was glad it was a happy occasion that made him don his second suit.

"Late enough to make an entrance, not late enough to be rude," Mom's friend Molly announced as she leapt out of the driver's seat and came around to the side door. Molly eyed Isaac. "Shouldn't you be inside? It's bad luck to see the bride before the wedding."

"I don't believe in that stuff," Isaac said impatiently and stepped forward to open the door himself.

"Okay, okay. Hold your horses."

Molly slid the door open and a second later, Isaac breathed, "Violet."

Jesse stepped to the side to get a look and felt his heart skip. Violet perched on the seat, a vision in a pale pink gown. Her wild hair had been drawn back from her face into some kind of fancy braid, aside from two spirals that framed her face. Mom had been teaching Violet girly stuff like how to dress and do her hair, but this was such a drastic transformation from the girl he'd come to know that he was momentarily dumbstruck.

Violet had an uncharacteristically bashful look on her face as she took Molly's hand and carefully stepped out of the van.

"You look..." Isaac cleared his throat. "You're growing up too fast, kiddo."

Violet flashed him a smile before she turned to help Mom out of the vehicle. Seeing his mom as a bride in a white gown and short veil made his chest tighten. Molly stood off to the side, capturing the moment with a camera as they took each other in.

"You two look so handsome," Mom gushed, grinning from ear to ear.

"And you..." Isaac shook his head, clearly at a loss for words.

Jesse understood completely. As Mom and Isaac leaned toward one another for a kiss, Violet made her way over to him.

"Do I look okay?" she whispered.

"Okay?" he echoed.

She tugged on her skirt. "No one's ever seen me in a dress before. I feel silly."

"You don't look silly," he reassured her. "You look..." Like Isaac, he struggled to come up with the words that would let her know she outshined every girl their age. "You're perfect."

Even as he inwardly castigated himself, Violet's face cleared.

"Really?"

"*Yes.*"

Violet gave him a giddy smile and patted his chest. "You look great."

He cleared his throat and eased away from her, worried she'd feel his heart racing. He thought he'd overcome those odd nerves he sometimes experienced around her, but for the first time in months, they were back.

"How's Dad?" she asked, glancing over her shoulder at their parents, who were having a moment.

"Nervous, but hanging in there," he said and then blurted, "You're wearing makeup?"

Violet jerked her head back around, eyes wide and startled. "You can tell?"

"Yes."

During their parent's whirlwind romance, they became best friends and were nearly inseparable. His favorite pastime was observing Violet, who wore her emotions on her sleeve. He'd come to know her face as well as his own and immediately picked up the subtle enhancements—her already long lashes were thicker, and her lips were a shiny, muted hue instead of her natural deep red.

"Don't tell Dad," Violet whispered.

"I think you'll get a pass today," he whispered back. "But if he does lecture you about it, blame Mom."

Violet's eyes danced with mischief. "Good thinking." Violet extended her foot so he could show off her fancy shoes. "Aren't they pretty?"

"Yes. And you painted your nails?"

"My first time ever! I got glitter nail polish." She wriggled her toes, so they sparkled in the sunshine.

"You two ready?"

Violet whirled and threw herself into her father's arms. "I'm so happy! I never thought this day would come."

Isaac kissed the top of her head. "Well, now that it's here, we don't want to waste a moment of it, do we?"

"No! Let's do this!"

Violet winked at Jesse before she grasped her father's hand and towed him up the stairs to the church, where everyone waited for them.

He went to Mom and grasped her hands. Thanks to a growth spurt, he was now taller than her.

"You were right to push for a wedding and not get married at the courthouse and rob us of seeing you like this."

Mom turned her face away. "I love you, son, but don't. I'm hanging on by a thread. Save it for after the ceremony, please. I'm going to bawl if you…"

He placed her hand on his arm and patted it. "Got it."

He heard the strains of a sweet melody as they climbed the steps. As they approached the open double doors, he saw Isaac and Violet reach the stage. She stepped to the left, while Isaac stepped to the right. When the music changed, everyone got to their feet. Mom's hand trembled on his arm as they made their way down the aisle.

It was a modest crowd who'd gathered to celebrate this day with them. After he placed Mom's hand in Isaac's, he stepped to his stepfather's side.

"We're gathered here today in celebration of Isaac Carr and Lynnette Sampson," Pastor Sonny began.

Jesse's gaze moved from Mom to Violet. She was so excited, the bouquet of flowers she held, shuddered. As the ceremony progressed, Violet's expressive face showed a kaleidoscope of emotions. When Isaac slid a ring on Mom's finger, Violet blinked back tears.

Violet had a hard, defiant shell that concealed the most fragile heart he had come across. Violet loved hard. Mom gave him the psychology behind it—that never having a mother and Isaac being physically and somewhat emotionally absent made Violet cling to him and Mom. She wanted them around all the time and fretted when they weren't together. That wouldn't be an issue anymore. Now, they would be together forever.

"I now pronounce you husband and wife. Isaac, you may now kiss the bride," Pastor Sonny announced.

The church exploded with whistles and cheers as Isaac dipped Mom for a dramatic kiss. Violet clapped so vigorously; petals littered the ground around her. When Isaac and Mom started down the aisle, he offered his arm to Violet. She took it and leaned into him.

"This is the best day of my life," she whispered.

As he looked down at her, he heard himself say, "Me too."

"ARE YOU *SURE* Y'ALL ARE GOING TO BE OKAY?" MOM ASKED.

"Yes," he and Violet stressed at the same time.

They'd debated about this for weeks. Mom and Isaac offered to make their honeymoon a family vacation, but he and Violet insisted they go on their own. Isaac had been surprised, but pleased, but Mom clearly didn't like the thought of leaving them behind.

"Mom, I just turned fifteen," he reminded her.

"So?"

He rolled his eyes. "You're just going for the weekend. The neighbors are watching out for us, and we can call 911."

"But..."

"Honey." Isaac wrapped his arm around her waist. "We have to go, or we'll miss the plane."

Mom gave in by throwing her arms around him and Violet and drawing them in for a tight hug. "You two are the best kids. I love you to pieces, you know that? Please be safe and if you need anything, call us. We can always come home and—"

Isaac covered Mom's mouth and carried her toward the door that led to the garage. "I'll try to keep her from calling you every hour. If you're going to throw a party, now's the time since the house is such a mess, we wouldn't know the difference—*ow*!"

He yanked his hand from Lynne's mouth.

"Don't listen to your father, kids!" Mom scolded. "Don't leave the stove on, and make sure the doors are locked before you go to sleep."

"Yes, Mom," he and Violet said dutifully as Isaac dragged her out the door.

"I love you!" Lynne cried.

"We love you more!"

"That's not possible!"

He and Violet watched from the doorway as Isaac placed Mom in the passenger seat. As the truck reversed out of the garage, their parents waved while Violet blew kisses until the door slowly came down.

"They actually left us," Violet said, stunned.

"Want to throw a party?"

She snickered as she closed the door to the garage and made a big show of locking it before she turned and surveyed their new house, filled with unwrapped furniture and stacked boxes. "Is this real life? Pinch me."

He tugged on that curl in front of her face that had been driving him crazy. "This is real, all right."

The last thing he expected was for her face to crumple.

"Vi? What's wrong?" he demanded.

When he drew her against him, she burst into tears.

"Did someone say something?" he demanded over the sound of her heart-wrenching sobs.

It had been a hectic day with their parents tying the knot, followed by a casual lunch reception, which finished just in time for Mom and Isaac to catch their flight. Violet hadn't seemed upset. On the contrary, she was so over the moon, she couldn't keep still. So, where was this coming from?

"Tell me what happened."

She shook her head.

He rubbed her back and was momentarily distracted by the soft, buttery material of her dress. "Come on. Talk to me. You know I hate when you cry."

"I just..." She twisted her hand in his shirt. "I'm..."

He ducked his head to hear her better and caught a whiff of something sweet and alluring. Violet had been experimenting with perfumes. This one was new and definitely his favorite.

"I'm scared."

Her confession brought his attention back to her weird breakdown. "Scared of what?"

She raised her tear-streaked face and tugged urgently on his shirt as she babbled, "I'm scared something's going to happen! I've never been so happy in my life. I kept thinking something was going to happen before they got married. They'd break up or someone would get into a car accident or..." She groaned and slumped against him. "I wake up every day, thinking this must be a dream. That I made you and Lynne up and—"

"Why can't this be real?"

"Because good things don't happen to me!"

He tugged on her braid, which was coming undone. "What do you mean, good things don't happen to you?"

Heartbroken green eyes searched his. "I wasn't enough for my mom to stay. Dad loves me, but he's never known what to do with me. He was relieved to drop me off with other families so he could go to work. I've never had a home or real friends, and then you and Lynne come along, and you're so great, and you actually like me and..." Fat tears slid down her cheeks. "I'm so scared something terrible's going to happen and this will all disappear."

He clasped her face between his hands. "Nothing is going to happen."

He saw the flash of anger on her face, so was prepared when she tried to jerk away.

"How do you know?" she snapped.

"Because I'm not going anywhere."

"But what if something happens between Mom and Dad?"

"Then we'll figure it out."

"It's not that simple."

"Yes, it is. You're just making it complicated."

She shoved at him. "I knew you wouldn't understand."

He clutched her shoulders and gripped so she would pay attention and stop fighting him. "I understand better than you think. You think you're the only one who's felt lost and lonely? Who thought you and Isaac were too good to be true?"

She went very still.

"Mom and I were miserable before you brought us back to life."

Her lower lip trembled. "Really?"

He gave her a little shake. *"Really."*

She sniffled and looked down. "I'm sorry. I'm having a hard time taking it all in. New mom, brother, *and* house?"

"We deserve it, Vi. Life hasn't been smooth sailing for any of us."

"I guess."

When she rubbed the back of her hand across her face, removing the last of her makeup, he slid an arm over her shoulders. "What time did you wake up this morning?"

"I couldn't sleep. I was too excited."

She didn't fight him as he led her down the hallway.

"And terrified something was going to happen?"

She hesitated before she shrugged. "Maybe."

"You're exhausted." Belatedly remembering her bedroom was still a disaster, he led her to his. "You should shower and get some rest."

Violet headed for his bed. "Sleep sounds good."

"You don't want...?" he began, but didn't bother to finish when she flopped on his bed in her fancy dress.

He eyed her for a moment before he picked up her foot to undo the strap of her heel. She struggled to sit up.

"Oh, I'm sorry," she began. "I can..."

"I got it," he said as her shoe clattered to the floor.

She propped herself on her elbows and watched as he took care of the other shoe as well.

He raised his brow when he saw the odd look on her face. "What?"

"Dad expects me to take care of myself. I'm not used to anyone treating me like a child."

"I'm not treating you like a child. I'm taking care of you. That's my job." When she frowned, he shared, "When my dad died, Mom was in shock. I had to feed her for a couple of days, even help her get dressed."

Violet's eyes widened.

"It's drummed into me to care for my family. I was brought up knowing when my dad wasn't around, I was the man of the house."

"I guess that's why Dad talks to you like you're an equal, even though you're only a year older than me," she mused and tipped her head to the side as she examined him. "Your dad must have been really special. I hear Mom say it all the time, that you're just like him."

Unconsciously, he mimicked his father's military stance and clasped his hands behind his back.

"You're the best brother a girl could ask for, Jesse Sampson."

Something about the way she said that made his throat thicken. He looked around for something to do, but he'd unpacked and arranged his room to his liking as soon as they moved in.

"Always taking care of everyone," Violet murmured as she settled back against the pillows. "Who takes care of you?"

He stiffened. "I take care of myself."

"Not anymore. You take care of me; I take care of you."

"I don't need anyone to take care of me."

"Yes, you do." She patted the empty space beside her. "Come lie down."

"What?"

"You may have gotten more sleep than me, but you're tired too."

"I'm okay."

Her eyes narrowed before she pouted and batted her wet eyelashes. "You're just going to leave me after I bawled my eyes out and confided my worst fears to you?"

He glared at her before he rolled his eyes and rounded the bed. When he stretched out beside her, she rolled into him. Her voluminous skirt flopped over his black slacks. He grumbled, even though her weight against him felt nice.

"I love you," she whispered.

He stopped breathing.

"I've said it to Mom, and she's said it to me, but you and I haven't... I just wanted you to know."

He couldn't speak past the obstruction in his throat, so he didn't say anything. Minutes passed. He stared at the ceiling and fought the pull of sleep but was just starting to drift off when she slapped his chest.

He jolted. "What was that for?"

"Aren't you going to say it back?" she demanded.

His mouth curved as he murmured, "I love you, Violet."

CHAPTER 3
JESSE

JESSE SNAGGED A SODA FROM A COOLER AND RETREATED TO THE shade. As he took a swig from the icy can, he took in the view. It was a beautiful summer day at the lake. Kids cannonballed off the pier under the watchful eye of their parents and the older kids who waited for their turn to ride one of the jet skis that someone had brought. The air was filled with gleeful screams, someone playing a guitar, and shouts from a football game.

He spotted Mom sitting on Isaac's lap near the grill. Isaac hadn't wanted to request time off from work to camp with church friends, but his smile said he was enjoying himself. Mom was a good influence on him. In the two years they'd been married, they had their fair share of disagreements, but they were happy.

"My turn!"

He followed the sound of Violet's voice and saw her wading through the water toward a group playing chicken. She stopped in front of Malcolm, a boy a year older than him. Malcolm leaned down to whisper something in her ear. Violet wore a one-piece bathing suit with shorts, but her back was completely exposed. Jesse's eyes narrowed as Malcolm's fingers brushed the base of her spine.

A second later, Malcolm sank beneath the surface, so Violet could hop on his shoulders. When Malcolm straightened, he reached up to steady Violet and took advantage of her position to grip her hips and smooth his hands down her legs. He playfully staggered, making Violet shriek and clutch at his head, the only thing available for her to hang onto. Malcom's broad smile said he was enjoying this a little too much for Jesse's liking.

He started forward as Malcolm and Violet faced off with Marissa, who was on Benny's shoulders. The guys moved forward so the girls could battle. Marissa was older and outweighed Violet by a good thirty pounds, but if he had to bet on either girl, his odds were on Violet. He was proven right less than five seconds later when Marissa toppled off Benny's shoulders and hit the water with a splash.

Violet did a celebratory shimmy as Marissa got back on Benny's shoulders. By the time he reached them, Violet had dethroned Marissa a second time.

Marissa sputtered as she came up for air. "Your sister's ruthless."

When he started to pass, Marissa grabbed his arm.

"You're taller than Benny. Maybe I can beat her if I'm on your shoulders."

He didn't answer her. His eyes were on Malcom. Instead of sinking into the water to let Violet off his shoulders, Malcolm coaxed Violet to slide down his front. Jesse's blood ran hot as Malcolm held Violet close while his hand moved over her bare back.

"Jesse?" Marissa prompted.

"Maybe later," he said shortly, and broke free of her to close in on his target.

"You want to ride with me on the jet ski?" Malcolm asked Violet.

"She's going with me," Jesse interjected.

Malcolm raised his head. Some of what he was feeling must have shown on his face because Malcolm immediately dropped his hand and eased back. "Hey, Jesse."

He grabbed the back of Violet's shorts and tugged her away from Malcolm.

"Violet knocked Marissa down twice," Malcolm shared.

"I saw," he said in a flat tone.

Malcolm held his gaze for a few seconds before he looked away. "I think I'll join the football game."

"You do that," Jesse said quietly.

As Malcolm headed toward the shore, Violet shaded her eyes with her hand and looked up at him. "Everything okay?"

He searched puzzled hazel eyes and knew she was oblivious to the liberties Malcolm had taken. As his gaze moved lower, his blood, already hot, went molten. From this angle, he could see down the front of her swimsuit. It took all his self-control to focus on her face and not the gentle swell of her breasts. The urge to go after Malcolm and put his fist in his face made him grind his teeth.

Violet cocked her head to the side. "Are you mad because I beat your girlfriend?"

"Ex-girlfriend," he growled and tugged on her strap. "I think you need to pull this up."

Violet stared at him. "Are you serious? I'm the most covered up girl here. I'm in a one piece *and* shorts. Did you not see Marissa's tangerine bikini? I was worried she was going to come out of her top when I pushed her in the water."

"I don't care what Marissa's wearing, I care what you're wearing. So, can you please…?" He tugged on the strap again.

"You're just as bad as Dad," she grumbled, though she did pull up her top so it covered her more adequately. "If it was up to you two, I'd still be shopping in the boy's department."

"That's not a bad idea," he said and grunted when she put her elbow in his stomach.

The days of Violet dressing like a tomboy were a distant memory. Though she still shied away from dresses, her clothes were now distinctly feminine. She dressed modestly, mostly to please Isaac, who looked pained when she wore anything too revealing.

"Are you really taking me on the jet ski?" Violet asked.

"Yeah, I'm next." He moved deeper into the water to flag down Logan, who was heading toward them.

"All yours," Logan said as he and his brother hopped off the jet ski.

He helped Violet on before he settled in front of her.

"You have to hold on to me," he instructed.

"Oh." She scooted forward and wrapped her arms around him. "Like this?"

"Tighter."

She attempted to crack his ribs as she tightened around him like a boa constrictor. "Like this?"

"Yup," he said in an even tone, and felt her arms tremble before she gave up and loosened her hold. "Ready?"

"Hold on."

He tried not to tense as she shifted around behind him to get comfortable. Plastered to his back as she was, he could feel the tiny, hard points of her nipples. Her thighs gripped him snugly. His hands tightened on the handlebars. The thought of her wrapped around Malcolm like this made his simmering temper go up a few notches. Over his dead body.

"Ready," Violet chirped.

He let out a long breath as he applied gentle pressure on the throttle. He glanced toward the shore and wasn't surprised to see Mom standing with her hands on hips. Isaac was reclined against the table, but made no motion to tell him he didn't have permission to take Violet for a ride. He held his hand up to reassure them that he would be safe before he headed out.

As they glided over the water, just the two of them, he relaxed. It had been a great weekend on the lake with friends and family. Summer was coming to a close. They would be back at school in two weeks. He was going into his junior year. Just two more years in Texas and then he would join the military. He stopped bringing it up because Mom tried to talk him out of it. She couldn't. He promised Dad he would follow in his footsteps. It was a done deal.

Violet smacked his stomach, disrupting his peace.

"Why are you driving like a grandpa?" she grumbled.

"I'm being safe."

"Come on, Jesse. How often do we ride jet skis? What if we don't do this again? We have this lake to ourselves. Let it rip."

"Mom would kill me."

"Mom isn't around."

He couldn't see her face, but he knew she was pouting. She lowered her voice to a tone she knew he couldn't resist.

"Please?"

"Just enjoy the moment, Vi."

"Maybe I should have gone with Malcolm," she muttered.

He craned his head around to look at her. "What did you say?"

She jutted out her chin. "You heard me. Why have all this horsepower if you aren't going to use it?"

She barely got the last word out before he gunned the throttle. The jet ski bucked beneath them. Violet let out a startled shriek, which immediately turned into a delighted whoop as they soared across the water.

"You're the best brother ever!" Violet screamed.

He grinned despite himself. Mom had tempered Violet's savage nature, but occasionally, her old recklessness made an appearance. It had gotten them in trouble countless times. He indulged her when he could so she wouldn't seek out trouble with a partner in crime who wouldn't have her back if things went south. Out of sight of anyone who would report back to their parents, he gave Violet the thrill ride she was seeking. He'd be damned if she asked Malcolm or any other guy for a ride.

As they made their way back to the pier, Violet squeezed him around his middle. "Can I drive?"

He hesitated. "You'll go slow?"

"Yes."

He didn't see it, but he knew she was rolling her eyes. "Fine."

He stopped so they could switch places. Once she was settled in front of him, he showed her the button for the throttle.

"Just apply a little pressure," he cautioned and bit back a curse when the jet ski jerked. "Vi!"

"I'm sorry." She giggled as she adjusted her grip until

they were gliding forward at an easy pace. "I'm sad we're leaving tomorrow. This has been so fun!"

"It has been," he said, as they approached their group of over forty people. "Dad's enjoying himself."

"He always does. I don't know why he puts up such a fight."

"He's a recovering workaholic. Old habits die hard."

"Marissa's waiting for you," Violet sang. "She's been changing her bikini twice a day. Have you noticed?"

"No."

Violet turned to give him an arch look. "Seriously? Each one she puts on is brighter than the last." Violet's voice dropped as she muttered, "And smaller. Her mom is so embarrassed."

He grunted. He dated Marissa for two weeks in sixth grade, and she had been trying to convince him to be her boyfriend again ever since. He liked her as a friend and did his best not to lead her on, but she made it clear to him and everyone else that she wanted more.

"Lara's also been trying to get your attention. Every time she sings, she looks right at you."

He'd noticed and started excusing himself or making sure he could duck behind someone until she was finished. Lara was pretty, sweet, and had the voice of an angel, but when she wasn't singing, she was painfully shy and had a stutter.

As he brushed Violet's wavy black hair out of his face, he smelled the soft floral scent of violets and rose. The already delicate fragrance was faint from her time in the water, but knowing Malcolm had probably caught a whiff of it reminded him what had pissed him off in the first place. He gripped her waist. "You want another ride, you come to me. I don't want you going with anyone else."

"Why?"

"Because I said so." As the image of her legs draped around Malcolm's face came back to him, he tacked on, "And no playing chicken again either, unless you're on my shoulders."

"You're so weird," she muttered.

"Promise me."

"Fine, *Dad*," she drawled as she killed the engine.

He flinched, not liking that label one bit, but before he could say anymore, she slipped off the jet ski into the water. He stayed put and helped two girls get on before he swam toward shore. Violet joined Mom and Isaac near the grill and made herself a plate of food. With his family occupied, he tracked down Malcolm, who was making his way back to camp. He waited until they had distanced themselves from everyone else before he called out to him.

"Malcolm!"

Malcolm stopped and looked over his shoulder. Jesse saw his brows come together in a frown before it was replaced with an easy smile.

"Hey, Jesse, what's up?"

"I just wanted to give you a friendly warning."

His pleasant tone belied the inferno in his chest. They were at a church event. He couldn't get in a fight with the worship leader's son, but he wasn't going to let what happened with Violet slide.

Malcolm blinked. "Warning?"

"Yeah." He kept a smile on his lips as he loosened his grip on his temper so the heat of it leaked into his eyes. "Touch Violet like that again, and we're going to have problems."

Malcom's mouth sagged before he said in affronted tones, "I'm sorry?"

"You think I didn't notice you slide her down your front or look down her bathing suit?"

He saw a flash of guilt before Malcolm puffed out his chest.

"I don't know what you're talking about."

"Yes, you do. If I see you do that with Violet or any other girl who doesn't know what you're up to, you won't like what happens. You got me?"

Malcolm stepped back with his hands up. "I'm sorry, man, if you thought I was being inappropriate. I never meant to—"

"See that you don't," he said shortly, and turned away before he ruined everyone's day by breaking every finger Malcom had dared lay on Violet's skin.

***

They gathered around the campfire to eat, play games, tell scary stories, and sing their hearts out. Everyone seemed to be having the time of their lives. Normally, Jesse would be in the thick of things, but he hadn't been able to shrug off his bad mood, even though Malcolm had taken his warning seriously and steered clear of Violet.

He sat on the fringes, observing, rather than engaging. His aggravation steadily increased as he watched his peers approach her throughout the night. He had never noticed how many male gazes followed her. Josiah tried to teach her how to play the guitar and spent a ridiculous amount of time positioning her fingers on the strings. He could tell within five minutes, Violet was over it, though she let Josiah talk to her for another ten before she excused herself.

When she made her way to the fire where they were making s'mores, Rhett offered her a toasted marshmallow on a stick. Violet reached for it eagerly, but her eyes flared when Rhett pulled it back and shook his head. Rhett said something. Violet grinned before she used her mouth to pull the marshmallow off the stick, which was obviously Rhett's condition for her to have it. Jesse was prepared to push Rhett into the fire, but Violet's laughter as she tried to eat the large marshmallow made him pause. He glanced around to see if Isaac or any other male thought what was happening was inappropriate, but everyone was in his spirits and oblivious to what was happening in their midst.

He raked his fingers through his hair. What the hell was wrong with him? His friends weren't trying to lure her out into the woods to have their wicked way with her. They were being overly attentive and toeing the line, but nothing that warranted getting their noses broken. That didn't mean he had to like it. She was too naive to see their true motives, but he did.

He was glad when Violet joined the women, but it wasn't long before some of the guys wandered over. When she rubbed her arms, Miles took off his hoodie and offered it to her. Violet blinked, clearly taken aback. Jesse shot to his feet, blood rushing in his ears. There was no way in hell Violet was going to wear some other guy's jacket. But Violet took the matter out of his hands when she politely declined Miles' offer and said she was turning in for the night.

Jesse fumed. He was angrier than he had ever been in his life. He was so pissed, if any of his friends came over to him, he wouldn't hesitate to put them in a chokehold. What was happening to him? He slumped in his chair and tipped his head back as he tried to calm himself. He'd always prided himself on being collected, pragmatic, and mature. He was none of those things right now. He wanted to ram his fists into something to take away the fire in his blood. Why? Because Violet almost put on another guy's hoodie.

He stared through the maze of branches to the twinkling stars and tried to think past the red haze. He had always been protective of Violet, but these amplified, aggressive emotions were dangerous. Since when did the sight of another guy touching her drive him into a killing rage?

He heard the chair beside him creak as someone dropped onto it before he heard, "You've been in a foul mood."

"So, you should leave me to it," he growled.

"Want to talk about it?" Logan asked cheerfully.

He clenched his jaw against the compulsion to fling his friend into the trees. "No."

"Do you want me to pray for you?"

He raised his head and glared at him. *"No."*

Logan drummed his fingers on the arm of the chair as he said, "Malcolm told me you threatened him."

He tensed. "It was a warning."

"You really think he was out of line with Violet?" Logan asked with a frown. "He's a good guy. It may have looked bad, but—"

"Don't, Logan. I saw him."

"He did it with others around. No one else thought what he did was inappropriate."

"No one was paying attention."

"Is Violet upset?"

"She had no idea what he was doing, but *I* do. I'm a guy."

Logan sighed and stretched his legs out. "I'm not saying you're wrong, but Violet's more than capable of standing up for herself if she was uncomfortable." He eyed Jesse's dark expression and sighed. "You have your work cut out for you if you police every interaction she has. What are you going to do, hide in the bushes when she goes on dates?"

"Who said she's going to date?"

Logan stared at him. "Are you hearing yourself?"

"She's fifteen!"

"Sixteen next month." Logan held up his hands when Jesse straightened. "Don't kill me. I remember the date because I went to her party last year." When Jesse switched his hostile gaze to the fire, Logan shook his head. "Violet's just a year younger than us. Why do you care if she dates? You do."

"She's a girl. It's not the same," he muttered.

"How old does she have to be before you let her date, Dad?" Logan dodged the soda can Jesse hurled at him. "Now, now. No littering or we'll get fined."

He surged to his feet. "I'm going to bed."

"You do that. I'll sit here a while and pray for you. I think you need it."

Jesse muttered under his breath and blinked rapidly so his eyes could adjust to the darkness as he made his way through the maze of tents. He unzipped his and fumbled with his phone for light before he flopped on his back, hands folded behind his head as he lay on his sleeping bag.

Logan's words knocked around in his head. Violet had never shown interest in his friends or talked about any boy in school that she had a crush on. She wasn't like other girls who wanted boyfriends to hold their hand during recess or make out behind the gym after school. Just the thought of her doing so made his blood pressure spike. Why did the thought of anyone asking her out make him feel like there was a demon clawing his insides, trying to get free?

Someone tugged on the zipper. "Jesse?"

He raised his head. "Violet?"

"I think Tina's getting a cold. Is anyone in there with you?"

"No."

He sat up and unzipped the tent. Violet crawled in, the tiny flashlight on her necklace revealing what she was wearing.

He grabbed a handful of the shirt that was four sizes too big for her. "Isn't this mine?"

"Yup," she said, supremely unconcerned, as she secured the tent and turned to examine his sparse setup. "Why is your tent so small? Or is it just that you're so big?"

"Just be grateful I have room, and you aren't being eaten alive by mosquitoes," he said testily as he unfolded his sleeping bag for her.

"Tina's been coughing nonstop. I don't want to get sick."

As Violet crawled around on all fours to spread out the sleeping bag, her shorts shifted, showing a flash of bright blue underwear. He resumed his position, flat on his back with his hands behind his head. Violet moved his backpack and rearranged things to her liking before she flopped beside him.

"Ouch."

He snickered. "Sorry, I didn't bring another sleeping bag."

She shifted. "I feel a stick in my back."

He closed his eyes as she fussed around. The flashlight on her neck swung, lighting up his eyelids briefly before she landed heavily beside him. He heard a click as she turned off the light on her neck.

"I should have grabbed my sleeping bag before I left,

but I didn't want Tina to feel worse than she already did. It's just for one night, right?"

When he didn't speak, she nudged him.

"Are you up?"

"Unfortunately."

"Why are you so crabby? Mom asked me if something happened. What's going on with you?"

"Nothing."

He could feel her eyes on him, though he knew she could see very little. The only illumination came from the distant fire, which penetrated the thin material of his tent.

"Did I do something?" she asked as she nestled against his side

"No," he said gruffly.

"Why are you so tense?" she complained, prodding his flexed arm.

He made a concentrated effort to relax.

"Tell me what's bothering you," she ordered, smacking his chest.

"Nothing's bothering me." He was very aware of her hand on his heart, which was picking up speed.

"Siblings aren't supposed to keep secrets from each other. They're supposed to tell each other everything."

He opened his mouth to say they weren't real siblings, but the words died on his tongue as the truth slammed into him. He didn't want her wearing some other guy's clothes, didn't want anyone arranging her fingers on guitar strings or trying to feed her because he saw her as his. She was his to touch and provide for, and these guys were encroaching on his territory, they just didn't know it.

"You know you can tell me anything, right?" Violet asked.

He jerked. "What?"

"About why you're angry." She peered at his face in the meager light. "Seriously, what's going on with you? You're acting so weird."

"It's nothing," he croaked.

"We used to be so close."

Violet sounded hurt.

"We're still close. You're practically on top of me," he muttered in a disgruntled tone, hoping and dreading that she would take the hint and give him some space. He was dying here. He stopped breathing when she propped her knee on his thigh.

"And we're staying like this until you confide in me," she declared.

"There's nothing to confide. I've just got a lot on my mind."

A pause and then, "You're thinking about school, aren't you?"

"I'm thinking about sports."

"Do you think about anything else?" she asked in a disgusted tone.

"No," he lied.

"What's there to worry about? You're always one of the best players on the team, no matter what you play."

"I don't want to take anything for granted."

Just as he anticipated, she immediately lost interest and yawned.

"You sure you aren't mad?" she asked sleepily.

"Yes."

She sighed. "If you weren't a guy, I'd think you were on your period. You're so moody."

He tunneled his fingers into her hair and massaged her scalp. "Go to sleep, brat."

"*You're* a brat," she countered fiercely before she went boneless. "That feels good."

He kept up the head massage until she drifted to sleep. He lay there, mind racing, as her familiar scent teased his senses. From the moment they met, he instinctively knew she was integral to his future. And he was right. Her existence grounded him, brought color back into his world, and gave him direction, purpose, and joy. He knew he loved her but had never acknowledged that his feelings extended beyond being brotherly until the sight of Malcolm's hands on her triggered violent, primitive instincts he hadn't even known he possessed.

He didn't want her legs draped over Malcolm's shoulders, he wanted them on his. And that look he had down her swimsuit... The image of her breasts kept flashing in his mind at the worst times—during prayer, while he was talking to Mom... It was wrong on every level, but the more he tried to suppress his fantasies, the more lecherous they became. Part of his anger was directed at himself for viewing her like Malcolm and the others. He tried to keep his thoughts pure—to see her as a sexless friend or stepsibling, but now that the blinders were off, his body reacted with a vengeance.

When his dick hardened in response to her nearness, horror speared his gut. He closed his eyes and tried to think of awful things to make it go away. He conjured up the day his dad died and the phone call that made Mom drop to her knees and scream in a way he would never forget. The normal sucker punch he received when he thought back to that day was a mere finger flick with Violet pressed against him. He thought of natural disasters, a car accident they passed on their way here, and his grandmother in her rocking chair, knitting.

It wasn't working. It was getting worse. He began to sweat, and it had nothing to do with the temperature. He tried to shift away but froze when she stirred. The last thing he needed was for her to notice his tented crotch. She would freak out, and rightly so. Here he was, pissed at his friends for shooting their shot, yet he lay beside her with a throbbing cock. Violet slept soundly because she trusted him. He wasn't going to break that trust by relieving himself while she lay beside him.

But his mind latched onto the idea and played out different scenarios in his head. His dick got so hard, it became painful. Gently, but firmly, he extracted himself from her. She made unhappy, annoyed sounds, but didn't wake. Slowly, he unzipped the tent so he wouldn't make too much noise and draw attention to himself. When he stepped outside, he took a deep breath of the cool night air before he strolled away from the congregation of tents, trucks, and RV's. He was relieved no one called out to him.

There was just enough light for him not to trip or twist his ankle as he navigated through the trees. He tried to banish the erotic fantasies by humming one of the worship songs they sang around the campfire not even an hour ago, but his mind fixated on what Violet would have done if she discovered his hard on. If her knee propped on his thigh brushed against it, would she have freaked out? He had no idea how much she actually knew about sex, but what if she shocked the hell out of him and grabbed it? Explored and pleasured him?

He stopped in his tracks and reached into his pants to grip his dick, which was leaking precum. He bit back a groan, braced his hand on a tree, and prayed he would hear if anyone approached before they saw what he was doing.

He bowed his head and let the forbidden floodgates

open. Images of Violet doing things to him and him doing things to her made him shudder. God, this was wrong, but he couldn't stop. *She's not really my sister,* he reminded himself as he climaxed.

"Shit," he hissed as he sprayed his cum over the trunk of the tree.

As the awful tension drained away, he hastily tucked himself in his pants and caught his breath. Guilt dulled the pleasure coursing through him. If anyone knew what he'd done... He straightened and peered through the darkness. But no one did. And Violet was clueless. No harm done.

He started back to camp and was relieved not to cross paths with anyone. He unzipped the tent and waited for Violet to stir. When she didn't, he crawled in beside her and turned on his side, facing away from her.

He took a deep breath and caught a whiff of his cum mixing with her delicate scent. He should have washed his hands. He should have slept in the SUV. He shouldn't have come back here. He should... Before he could leave, she fit her body to his back, spooning him and draping her arm over his middle. He clenched his jaw and closed his eyes. He'd already come. He should be okay for the rest of the night.

HE WOKE ON HIS BACK WITH VIOLET'S HAIR TICKLING HIS NOSE and her knee once again inches from his aching cock, which was hard enough to use as a hammer. Groggy and horny, he wasn't as gentle moving her off him as he'd been last night.

"Wus going on?" she moaned.

Her raspy tone made his hard on worse. He tore out of the tent to discover the sun was just coming up. He wasn't pleased to see a handful of adults, including Isaac, standing around the dying fire. Isaac straightened like he wanted to talk to him. Jesse slashed his hand through the air and turned in the opposite direction. He hoped Isaac thought he had to take a leak. He did, but he also had to take care of his throbbing dick before he faced anyone.

Being half awake dulled the shame of jacking off to Violet again. It didn't take much for him to blow his load, not when he had the pleasure of moving her dead weight off him and her scent was imbedded in his clothes. Her skin was so soft. Why did it feel so different from his own? If he ever had the opportunity to put his mouth on her...

He tipped his head back and let out a moan that came out louder than he intended. The shock of it ruined what would have been one of the best orgasms he'd ever had. He had just enough time to piss and put himself away before someone called his name.

He hoped he didn't look like the pervert he felt he was as he faced Isaac. "Morning."

"Morning." Isaac cocked his head to the side and gave him a considering look. "Are you okay?"

"Yup."

"Mom said you weren't yourself yesterday."

"I'm fine."

That reassurance was enough for Isaac, who turned back to camp. "We could use your help loading up."

"Sure." They reached the clearing when he decided to disclose, "Violet's in my tent."

He watched Isaac out of the corner of his eye, curious if his stepfather would sense that something was amiss. He'd seen straight through Malcolm and his friends yesterday. Would Isaac sense his feelings toward Violet had changed?

Isaac's brows drew together. "I thought she was sharing a tent with Tina."

"Tina was coughing so Violet bailed and came to me."

Isaac nodded and clapped him on the shoulder. "Good. Let's get to work."

He blew out a breath before he fixed a smile on his face and greeted Pastor Sonny.

THEY WERE ABOUT FIFTEEN MINUTES FROM HOME. THE SUN WAS setting, Isaac was behind the wheel, and the open windows let cool air circulate through the cab. Mom and Violet fell asleep about a half hour ago. The only sound in the SUV was the whistling wind and country tunes on the radio.

He spent the morning helping the men load trucks and trailers with camping equipment until he spotted Violet trying to take down his tent. When he rushed over, she gave him a sheepish smile as she gestured to the mess she'd made.

"I wanted to help, but I have no idea how..."

"No problem. I got it," he said, and knelt to pull out a stake anchoring the tent to the ground.

"Thanks for letting me invade your space."

When she groaned, he glanced back and saw her stretch. His shirt lifted to show her tiny gray shorts.

"Anytime," he rasped and turned back to his task.

"Did I dream it, or did you leave the tent several times?"

He fumbled with a pole. "I had to take a leak."

"Hmm."

His head jerked up. "What's *hmm* mean?"

The look she was giving him made him break out in a cold sweat. She couldn't know...

"I thought you might have rendezvoused with Lara or Marissa."

She was so far off base that he gawked at her before he shook his head. "No."

"They were hoping you would ask one of them out before we started school."

"I'm not interested in them."

"Aha! But you are interested in someone?" she asked with great interest.

When he realized he'd been staring at her mouth for a few seconds, he forced himself to look down at what he was doing. He cleared his throat. "I'm not interested in anyone."

"I'm going to find out at some point. You won't be able to hide it from me!" she called over her shoulder as she headed to the bathroom.

He worked until Mom forced him to take a break and eat something.

"You seem troubled, son."

He hadn't been able to meet her eyes as he reassured her that he was fine, just tired and ready to go home. If she only knew... He didn't bother telling Mom that Violet slept in his tent. It wouldn't occur to her that anything inappropriate would happen because she saw Violet as her blood daughter. But she wasn't. And he wasn't truly her brother.

He glanced at Violet who slumped against the door, fast asleep. He considered offering his hoodie for her to use as a pillow, but saw they were already in their neighborhood. As the SUV went over a bump, her breasts bounced. He quickly looked away, inwardly cursing. He was so screwed.

Now that the paper-thin platonic wall had disintegrated, it was impossible to switch his mind back to seeing her as a sibling. Thankfully, only he and God knew that he'd crossed a mental boundary. At least he hadn't done something monumentally stupid like jack off in the tent or cop a feel. He wasn't *that* far gone. He had to find a way to act normal around her because it wouldn't take long for her to notice he was acting different. They were extremely close, and he didn't want to risk ruining their relationship by exposing his feelings or introducing things she wasn't ready for or interested in if she truly saw him as a brother.

He straightened as Isaac pulled into the garage beside Mom's SUV. Neither Mom nor Violet stirred as the garage door came down.

"We can unload tomorrow," Isaac said as he hopped out of the SUV and eyed his sleeping wife. "You got Vi?"

His stomach clenched. "Yeah."

Mom and Violet were heavy sleepers. He had been carrying Violet to bed or cars or wherever she happened to fall asleep ever since their parents got together. This was nothing out of the ordinary. Or, it hadn't been until he realized staring at her too long could make him hard.

He got out of the SUV and came around to Violet's side. Dad draped Mom over his shoulder. He used the same hold on Violet and followed Dad into the house, detouring to Violet's bedroom while Dad continued down the hallway to the master bedroom.

He hit the light switch with his elbow, illuminating Violet's pastel bedroom. He flicked back her covers before he gently deposited her in bed. She smiled as she sank into the plethora of pillows.

"You're the best," she murmured with her eyes closed.

He mock scowled. "You made me carry you when you could have walked?"

"Umm hmm."

"Like I said, you're a brat," he said, trying to sound irritated as he brushed her tangled hair away from her face.

"But you love me, anyway, don't you?"

His hand stilled before he retracted it.

Her brows bunched together. "Jesse?"

"You know I do," he said gruffly.

She sighed as she turned on her side and burrowed into her pillows. "I love you, too."

"Sleep tight," he said before he turned off the light and went through their connecting Jack and Jill bathroom to get to his room. He flopped on the bed and stared at the shadowed ceiling as he came to terms with the fact that his life had just turned upside down.

CHAPTER 4
JESSE

4 MONTHS LATER

Jesse lay in bed with Violet's panties wrapped around his cock. He snagged it from her hamper before he joined the family for dinner.

A few months ago, he stumbled across Violet's underwear that she'd dropped after her shower. He didn't kick it under the counter or discreetly toss it into her hamper. No, he'd picked it up and proceeded to jack off in the sink.

Taking her underwear had become a habit. Every couple of days, he stole another. His unhealthy fetish went into overdrive when Mom took Violet shopping for her sixteenth birthday and bought her an array of underwear in different styles and patterns.

He stroked his cock but couldn't bring himself to climax. He brought her underwear to his mouth and gnawed on the crotch, whining like a dog, desperate for more of her taste, but he'd sucked it clean. He knew it was sick. He knew it was wrong, but he couldn't stop. Four months ago, he'd been a normal, happy, healthy teen, but that camping trip changed everything. He wished he'd remained ignorant of his feelings and the blinders had stayed on. Guys who thought it was shitty to be in the friend zone had no idea what utter hell it was to have the love of their life see them as their brother.

How was he supposed to regulate his emotions when his days started and ended with her? He woke to the sight of her brushing her teeth or doing her hair in their shared bathroom. Before she went to bed, she usually sought him out for a hug. He started giving her side hugs so she wouldn't know the effect she was having on his body. Her signature scent of violets and rose lingered in his room, car, and on the shirts and hoodies she borrowed. They drove to and from school together and hung out with the same people. The only time he wasn't with her was during class or practice. He had no respite from her and the worst part was, he didn't want one. He was a glutton for this exquisite torture.

His friends had been ribbing him for dismissing every girl who flirted with him. If only they knew the girl he wanted was the same one they did. None of his friends dared ask Violet out, but he knew it was coming. It was just a matter of time. And when it did, he had no idea how he was going to cope.

Violet had blossomed into a girl that would draw the eye of any straight male, even if she wasn't their type. Thankfully, his reputation of being an overprotective brother and Violet being known as a good, Christian girl kept most boys at bay. She was also studious and intro-verted and shied away from the spotlight. He was grateful she didn't try out for cheerleading. There was no way he would have been able to focus with hundreds of guys ogling her in that tiny uniform.

He tossed his arm over his face and blew out a frustrated breath. His body raged 24/7, his hormones whipped into a frenzy by her constant presence. Everything she did, however innocent, his mind interpreted as sexual. At dinner, Violet had a glass of eggnog. When some of it dribbled down her chin, it looked so much like cum that he'd lost touch with reality and reached under the table to grip his hardening cock before he remembered where he was.

When they were watching TV, she started doing these crazy yoga stretches in front of him. Thankfully, Mom called Violet to the dining table to help with crafts for her kindergarteners. He retreated to his room, only for Violet to ask him to get something out of storage. She barged in a second time because she needed help with her math homework. He tried to distract himself with a book and then a movie. He tried to seek refuge in sleep. Nothing worked. When everyone finally retried, he unearthed his most recent acquisition, but even her underwear couldn't get him off.

He jumped out of bed and pulled on sweats before he padded into the bathroom. He flicked on the light and splashed his face with cold water to snap himself out of this awful frenzy. He was beating his dick so often, he considered asking his friends how often they did it. Would they guess that his constant state of arousal was because of Violet? He couldn't risk anyone making that connection, so he kept it to himself.

He scanned the vanity for something of hers that would get him off, but there were just hair ties, bobby pins, and other things that did nothing for him. He winced as his dick pulsed, begging for release. He eyed her towel and leaned over to smell it. There was an earthy scent mixed with her sweet pea body wash. He wrapped the damp towel around him and began to thrust. A minute later, he let out a frustrated hiss. It wasn't enough!

As he began to open her drawers, desperately looking for something of hers that would aid him, he realized how much noise he was making. He eyed the door that led into Violet's room and pressed his ear to it. Silence.

A wicked idea formed that was so provocative, his cock wept in anticipation. His heart thudded in his ears. As he reached for the door handle, the magnitude of what he was about to do hit him full force. Fantasizing about Violet was one thing, stealing her underwear was another, but sneaking into her room in the middle of the night?

I'm just going to make sure I didn't wake her, he told himself. But even as he turned the doorknob, he knew that wasn't true.

Her door wasn't locked. There was no need to since they trusted one another and had a double knock policy that prevented any awkward situations.

He turned off the bathroom light and let the door swing open. He waited for a gasp or the sound of Violet sleepily asking if something was wrong, but nothing happened. He stood there for a full minute, warring internally, before he stepped out of the shadows.

He cursed the colorful Christmas lights that Mom and Violet had strung around her room for the holidays. If Violet opened her eyes, there was nowhere to hide. She tended to be a heavy sleeper, but there was always a chance that she could wake like she had when he left the tent to jerk off.

He approached the bed cautiously, blood rushing through his veins, making his skin itchy and hot. His ears were pulsing, and a trickle of sweat slid down his spine. This was dangerous—the riskiest thing he'd done thus far.

If he was caught, the results could be catastrophic. That possibility should have made him leave, but his need was too great. He couldn't think straight.

He held his breath as he took her in. Violet lay on her side facing him. She wore a pink long sleeve shirt with her hands stacked beneath her cheek. His mouth quirked. She was adorable. He listened to the rhythm of her deep, even breaths and found himself matching her. Amazingly, his clamoring demons began to settle. Maybe being near her was enough, and he wouldn't need to compromise his morals by...

Violet let out a little moan before she flipped to her back. The colorful Christmas lights gilded her face, highlighting her full lips, which were slightly parted. He focused on her rising and falling chest. It was clear she wasn't wearing a bra. Her nipples were hard and pointed straight to the ceiling.

Even as he called himself every vile name he could think of, he sank his hand into his sweats and began to stroke himself. It didn't take long. Being in her room and seeing her face instead of conjuring it in his mind sent him soaring over the edge. *I'm going to hell,* he thought as his climax hit. He bit his lip to stop his moan and staggered at the sheer intensity of it. He put his hand out to brace himself before he realized he would jostle the bed and wake her. Terror made him light on his feet. Swiftly, he righted himself and backed into the bathroom without taking his eyes from her. He closed the door and waited several seconds to make sure he was in the clear before he flipped on the light.

Chest heaving, he stared at the closed door, unable to believe what he'd just done. He'd just crossed another line, one that could put him behind bars. Cursing, he stripped off his shirt, sweats, and ruined underwear and stepped into the tub. He tipped his face up to the hot spray. His behavior was escalating at an alarming rate. He was scaring himself.

Should he get help? The thought of broaching such a topic with Isaac or his mom made him ill. They wouldn't understand. What if they told Violet? That sent a bolt of panic through him. He didn't want to destroy what they had. He would rather have her platonic love and affection than have her look at him with pity or, worse, have her distance herself because she didn't feel the same.

Sometimes when she looked at him, he thought he saw something more, but he wouldn't act unless he was one hundred percent sure, and he wasn't. Unrequited love had to be one of the most excruciating human experiences. In church, they discussed love like it was this gentle, peaceful emotion that aligned your life and made you whole. Love was driving him demented. It was a cruel, ruthless master that drove him to do all sorts of twisted, depraved things. Love was an incessant hunger, a thorn burrowing ever deeper in his heart. His love had no bounds—no line he wouldn't cross, nothing he wouldn't dare for a few hours of peace from the all-consuming pain. Several months ago, his behavior would have been abhorrent. Now, he was creeping into her room and jacking off like a pervert. What next?

But you didn't get caught. She didn't wake, and now you can finally sleep, he reasoned with himself. At least he hadn't touched her... The thought of putting his hand on her pert breast made his cock twitch. His inner sicko urged him to go back to her room for one more hit. *It's late. The chances of her waking are slim. One more look and you'll never do it again.*

He cut off the water with a vicious twist and wished he could shut off the despicable thoughts running through his mind as easily. His father had drummed into him the importance of discipline, integrity, and honor. All of that had fallen to the wayside. He didn't know who he was anymore. All he could think about was her. Being in constant proximity to someone he was in love with and who was completely oblivious was like being in purgatory. He was forever burning, in agony, and he was starting to lose it.

He wrapped a towel around his waist and slicked back his hair. Now that his mind wasn't clouded by lust, the answer was obvious. If he couldn't have the girl he wanted, he had to find another. Even though the thought was distasteful, what would be even worse is if desperation caused him to do something unforgivable that ruined their relationship. He had to redirect his fixation for both their sakes. It was the only sane solution.

When he got into bed, he closed his eyes and tried to ignore the quiet, insidious voice that fanned the flame of dark desires he was desperately trying to keep at bay.

CHAPTER 5
VIOLET

Violet sung along to the upbeat playlist she created to keep her motivated when she had to cook, clean, or do laundry. Her clean clothes pile that she'd ignored for almost two weeks was driving Lynne crazy, so she'd finally given in and was folding and sorting.

She paused frequently to check her group texts. Her nerdy friends were asking if anyone had finished a project that was due next month, while her girlfriends gossiped about crushes and boyfriends. The group chat she was in with Jesse and their mutual friends asked if they wanted to go to the movies on Friday. Jesse hadn't responded. She could hear the TV going in the living room and the low rumble of Jesse and Dad's voices. Since it was Wednesday, there was no rush for him to answer, but she suspected he would say yes.

She hung her tops and jackets in the closet before she carried neat stacks of clothes to her drawers. As she surveyed her underwear, she frowned. She walked around the bed and looked under it to make sure she hadn't missed any stray clothing before she went to her hamper and dug around.

It was the strangest thing… Certain panties had an uncanny habit of disappearing during a wash cycle and reappearing during the next. It was hard to be certain since she didn't do laundry consistently, but sometimes she'd wash a specific pair for an outfit and when the day came, she couldn't find them. The panties always magically reappeared at some point, but sometimes she felt like someone was pranking her. But why would anyone take her underwear? Even stranger, why would they fold and put them back after using them?

A series of chimes on her phone distracted her from her bizarre underwear problem. *Vi, what's going on with you and Tobias? Allison said she saw him pass you a note in class?!*

You and Tobias? Since when?

I've never even heard him talk.

OMG, what did the note say?

Tobias was a quiet guy she had History with and who haunted the school library. They crossed paths often, since she hung out after school when Jesse had practice. Tobias was always scribbling in a notebook. One day, she asked him what he was writing and was dumbfounded when he showed her pages of poetry that sounded like Shakespeare. Tobias was awkward and terribly shy, but when he was talking about poetry, he became animated and incredibly passionate.

Tobias and I are just friends. He's a poet, she shared. *He's been asking for my opinion on some of his work.*

There was a long pause as the girls digested this. She hadn't known how to react when Tobias started asking her for feedback. She'd been flattered but had no idea what the poems meant. Knowing how much his art meant to him, she didn't want to hurt him, so she said things like, "powerful," "moving," or "I really like the direction you're going in." That seemed to be enough for Tobias.

Are the poems about you? Marie asked.

That had occurred to her, especially when a few mentioned a girl with hair that mimicked the ripples on the surface of the ocean and eyes the color of amber. But he'd also handed her poems that spoke of ravens, dragonflies, and roses, so... *I don't think so. I think he's just happy to share them with someone.*

He's in love with you, Georgia gushed and added a row of heart emojis.

"Lights out, honey," Mom called through her closed bedroom door.

"Okay!" she called and rolled out of bed to brush her teeth.

Although she was getting a little too old for Mom to give her a bedtime, she didn't fight it. No matter how much sleep she got, mornings were always a struggle for her. Somehow, Jesse managed sports, school, and homework effortlessly on only four or five hours of sleep. Everything came so easy to him. If she didn't love him so much, she'd hate him for being so perfect.

She hopped into bed and turned out the light, but continued texting. When most of the girls signed off for the night, she rolled her eyes when Georgia started messaging her directly. Her friend was convinced that Tobias had a crush on her and that she was in denial. When she insisted they were just friends, Georgia demanded to see his poems to determine for herself whether they were about her or not.

She hadn't realized how much time had passed until

she heard Jesse and Dad making their way to their rooms. She heard Jesse's door close and, ten seconds later, her parent's door at the end of the hall.

She yawned and placed the phone face down on the nightstand, unable to continue debating with Georgia. She'd tell her friend she'd fallen asleep, which they both should be doing right now. Why had Allison brought that up? Now, the girls would be watching her and Tobias like hawks in class and Georgia, being the bold, curious soul that she was, may ask Tobias outright if he was in love with her. She sighed. She'd make sure to talk to Georgia tomorrow before she pounced on poor Tobias.

She pulled the covers up to her chin, turned on her side, and tucked her arm under her pillow just as the bathroom door swung open. She blinked, sure her eyes were playing tricks on her. Did the door open on its own? Just as she was about to raise her head to get a better look, Jesse stepped into her room. She opened her mouth, but whatever she meant to say was forgotten when she registered that he wasn't wearing any bottoms.

Her eyes snapped shut, but the image of his penis jutting out beneath his t-shirt was burned in her brain. What was happening? Did he forget to put on pants before he came to talk to her? Was he sleepwalking? His footsteps were muffled by the carpet, but she felt a soft whoosh of air as he stopped beside the bed.

She waited with bated breath for him to reach out and shake her awake, but he just stood there, hovering. Did he know she was awake and wanted her to acknowledge him? But why would she when he was half naked?

She heard a long, deep inhale. Was he *sniffing* her? No, he couldn't be. Why would he...? Jesse's muffled groan scrambled her thoughts before she heard an odd noise, something she couldn't place. A minute that felt like an eternity passed before curiosity got the better of her. A nightlight placed near the foot of the bed allowed her to see what was happening when she cracked one eye open.

Shock reverberated through her. Jesse was touching himself. No, not just touching, but stroking rapidly.

This had to be a freaky hallucination, or maybe she'd fallen asleep and this was a nightmare. This couldn't be happening in real life. Jesse couldn't be standing beside her bed, masturbating. She closed her eyes, unable to comprehend what was happening. She willed herself to wake up, but the dream continued. She lay there, paralyzed in her body, as the sounds of Jesse pleasuring himself assaulted her ears. It went on and on. She didn't know what to do, so she played dead. She didn't realize she was holding her breath until her lungs protested. She panicked when she had to take a gulp of air, but thankfully, she wasn't the only one who gasped.

Jesse made a noise, almost like he was in pain. Unable to bear the suspense, she peeked again and saw him grip the head of his penis. When his breath hitched, her gaze rose. The primitive elation on his face made her insides squirm. A grunt was her only warning before something spurted on her sheets. She was too stunned to flinch when some of it hit her cheek.

Jesse panted as he spread what he'd spilled over her bed. When his hand came toward her face, she stopped breathing. His hand stopped inches from her face, fingertips twitching before it retracted.

A flash of light scared the bejesus out of her. She clamped her eyes shut, terrified he'd seen them open. She would just die if he... She heard a soft scrape and then nothing. *What the hell was happening?* She opened her eye just a sliver. Jesse's face was illuminated by her cell phone in his hand. A message must have come in, which is why it lit up and caught his attention. He scrolled on her phone. She frowned, surprised he knew her password. He grunted and set the phone facedown as she'd had it before he turned on his heel. Her stomach flipped at the sight of his muscular butt as he disappeared into the bathroom and closed the door soundlessly behind him.

The bathroom light came on. The water ran. She heard the normal sounds of him brushing his teeth and using the bathroom before she heard his door close as he exited into his bedroom.

Violet stared at the closed door, unable to process what just occurred. She pinched herself. The tiny bite of pain assured her she was very much awake, unless her mind could mimic pain in a dream. But there was evidence... She reached out to touch her sheets, but before she made contact, she stopped. The foreign substance on her cheek suddenly burned white-hot. Stomach tight as a fist, she wiped away the tiny droplets with her sleeve and turned her back on her damp sheets and scooted to the far side of the bed.

She closed her eyes and let out a shaky breath. Even though she'd witnessed it with her own eyes, she didn't want to believe it. Jesse was her brother. He wouldn't... She pulled the covers over her head. Maybe she was coming down with something. She had to be to imagine something so deplorable. Jesse was a saint, the poster boy of their high school and church. He had never shown an ounce of depravity or perversion. This wasn't him.

She clasped her stuffed longhorn to her chest and buried her face in its fur. This didn't happen. It couldn't have. She drew her knees up to her chest and willed her mind to erase the past fifteen minutes from her memory banks.

Violet stared blearily at her reflection as she brushed her teeth. She had no idea if she'd gotten any sleep. It didn't feel like it.

Jesse's double knock startled her. She hesitated, before she said, "Come in."

She tapped her toothbrush on the edge of the sink to remove excess water as Jesse entered.

"Morning," he said.

"Morning," she returned and set her toothbrush in its holder and reached for her hairbrush.

"Mom made breakfast if you're hungry," he said.

"Okay."

He reached for his comb. She kept her eyes trained on herself as he styled his hair with just a few passes. He was already dressed in jeans and a dark gray sweater. She frowned when he put on a hat. Why brush his hair if he was just going to cover it?

"Are you okay?" he asked.

"Yup," she said without looking at him.

"You sure?"

"Mm hmm."

There was a long pause. She felt the intensity of his gaze before he said, "I'm ready when you are."

When he left, closing his door behind him, she stared at the place he'd been standing. She hadn't inspected her bedsheets this morning to confirm her fever dream. She couldn't handle that, so she ignored it, just as she had Jesse.

She was worried that looking at him would revive those graphic memories she was trying to repress.

"I'm out, kids! Have a great day! Stay safe!" Mom called as she headed out the door.

"Love you!" Jesse shouted.

"I love you more!" Lynne hollered back.

Despite herself, Violet's mouth curved. She and Dad never used to say the L word, but thanks to Jesse and Lynne, it had become a daily declaration she never tired of hearing. The familiar ritual eased some of her tension. It was just another day. Everything was the way it should be. And she had to get going.

She gave up on her hair and pulled it back with a clip. She rushed into her bedroom and dressed in jeans and a sweater like Jesse to combat the chilly February morning.

When she made her way to the kitchen, she spotted Jesse outside, wheeling their elderly neighbor's trash can to the street. On his way back to the house, he was hailed by two women power walking. Violet couldn't hear what they were saying, but she didn't need to. The women's broad smiles and the way they patted his arm told her they were impressed with his thoughtfulness.

She'd heard it for years—adults praising Jesse for being so helpful, kind, and responsible. It wasn't an act. Jesse was the same at home as he was at school and church. He was a natural leader. People gravitated to him, unconsciously sensing his grounded nature. He was everything everyone believed he was and more. She knew for a fact that he was a genuinely helpful, sweet guy. He had made her life immeasurably better. She had been so insecure, so terrified of things going wrong. His steadfast patience, love, and support healed wounds she didn't know she had. It took years for her to accept that this was her real life, and it wouldn't dissolve when Mom and Dad had a fight. She didn't want anything to change. Not now, when she finally had everything she'd ever wanted and more.

As Jesse started up the driveway, she hastily made herself a breakfast sandwich. By the time he opened the door, she had the leftovers in the fridge with a note for Dad when he came home from work.

"Ready?" Jesse asked.

"Yup."

She braced one hand on the wall as she shoved her feet into her boots.

"That's the second time you've said that this morning," Jesse observed.

"What?"

"Since when do you say yup?"

She shrugged as she made her way to the SUV. Mom bought a small, fuel-efficient car once Jesse got his license and let him take the SUV since he usually needed the extra room for his sports equipment.

She settled her backpack on the floorboard and belted herself in as Jesse got behind the steering wheel. He fiddled with the radio as they made their way out of the neighborhood. She unwrapped her breakfast sandwich and stared out the window as she tried to think of the day ahead and not about anything that could ruin her picture-perfect life.

"Did you see that text about Brody and the others going to the movies on Friday?" Jesse asked.

"Yes."

Several seconds passed before he asked, "You want to go?"

"I don't know," she heard herself say.

"You told me a couple of days ago, you wanted to see that movie."

"I know, but…" She waved her half-eaten sandwich. "I can always see it later."

"There's no reason for you to see it later unless you have other plans this weekend?"

"Maybe. My friends were talking and…" She shrugged.

"You need me to drive you anywhere?"

She shook her head. "No, I can catch a ride."

"I don't have to go to the movies. I can take you wherever you need to go."

She relaxed a little. He sounded like himself. Helpful, supportive, sweet. "No, you should go to the movies. I'm sure it'll be fun. You can tell me if it's good."

"I'd rather you come with us. When you know what you're doing with your friends, I'll decide what I'll do."

She didn't know what to say, so she finished her sandwich in silence and crumpled the foil into a ball. Lost in thought, she didn't realize she hadn't said a word until he parked the car, and she undid her seatbelt.

"You okay?" Jesse asked.

"Of course." She scanned the crowd for her friends. She was relieved to be at school, where she had classes and numerous things to distract her. She reached for her backpack and froze when Jesse touched her arm.

"You don't seem like yourself this morning."

"I didn't get the best sleep," she said and pushed her door open, eager to escape.

"Hey."

"Yeah?" she asked, tugging on her backpack zipper, even though everything was secure.

"Look at me."

She mentally braced before she turned her head. She wasn't sure what she was expecting. Of course, he hadn't changed overnight. His face was the same—chiseled jaw and what some of her friends called perfect lips. When they met, he'd been four inches taller than her, but now he towered over her and most of their peers at six foot three. Sunlight hit striking sky-blue eyes that stood out even more because of his dark brows and hair. She searched his face for an explanation for the disturbing images in her mind, but all she could see was baffled concern.

"Are you sure you're feeling okay? You're pale."

She didn't have time to stiffen as he cupped her cheek.

"Are you coming down with something?"

She gave him a bracing smile. "I'm feeling a little better now."

He cocked his head to the side and dropped his hand. "You should have stayed home."

"I have a test today."

"You could always make it up."

"No need," she said and waved as a girl approached the SUV. "Your girlfriend's coming."

He didn't turn to look. "Who?"

"Sasha."

"We're not official," he said shortly. "If you need me to take you home..."

"Yes, I'll call you, but I'm sure I'll be fine, Dad."

She grimaced at the last word she'd tacked on, but Jesse didn't notice because Sasha was knocking on his window. Violet slipped out of the car and slung her backpack over one shoulder as Sasha drawled, "Hey, handsome."

She walked away before she heard Jesse's response. She wasn't sure what had come over him, but in the past few weeks, he'd gone into a dating frenzy. When he didn't have practice or a game on the weekends, he usually spent it with the girl of the week. Sasha was the first to pass the two-week mark. When she asked him why he was suddenly playing the field, he'd said it was necessary. She wasn't sure what that meant and hadn't been interested enough to push for clarification since she was sick of hearing about his love life from her friends who were dying to be included, even if it was just for a day. Unfortunately for them, Jesse was dating only juniors or seniors. She was grateful. She didn't want to have to console her friends when Jesse moved onto someone else.

"Vi!"

Georgia stood beside her yellow Fiat, waving frantically. One glance at her friend was all it took to know what was on her mind. Her life had taken an outlandish turn while Georgia was still stuck on Tobias and his nonexistent crush.

"You left me hanging last night!" Georgia exclaimed as she hooked her arm through Violet's.

"I passed out," she said apologetically.

"I'll forgive you if you let me see one of Toby's poems." When Violet gave her a level stare, Georgia sucked her teeth. "What if he's carefully crafting these poems to express how he feels, but you're too stubborn to see it?"

"And if they are just poems and not secret love letters?"

"That's why you have me!" Georgia said cheerfully.

Her brow arched. "Because you're a whiz at poetry?"

"No, but I *am* a whiz when it comes to love."

Violet frowned. "You've never had a boyfriend."

"Exactly! Those who can't fall in love are fated to spot it miles away for everyone else."

Before she could respond to that, someone pressed against her other side.

"I see Jesse's still with Sasha," Marie whispered.

Georgia held up her finger like she was trying to figure out which way the wind was blowing. "My senses say they'll call it quits before the end of the week."

"I think they make a cute couple," Marie said.

"You say that about every girl he's with."

"And I'm right!"

"He's hot. He could choose someone butt ugly and his looks would bring her up three levels."

"Georgia!" Violet and Marie exclaimed, appalled.

"You know I'm right." Georgia glanced around to make sure no one was listening before she murmured, "Is it just me or does Jesse look bored out of his mind, no matter who he's with?"

Violet stiffened. "What do you mean?"

"I *mean*," Georgia emphasized, showing off her pink braces. "He's going through these girls like hotcakes because they aren't who he really wants."

"That's crazy. Why pick them in the first place if he's not interested?" Marie asked.

"I don't know." Georgia bumped Violet with her hip. "Why don't you ask him who he's really stuck on and go for her instead of breaking all these girls' hearts?"

Violet made a face. "Can we not talk about my brother's love life and speaking of, please don't go up to Tobias and ask him if he's in love with me."

"But," Georgia began, but the bell rang, saving Violet from having to hear any more of Georgia's insane theories.

***

Violet decided not to go to the cafeteria for lunch. Her sleepless night was catching up to her. She wasn't in the mood to run into Jesse or be harassed by Georgia. She detoured to the library, which she could always count on for peace and quiet. She nodded to the librarian and got a nod in return before she walked on the outskirts, looking for a cozy chair to curl up in for twenty minutes.

As she neared the back, she spotted Tobias in his normal spot. Her mood perked up a bit. Tobias may be a little eccentric, but he was kind and didn't mind sitting in silence. She didn't technically want to be alone, so finding him here was great. As she approached, she realized he was talking to someone out of her line of sight, and he looked upset. She slid into an aisle and peered over the books to see who he was talking to. Her mouth dropped when she spotted Jesse. What the *heck*? She didn't think Jesse knew Tobias. What could they possibly be talking about?

Jesse must have asked Tobias a question because he nodded adamantly. Satisfied, Jesse turned on his heel and walked down the main aisle. Violet made sure to exit the row and hide at the end of the bookshelf so he wouldn't see her. When the coast was clear, she hurried toward Tobias, who was on his feet and gathering his notebooks.

"Tobias."

He visibly stiffened and didn't turn to look at her as he tossed his bag over his shoulder.

"Tobias?"

He started for an exit door that led outside.

"Hey!"

She rushed after him, aware that several heads shot up from the cluster of work tables.

"Tobias, wait!"

She jogged to catch up to him. He didn't look at her, but kept his gaze fixed straight ahead.

"What happened?" she demanded.

"I never meant to make you uncomfortable," he said stiffly. "I apologize. It won't happen again."

"Uncomfortable?" she echoed. "What are you talking about?"

"Your brother said I was making you uncomfortable with my poems. I won't bother you with them anymore."

She was so taken aback, she stopped in her tracks. Tobias continued across the field, putting as much distance between them as possible. Why would Jesse lie about Tobias' poems making her uncomfortable? How did he even *know*...? An image of him scrolling through her phone after he orgasmed flashed in her mind. The confirmation she hadn't wanted smacked her in the face. This was proof positive that he'd read her messages with Georgia, which he would have been unaware of if he hadn't come into her room last night.

She stood there, staring into space as her phone chimed. Mind awhirl, she reached for it and wasn't pleased to see a message from the person who was responsible for her current distress.

Where are you? I bought you soup.

She pocketed her phone and made her way back to the library. She got several sidelong glances that she ignored them as she staggered to a one-person desk. She placed her backpack on top of it and used it like a pillow, burying her face against the cool nylon. What was happening to her life? Yesterday, everything was fine. Everything was *right,* and now everything was going topsy-turvy. Her brother, who she thought she knew better than herself, had gone rogue.

The bell rang. Immediately, those around her began zipping up backpacks. She forced herself to get up and follow the crowd into the hallway. She made her way to her next class and took a seat at the back instead of the front where she usually sat. Her friends spotted her and made their way over with puzzled expressions.

"Why are we sitting back here?"

"I didn't get much sleep last night. I'm worried I'm going to fall asleep in front of Mrs. Gindler," Violet said in a monotone.

She frowned as she spotted Marissa weaving through the desks.

"You don't have this class," she said.

"I'm at the lab down the hall. Jesse told me to give this to you," Marissa set a paper bowl on the desk before she left, giving the teacher an apologetic smile.

Violet wrapped her cold hands around the bowl, knowing without sniffing it that it would be her favorite lentil soup. When Mrs. Gindler called their attention to the board, she obeyed, but didn't hear one word the teacher said.

***

"Violet."

She jolted awake at the sound of Jesse's voice. She raised her head to see him coming around the couch where she had been napping.

"What time is it? You're done with practice?" she mumbled, fumbling for her phone.

"You shouldn't have asked Georgia to give you a ride home. I would have skipped practice if you didn't feel well." He brushed her hair aside to feel her forehead. "What is it? Do you have a fever?"

"Migraine," she muttered, pushing his hand away.

"Migraine? Do you have your...? No, not for another week," he muttered.

She peered up at him through one puffy eye. "What are you talking about?"

"Nothing," he said gruffly. "Did you take something?"

"Yes, I just need to rest. Stop fussing."

There was a short pause, and then he asked, "Are you washing something?"

Her heart skipped. "I tossed my bedsheets in the wash. Can you hang it when it's done?"

"Sure. Do you want anything to eat?"

"No. I just need to sleep."

He stood over her for a moment before he pulled her into a sitting position.

"What are you doing?" she grumbled.

"Taking care of you."

He sat and pulled her down, so she lay with her head on his lap.

"I'm not really sick."

"If you weren't sick, you wouldn't be so pale. You should have stayed home today." He absently stroked her hair. "Did Marissa drop off the soup?"

"Yes."

"Why couldn't I find you at lunch?"

She closed her eyes. "I got held up talking to my teacher. I decided to go to class early and get some studying in."

"Hm."

"Hm, what?" she said testily.

"I went by both classrooms. I didn't see you."

"That's odd," she said, words slurring a little as she unwillingly relaxed under his soothing touch.

"Must have missed you," he said in a low voice.

"Must have."

"Next time you don't feel good, you tell me. You don't

tell your friends to take care of you. That's my job, remember?"

"But…"

"Next time I'm sick, you can baby me."

She peered up at him. "But you're never sick."

"I'll pretend so you can pay me back."

She snickered. It was impossible to stay angry at him. He was so ridiculously caring and protective. Before she realized she needed something, he provided. That had to be why he said what he had to Tobias. He'd misinterpreted her texts with Georgia and thought Tobias was bothering her. She would seek out Tobias and apologize for what Jesse said and reassure him that she hadn't been uncomfortable.

As Jesse's fingers tunneled into her hair, the confusion and turmoil she carried throughout the day slipped away. This was the Jesse she knew. The Jesse she loved. The brother she'd come to depend on. For three years, they'd been deliriously happy. For the first time in her life, she felt safe and stable. She needed everything to stay the way it was.

Last night was an aberration. Whatever had possessed Jesse to enter her room and do what he had, wasn't him. Everyone made mistakes. She couldn't let one action ruin their relationship. She wouldn't. She chose to forgive and forget and erase it from her memory.

Decision made, she relaxed completely and allowed herself to enjoy Jesse's comforting touch. She needed everything to go back to normal. She couldn't accept the alternative.

CHAPTER 6
VIOLET

3 MONTHS LATER

"So, honey, have any boys caught your eye?"

Violet whipped her head around to make sure Dad wasn't within earshot. She spotted him in the backyard, tossing a football with Jesse as they kept an eye on the grill.

"Mom!"

Lynne threw back her head and laughed. "Your father knows you're going to date someday."

"He literally told me a week ago, I can't date until I'm thirty."

"He's kidding."

"He isn't," Violet said flatly.

Lynne flicked a hand covered in flour. "I'll take care of that for you." She bobbed her brows. "So? Is there anyone you want to tell me about?"

"Not really."

Lynne looked disappointed. "Really? When I was your age, I had a crush on a dozen boys."

"I..." She carefully measured out the ingredients for one

of three buttermilk pies they were making. "I'm just focused on school."

"Huh."

"What?" Violet said defensively.

"Not that I want this to happen," Lynne drawled as she arranged her dough in the dish and began to pinch the edges. "But I was your age once. I keep expecting you and Jesse to rebel at some point, but you two are the most well-adjusted, strait-laced, responsible teenagers I've ever met. My friends are convinced we've either drugged you two or we're hiding some dark family secret." Lynne shrugged. "I tell them we're just blessed to have such levelheaded kids."

Violet fixed a smile on her face that she hoped concealed the way her stomach curdled. "We still have time to disappoint you. I have two more years of high school and Jesse... he might go nuts his senior year."

Lynne glanced into the backyard with a proud smile on her face. "I doubt that."

Violet turned on the mixer to stop any further conversation on the topic.

They'd just put their pies in the oven when Jesse and Dad came in with the meat they cooked on the grill. As she set the table, Dad spun Lynne and gave her a loud kiss. Once they were seated, she took Jesse's hand on her left and Lynne's on her right as they bowed their heads to pray. She tried to ignore the distracting brush of Jesse's thumb stroking her skin as Dad blessed the meal.

"Lord, thank you for everything you've given us. Thank you for providing for us and blessing our family. Protect us as we begin a new week. Give us wisdom and strength to see us through. Amen," Dad said.

"Amen," they said in unison.

It was a lazy Sunday evening with delicious food and

stimulating conversation. They discussed Pastor Sonny's message at church that day in length before they moved onto what was going on in the community and their schedules for the week. Dad and Jesse were too impatient to let the buttermilk pies cool properly. They each dug into their own, while she and Lynne were satisfied with a slice. Dad had to turn in since he had such an early shift.

When Lynne yawned, Violet offered to clean up. Lynne gave her a grateful smile as she and Dad headed down the hall with their arms around each other.

Violet eyed Jesse's pie, which was more than half gone. "You aren't going to eat it all in one sitting, are you?"

"I could."

"Don't," she warned. "Because Mom will come after you with a knife if you scarf down our pie, too."

"You wouldn't tell her it was me, would you?"

"I would," she said, tipping her nose in the air as she carried dishes to the sink.

"You're heartless. You know this is my favorite," Jesse said as he gathered the rest of the plates and piled them in the sink.

"Maybe you should have pie instead of a cake for your birthday this year."

He froze. "Give up German chocolate cake?"

She crossed her arms over her chest. "What's it gonna be?"

"Can't I have both?"

She tilted her head to the side as she considered. "I could bake for your birthday instead of buying you stuff you never use."

"I use what you give me."

"You used that nice shirt *once*."

"Because I outgrew it within six months."

"And the cologne?"

He shrugged. "I sweat too much. It doesn't last."

She took in the sweat stains on his shirt that clung to his athletic physique and wrinkled her nose. "I can finish up here. You should shower."

He spread his arms wide. "Can I get a hug first?"

She held her hands up as she backed away. "No! Stay back!"

"I just want to thank you for making my favorite pie."

"You just did," she pointed out. "There's no need to touch me."

He moved swiftly, but so did she. She ran to the living room and put the couch between them.

"Jesse." She tried to sound stern, but a nervous laugh escaped. *"Don't."*

His speed never failed to shock her. When he darted around the couch, she let out a panicked yelp. He picked her up and pinned her on the couch.

"I'm going to tell Dad!" she yelled into his chest.

"Promise me you'll make me cake and pie for my birthday, then I'll let you go."

"No!"

He put more of his weight on her, sinking her into the cushions.

"Fine, I promise!" she croaked.

He sat up and grinned down at her. "You're so easy."

She glowered and made a show of smelling herself, even though his scent wasn't as repulsive as it should be. "I'm going to get you back for that."

He climbed off her, stripped off his shirt, and draped it over his shoulder. "Looking forward to it."

As he strolled away, she lay there for a second, before she gave herself a shake. She'd seen Jesse shirtless countless times during practice, while camping, exercising, or at the beach. There was no reason for the sight of his naked torso to make her stomach jitter.

She stored the leftovers in the fridge, cleaned the kitchen, and washed the dishes. By the time she entered her bedroom, Jesse was out of the shower. She grabbed her pajamas and did the double knock on the bathroom door to make sure the coast was clear. When she didn't get an answer, she entered and eyed Jesse's door as she stripped.

After her shower, she put on lotion before she brushed her teeth and re-entered her bedroom. She sat at her desk and worked on an essay that was due on Friday, before she double-checked her backpack to make sure she had all her homework assignments for tomorrow.

With just one month of school left, projects were coming to a close. There was a flurry of tests and then they would be on summer break. The year had passed in a blur. Next year she would be a junior. She couldn't wait! This year she'd been Student Body Secretary. Maybe next year she could be Student Body President? Would her peers vote her in? There was only one way to find out. Dad hadn't let her attend prom this year. Maybe Mom could talk him into letting her go next year?

My friends are convinced we've either drugged you two or we're hiding some dark family secret.

Lynne's voice echoed in her mind as she climbed in bed and pulled the covers up to her chin. From the outside looking in, she knew that they looked like the perfect blended family. They attended church every Sunday, Mom and Dad were happy and in love, and she and Jesse were as close as blood siblings. Jesse got a lot of attention for being a star athlete and was a great student on top of that. They both were. Everything was perfect.

Or, it had been before she discovered Jesse's nighttime habit.

By day, Jesse was an honorable Boy Scout. He never touched her inappropriately. He never even looked at her in a way that made her uncomfortable. He seemed as open and loving as he'd always been. When she looked into his eyes, there was nothing deceptive, lecherous, or evil. She couldn't make sense of it.

The visits were sporadic. Sometimes days would pass without incident, allowing her to believe it was a thing of the past, only to be roused in the middle of the night by the sound of him jerking off.

She tried to go to bed early, hoping she would be too deeply asleep to hear him come in. But the stress of wondering if tonight would be one of those nights kept her wide awake. She considered locking the bathroom door to bar him from her room, but then he'd know she knew. And, for some reason she couldn't fathom, that was worse than enduring the deed.

The sounds of him masturbating were burned into her brain. She knew from the rhythm of his strokes and breathing patterns when he was close to climax. She catalogued every sigh, moan, or grunt. Some nights, he came immediately. During others, he struggled. Those were the worst because ten minutes felt like an hour when she was playing dead.

He was becoming bolder. He went from spilling on her sheets to now coming on her face. It took every ounce of control she possessed not to react. She was terrified that one day, she would flinch, open her eyes, or say something.

Initially, it seemed Jesse regulated himself to once or twice a week. Now, that amount had doubled. He was also becoming more impatient. One night, she'd barely been in bed for fifteen minutes before he came in. And he wasn't as quiet as he used to be. She had always been a sound sleeper, but not *that* sound. He couldn't be trying to wake her, could he?

Even if she was truly ignorant to his nighttime shenanigans, at some point she would have questioned why she woke with stuff caked in her hair or had sticky, flaky patches on her skin. What if she'd naively asked Lynne about the stains on her bedsheets? She moaned into her pillow.

If only he would stop, then everything could go back to normal, and she wouldn't feel... Her legs clamped together as her core pulsed. It was humiliating and revolting, but somewhere along the way, her body began to react to the nightly ritual. Most nights, after he left, she had to...

She balled her hands into fists as self-loathing swamped her. It was all his fault. Before this, she rarely thought about sex. She never explored her body or tried to figure out how things worked. Because of him, she now knew what a man's penis looked like and what cum tasted like. One night, she'd gotten so aroused that she humped her stuffed longhorn. The next day, she washed him, but she didn't look at him the same and suspected the feeling was mutual.

It was so confusing to feel one way and have her body react in another. To overcome the excruciating shame and guilt, she rationalized that what happened during these interludes didn't count. That went for Jesse as well. The creeper who slipped into her room and did perverted, wicked things was a totally different person from her beloved brother. Once the sun rose, the dark, degenerate entity that possessed him at night evaporated and wiped the slate clean.

An hour passed. She lay on her stomach, a little rebellion on her part. When another hour crawled by, relief mixed with irritation. She wished he had a predictable schedule, but the times and days varied, so there was no way to predict anything. As another twenty minutes inched by, she concluded that Jesse had conquered his demons for the night, which left hers to deal with.

She flipped onto her back and slid her hand down her primed body. She rubbed herself through her pajama shorts and underwear. An image of his body that he'd casually revealed in the living room appeared in her mind, along with the memory of his weight pinning her to the couch. She bit back a moan as she arched her hips into her hand.

As pangs of conscience smothered her sexual desire, she tried to replace Jesse's face with another boy, as if that would make it less sinful. But it was impossible to picture anyone else when Jesse had awakened her libido. Her passions now revolved around him.

All the things her friends found attractive about him, she found herself inspecting for herself. The lips they thought were perfect, she'd seen him bite during orgasm. His athletic build gave him a body that didn't need to be covered up. She didn't know why he insisted on wearing a shirt during his visits. She wanted to see his body in its entirety and hated how often she harped on that detail.

She was terrified her friends could read her dirty mind and sense that she'd changed. But, like their parents, her friends seemed oblivious to any undercurrents between them. But why should they pick up on anything when she couldn't? Jesse treated her the same as he always had. There was no trace of the desperate hunger that brought him to her night after night. It was unsettling and made her question her sanity. She wished she could confide in someone about what was happening to her, but she didn't dare.

As she approached the finish line, her toes curled. As she prepared for take-off, movement off to her left made her freeze. The bathroom door swung open, and Jesse's familiar shadow appeared before she could retract her hand. She closed her eyes and hoped the comforter looked like it was merely bunched over her crotch so he wouldn't realize what she'd been doing.

He stood over her for a moment before he leaned down and inhaled. This was another part of the ritual, but tonight it sent a streak of panic through her. He couldn't smell her arousal, could he? She died a thousand deaths as he took another, longer inhale. *Just get on with it*, she silently screamed.

"Shit," he whispered.

Her eyelids flickered. She was shocked by his curse and the fact he'd actually spoken. Normally, all she heard were muffled, involuntary sounds, but hearing his voice tore the seams between this alternate reality and real life.

The wet sound of him stroking himself made her clench her teeth. It was the worst punishment to act like a lifeless doll when she was so close. Why had she wasted so much time wrestling with herself? She could have come and been asleep hours ago. Then, she wouldn't have to listen to the sounds he was making that made the space between her legs so slippery she may need to change her bedding.

Jesse's stifled moan unraveled her shaky control. She pressed on her clit, but it wasn't enough. She needed that back-and-forth motion. Jesse wouldn't notice, would he? He was focused on his own needs, and he was making enough noise that she knew he was close too. Moving as little as possible, she began to rub and was rewarded with a delicious wave of prickling heat. She sucked in a breath and heard Jesse do the same. She found herself matching Jesse's strokes. This was wrong on so many levels, but she was past the point of caring. Her heart soared. This was going to be the best orgasm she'd ever had.

"Violet."

She obeyed without thinking. Her eyes popped open and collided with Jesse's, which were dark, glittering pools. As always, he wore his shirt, and his cock jutted beneath it. He was close. She could tell from the way he was jerking on the head of his penis.

As she realized they were staring at one another, and they'd broken their unspoken pact, a bolt of heat lanced through her. Her climax bubbled up. She gasped for breath as her eyes began to roll.

"Shit," she heard again.

When the head of his cock touched her lips, they instinctively parted, allowing him to spill into her mouth, while remnants dribbled down her chin and cheek. Even in the midst of her orgasm, his gut-wrenching groan freaked her out. Their parents were going to hear!

As the hot euphoria of her climax faded, cold horror came charging in. She lay there, trying to control her breathing as her heart hammered so hard in her chest that she trembled from the force of it. Not wanting to face the consequences of her actions, she went motionless again, like a stupid animal who'd made a foolish move and hoped they would blend back in with their surroundings before the hunter took its shot.

Jesse didn't move for several minutes. Neither did she. She didn't even swallow, she was so determined for him to believe her looking at him had been a figment of his imagination. She willed him to walk away and continue the pretense.

She was so attuned to him, she sensed the moment he moved, even though he didn't make a sound. There was a light snick of the bathroom door closing. Jesse didn't wash his hands or use the toilet but went straight through to his bedroom and closed that door too. Everything went still and quiet and tranquil, as if what just took place between them never happened.

She finally swallowed. Was it her imagination, or was his cum sweeter? Was it because of the buttermilk pie? Dismayed over her thoughts, she sat up and feverishly scrubbed her face to remove all traces of him. The urge to shower and gargle with mouthwash was overwhelming, but the bathroom was neutral territory. Why did she have a feeling, if she went in there, he would try to talk to her? She would die if he did.

She rushed over to her drawer and got a new set of underwear and pajamas and tossed her ruined ones into the hamper. When she climbed back into bed, she huddled under the covers and writhed in anguish.

Her worst fears came true. Jesse's secret—now, *their* secret—was out in the open. She allowed herself to be enticed into participating in his twisted fantasy, which had abruptly transitioned into something else. Something terrifying. Something that could never be. This is what happened when she let her body make stupid decisions! This wasn't her and it wasn't him. They were good kids, *Christian* kids. This went against everything they believed in. What were they doing?

Tomorrow, she would put a stop to this. What was done in the dark had to stay there. She wouldn't allow it to see the light of day and change their relationship.

CHAPTER 7
JESSE

LOOK AT ME, BABY. OPEN YOUR EYES SO WE CAN FINALLY TALK, HE silently begged, but Violet's eyes remained closed.

He wanted to sweep her up in his arms and shout for joy, but the fact that she'd gone back to feigning sleep didn't bode well. He sensed her distress but couldn't make sense of it. They didn't have to hide this anymore!

Over the past weeks, there had been times when he swore he saw her eyelids flutter or random body movements that led him to believe she was awake. He'd been pushing it lately, willing to risk it all to discover whether he was losing his mind.

Tonight, when he came into her room and tried to catch her scent, he detected something that shouldn't have been, something that reminded him of what he'd found smeared on several of her used underwear. Arousal. It sent his body into overdrive. He'd noticed the odd bunching of the covers over her crotch, but thought nothing of it, until it shifted. It took him only a second to figure out what she'd been doing before he entered. When her hand began to move in telltale circles, his heart stopped.

It had been a calculated risk to say her name. He said it loudly enough to rouse her if she'd been asleep, but when her eyes flew open, they were alert and glazed with lust. And then she started to climax. He hadn't been able to resist her open mouth. It was the most satisfying orgasm he'd ever had.

Please, baby. I'm dying here, he thought. He reached out to touch her but stopped when he noticed she was trembling. The urge to comfort her was overwhelming, but his need to put her at ease was stronger. Reluctantly, he retreated.

He walked through the bathroom to his bedroom and leaned against the door. His initial blast of elation had morphed into disquiet, but he wouldn't let that get him down. He would give her the space she needed this evening and talk it out tomorrow. He worried that she may always see him as a brother but tonight proved otherwise. She declared her feelings in the best way possible—by masturbating right alongside him.

He wanted to roar in triumph. He wanted to hold her on his lap and confess how much he loved her. How much he had been holding back. Nine months he'd kept all of this bottled up inside of him. He worried constantly that she or someone else would deduce how he felt about her, but that was at an end. God had mercy on him and made her want him in return. He no longer needed to date other girls in a futile attempt to dilute his obsession or use religion as an excuse for why he didn't go all the way with them.

He flopped on his bed and folded his hands behind his head and replayed her orgasm—eyes rolling, legs jerking beneath the covers in involuntary response, and her beautiful face covered in him. His heart swelled, felt like it was about to burst. Violet wanted him. He wasn't sure what their next step was, but it didn't matter because they were finally on the same page.

———

His hand flexed on the steering wheel. He wasn't sure what to expect from Violet this morning, but the bright smile and upbeat, inane chatter wasn't it. From the moment she bounded out of her bedroom and for most of the ride to school, she talked about a range of topics—everything but the one thing he wanted to discuss. He couldn't get anything in edgewise. He decided to let her take the lead, but he had no idea where she was going with this.

"You have games on Tuesday and Friday, right?" she asked distractedly as she typed on her phone.

"Yeah."

"All righty."

He waited a second before he asked, "You're coming, right?"

"I'm not sure. My friends asked me to do something Friday night."

On cue, her phone chimed.

"Who's texting you?"

"Georgia and Allison and..."

Another chime sounded.

"And?" he prompted as he turned into the school parking lot.

"Huh?" Violet looked around and waved when she spotted her friends. "There they are!"

He parked and tried to tamp down the flurry of emotions in his chest as she prepared to leave. "Violet."

"Yeah?"

"Hang on a minute."

Her body visibly stiffened. The unease he dismissed last night came back full force. He assumed they could finally talk openly, but Vi clearly wasn't ready.

"Look at me."

She made eye contact with him several times this morning, her eyes filled with rabid good cheer. Not now, though. They were more green than hazel, a sure sign that her temper was on the rise.

"What, Jesse?" she asked impatiently as her cheeks bloomed with color.

He wished he could touch her, but in the mood she was in, he had no idea how that would be received. She was skittish and on edge and couldn't make it plainer that she wanted to get away from him. What the hell was happening?

"Is everything okay?"

His voice was gruff with panic. He had the crazy urge to keep her in the car and drive to some secluded place where they wouldn't be interrupted so they could sort this out.

"I'm fine. I'll see you later," she said and slid out of the vehicle.

He didn't move as she hurried over to her friends. He sat there for a full minute, his mind racing. She'd been with him every step of the way last night, so what was the issue? Had she just become aware of his feelings and her own? Did she need more time to wrap her mind around this? He wished she would tell him, so he wasn't left feeling like everything he wanted was slipping through his fingers before he had a chance to grab hold of it.

Her feelings had changed somewhere along the way, she just didn't want to admit it. For weeks now, he'd sensed a subtle change in her gaze. She thought he wouldn't notice, but he was so aware of her, he felt the weight of her intrigued consideration during his games, on their commute to school, and when they watched TV. He thought he might have imagined it, but after last night, he was certain. To help her along, he stripped in front of her whenever possible, like yesterday after pinning her on the couch. Was she worried about what people would say? Their parents? He didn't care what they faced if he had her, but Violet didn't feel the same. So, where did that leave them?

He hissed through his teeth as he stepped out of the SUV and resisted the urge to slam the door. He wouldn't push it for now. Pressuring her would only cancel the progress he'd made. He'd lasted this long. He could wait a little longer, especially with last night's victory under his belt.

Good things come to those who wait, he reminded himself.

***

"So, this is where you're hiding."

He turned to see Brody enter the gym.

"Hiding?" he echoed before he turned back to the hoop and took his shot.

Brody let out a disgusted sound as he made his way across the court. "Are you practicing for the NBA?"

"You know I'm going into the military."

"I was hoping you changed your mind," Brody muttered.

"I haven't."

He retrieved the ball and dribbled back to his spot to make another three-pointer. Brody placed himself beneath the hoop and passed him the ball. Several minutes passed before he noticed the odd look Brody was giving him.

"What?"

"You're taking this well."

He frowned. "Taking what well?"

Brody did a hook shot before passing the ball to him once more. "Violet."

He tensed. "What about her?"

He texted her to see if she wanted to go off campus for lunch. He hoped if she wasn't ready to talk, she'd still want to spend time together. She hadn't responded, which put him in a foul mood. He had no idea where he stood with her, and it was driving him crazy. He'd taken refuge in the gym during lunch to clear his head.

"I thought it was a rumor, so I didn't bother asking you about it, but I saw them with my own eyes." Brody shook his head. "Out of all the guys she could pick, she chose *him*? That loner who hides in the library?"

He tucked the basketball under his arm. "Tobias?"

Brody made a face. "Is that his name? He can't even make eye contact with anyone, and your sister looks at him and thinks, 'Hey, this guy should be my first boyfriend?'"

His heart slammed against his ribs. "Who says Violet's dating him?"

Brody stared at him. "I saw them."

He took a threatening step toward his friend. "Saw them *what*?"

Brody held up his hands. "Chill, bro."

"Tell me what you saw!"

"They were holding hands in the cafeteria." Brody searched his face. "I thought you knew."

He threw the ball at his friend before he snatched his backpack and stalked out of the gym. *She wouldn't do this to him*, he thought as pain and fury seared his chest. The bell rang, flooding the hallways with students. He went against the crowd to reach the cafeteria, but by the time he got there, it was empty. He broke into a run to get to Violet's next class. Several people called out to him and a teacher told him to slow down, but for once in his life, he ignored everyone. Brody had to be mistaken. There had to be another explanation for Violet holding Tobias' hand. Like, the kid had suddenly gone blind, and she was leading him around because no one else would, or something. She wouldn't date. Not now and not *him*.

He turned the corner as the second bell rang and stopped in his tracks. Tobias and Violet stood outside of her class. Violet was smiling at Tobias like... Like she should be smiling at him. Tobias grasped Violet's hand and pecked it before he scuttled down the hallway. Violet had a bemused look on her face before it morphed into a delighted giggle.

As if she sensed his presence, she looked down the hall to where he stood. Her eyes widened and her amusement vanished. He started toward her to get some answers, but she took a step back and raised her hand in a stopping motion before she disappeared inside her class.

What the fuck?

The third and final bell rang. Teachers came out to close their doors. One of them noticed him standing there and frowned.

"Mr. Sampson? Is something wrong?"

"No," he said and pivoted on his heel.

His temper, something that hadn't been provoked since last summer, threatened to break free. Why would she suddenly decide to date after what happened last night? And why choose a creep like Tobias? The guy spent his days in the library or in empty classrooms, scribbling in a notebook and talking to himself. He told Tobias to steer clear of Violet, but apparently Tobias hadn't taken him seriously. Or, had Violet sought him out? The thought incensed him so much that he smashed his fist into the building, bruising his knuckles, but he didn't notice.

He was in no mood to sit in class. He walked toward the parking lot, nodding to the security guards who knew him by name. His reputation as a good student and athlete allowed him to walk off property without being asked if he had permission.

It took extreme discipline not to give into his demons as he navigated out of the parking lot and rode gently over the speed bumps. It wasn't until he was on a deserted country road that he slammed on the accelerator and let the engine release a roar that he silently echoed. He drove to a park. The sound of his phone chiming made him dig through the zippers to find it.

Madyson: *I couldn't find you at lunch. I have a surprise for you.*

Madyson: *Do you want to go to a concert in San Antonio this weekend?*

He tossed his phone on the seat, slammed the door, and paused. He'd been dating Madyson for a couple of weeks. He planned to break it off with her, but there'd been no need to rush. Is that why Violet decided to date? Because he was? Did she think last night meant nothing to him?

He scowled as he headed for the trail. Running always cleared his head and right now, he needed all the help he could get with his emotions clamoring. He should have pushed the issue this morning during their ride to school. He should have just laid it out and found out what was going on in her head instead of being blindsided like this.

To expel the black rage threatening to consume him, he

ran full out. Was it a coincidence that Tobias asked her out today, or was this something Violet had orchestrated? His chest burned, and it wasn't from his pace. Tobias didn't have the balls to ask her out, which meant Violet had done this deliberately. Why? To punish him for dating other girls? But that look Violet gave him in the hallway wasn't smug or defiant. She'd been alarmed to see him and ran from him for the second time today instead of talking to him. That fucking burned him.

He slowed and continued along the trail at a jog instead of the breakneck sprint he'd started with. The run had taken the edge off his anger, though it still heated his brain. But he was thinking a little more rationally.

So, she was hellbent on ignoring what happened between them and decided to date Tobias. If Violet wanted to date, he didn't have the right to protest or be upset when he'd dated... and done other things while pining for her.

How would Isaac react to Violet's sudden decision to date? He secretly wanted Isaac to forbid it, but that was hypocritical and selfish on his part and when they came out to their parents in the future, that would apply to him as well.

He grimaced. Why the anti-social poet, though? What did she see in him? Abruptly, his bad mood lightened a bit. Better Tobias than one of his friends. Tobias had no game. He was awkward and weird, and it wouldn't last. Violet was just testing the waters. She wasn't truly attracted to Tobias. He was a filler, just like his girlfriends had been. But he used other girls to temper his fixation on Violet while she was deliberately bringing other guys between them. Why? Because she didn't trust what was between them? Was she too self-conscious of what others would say?

He gritted his teeth at the realization that his suffering

wasn't at an end, but another beginning. Violet wasn't as deeply enmeshed as he was. If she was, she wouldn't care what others would say or think. She wouldn't care about the consequences. But she did. He still had a long way to go to convince her they were meant to be together.

He slicked back his sweaty hair as he made his way back to the parking lot. Her stunt still grated, but throwing a fit over her dating or forcing her to acknowledge their sexual attraction to each other would only make her dig her heels in and reinforce whatever reservations made her do this in the first place. He had to stand back and let her explore and experiment. Violet was a good girl. She wouldn't go too far. She wanted the freedom to choose. He could understand that, even if he didn't like it. If part of this was revenge for the girls he dated, he would let her have it.

He was confident it wouldn't take her long to realize that their connection was special. No one suited her like he did. He knew her better than she knew herself. He adored everything about her and would do anything for her, even let her date other guys, though it would drive him crazy to see anyone touch what was his. She would come to him when she was ready. And once he claimed her, that would be it for both of them.

CHAPTER 8
VIOLET

4 MONTHS LATER

VIOLET FROWNED AT THE COMPUTER SCREEN, WHERE HER unfinished article for the school newspaper was laid out in incomplete paragraphs. She'd been sitting here for at least twenty minutes and hadn't changed one word. She stared at the screen, her mind a million miles away. The steady clicking of her pen gave away her agitation.

Someone stuck their head into the empty classroom, capturing Violet's attention. She sat up, a smile breaking across her face as the boy entered and came toward her.

"What are you doing here?" she asked her boyfriend as he stopped beside her.

"Looking for you." Tucker leaned down to give her a swift kiss. "Let's get out of here."

She didn't hesitate. She saved her work, shouldered her backpack, and felt her stomach flutter when he wrapped an arm around her waist.

"Jesse has practice, so I knew you'd be around here

somewhere," Tucker said. "It took me a while to find you. Since when do you hide out in Mr. Halstead's classroom?"

"How'd you know I was hiding?"

He cocked his head as he looked down at her. "I was kidding."

"I wasn't," she said sourly. "Is there something on my face?"

Her boyfriend's brows arched. "I'm sorry?"

"I swear, people have been staring at me funny all day."

She blew out a breath as they left the building and headed toward the deserted parking lot. When she began her junior year with Tucker as her boyfriend, it caused a sensation. Tucker was a senior and lead singer of his band with a notorious reputation. Tucker may be known as a bad boy, but around her, he was sweet and attentive. After several weeks, people were finally getting used to seeing them together but today felt like day one all over again. She didn't understand it.

"I haven't done anything out of the ordinary, and I'm not wearing anything scandalous," she said, gesturing to her blouse and shorts.

Yes, the blouse was a little more fitted than what she'd gone for in the past, but compared to her classmates, her clothes were still modest and conservative. She'd been stared at so intently, she excused herself to go to the bathroom to make sure she didn't have a stain or rip in her clothes. She told herself it was all in her head until she heard her name said three times in her last class. The temptation to confront her classmates was strong, but what could they possibly be gossiping about? Her conscience was clear... for the most part.

As Tucker's eyes moved slowly and deliberately over her body, she gave him a little push as her cheeks flushed.

"Stop looking at me like that!"

"Like what?"

"Like..." She flapped her hands, unable to bring herself to say it out loud. "You know!"

"Like you're gorgeous? Like I want to strip you naked?"

"*Tucker!* You can't say that!"

"Why? It's true. You have nothing to be self-conscious about. They're just jealous because you're a knockout."

Her heart leapt when he patted her butt. She glanced around self-consciously, but there was no one around to witness Tucker's inappropriate PDA. Tucker felt like her first "real" boyfriend. Tobias and the others she briefly dated had been more friend than boyfriend, but Tucker made it clear from the start that he wanted much more. He kissed her on their first date and wasn't embarrassed to touch her in public. It was exciting and thrilling. She allowed him to go further than anyone else, though she hadn't gone *all* the way. The fact that she considered allowing him to be her first was shocking when she'd vowed to save herself for marriage. But with her sexual frustration mounting, Tucker was a much-needed, healthy outlet she could indulge in without feeling guilty.

Tucker led her toward his Bronco parked in the back corner of the mostly empty lot and opened the passenger door for her. When she made no move to get in, his eyes narrowed.

"You know what my dad said."

Tucker made a terrible first impression when he sped through their neighborhood after picking her up. Dad hadn't ordered her to break up with him, but she wasn't allowed to get in a car with Tucker. If they wanted to meet up, someone had to pick her up or drop her off.

Tucker rolled his eyes. "I swear, I won't speed again."

"If my dad finds out I got in a car with you, I'll be grounded for life."

"He won't find out."

"Jesse will tell him."

Tucker glanced at his watch. "He won't finish practice for another hour. I can bring you back before he's finished. He won't even know you left campus. You can say you were in the library the whole time."

Her insides twisted. This was just the sort of thing Dad had lectured her about—her boyfriend encouraging her to lie and break the rules. All the males in her life unanimously disliked Tucker. Her father, Jesse, and her guy friends had protested the moment they started dating, but they didn't see what she did.

Tucker's band played a set at a concert she and her friends attended this summer. They hung out after, and the rest was history. Tucker was so different from everyone she knew. He had big dreams of becoming a rock star. She loved listening to him talk about music and his plans to travel the globe. Being around someone who had such large aspirations made her reexamine her own future. He was free, liberated. Not bound by the constraints of religion or the weight of family expectations. Being near him made her feel like she could be a different person... But she wasn't willing to break all the rules just yet.

"I'm sorry, but I don't want to lie to Jesse or my dad," she said.

Tucker didn't do a good job of hiding his irritation.

"You're lucky you're hot," he growled and tugged her toward him and boxed her in the open doorway of his car. "You're driving me crazy."

"I don't," she began, but was cut off when his mouth covered hers.

He kissed her deeply. She was dimly aware of her backpack falling to the ground as he pressed himself against her, so she couldn't fail to feel his erection. She gripped his shirt as the space between her legs pulsed.

"Don't you want me?" Tucker panted as he brushed kisses over her cheek and gripped her ass.

"Of course I do," she whispered and tipped her head back to give him better access. God, she needed to be touched like this. She was starving, burning up. There were so many desires trapped inside her. So much she wanted to set free, so much she wanted to experience.

Guilt cut through her carnal desires. Good Christian girls didn't let their boyfriends put their tongues in their mouth or let them touch their butt. A good Christian girl would stop this and walk away. She stayed where she was. She hadn't been a good Christian girl for a while now. On the surface, not much had changed. She attended church, had the same friends, and continued to be a dedicated student. But no one knew the dark secret she shared with her stepbrother.

Jesse's visits continued. He hadn't been put off by her dating, as she'd hoped. They presented a wholesome image to the world while he crept into her room at night, and she pretended to be asleep. She hated that no matter who she dated, Jesse was still in the forefront of her mind. But she finally had a boyfriend who didn't treat her like a princess or a good girl. Tucker treated her like a woman, giving her the opportunity to act on her pent-up desires.

"You feel so good," Tucker rasped as he gripped her breast.

She arched into his touch.

"God, you're so hot for me. Let's get out of here."

"I can't," she said breathlessly and glanced around,

reason asserting itself now that he wasn't kissing her. "We can't do this. Somebody might see! I have to..."

In a sudden move that took her by surprise, he picked her up and carried her to the back of his Bronco and pinned her against the cool metal.

"Now, no one can see us," he said huskily.

She stared at the surrounding trees, which gave them a false sense of privacy, before she looked back at Tucker, who was staring at her with a determination that made her tense. "Tucker, I can't..."

"You're not ready to give me your cherry yet," he said impatiently. "But I can give you a preview of what you're missing."

She braced her hands on his shoulders. "What are you talking about?"

"Let me show you," he cooed as he undid the button of her shorts.

She grasped his wrist, eyes wide. "What are you doing?"

"Making you feel good," he said against her lips. "Come on, give me this at least. Let me touch you."

"Y-you want to touch me *there*?" she whispered, scandalized.

He stared at her for a moment before he shook his head. "You're such an innocent. It's a miracle no one's got to you before now. I guess I have Jesse to thank for that."

He tested her grip on him before he pulled down her zipper. This was dangerous. She knew that, but she couldn't find the will to stop him as he lifted her shirt to examine her underwear.

"Of course you're wearing pink," he said with masculine approval. "So pretty and perfect."

"Tucker?"

She wasn't sure if he kissed her because he heard the

uncertainty in her tone. If that was so, it was a good strategy. It was wiped any thought of resistance from her mind. She sensed his excitement and urgency as his hand brushed over the front of her. She gasped and was thankful for his bumper, which gave her something to sit on when her legs gave out.

"I'm going to make you feel so good," he panted as he adjusted his hand. "I want you to come on my fingers. God, you feel…"

One minute he was pressed against her and the next, he was gone. She opened her eyes and stared at the empty space where Tucker had been without comprehension before she heard a shout and then a strange scuffling sound. She rose on shaky legs, rounded the vehicle, and stopped in her tracks.

Jesse straddled Tucker, who was splayed out on the pavement. Even as she watched, Jesse drew back his fist and rammed it into Tucker's face. Tucker's head snapped back and collided with the pavement with a sickening crack. Jesse landed two more forceful blows before she came out of her horrified stupor.

"Jesse, stop!" she screamed.

Blood spurted as he landed another punch before she caught his swinging arm.

"*Stop!*"

Her desperate shriek finally seemed to penetrate the haze. Jesse stilled. Tucker's face was covered in blood from a split lip, a broken nose, and what might be a shattered cheekbone.

"What the hell, Jesse?" she whispered, shaken to the core.

As Jesse rose, she collapsed beside Tucker to make sure he was all right, but before she could touch him, Jesse roughly hauled her to her feet. She hauled in a breath to yell at him, but the chilling look on Jesse's face wiped her mind clean.

"Touch her again, I'll kill you," Jesse said with chilling softness.

Her mouth dropped. "Jesse, he—"

He ignored her and began to tow her across the parking lot. She dug in her heels.

"I'm not," she began before Jesse turned, crouched, and tossed her over his shoulder. She braced her hands on his back so she could see Tucker. "He isn't moving!"

"He's alive," Jesse said curtly as he set her beside the SUV and yanked the door open. "Get in."

She gawked at him, unable to believe what he'd done. She had no idea he knew how to throw a punch, much less how to systematically beat someone to a pulp. Tucker had been in his fair share of fights, but Jesse had incapacitated him with shocking ease. She didn't know Jesse had that level of violence in him, but the splatter of red on his shirt, arm, and hand said different.

"Why did you do that?" she demanded.

It was an unfortunate moment for her gaping shorts to drop to her knees. In the time it took her to haul them up and fasten them, Jesse had crossed quite a distance on his way back to Tucker to finish what he started. She wrapped her arms around his waist and pulled back with all her might.

"Jesse, *don't!*"

He stopped, but didn't turn back to the car. She was very aware that if he wanted to, he could continue to beat the crap out of Tucker and there was nothing she could do about it. His chest pumped as he tried to rein in his temper. He was angrier than she had ever seen him.

"Jesse?"

"Get in the car."

His voice trembled with rage. She hesitated before she loosened her hold on him. She felt a modicum of relief when he turned from Tucker's prone form to follow her back to the car. She warily eyed his blank expression as she climbed in. He held the door open for her out of habit. She flinched, even though he didn't slam the door. She almost wished he had.

As he stalked around to the driver's side, she turned in her seat and was relieved to see Tucker sitting up and clutching his head with both hands. She hoped he was okay. If she had her phone, she would have texted one of his friends to check on him, but it was in her backpack on the other side of Tucker's Bronco. Considering what just happened, her backpack didn't seem all that important at the moment. As Jesse got in, she faced forward.

"Did he force you?" Jesse spat as they left the parking lot.

Her head whipped toward him. "F-force?"

"Did you want him to touch you?" he clarified impatiently.

For a second, she considered lying before the telltale wetness between her legs and honesty made her confess, "Yes."

Jesse didn't say a word, but his temper filled the cab, making her heart skip erratically. She ran a shaking hand through her hair. "I'm sorry. I don't know what I was thinking."

"Don't talk," he said harshly. "Before I crash the car."

Sick to her stomach, she looked out the window, and bit down on her lower lip until she tasted blood. Jesse thought Tucker was forcing her? His reaction was understandable if that's what he believed, but she wished Jesse asked questions before he got physical with her boyfriend. She buried her face in her hands. This was all her fault. Anyone could have come by. It just so happened that it was Jesse who interrupted them. Everything happened so fast that her mind was still spinning.

They didn't exchange a word the whole ride home. When Jesse pulled into their driveway, he braked hard enough to make her rock forward, so her seatbelt locked. She cast him a wide-eyed look he didn't notice since he got out of the car and, this time, slammed the door behind him.

She sat there for a moment, unsure what to do. It wasn't until he disappeared inside that she realized Dad could be home. The bolt of fear that struck her caused her to undo her seatbelt and sprint after Jesse.

She burst through the front door and took in the empty living room and kitchen before she raced down the hallway. She got a glimpse of Jesse in his bedroom as she made her way to the end of the hall. She was relieved to see her parent's room was empty, and her father wasn't sleeping after a long shift.

She made her way back to Jesse's room, nervously plucking at her top as she stopped in the open doorway. He paced manically, a far cry from his controlled, athletic grace. She was at a complete loss on how to fix this, especially when she and Jesse weren't on the best terms.

They'd grown apart this summer. Jesse attended sports camps, helped renovate the church and went dirt biking, hunting, and fishing while she spent her time with whoever she was dating and her friends. Mom and Dad had remarked on her suddenly full social calendar, but they'd been happy for her rather than disappointed. Little did they know, she was doing it to avoid Jesse and exhaust herself so she could sleep through his visits.

It had been a sound strategy, but it hadn't had the desired effect. Her body still responded to Jesse despite the emotional distance and distractions she'd placed between them. The shame of being sexually attracted to her step-brother caused her to give Tucker privileges she otherwise wouldn't have if her hormones weren't running amok.

She glanced at the clock. Mom would be home in an hour and a half. She had never been more grateful that Lynne helped with after school programs. She wasn't sure when Dad would be home, but she would do anything to gain Jesse's promise not to tell him what she'd done with Tucker.

Her father would lose his mind. Would he take matters into his own hands and go after Tucker with a gun for daring to touch her? When she decided to date Tobias, she went to Lynne first, who made good on her promise to handle Dad. Though it clearly pained him, Dad allowed her to date on one condition—that she wouldn't allow any boy to pressure her to do anything she wasn't comfortable with. That was Dad's way of telling her she wasn't allowed to have sex. She hadn't gone all the way with Tucker, but that wouldn't matter to Dad. Imagining his reaction made her sweat. The thrill of breaking the rules and treading into forbidden territory had long since faded. Now, all she could think of was the consequences.

"What the hell were you thinking?"

Jesse's words, dripping with disgust, made her hang her head.

"I'm sorry."

"Sorry?"

Out of the corner of her eye, she saw him feverishly rake his fingers through his hair.

"If I hadn't seen it with my own eyes, no one could have convinced me that you would let him touch you like that."

A ripple of defiance stole through her. "Why not? He's my boyfriend! I'm *seventeen*. Other girls..."

He pivoted to face her.

"You aren't like other girls! You're better than that."

She swallowed hard and averted her gaze.

"Or I thought you were."

The verbal blow stole her breath. Jesse had never been intentionally hurtful, but that stabbed her straight through the heart and momentarily distracted her from their parents' impending arrival. Before she could think of a response, Jesse whirled and sank his fist into the wall. She gasped, hands over her mouth, as he retracted a hand now covered in not just Tucker's blood but his own. She thought that would be the end of it, but when he pulled back his fist again, clearly about to pummel the wall to bits, she rushed forward. She hauled back on his arm, stopping the force of his punch so he merely cracked the wall instead of creating another gaping hole.

"Please stop," she begged.

He shrugged her off as if he couldn't stand her touch, as if she was contaminated. He skirted around her, looking anywhere but directly at her. Once again, he ran his fingers through his hair, not registering the dust, plaster, and blood that was getting all over him.

"You're hurt," she said quietly.

He began to pace again, head bent, hands flexing at his sides.

"Let me clean your hand."

No response. No reaction to her voice. Cautiously, she

started toward him. She had to snap out of this agitated state. This wasn't the Jesse she knew. For nine months, she'd known there was more to him than what he presented to the world, but somehow, this side of him was more shocking than the late-night visits. Anger wasn't a part of his makeup. Neither was violence. Seeing both made her feel like she was talking to a stranger.

"What can I do?" she whispered, willing to do anything to make this right.

"You should leave," he said in a flat monotone as he stared at the floor.

"Jesse."

"I thought I knew you better than I knew myself. I never thought you would let anyone…"

His leg flashed out, sneakers colliding with an old dresser that shuddered, but otherwise didn't move. Encouraged by this, Jesse kicked it again and then kneed it in a move that she knew would hurt tomorrow. Knowing even in the depths of his rage that he would never hurt her, she inserted herself between him and his target. Just as she expected, he immediately backed away from the dresser, which was apparently indestructible.

Despite the wild look in his eye, she reached for him and clasped his face.

"Stop hurting yourself," she pleaded.

He tried to jerk away, but she wouldn't let him, tightening her hold and matching the steps he took to put distance between them.

"Look at me," she ordered.

He looked over her head, jaw set. Her eyes filled with tears as she stroked his cheeks.

"Please."

He tugged her hands from his face. Knowing he was

about to push her away, she plastered her body against his. He went rigid.

"I'm sorry that I put you in that position. I'm sorry you had to see... I wasn't thinking." A tear slipped down her cheek. "Please don't be angry at me."

"Step back," he said coldly.

The compulsion to obey was strong, but she stayed put. The moment she backed away, he would continue taking his anger out on the room, which would make it impossible to keep anything from their parents. She needed him cool and rational. She didn't know what to do with the Jesse before her, who was trembling with the need to wreak havoc. All she knew was he wouldn't hurt her, and although he wanted space, her presence was the only thing stopping him from going nuclear.

"Please don't tell Dad," she said.

He glared at the wall and didn't respond.

"I swear, I won't do it again."

Again, nothing.

"Jesse." She went on tiptoes to force him to look at her, and when that didn't work, she yanked his head down. Stubbornly, his gaze remained averted. Anxious, frustrated, and exasperated, she did the only thing she could think of and brushed her mouth against his. Stormy blue eyes immediately snapped to hers. She jerked back, hands dropping away, stunned by her own impulsivity. What the hell was she *doing*? First Tucker and now she was kissing her stepbrother. What was happening to her? She backed away, twisting her hands together, cheeks hot.

"Is that how you get your way these days? With kisses?" Jesse asked in a cynical tone.

Her mouth dropped before she glared at him. "No!"

"Then what was that?"

She flung her hands in the air. "I just wanted you to calm down!"

"So, you kissed me."

Her stomach writhed. "I-I don't know why I did that." When he continued to stare at her, she snapped, "We've kissed on the lips before."

"By accident."

"Yes, well, so was this."

His eyes narrowed. "You really think I'm not going to tell Dad what happened today?"

"I don't know why you would." She was relieved to return to their real problem. "You'd be in just as much trouble as me! You beat the crap out of him! Dad won't—"

"Dad's going to pat me on the back, and you know it. Dad warned you about boys like Tucker. Boys who will take advantage of your inexperience to pressure you into something you aren't ready for."

She crossed her arms over her chest and jutted out her hip. "Who says I'm not ready? I know what I want!"

His eyes darkened. "Do you?"

"Yes!" she said defiantly. "I'm not a little girl. I'm going to be a senior next year. I'm allowed to experiment if I want to! If I want him to..."

He closed the distance between them in two strides. She fell silent as he towered over her.

"You want him to what?"

Something about his tone caused the fine hairs on her nape to rise. The only sound in the room was her rapid breathing. As he stared at her, not speaking, her nipples hardened into points so sharp, they hurt. Embarrassed and confused, she stepped back and collided with the massive dresser.

"You want to experiment?" he asked softly as he crowded her.

She swallowed hard, heart thudding in her ears as she tried to think. His hand moved between them. She went cold when she felt a tug on her shorts. When he began to pull down her zipper, she clutched his wrist and shook her head. He held her gaze as he nudged her shorts down. Her breath halted when he cupped her like Tucker had. His fingers pressed against the gusset of her underwear. Not penetrating, but firm enough to push the material between her lips.

"How much have you experimented?"

His voice, rough with anger, caused her insides to clench. Warmth pooled low. To her horror, she felt herself secrete. She held her breath, hoping he wouldn't feel her underwear dampen, but a second later, his fingers shifted, rubbed, and then his expression hardened.

He brushed her underwear aside and slipped a finger inside her. She let out a strangled yelp and banged into the dresser in a desperate bid to get away, but Jesse was relentless. His finger sank so deep, her mouth opened on a silent gasp.

"You're soaked," he growled against her temple and hissed when her pussy bathed him in more honey. "Christ."

"I..." She closed her eyes as another finger joined the first. "Jesse."

"How many times?" he growled.

She grabbed fistfuls of his shirt and tugged, unable to utter a single word. Her mind was whirling, emotions spiraling, back arching as he caused her womb to weep. She went on tiptoes as he sank deeper than her hairbrush ever had.

"How many times?" he bit out.

"I... I don't know," she babbled as her shorts dropped to her ankles, allowing her to spread her legs, which he immediately took advantage of.

"You've done it so many times, you didn't keep count?"

His voice was so guttural she could barely understand him, but what he was saying didn't matter when he was fingering her. Was this really happening? It couldn't be. It was broad daylight. Jesse never did anything sexual during the day, but there was no denying he was definitely touching her.

Shock made her lightheaded. Jesse caught her as she began to sway. Her head swam as he picked her up and settled her on his bed. Her legs hung over the side as she lay on her back, chest pumping as she tried to wrap her mind around what was happening. She jerked as her underwear was dragged down her legs. When she heard a zipper being undone, she stopped breathing. She felt the coarse brush of his jeans against her shin as he stepped out of them.

"Jesse?" she whispered.

A large hand cupped the back of her knee and began to lift it, spreading her wide. Her hands dove between her legs to cover the heart of her that had been touched for the first time today by two different boys within the same hour. She should stop this. She should talk some sense into him, but one look into blue eyes that still glittered with banked rage made her body pliant in instinctive submission.

"I was so patient. I thought we had an understanding, but you gave yourself to him," he growled as he dragged her ass to the edge of the bed.

"I..." she began, but her mind went blank as something began to enter her. She looked down the length of her body as Jesse gripped her hip, holding her still as he fed his dick into her with his bruised, bloody hand. Belatedly, she tried to scoot away to stop him, but his hold tightened, keeping her in place.

The tendons in his neck stood out as he bared his teeth and eased his way in. He still wore his white t-shirt, splattered with specks of red. His nipples stood out starkly as he stared down at where they were joined. He braced himself over her, the gold cross on the chain around his neck dangling over her face as he buried himself inside her. His groan drowned out her own.

"Jesse?"

"How could you?" he panted as he withdrew and gently began to drive in again. "How could you do this to me?"

As her unused channel spasmed in pain, she grasped his shirt, feet kicking for purchase as her body tried to adjust to his invasion. Panicked tears leaked out of the corner of her eyes.

"I don't know what you're..." Her voice died as he speared her core, tearing through her hymen.

Jesse went rigid, and then his head came up. He stared down at her, eyes wide with astonishment. Every ounce of anger drained away to be replaced with anguish. He cupped her wet cheek with a shaking hand.

"You're a virgin?" he whispered.

She nodded jerkily.

He rested his forehead against hers. "God, I'm sorry. I'm so sorry, baby."

He chanted his apology while she lay rigid as a board beneath him. She was dimly aware of the sound of kids playing basketball in the street. His blinds were up. There was a bush obscuring part of his window, but if anyone looked in, they'd see...

"Look at me."

Her skittering thoughts halted. She met his gaze as

he stroked back her hair. He looked like her brother again. Composed, gentle, affectionate. But he was inside of her, and he hadn't pulled out yet. She could feel his dick pulsing inside of her like a piece of heated steel. Now that the pain was receding, it felt... okay.

"You never..." he began unsteadily and then hissed and closed his eyes as his dick twitched inside of her.

"That was the first time he ever touched me."

His eyes shot open and bored into hers. "And that's the last time. No one's ever going to touch you but me." His gaze moved over her face and landed on her lips. "You don't know how long I've been waiting for this." His hips moved and when she didn't flinch, his breath hitched in excitement. "I'm sorry. I need this."

She didn't make a sound as he began to move. She knew he was larger than other boys his age and had witnessed his strength, but she had never experienced both until now. He was going too deep, too fast.

"Jesse, you're hurting me," she whispered.

He didn't slow down. He was deaf to anything but the urges of his body and ruthlessly sought relief.

"Jesse!"

She pushed and when that got no reaction from him, her hands slipped under his tee and raked over his back. That only seemed to spur him on. She fought him in earnest, scared and in agony, but Jesse was oblivious to both. When he finally climaxed and slumped on top of her, she was covered in cold sweat.

He eased to the side so she could take a full breath. Pinned partially beneath him, she stared at the ceiling, battered, shaken, and numb. This wasn't supposed to happen. It couldn't happen. But it had. Now, what?

Jesse lay on his side facing her. She tensed as he splayed his hand on her quivering abdomen.

"I'm sorry."

She wasn't sure whether he was sorry for what he'd just done, how rough he'd been, or believing she hadn't been a virgin. It didn't matter. Nothing did anymore.

He gripped her face and tipped it toward him. Sated, heavy lidded eyes searched her blank, tear-streaked face.

"I'll make this up to you," he vowed as his thumb passed over her bottom lip.

The only way he could make this up to her was if they pretended that it never happened. As if he'd heard her thought, he grimaced.

"I'll never forgive myself." He stroked her cheek. "I promised myself I'd never hurt you, that I'd always protect you. I failed on both counts today, and I can't take it back. Can you forgive me?"

She nodded without thinking it through. Accepting his apology was a reflex, something that had been drilled into her by going to church her whole life. Nothing was so egregious that it couldn't be forgiven, even this... She gulped back tears as she began to shake.

Jesse drew her against him. Even though he was the cause of her pain, she wrapped one arm around him and sobbed against his throat as everything that had happened over the past hour overwhelmed her. He stroked her hair and apologized over and over.

"I swear, Violet," he breathed fervently. "I'll never—"

She turned her head and latched onto his mouth. She wasn't sure whether she did it because she didn't want him to make rash promises, or because she wanted a different type of comfort. Either way, it did the job. The talking stopped, and the physical reassurance she desperately needed after he'd used her body so brutally came in the form of a gentle, almost reverent kiss.

She had kissed a few boys, but most of her experience came from Tucker. He was a playboy and had great technique, but there was something about the way Jesse kissed her, as if she was made of fragile glass, that soothed the trauma of her first time. That hadn't been him. That was his dark alter ego that paid her midnight visits. This was Jesse, the one who clasped her face as he kissed her, as if she was the most precious thing in the world to him.

Kissing other boys caused her tummy to flutter, but with Jesse, she felt like her world was spinning. He kissed her with an absorption that blocked out everything else. He didn't stop, even to let her catch her breath.

When his fingers probed between her legs, she stiffened and tried to push his hand away.

"Let me do this for you," he breathed against her lips.

She was prepared for more pain when his finger slid inside her. To her surprise, it evoked a pleasant, familiar throb of desire.

"Does that feel good?"

She bit her lip.

"Violet."

Her eyes opened and stared into his.

"Tell me how it feels."

He wasn't angry, but his intensity was back. She flushed under his dissecting gaze as her awareness flared out, reminding her where they were and that soon Mom and Dad would be...

Jesse's thumb rubbed her clitoris. She let out a stifled shriek and bucked.

He kissed her cheek. "Yes, let me know what you like. I want to make you fly."

He asked her for guidance on how he was making her feel, but words were beyond her. Her moans, gasps, and shudders led him instead. When she finally came, she bit her own forearm to stifle her scream.

"Good girl."

She heard Jesse's satisfied tone from a long way off. She felt his hand smoothing what was dripping out of her onto her belly. Her eyes fluttered shut against her will.

"Jesse," she slurred.

He kissed her temple. "Everything's fine. Go to sleep."

"But I..."

He covered her mouth with his. Their tongues dueled before her mouth went slack. He broke the kiss, chuckling, and kissed her forehead. "Sleep, baby."

<hr>

SHE SWAM UP FROM THE DEPTHS. HER BODY ACHED LIKE SHE HAD the flu. Was she ill? She opened her eyes and took in her surroundings. The room was dark, but a nightlight oriented her in her bedroom.

She listened, but no voices drifted down the hall. Had she missed dinner? She braced her hand on the bed to sit up and felt an unfamiliar, dragging pain between her legs. Her breath caught in her throat as graphic visions whizzed through her mind. Her hand slid over her body and stilled. She was no longer wearing a top or shorts. She was in one of her nightgowns. Her brows drew together. *Was* it a dream? Her fingers pressed between her legs, but there was no sticky residue. She was clean, but tender and achy. Why couldn't she remember?

She threw back the covers and went into the bathroom. She didn't turn on the light but went to Jesse's door and put her ear to it before she stepped through. Jesse's room was dark, but the door leading into the hallway was open, allowing her to see that the room was empty. Frowning, she peered at the made bed, which had sheets tucked so tight, she could bounce a quarter off it.

Worried that she was losing her mind, she entered the hallway. The door to her parents' domain was closed, indicating one or both of her parents had turned in. What time was it? The living and dining room were empty, but there was a lone lamp on. She peered at the numbers on the microwave but was distracted by an unfamiliar flickering light in the backyard. Jesse stood by the fire pit. She stared at him through the glass, heart thudding in her ears, palms damp with anxiety.

As if he sensed her, he half turned. With the fire behind him, she couldn't see his face, but he beckoned her outside with his hand.

She hesitated before her need for answers and confirmation pushed away her uncertainty. She slipped on sandals as she crossed to him. He held out his arm as she neared. She didn't hesitate to tuck herself against his side.

"Feeling better?" he asked.

She stiffened. "I'm fine."

He stroked her arm. "That's good to hear."

She hovered on the precipice, wanting to know if what her mind was shrieking at her was true, but she didn't voice it. Instead, she huddled beneath the umbrella of denial and let the flames of the small fire hypnotize her. She absorbed Jesse's strength and warmth. She didn't want things to change between them. This was familiar, comfortable, meant to be. That other stuff was titillating, but wrong on every level.

Her eyes narrowed as she spotted something in the fire.

She took a step forward. "There's a…" She fell silent as she got a better look. Her heart lodged in her throat. "Is that my top and shorts?"

"And underwear," Jesse confirmed.

She whirled to face him. "Why are you burning it?"

His eyes were a mix of blue and orange flame.

"You know why."

She crossed her arms. "No, I don't."

"Every time I'd see those shorts or top, I'd think of Tucker."

Her breath stalled. Her face drained of all color, and she swayed.

"Hey." Jesse drew her trembling form against him. "You aren't okay. You should be lying down."

Before she could speak, he picked her up and started toward the house.

"I told Mom and Dad you weren't feeling well. Dad's shift went long, so he went straight to bed. Mom made soup and then turned in. Are you just sore or do you need—"

"What did you tell them?" she hissed.

"About what?"

"About what?" she echoed shrilly. "About your bruised knuckles, the hole in your wall, Tucker and…" Her throat constricted as she thought about what happened between them.

"They didn't see the hole. I moved something in front of it until I can patch it up. They didn't notice my hand, and there's no reason for them to hear about Tucker. As far as they know, I brought you home from school, and you went to bed because you weren't feeling well."

He carried her into the house and settled her at the table before he made his way to the kitchen, where he busied himself at the stove. He sounded so matter of fact, so controlled and blasé, as if losing his temper and taking her virginity was nothing out of the ordinary. She didn't know how to feel or behave. He was acting as if nothing had changed, so maybe it hadn't?

He brought her chicken tortellini soup and bread rolls and made a bowl for himself.

"Do you want tea?" he asked.

"Water's fine," she said awkwardly and stared at the pills he set on the table. "What's this?"

"Ibuprofen."

Her cheeks heated as she swallowed the pills. As he began to eat, she took in her familiar surroundings. Everything looked as it should, but she felt different, like she'd gone to Narnia for a year and came back to find she hadn't missed a second. But that's what she wanted, right? For everything to be as it should?

She glanced at Jesse. His blood splattered shirt had been replaced with a pristine white tee and sweatpants. His gold cross was on display. The memory of it swinging back and forth as he thrust inside her made her womb clench. She clamped her thighs together and blew on her spoonful of soup before she took a bite. It was delicious. She hadn't eaten since lunch, and it was now... She glanced at the clock. Almost eight.

"Do you want anything else?"

She focused on Jesse to discover he had inhaled his soup. Her mouth twitched. "No, thank you. I'm still working on it."

He grinned at her. "Sorry, I was starving."

She went solid as he kissed her forehead and got to his feet. Her eyes followed him to the kitchen as he rummaged in the fridge. If she hadn't been an active participant in what happened today, she wouldn't be able to sense that anything had happened. There were no strange undercurrents or awkwardness. Jesse was back to being the affectionate big brother and she... She looked down at her soup. She was going to resume playing her part of younger sister. That was best for everyone.

"You don't like it?"

She jolted as Jesse's question broke through her hazy musings. "No, it's great. I guess I'm still tired."

He gave her a sympathetic look as he brushed back her hair. "You want me to run you a bath?"

Even this question wasn't out of the ordinary, since she and Lynne talked openly about their periods. Jesse didn't mind pampering them or being sent to the store for pads or tampons, while her father flat out refused.

"No, I'm okay. I'll just finish what I can and turn in," she said lightly.

"Okay." He glanced outside. "I have to watch the fire."

"Yes, you do that." When he turned away, she hesitated before she asked, "Did you burn anything else besides...?" Again, she blushed like a virgin. She wasn't anymore, so she would have to get past her embarrassment.

Jesse raised a brow. "Should I have?"

"I don't know." She broke eye contact and wrapped her foot around the leg of her chair. "Your sheets? Were they stained?"

"No."

She didn't hear him move, so wasn't prepared for the hand that grasped her chin. She felt her face turn beet red as he stared down at her.

"I got the blood out of them," he said in a low rumble that made her nipples hard. "You don't need to worry."

"You dressed me," she whispered.

"I knew Mom would want to check on you. She couldn't find you naked."

Very practical on his part, but, "You cleaned me."

His gaze fixed on her mouth. "Seemed like the proper thing to do."

His eyes rose to hers. Her heartbeat accelerated.

"Is there anything else you want to ask me before I tend to the fire?" he asked gently.

She shook her head. His finger slid along her jaw before he turned away. She turned back to her soup and ate mechanically before she put her bowl in the sink. Habit made her clean up the kitchen and wash the dishes. She glanced outside and saw Jesse staring contemplatively into the fire. What was he thinking? Did he feel like his life turned upside down, or was deflowering his stepsister something they would forget ever happened? That they would never speak of, like his late-night visits?

While she brushed her teeth, she scanned the bathroom for any sign of their hookup, but everything looked boringly mundane. She wished she had her phone to see if there was any word from Tucker. Had word already gotten out of Jesse fighting Tucker?

It wasn't until she swallowed her birth control pill that her eyes flew to the mirror, wide as saucers. Holy shit. She had been put on birth control a year ago to regulate her heavy, painful period. It never occurred to her that she would need it for its main purpose. She went cold with terror at the thought of getting pregnant. She was a Christian. It had been drummed into her that life was sacred and to be protected and preserved at all costs. She didn't believe in abortion, but if she was accidentally impregnated by her stepbrother, she would have no choice but to... Bile rose.

She swished mouthwash to banish the taste from her mouth before she staggered to bed.

She tunneled under the covers and clasped her stuffed longhorn to her aching chest. She made a lot of stupid decisions today. The repercussions were steep, but they could have been much worse. Unfortunately, Tucker got the worst of it. Was he pissed at her? She hoped he hadn't been hurt too badly. And her consequence had been to lose her virginity. Not to the man she thought, but the most unlikely person imaginable. Even as pangs of anxiety washed over her, memories of Jesse in the throes distracted and made her body tingle.

She banished such sinful thoughts and thanked God that Mom and Dad were unaware of what happened this afternoon. Although she was worried about how she and Jesse would deal with each other moving forward, she was too tired to fight the tug of replenishing sleep. She gave in to oblivion with a soft sigh.

CHAPTER 9
JESSE

Jesse stood beside Violet's bed. Thick lashes rested against her cheeks and her mouth was parted slightly, letting him know she was deeply asleep.

She was his. Finally.

He brushed her hair back as he marveled at the strange string of events that led to the consummation of their relationship. In the middle of practice, one of his teammates told him that Tucker had bragged about taking Violet's virginity and sharing her with his bandmates. The way the rest of the team avoided his gaze told him everyone had heard the lies Tucker was spreading, but no one had the balls to tell him except Reggie.

He hadn't thought twice about stalking off the field, changing out of his uniform, and tossing his gear in the car. It was sheer coincidence that he spotted Tucker's Bronco and saw two people on the side of it. Even as he started toward them, they'd moved to the back of the car. The last thing he expected to find was Tucker with his hand in Violet's pants.

He'd taken great pleasure in smashing his fist into Tucker's pretty face. He would have killed him with his bare hands if Violet hadn't stopped him. He knew about Tucker's playboy reputation and had wrongly assumed Violet would break it off if Tucker pressured her sexually. It never occurred to him that Violet would welcome his advances.

As the rage flooded back, he slid his thumb into Violet's mouth to calm him. She jerked back, but he followed, unwilling to give her space. He rubbed his thumb over her tongue, encouraging her to suck. When she reflexively obeyed, he bit back a groan and buried his face in her hair spread over the pillow.

He fooled around with his fair share of girls but never slept with any of them. He hadn't wanted to. He'd been saving himself for her. He thought they had an unspoken understanding. The betrayal and pain that consumed him was something he never wanted to experience again. He drew in a steadying breath and was comforted by her bewitching scent he couldn't get enough of. It didn't matter that Tucker had his hand in her pants first. He was the only man who had been inside her. That's all that mattered.

Today, Violet finally made her move. She kissed him. From the mortified expression on her face, she hadn't meant to, but he was damn glad she had. That impulsive kiss funneled his anger into lust. If only he'd known she was acting on instinct or desire rather than bribing him to keep quiet. Thinking she was using wiles she learned from Tucker to manipulate him, he'd been coarse, rough, out of line.

Violet let out a pitiful whimper. He nuzzled her, wondering if she was having a bad dream or if she was in pain despite the pills he'd given her. He felt a flash of regret that her first time hadn't been the gentle, loving experience she deserved. If only he'd known she was a virgin... But catching her and Tucker red-handed, he wouldn't have believed her if she'd said so.

Assuming she'd given herself to Tucker first and considering how slick she was, slow and tender had been the furthest thing from his mind. And even when he realized she was a virgin, he'd denied himself for so long that he hadn't been able to hold back the force of his need. With all that rage still pumping through his system from dealing with Tucker, he'd been primitive and savage. Violet didn't accept his claim meekly. She fought him. It had been an exhilarating, eye-opening experience. It wasn't romantic, but it was perfect because it was them, stripped of all civilization. Violet rose to the challenge and after, still trusted him with her body and allowed him to bring her to orgasm. He'd never been more grateful that he'd practiced on other girls beforehand. Violet came so hard; she passed out cold.

Knowing their parents would be home soon, he cleaned and dressed her. He didn't have time to inspect her the way he wanted. Instead, he put her in bed before he stripped off his sheets and rearranged his room to cover the hole that would prompt questions he couldn't answer. Once his bedding was in the wash, he checked on Violet, which led to him jacking off on her. He'd just cleaned her face with a cloth when Mom arrived.

"What's wrong?"

"Vi isn't feeling good," he said in low tones, and hoped Violet wouldn't wake at this inopportune moment.

He felt like he was coming out of his skin as Mom approached the bed and brushed back Violet's tangled hair. He prayed to God he got every drop of his cum as Mom pressed the back of her hand against Violet's damp fore-head and cheek.

"She feels feverish," Mom said with a frown. "Has she taken anything?"

"No, she was hoping to sleep it off."

"I'll make soup," Mom said.

As Mom walked to the door, he couldn't resist doing one more pass over Violet's face with the washcloth. When he looked up, he saw Mom in the doorway, watching him with a fond smile.

"You're such a good brother," she'd said before she walked away.

He was never meant to be her brother. He'd known from the moment he laid eyes on her that he was destined to be more. It was everyone else who had it wrong, not him.

Jesse straightened and withdrew his thumb from Violet's mouth. He vowed to give her time to recover, but he was hard as a rock. He pushed his pants down and grabbed Violet's hand and curled her fingers around him. He moved her hand along his length and shuddered in absolute bliss. Her tiny, silky fingers felt amazing and with the memory of what it felt like to be inside her heating his blood, it didn't take long.

He tipped his head back, gasping, as he climaxed. He spread his cum over her skin and held her face still as he sank his tongue into her mouth. She mewled and tried to get away, but he held her captive until she surrendered.

He eyed the closed door. There was still a chance that their parents would check on her. It was risky as hell for him to come into her room, but he couldn't resist.

He tucked himself away and gave her a swift kiss. She frowned, face scrunching up in what looked like disgust, before she turned her back to him. He grinned as he stepped back.

When she joined him by the fire pit, pale, dazed, and confused, he sensed her questions, but she didn't voice them. He had to tread carefully. They had gone astray before. He wouldn't allow that a second time. He would begin his campaign tomorrow and show her how their relationship was always meant to be.

CHAPTER 10
VIOLET

VIOLET WOKE BEFORE DAYLIGHT. SHE TIPTOED INTO THE bathroom and washed her face and teeth before she left her bedroom. She was surprised to see a glow from the dining room and found Dad sitting at the table, reading his Bible.

"Hey, kiddo. How are you feeling?"

"Okay." Her heart was in her throat as she came forward and gripped the back of the chair. "What are you doing up so early?"

"God woke me up, told me I needed to read the Word." He tapped the open Bible. "Mom told me you weren't feeling good yesterday. I checked on you before I turned in, but you were out. I prayed over you."

She gave him a tremulous smile. "It worked. I feel much better."

He pulled out Lynne's chair. "Coffee?"

She made a face. "No!"

He chuckled. "Cocoa it is."

She sat as he went to the kitchen. She tucked her hands between her thighs as Dad made her a comfort drink. She thought that just by looking at her, people would be able to tell some monumental change had happened, but even her sharp-eyed father didn't seem to think anything was amiss. That was a relief.

"There you go."

She grinned when Dad set a mug heaping with marshmallows in front of her. "Thank you."

She popped a few in her mouth before she realized Dad was watching her closely. She froze.

"What?"

"When Lynne told me you weren't feeling good, I thought something else may have happened."

Her pulse skipped. "Like what?"

"I don't know." He took a long draw on his coffee. "I thought, maybe, boy troubles?"

She wrapped her hands around the mug and stared at the quivering marshmallows.

"Vi?"

She met his serious gaze.

"You rarely get sick. Is there something you want to tell me?"

"Tucker and I broke up," she heard herself say.

She hadn't realized she'd made a conscious decision until the words left her mouth. She'd been trying not to think past getting something to eat—the primary reason she'd gotten up at this hour. Apparently, her mind had made some decisions while she slept.

Even if Tucker didn't hate her for Jesse beating the hell out of him, she wasn't the same person she'd been yesterday. She couldn't act as if nothing had happened. Jesse was partially right. Tucker had been pressuring her sexually and eventually, she would have given into him, and it wouldn't be because she had any deep feelings for him. It would be to assuage her body's needs. Now that Jesse had done that for her, there was no need for her to use these boys as a distraction or outlet. All these months of emotional turmoil had been washed away by yesterday's events. She was a new person and had officially stepped into womanhood.

"I thought that may be the case," Dad said.

She narrowed her eyes. "You're smiling."

"Can you blame me?" He held up a hand before she could say a word. "I'm sure Tucker's a good kid, but I don't like the way he treated you. He always had an arm around your neck like you were his property..." He shook his head. "You want a guy who looks after you and respects you. Tucker only cared about himself. You can do better."

She pushed her marshmallows down into the hot cocoa.

"You want to tell me why you broke up with him?"

"No."

"Maybe you should take a break from dating." When she gave him a level look, he tacked on, "Or date one of the guys from church, so I don't have to worry so much."

"Morning."

They turned their heads as Jesse entered the dining room with messy hair and a wrinkled shirt. Jesse came straight to her. Her stomach clenched as he clasped her face between his hands.

"You feel okay?" he asked.

She gripped his hand, very aware of Dad watching them. "I'm fine. Just hungry."

Jesse nodded and kissed her forehead. "I'll make you something." He moved to Dad and clapped him on the back. "What about you?"

"I can eat."

She cut into her melted marshmallows with her spoon, dunked them in cocoa and shoveled them in her mouth.

"Vi said she had boy problems. You know anything about it?" Dad asked.

She choked as Jesse turned away from the open fridge with an egg carton in his hand.

"Boy problems?" he echoed.

"She said her and Tucker are done."

"Dad!" she exclaimed and swatted his arm.

"What? I'm spreading the good news. We've all been worried, especially Jesse. He didn't tell us about Tucker's background, but I didn't need him to. All you had to do was look at the kid to know he was bad news."

"I get it!" she said loudly. "It's over."

He looked up at the ceiling and murmured, "Thank you, Jesus."

She was considering kicking him when Lynne appeared, tying the sash of her robe over her nightgown.

"Everything okay?"

"Yeah, we're just thanking God for answering prayer," Dad said.

Before she could make a retort, Lynne clasped her face, just as Jesse had.

"How are you feeling, honey? Do you need to stay home from school?"

"No, I'm back to normal. I'm just hungry."

"I'm on it, Mom," Jesse called out.

Mom patted her cheek before she gave Dad a kiss and made her way to the kitchen. She gave Jesse a hug before she grabbed a cup of coffee and settled at the table.

"Do you have a scripture for us, Isaac?" Lynne asked.

"I opened my Bible to this." Dad bent over the page and tapped a passage. "Ecclesiastes 3: 1-8. There is a time for everything, and a season for every activity under the heavens: a time to be born and a time to die, a time to plant and a time to uproot, a time to kill and a time to heal, a time to tear down and a time to build..."

Lynne nodded as Dad read the passage that described the ever-changing seasons of life.

"There's a time to tear and a time to mend, a time to love and a time to hate, a time for war and a time for peace," Dad finished and cocked his head to the side as he contemplated the highlighted passage. "I've had my fair share of worries and internal battles lately. I'm always trying to control every outcome and prepare for what I think will happen."

Violet was caught off guard when Dad suddenly grinned at her.

"But there's no need to worry. God heard my prayers and answered them. What isn't meant to be, God won't allow."

Her mouth dropped. "Dad!"

"Did I miss something?" Lynne asked with raised brows.

"Vi broke up with her wannabe rock star," Dad shared with unashamed delight.

"Oh, honey, is that why you weren't feeling well yesterday?" Lynne asked with great sympathy as she reached across the table to pat her hand.

Jesse plopped a plate of pancakes in front of her and Mom. "Better eat them while they're hot."

<hr>

She was putting the finishing touches on her makeup when Jesse double knocked on the bathroom door. Before she could say he could come in, he did so, startling her.

"You sure you want to go to school?" he asked. "You don't have to if you'd rather stay home and rest."

She lifted her chin. "I'm fine."

He held her gaze. "You don't have to pretend with me. I know I hurt you yesterday." His eyes moved over her face as he reached out and gently stroked her side. "In more ways than one. I want to make sure you're okay."

She swallowed hard, eyes watering slightly at his tenderness. "I really am okay."

Whatever he saw in her eyes must have reassured him because he nodded.

"I'm ready when you are," he said and left without another word.

She stared after him, heart thudding in her ears, every nerve ending buzzing. Everything was the same and yet... not. He wasn't ignoring what happened, but he also wasn't discussing it in detail. She was grateful and confused.

Once she was in her bedroom, she automatically looked around for her backpack before remembered where she left it. She wished she knew what to expect at school today. She suspected Tucker wouldn't show his bruised face... Unless he decided to report Jesse's unprovoked attack to the school? Had anyone witnessed what happened? Were any rumors circulating? Had Tucker tried to contact her?

With countless questions crowding her mind, she headed down the hall. Mom was already gone and after a quick scan of the kitchen and living room, she headed outside where Jesse was already in the SUV. She walked toward him, feeling naked and awkward without her backpack.

She slipped into the passenger seat and buckled herself in. Jesse had the country station on. She tried to get lost in

the music, but her mind was overwrought as she anticipated what the day would bring.

"Where's your backpack?"

"It was on the side of Tucker's Bronco. I hope it's still in
the parking lot," she said, rapping her fingernails on the
door.

"Hopefully, someone turned it in."

"Yeah."

There was a long pause before he asked, "You're
breaking up with Tucker?"

The toe of her right shoe tapped restlessly. "Yes."

"That's good."

She waited for him to elaborate, but when he didn't, she
didn't pursue it. Instead, she asked, "You aren't worried
you'll get in trouble?"

"For what?"

She finally looked at him. He wore a white shirt with
jeans and a navy hat pulled low over his eyes. The gold
cross on his chain gleamed on his chest.

"For assaulting someone," she said sharply. "You could
get kicked off the team for fighting. What you did to Tucker
could get you banned from sports completely."

"I had cause."

She tensed and balled her hand into a fist as she
reminded him quietly, "He didn't force me."

A hint of the rage he displayed yesterday crossed his
face as he shot her a hard, glittering look. "Don't, Vi."

"I'm just being honest! If you get pulled into the
office..."

"I won't."

"How do you know that?"

"Because Tucker had it coming and he knew it. Why do
you think I walked out of practice yesterday?"

She straightened, this new piece of information catching her totally by surprise. Jesse should have been occupied with football practice. That's why she took leave of her senses and allowed Tucker to take such liberties. She was so rattled, it never crossed her mind why Jesse had stumbled across them in the first place.

"Why'd you leave practice?" she asked.

The muscles in his forearms flexed as he tightened his hold on the steering wheel. "I had a bone to pick with Tucker, but once I found you two, why I was looking for him no longer mattered."

"So, you weren't looking for me, you were looking for him," she clarified.

"Yes."

"And you weren't expecting to find me with him."

He shifted restlessly in his seat, yesterday's aggression permeating the air.

"No."

So, the events that unfolded yesterday wasn't because of her, as she thought. Jesse was already angry enough with Tucker to leave practice. Catching Tucker fingering her set off Jesse's temper, which was the driving force behind his behavior. If she hadn't been in that compromising position when Jesse found them, she would still be a virgin today.

Feeling suddenly ill, she looked out the window and was relieved to see they had reached school. She scanned the parking lot, but there was no sign of Tucker's Bronco.

When she pushed open her door, Jesse said, "I'll come with you to lost and found."

Apparently, he didn't see her backpack either. As they made their way toward the cluster of buildings, she eyed the other students. No one pointed or came running up to them to confirm any juicy gossip. When their friends called out to them, she and Jesse raised their hands in acknowledgment, but they didn't stop to chat. Again, everything seemed normal. Freakishly so.

She didn't have high hopes that her backpack had been turned in, but to her immense relief, some angel had done the right thing. She immediately plunged her hand into the front pocket and said a silent prayer of thanks when she found her phone. As they walked out of the office, she scrolled through her messages and was relieved not to see anything out of the ordinary. By some miracle, the atomic bomb that went off in her life yesterday had gone unnoticed by anyone else.

"Vi."

She looked up with a frown. Jesse was looking down at her with a strange look on his face. "What?"

"Any word from Tucker?"

"No."

Jesse nodded. "That's good."

When the bell rang, he squeezed her arm.

"I'll see you later."

She watched him walk away. Faithful Marissa materialized at his side. Jesse hadn't dated after he broke up with Madyson four months ago. He'd been single for some time, which had caused quite a lot of speculation and gossip. Girls fawned over him, desperate to win his favor, but he seemed immune to their charm.

She turned in the opposite direction to go to her first class. She wasn't sure why her chest was tight or why her eyes began to water. She dabbed at the corner of her eye and fixed a smile on her face. All was well. Yesterday happened. She couldn't take it back and if she could, would she? She crossed the threshold into womanhood. Today, she was wiser and more mature.

So why did she feel so lost and lonely?

Want to get lunch somewhere?

She didn't respond to Jesse's text for two periods. She wasn't sure whether she should keep her distance from him or not. He had taken everything in stride, but that feeling of calm acceptance she woke with was beginning to wane.

Her friends were talking and laughing around her, but she felt disconnected, like her normal frequency was off. It was clear that they hadn't heard anything about what happened between Jesse and Tucker. They would have bombarded her otherwise. Georgia asked about Tucker during recess. She said they'd had a fight and were on a break. Her friends rubbed her back and gave her sympathetic hugs. The urge to confide in them was so strong, she had to excuse herself from their huddle.

In her next class, she noticed she was still getting odd looks like she had the day before. She kept her attention on her assignment and tried to ignore the paranoia that everyone could see right through her. If anyone knew that she, Violet Carr, had lost her virginity yesterday, *no one* would be giving her intense stares. They would be gawking. And if they knew who she'd lost it to...

"Are you sure?" someone whispered. "No. *Violet?*"

Her back stiffened as someone a row back gossiped about her. She reached for her phone and accepted Jesse's invitation to get lunch off campus. She had to get out of here.

The moment the bell rang, she dashed out the door and jogged to the parking lot. Jesse was already behind the wheel. She wasn't hungry, but the strain of appearing normal when she felt anything but was taking its toll. She was terrified she would accidentally blurt out something to her friends and once that happened, there was no taking it back. Better to be with Jesse. At least she didn't have to pretend with him.

"Hey," he said as she tossed her backpack on the floor and hopped into the passenger seat.

"Hey," she replied and rolled down the window for some fresh air.

"What do you want to eat?"

"Anything."

"Mexican?"

"Sure," she sighed.

"Are you okay?"

"Yup."

Jesse stopped by a well-known taco place. She surveyed the menu and jolted when Jesse touched her back.

"Know what you want?" he asked.

"Uh, can I get chicken tacos, and I'm going to grab an iced tea from the fridge."

He nodded and jerked his head, indicating for her to sit. She nabbed her drink before she sat at a glossy round table. Jesse stood behind two stocky construction workers. She found herself comparing Jesse's build to the grown men. Jesse's broad shoulders and military stance made him appear much older than his eighteen years. He had also put on some muscle while helping to rebuild the church this summer. He had a knack for it and had been working with a general contractor as an apprentice on the weekends.

Her eyes moved over him, taking in the well-fitted jeans and trim waist. As her eyes moved up, she spotted something above his collar. She half rose from her seat before she sat, hands over her mouth, as she stared at the scratches she'd left on the back of his neck. The urge to lift his shirt and inspect his back was overwhelming.

As Jesse stepped up to the counter, the cashier adjusted her black hat and blushed. Jesse smiled kindly at her and gestured at the board as he ordered. Jesse was back to being the nice guy. The helpful guy who held doors open for people and was always willing to lend a helping hand. No one would believe that he had an explosive temper, one that could ignite without warning. Thinking of the hunger in his gaze as he pinned her to the bed made her clamp her legs together and slant them to the side as her core pulsed. He'd been ruthless yesterday. Determined. She was still having trouble believing it happened. There was no visible mark on her to prove it hadn't been a bizarre figment of her imagination, but her mark on him was irrefutable proof of the intense battle they'd waged.

Jesse set his drink on the table and cocked his head to the side. "What?"

She bit her lip and gestured for him to sit before she reached out and gingerly touched his neck. She traced the mark, knowing he'd bled for it to still be there today.

"Did anyone say anything about your neck?"

"No."

"There's," she swallowed nervously, "marks."

He held her gaze as he rolled his shoulders. "That's not the only one."

"I'm sorry."

"I deserved it."

She flicked water droplets from her sweating can of iced tea. "It must hurt."

"It was worth it."

She looked away as her heart lurched into her throat.

"Vi."

Reluctantly, she looked back at him.

"Have you heard from Tucker?"

She shook her head.

He nodded, apparently satisfied.

"I was thinking of texting him we're over, but I'd rather talk to him in person."

"He knows."

"Still."

Jesse opened his mouth to argue, but the cashier called his name. Violet shook her head as the girl fussed over him before handing over a bag with their food. As Jesse turned, he headed toward the door. Surprised, Violet got up and followed him.

"I thought we were going to eat here."

"I know a better place," he said.

She thought he was going to stay in the school's vicinity. To her surprise, he drove quite a way before pulling into a deserted park.

"Where are we?"

"I come here to run on the trail."

She frowned. "When do you come here?"

"During lunch or after school if you catch a ride home with someone. It's out of the way, so it's rarely crowded."

"It's nice," she said as she handed over his massive burrito.

They ate in companionable silence, taking in the squirrels, birds, and a lone jogger that passed. When she finished her food, she tossed her trash in the plastic bag, sat back, and closed her eyes. She raised her face to the cool breeze that came through both of their open windows and let out a long sigh.

She thought her life had turned upside down, but what had really changed? She and Jesse were okay. She assessed the vibes in the car and detected nothing bad. There had been tension between them when she started dating, but now it was gone.

She had enjoyed Tucker, but wasn't upset about breaking up with him, which reaffirmed that she had been scratching an itch that no longer existed. The only thing she'd lost was her innocence, and girls lost that every day. Not to their stepbrother, but there was no erasing that fact. It would never happen again, so there was no sense in bemoaning the series of unfortunate events that resulted in her and Jesse having sex. In retrospect, insisting that she knew what she wanted and that she was old enough to experiment had contributed to Jesse losing control. He hadn't meant to go that far. Maybe he meant to teach her a lesson that had spiraled out of control?

"Vi."

She turned toward his voice with her eyes still closed. The last thing she expected was to feel his lips on hers. Her eyes flew open, and she straightened in her seat.

"Jesse, what...?"

He brushed his mouth against hers lightly, teasingly. She blinked, befuddled and alarmed by the spurt of heat that shot through her body.

"Don't think," he said against her lips. "Just feel."

"But..."

He cut her off as he covered her mouth with his. She didn't have a chance to think. His lips on hers short-circuited her brain. The tingling numbness that came upon her during his midnight visits engulfed her. Jesse's response to her paralysis was to deepen the kiss and replace the chill with scorching heat. She tried to mentally detach from what was happening, but the feelings he evoked wouldn't allow it. They lured her in and bathed her in sensation. When she whimpered, he broke the kiss to nuzzle her affectionately.

"It's okay, baby," he cooed. "I'm not going to hurt you."

She gripped his wrist as she tried to catch her breath. "I know that, but we can't—"

He brushed his thumb along the apple of her cheek. "There's a time for denial and a time for acceptance."

His spin on the scripture Dad had shared this morning made her heart skip.

"A time for restraint and a time to indulge." Jesse kissed the corner of her mouth. "It's our time, Violet. Stop thinking and *feel*." He brushed his lips against hers. "Open your mouth."

She parted her lips before she thought better of it. Jesse didn't give her time to change her mind. He took advantage of her obedience and sank his tongue into her mouth before he clasped her nape and drew her over the console, ignoring the fluttering hand she placed on his chest.

He kissed her with an absorption that made everything else cease to exist. She was lost in a maelstrom of feeling. She had never experienced anything like it. There was tenderness, desire, and a desperate urgency that seeped from him to her.

There was no thought of consequences or right and wrong. There was only mounting desire and the over-whelming need to do something about it.

When Jesse finally drew away, she clutched at him because she felt like she was teetering on the edge of a precipice. It took her a second to remember where they were, since she'd completely lost touch with her surroundings.

Jesse searched her eyes and cupped her flushed cheek. "You feel it, don't you?"

She swallowed hard, nodded. She thought she saw a flash of relief before he rested his forehead against hers.

"After school, I'll take care of us, okay?"

When she didn't respond, he tensed. He cupped her chin and searched her glazed eyes.

"After school," he repeated, voice dropping as his temper ignited. "You with me?"

"Yes."

He gave her a hard kiss before he pulled back. "Don't think."

As he turned the key in the ignition, she faced forward and dazedly fastened her seat belt. Thinking was beyond her at the moment.

Neither of them said a word as Jesse raced back to campus. They pulled into the parking lot as the second bell that signaled they should already be in class rang. As she bailed out and prepared to run to class, Jesse called, "Vi!"

She pivoted to face him.

"You with me?"

He had an odd look on his face she couldn't interpret and didn't have time to decipher because she was late.

"Yes," she shouted, exasperated, before she took off.

CHAPTER 11
JESSE

"Is it true?"

Jesse looked up from his notebook to find Blaine, Anton, and Brody in front of his desk. They were staring at him avidly as if... He straightened and crossed his arms over his chest as he leaned back in his chair. "Is what true?"

"That you beat up Tucker?" Blaine blurted and got elbowed by Anton.

Jesse narrowed his eyes. "Where'd you hear that?"

"One of the guys in Tucker's band said you jumped him in the parking lot after school yesterday. Did you?"

Brody eyed Jesse's bruised, swollen knuckles and drawled, "That's what I would have done if I heard the nasty rumors he was spreading about my sister. Me and some of the boys were thinking of kicking Tucker's ass, regardless of whether it's true or not."

"It's not true," Jesse snapped.

"It isn't?" Blaine asked and took a step back as Jesse shot to his seat.

"Violet never slept with him." The memory of him claiming her virginity made his dick twitch. He sat before any of them noticed he was getting an erection. "She's breaking up with him."

"Because she heard what he said about her?"

"No," he growled and fixed them with a level look. "She came to the conclusion that he's a dick all on her own. I don't want her to hear what Tucker said about her. It'll just upset her."

"How are you going to stop her from hearing about it? It's all over school."

"By countering it with the truth. She wouldn't sleep with him, so Tucker started that rumor to ruin her reputation. It's as simple as that."

Anton and Blaine glanced at one another before they left to spread the word, leaving Brody behind.

"I would have had your back if you asked me to come with you," Brody said.

"I know."

"Coach Rick was pissed you took off like that."

"I apologized to him this morning."

"How much damage did you do?"

Jesse flexed his sore hand. "Enough. I wanted to do more, but it's probably best I didn't. He'd be in the hospital, otherwise. He'll think twice before he pulls a stupid stunt like that with Violet or any other girl."

Brody shook his head. "I hope Violet learned her lesson, but I have a feeling she didn't. What does she see in these losers?"

He had no idea, but if he had any say in it, Tucker would be the last guy she ever dated.

Brody filled him in on what he missed at practice yesterday and their upcoming game before he was cut off by their teacher, who called their attention to the board. As

Brody took his seat, Jesse slouched in his chair and stared at the clock.

Why the hell had he brought them back to school? He should have taken Violet home. Giving her two class periods to think was dangerous. The last time he thought they were on the same page, she started dating Tobias. He wouldn't stand aside this time. He couldn't. Not after having her. Not after being inside her. Not when he was so close to having all of her.

He felt like he was walking a tightrope. He was afraid of coming on too strong and scaring her or giving her too much space, allowing her to come up with more obstacles to throw in his path.

For four months, he'd been forced to watch her date the most bewildering lineup of guys imaginable. They were the bottom of the barrel, the invisible one's other girls dismissed without question. Even his friends grumbled about her bad taste and asked him why he allowed it, but Violet was deaf to anyone's advice. He knew it would be difficult to see her with Tobias. Little did he know, he was just the first, with each guy getting progressively worse until Tucker came along.

Tucker was the only one bold enough to kiss and pet Violet in front of him. The sight made him physically ill. He suspected Tucker did it deliberately to see if he would do anything. He wanted to, but he didn't want to give Violet any more reason to avoid him as she'd done all summer, and she'd seemed genuinely happy. The only thing that kept him sane was believing she wouldn't go beyond chaste kisses.

His aggression in sports had increased. He did his best to fill his days with as much activity as possible. At night, he staked his claim in the only way he could. They never had a replay of Violet touching herself or waking up when he was in her room, though he'd done his best to make that happen.

The need to check on her was hammering at him. She said she was with him, but what if she changed her mind again? He dragged his sneakers restlessly across the floor as his heartbeat accelerated. Then he would find a way to change it back again.

The fact that she joined him for lunch was a good sign. It had been a calculated risk to kiss her at the park. She'd been shocked and resistant at first. He kept his kisses light, almost teasing to draw her in. It didn't take long for her to respond and then came that sweet acquiescence that frayed his control. He had to stop, or he would have taken her right there in the car. Her look of dazed pleasure was one he intended to see often.

Violet wanted him, but she didn't want to want him. She'd done her best to keep their relationship platonic, but yesterday he broke through. He wasn't going to let her withdraw. She was just as susceptible to their chemistry as he was. He'd chain her to him with bonds of the flesh and fulfill sexual desires she tried to keep hidden. She so badly wanted to be a good girl, but she wasn't, just like there was another side to his wholesome facade. He had to destroy Violet's image of him as her brother and make her see him as a man. He would make her love *him*, regardless of the title he carried.

Eight minutes left.

Mom finished work in an hour and a half, maybe two hours. Dad had the day off, but mentioned he was helping someone from church and wouldn't be back until dinner. They would have the house to themselves. Would Violet let him touch her? If she allowed him another chance between her thighs, he wouldn't waste it.

He lifted his hat to comb his fingers through his hair and touched the back of his neck where she'd left her mark. He took a picture of his back in the mirror last night, mesmerized by the chaotic pattern she'd created, which would fade all too soon. Under other circumstances, he would have loved showing off her brands in the locker room, but he couldn't afford rumors to spread when he was supposedly single, so he would have to be mindful of such things in the future.

The teacher eyed him but made no comment as he rose and slung his backpack over one shoulder. He was halfway to the door before the bell rang, signaling school was over. Blaine called his name, but he didn't stop. He briefly debated whether he should go to Violet's class or wait by the car, but he didn't want to risk missing her. In the end, he headed to the parking lot.

He leaned against the SUV and searched the crowd for Violet or her friends from her last class. Minutes passed. He was about to go hunting when he saw Violet crossing the parking lot with Lettie. His fears evaporated when Violet made eye contact and gave him a smile. His heart thundered in his ears as she said goodbye to her friend and made her way over.

He waited until she had hopped into the SUV before he climbed behind the steering wheel. Violet stared straight ahead with her hands clasped in her lap. *Nervous*, he deduced, but he could work with that. She hadn't run or gone into another bout of denial. She came to him. That's all that mattered.

The adrenaline rush made it difficult to concentrate. *Please may Mom and Dad not be home*, he silently chanted. When he pulled into the driveway, he opened the garage to make sure their parent's cars were missing and said a prayer of thanks when he saw they were gone. He turned toward Violet with a silly grin, but she was already closing the passenger door and heading to the house. He'd spent the drive running all sorts of scenarios through his head and hadn't said one word to her.

He jogged after Violet and caught a glimpse of her heading down the hallway. He checked to make sure they were truly alone before he stood in the open doorway to her bedroom. She took out her binder and set it on the desk. The sight of her trembling hands reminded him that he needed to tread carefully.

"Vi."

"Hmm?"

"Look at me."

She went motionless. The long silence and sudden awkwardness that filled the air made him move quickly. He let his backpack drop to the ground and strode toward her. He clasped her face and gently lifted it.

"Violet."

Her lashes lifted, revealing her eyes had turned green, a sure sign that she felt conflicted. He leaned down and rested his forehead on hers.

"It's me, Violet."

"I know," she rasped. "But this is so..." Her eyes glistened with tears.

Declarations she wasn't ready to hear clogged his throat. He swallowed them and murmured, "Do you trust me?"

She blinked, the question clearly taking her by surprise before she nodded. A tear hovered on her lower lashes. He brushed it away before it could fall. Tears had no place here unless it was tears of joy.

"I won't hurt you," he promised.

"I know."

He covered her mouth with his and felt her jolt, but she didn't try to break away. Encouraged, he tilted his head to deepen the kiss. When her mouth tentatively parted, he immediately accepted the invitation. She tasted of bubble gum and iced tea. She was more addicting than German chocolate cake.

He backed her against the wall, hands sliding from her face into her hair. He angled her head the way he wanted and claimed her mouth.

"Kiss me back," he breathed.

She was passively allowing him to do what he wanted, but he wanted her active participation. Demanded it, in fact. Violet had matured from the impulsive wild child he met at fourteen, but her true nature still lurked beneath the surface. He didn't want just the sweet parts of her. He wanted the competitive savage who would do anything to win and the warrior who marked up his back. He wanted the vulnerable, lonely girl who had unabashedly claimed him as her friend the moment they met. And he wanted the dirty girl who had touched herself and masturbated right along with him. She was holding back, and he wasn't going to allow it.

He brushed kisses along her jaw. "How does this feel?"

She swayed as he sucked on her earlobe.

"Tell me," he growled and squeezed her hip to beckon her out of her head.

"It feels good," she said so quietly, he wouldn't have been able to hear her if he wasn't pressed against her.

"And this?"

When he put his hand on her breast, she went very still.

"How does this feel?" he pushed.

"Um…"

When his thumb brushed over her nipple, her stifled gasp was music to his ears.

"How does this make you feel, Vi?"

"Hot," she said in a strangled tone.

"And this?"

He placed a wet kiss on her neck and felt her body vibrating under his hands.

"Makes me weak," she whispered.

That's all he needed to know. He stepped back. Immediately, her nerves came back, but he didn't give her time to get her defenses in place. He crouched and hoisted her over his shoulder.

"Jesse?"

He didn't answer her because it was taking all his discipline not to toss her on the floor and sink himself inside her.

He closed her door to the bathroom. If their parents came home and saw his bedroom door closed, they wouldn't think anything of it. If they went to Violet's room and saw the bathroom door closed, they would assume she was in there. It would buy them a few minutes to get themselves situated if they needed it. Also, he wanted her in his bed. Tonight, he would go to sleep not just with the memories of what they were about to do, but the physical proof soaked in his sheets. He couldn't wait.

He set her on the edge of his bed. She looked up at him, clearly unsure, but battling it back for him. Humbled, he leaned down and kissed her forehead. When she closed her eyes and kept her face turned up to him like a flower seeking the sun, his heart melted. He ignored the demands of his body as he stroked her rigid back and kissed every inch of her face until she was completely relaxed.

"Arms up," he said quietly.

Her eyelids lifted. Green eyes surveyed him for a moment before she obeyed. The blast of triumph that ripped through him caused his hands to shake. He grasped the bottom of her shirt and lifted it, uncovering every exquisite inch of her. She held his gaze for a moment before she blushed and raised her hands to cover her breasts, encased in baby blue satin.

"No, don't do that," he admonished, twining their fingers together and holding her arms wide so he could take her in.

"Jesse!" she protested, twisting and hunching in an attempt to hide her bare upper half.

He couldn't believe she was self-conscious about her body. She was gorgeous.

"I don't think," she began.

To squash her nerves and rising panic, he flattened her on the bed and took her mouth to stop the words he didn't want to hear. To his surprise, she kissed him back with a fervor that made his dick throb. She was channeling her anxiety into sexual aggression, which was just fine with him. But he underestimated the effect her enthusiasm had on him. She was setting him alight! He detached their mouths and moved down her body so he could retain some semblance of control. He wanted this to last, and he was determined to examine her body.

He kissed his way down her neck, inhaling her heavenly scent. As his tongue traced her collarbone, she quivered and then went lax beneath him. Her breasts were so sensitive, even lightly nuzzling them made her squirm and gasp. When he slid even further down, hands smoothing along her sides, he suddenly stopped and buried his face against her quivering stomach, unable to believe this was really happening.

Her fingers sank into his hair. "Jesse?"

Emotion swelled in his chest, making his eyes sting. He lifted his head and looked up the length of her body. As their eyes met, hers flared before her expression softened. She didn't say a word as she stroked his cheek. Time stalled as their spirits realigned with one another. This was meant to be. Did she feel the rightness of it? There was just him and her. It wasn't just sex, though desire plagued him night and day. Their connection was magnetic, an unstoppable force. She was the moon, and he was the ocean, obeying her push and pull—forcing him to withdraw or flood the shore. He was defenseless against her, a slave to the bond that snapped into place at fourteen. She was everything to him, but did she feel the same? He turned his head and kissed her palm. He would show her how much she meant to him; how much he adored her. No one would ever love her more than he did. It was time to prove it.

He continued his reverent exploration. He gripped her tiny waist as his lips dragged over the silky skin of her stomach before tracing her hipbones with his tongue. When he undid the button of her jeans and pulled down the zipper, she stopped breathing. Discovering she wore matching underwear made his mouth water. He took off her shoes and socks and when he tugged on her pants, Violet hesitated before she lifted her ass, allowing him to drag them off.

He knelt at the foot of the bed with Violet splayed out before him, clad in just a bra and panties. He saw her naked yesterday, but he hadn't been able to admire her. Now, he did.

God took his time with her. Her face alone was portrait-worthy, but her body surpassed those he'd seen in movies, magazines, or TV. Nothing compared to flesh and blood. She had breasts that he now knew fit perfectly in his hand, a small waist, wide hips, and thighs that some guys would have labeled as too thick, but he loved them. They were feminine, muscular, and strong. Her skin was still tan from the summer.

As his hand brushed over her satin covered mound, she clamped her thighs together. His lips quirked as he kissed the tops of her thighs to coax them to part while he massaged her calves.

He'd been fantasizing about this for over a year. After jacking off with her underwear and trying to lap up what she left behind, he could now partake directly from the source. He intended to go slow. To savor and seduce, but the smell of her arousal made him salivate.

"Come on, baby. Spread your legs for me. I need to taste you," he said hoarsely.

"Taste *what*?" Violet demanded, bracing herself on her elbows to gawk at him.

"You liked my fingers in you?"

She bit her lip when his thumb dipped between her thighs.

"Did you?" he demanded

"Yes."

"You're going to like my mouth on you even more."

"*What?* No way!"

He gripped her waist to stop her from scooting up in bed. "It'll be good, I promise."

"That's gross! Why would you even want to...? My answer's no!"

When she started to struggle, his shaky control

snapped. He yanked the drenched underwear down and off. When he pried her legs apart, she sat up, her cheeks flushed with mortification and anger.

"Jesse, don't you dare—"

Her voice cut out as he put his mouth on her. The vibrant taste of her burst on his tongue. Stealing her underwear versus being between her thighs was like someone describing what a dish tasted like rather than sampling it himself. There was no comparison, and he was starved. He ignored her panicked voice and fluttering hands that pushed at his head and smacked his shoulders. He wasn't going anywhere.

He'd never done this before, so it took him a while to figure out what he was doing, but he figured he was on the right track when she let out a strangled shriek and fell back on the bed.

"Oh my God, please stop," she begged.

He had no intention of stopping, not when he was finally drinking nectar straight from her, as God had intended. He was mesmerized by the rolling movements of her body and loved the tortured, helpless sounds she made. He drowned himself in her and rode her restless hips.

Violet threatened, begged, then sobbed as she yanked at his sheets, lost in the throes. He watched her fight her orgasm and him, but in the end, had no choice but to surrender. When she climaxed, her piercing scream hurt his eardrums. When her slick walls contracted, he slid his finger in to give her pussy something to grip onto.

When her orgasm passed, she tried to turn on her side to get away from his mouth and pushed at him with weak, shaky hands.

"Please, Jesse. I can't take anymore."

"I'm almost done," he soothed.

He finally stopped not because he was satisfied, but because he was ready to burst. He shot to his feet, shucked his shirt and shoved down his underwear and jeans. He didn't have the patience to kick off his shoes or step out of his pants but leaned forward and slid inside her. Violet moaned as he penetrated her tight channel. Her eyes flashed open as he kissed her, forcing her to taste herself. She tried to turn away, but he wouldn't let her.

"You're perfect," he panted. "The best thing I've ever tasted. I'll never get enough."

She bared her teeth as he sheathed himself.

"How does it feel to have me inside you?" he said harshly.

"Incredible," she breathed, wrapping her arms and legs around him, taking him even deeper and running her hands over him.

He jerked as if she'd put her mouth on his cock. "Vi, don't…"

Eyelashes wet from tears she'd wept in ecstasy, lifted as she glared at him. "So, you can touch me, but I can't touch you?"

"I'm going to come."

She licked his lip. "So, come."

That's all it took. He spilled at her command, just from the wonder of being inside her. He slumped on top of her and buried his face in his sheets, groaning that he hadn't lasted. But it was difficult to be truly disappointed with Violet beneath him and her fingertips caressing his skin.

"I didn't know," she whispered.

"Know what?" he muttered.

"That people put their mouths…"

As her inner muscles fluttered around his dick, he raised his head to look down at her. Her eyes were glassy from her orgasm and despite all they'd done, she still looked a little embarrassed.

"You didn't know about oral sex?"

She shook her head, eyes wide.

"We're gonna do it often," he stated, brushing his lips over hers.

"We are?"

Detecting the eagerness she tried to conceal, his mouth curved. "Yeah." When she squirmed, he raised a brow. "Want me to do it again?"

Her cheeks bloomed with color. "No!" she said adamantly, but her body said otherwise.

Violet wasn't a good girl, thank God. His dick twitched with renewed life.

"Jesse."

Her tone warned him before he saw the uncertainty creeping back.

"I don't know if we should…"

"Do you like what I do to you?" he interrupted.

She blinked. "I…"

"It's a yes or no answer."

When her eyes slid away, his heart stopped.

"Violet." He cupped her cheek to get her attention. "Tell me you like what I do to you."

"I do, but…"

He thought they were of one mind, but she was slipping away while he was still inside her. How could she not realize what was between them was a gift, not a curse? He instinctively knew it would never be like this with anyone else. She was it for him. Why didn't she realize that? Terror that he would lose her stoked the ashes of his temper.

"We don't have to make any decisions right now or share what's happening between us. We have time to explore each other and just be." He searched her eyes. "Have you felt this way with anyone else?"

She shook her head. The relief that passed through him made him drop his forehead on hers. He wasn't alone in this. She may not be ready to commit to forever, but she was willing to let him in. For now, that's all that mattered. Everything would fall into place. He would reel her in so gently, she wouldn't realize she'd been caught until it was too late.

"What we have is special, once in a lifetime. It would be a crime to ignore it."

Her vulnerable expression altered, became impish. "Crime?"

He tugged on her bra, so her breast popped out. "A *serious* crime."

He was done talking about this. There were far more important things to do, like pay homage to her neglected breasts. Her expressive face was such a turn on. She couldn't conceal her reaction to what he was doing to her. He hardened inside of her and soon, was grinding against her.

"Kiss me," he ordered.

She pressed her mouth to his. At his gruff encouragement, she grew bolder and more confident. When her tongue darted into his mouth, he groaned.

"Yes, that's what I want. Give it to me."

This time, she was with him every step of the way. The air was permeated with the smell of sweat, sex, and her unique blend of violets and rose. She quickly picked up his rhythm. He raised his head to look down at her. Her hair was spread over his sheets, she was clutching at him with both hands, and her breasts were bouncing with each thrust. Her eyes were bleeding back to hazel. She was flushed with passion. She held on to him as if she were afraid of being tossed into the abyss. She stared at him with a mixture of fear, wonder, and need. He got off on all of it.

When he felt himself getting close, he rubbed her clitoris, wanting her to come with him.

"Tell me how this feels," he said against her lips.

Her eyes fluttered shut. "It feels..." She flinched and clutched at his biceps as her hips bucked against his hand. "Like I'll die if I don't... Oh, God. *Jesse*."

Saying his name in that thready tone made him giddy. "Say it again."

"Oh my God."

"My name," he growled and stopped his ministrations so she would give him what he wanted.

Her eyes opened, stormy green chasing away the hazel. "Jesse."

"Jesse, what?" He couldn't resist teasing her when he was between her legs and his fingers were slipping through honey that was all for him.

"I want..."

She didn't bother finishing her sentence but brushed his hand aside and took over the motion he'd been doing.

He was stunned for a moment as one of his fantasies materialized right before his eyes. "That's my girl. Make yourself come."

"Jesse," she breathed before she convulsed.

He ground against that bundle of nerves, prolonging her climax as she wrapped her arms around him and shuddered like a survivor being rescued from a shipwreck. This time, it took him longer to come. He set a decent pace and when he finally orgasmed, he was out of breath and immensely pleased. He collapsed on top of her, but made sure to move his top half to the side so he wouldn't smother her.

He was sated to his bones, and a had a feeling that Violet was finally on the same wavelength. She was completely relaxed beneath him, the physical exertion calming her overactive mind.

A few minutes passed before he reluctantly peered at the clock. Damn it. He wished they could stay like this for days, but life was still chugging along, propelling them forward.

When he forced himself up and knelt on the bed, Violet gave him a quizzical look, which turned indignant when he unceremoniously spread her legs.

"Jesse!"

Her mortified tone made him grin, but his eyes were on his semen that spilled from her. Prompted by some primitive instinct, he pushed it back in and, when it poured out again, spread it over her skin. He wanted her covered in him. Thankfully, she didn't fight it. She watched him from beneath half lowered lids until he regretfully noticed the time again.

"If we're lucky, we have about ten minutes before Mom comes home," he announced.

"What?"

He wasn't surprised when she jackknifed up and ran to the bathroom. He finally kicked off his clothes and stretched out on the bed. He considered joining Violet in the shower, but had a feeling she wouldn't like that. He closed his eyes and drifted with a smile on his face. His dreams were finally coming true.

CHAPTER 12
VIOLET

VIOLET PUT THE FINISHING TOUCHES ON HER MAKEUP BEFORE SHE backed up to take in her appearance in the bathroom mirror. For church, she donned a dress she normally reserved for special occasions. The dress ended at mid-thigh, which Dad wouldn't like, but the length was counterbalanced by the long sleeves and modest neckline. She gave the tiered skirt a swish, admiring the ruffle detail that in the past made her feel silly. But her mindset had shifted over the past few days. She had never been more aware of her femininity and for the first time in her life, she was fully embracing it.

She slid the heart pendant that Mom and Dad had gifted her on her sixteenth birthday back and forth along the fine gold chain as she eyed her reflection. Last week she attended church as a virgin and this week, she returned with more sexual experience than anyone who had been initiated four days ago should. But Jesse wasn't just an overachiever in sports and academics. She'd known from his nightly visits that he had a high sex drive, but the physical reality was another thing entirely.

When they attended school on Friday, she did her best to act normal. She thought she was doing a good job until she caught the odd look Marissa was giving Jesse. She glanced at him and found that he wasn't listening to the conversation but focused completely on her. The make out session on the way to school had been brief and unfulfilling, and Jesse was clearly still feeling the effects of it. One look at his heated gaze was all it took for her to get embarrassingly damp. He was going to give them away! She promptly excused herself from the group and managed to avoid him until lunch, when he yanked her into an empty classroom.

"Why aren't you answering my messages?" he demanded.

"I think we should steer clear of each another until things calm down."

He cocked his head to the side. "Calm down?"

She was too embarrassed to bring up the way he'd been looking at her earlier, so she gestured to her hard nipples, which were aching for the attention he paid them the previous day. The connection between them had always been strong, but now it was tuned to a frequency so raw and sensitive, it was difficult to be around each other without touching. Last night at dinner, they studiously avoided eye contact. Watching TV together was out of the question. Jesse expended energy by shooting hoops on the driveway with Dad, while she went to her bedroom to give her overstimulated senses a break.

"I need some time to adjust. This is a lot." That was a vast understatement, but it was the best she could come up with when Jesse was looking at her like he wanted to eat her alive. Her unfettered response would have been embarrassing if it wasn't obvious that Jesse wanted her just as much.

"I'll give you space after," Jesse said.

She frowned. "After what?"

He'd shoved her into a janitor's closet for some heavy petting. At some point, he put her hand on him. She got the hang of it quickly. It wasn't long before he begged her to put him in her mouth. Remembering how much pleasure she got from him going down on her yesterday, she was eager to make him feel the same.

He whispered what he wanted her to do, and she accomplished her goal as the bell sounded, signaling lunch was over. Despite her worries about being caught, Jesse turned on the light to watch her swallow and lapped up what spilled over. When she tried to leave, he pinned her against the wall and French kissed her until she was dizzy before allowing her to go to class.

Jesse had a football game that evening. She rode to and from the game with Mom and Dad, while Jesse caught a ride home with a teammate. When he came into her bedroom, high on his win, and tried to kiss her, she freaked out.

"You can't do that when Mom and Dad are home!" she said, scandalized.

"Fine. Tomorrow."

She didn't know what he meant by that until he told Mom over breakfast that they were going for a drive and then meeting up with friends to see a movie. Mom smiled and told them to have fun.

"Who are we meeting up with?" Violet asked when she climbed into the passenger seat.

"No one. I lied."

"You did? Why?"

"I can't tell Mom what we're really going to do."

Her heart thudded in her ears. "What are we going to do?"

His eyes glittered under heavy eyelids. "I guess you'll find out, won't you?"

Part of Jesse's lie was true. They went for a drive. To her surprise, he drove out of the city limits. When Jesse got his license, they had practically lived in the car, high on their newfound freedom. They thoroughly explored the Texas Hill Country and neighboring quaint towns. This was a throwback to a simpler time. She didn't say so, but she was relieved to get away from home and the constant fear of being discovered. She hadn't realized she needed a time-out from the rest of the world, but Jesse delivered without being asked.

She spoke very little during the nearly two-hour drive. Her mind still struggled to process everything that had happened in the past few days and the potent sexual chemistry that strummed her nerve endings. She was pleasantly surprised when Jesse pulled up to a beautiful lake and delighted when he pulled a thick blanket and cooler from the trunk. Beneath the shade of some trees, they had a picnic. They lounged on the blanket, chatting about everything and nothing as they ate and gazed at the water.

It seemed inevitable that Jesse would touch her and that she would lift her face for the kiss she'd denied him the night before. He lowered her to the blanket and drowned her in sensuality. There was no thought of denying him or herself. He told her not to think, and she wasn't. That was beyond her. Her principles and sense of propriety were lost in the undertow of a passion that overpowered all else.

Jesse was irresistible. Playful, indulgent, generous,

persistent. He seemed intent on giving her as much pleasure as possible and was painfully fascinated with her body. She felt the same, though Jesse had to come twice before he allowed her to explore him as thoroughly as he had her. The day passed by too quickly, and before she knew it, they were heading home.

Dinner passed in a lust-hazed fog, but she came to when Mom cupped her flushed cheek and said, "It looks like you got some sun. Did you have fun today?"

"Lots," Jesse answered for her.

She didn't have to look at him to know he wore a broad grin. She resisted the urge to kick him under the table and avoided looking at Dad.

"What movie did you see?" Mom asked.

She felt a burst of alarm that was immediately canceled out by Jesse, who said, "We ended up driving further than we anticipated. The spot on the lake was so nice, we thought it would be a shame to leave after only an hour, so we stayed and canceled our other plans."

She was grateful yet taken aback by his glib tongue. When had Jesse become such a proficient liar?

The door to her left opened, bringing Violet out of her reverie. Jesse stepped into the bathroom, dressed in gray slacks and a black button-up shirt for church. He went motionless when he spotted her. As his eyes moved over her, she grinned and did a spin so he could get the full effect. When she stopped, she saw Jesse had closed his door and was undoing his belt.

Her heart leapt in treacherous anticipation, even as she blanched. "What are you doing?"

"What does it look like?"

She took a step toward the safety of her bedroom. "I

told you; I'm not doing anything while Mom and Dad are around!"

"They're eating breakfast."

"I don't care!" she hissed.

She tried to escape into the safety of her bedroom, but he wrapped an arm around her middle, pulling her back while firmly closing her door.

"Jesse," she groaned as he turned her to face him and backed her up to the vanity. "We can't."

"Don't you want me?" he asked huskily.

She wanted him so badly, it scared her. "We're going to church!"

"That's not what I asked you."

He cupped her jaw, his piercing blue eyes making her stomach jitter. The way he focused on her as if there were no one else in the world was thrilling and unnerving. Did he start out this intense with every girl he was with? The stab of jealousy gave her the strength to yank her chin out of his hold. He frowned, but didn't back off.

"Tell me you want me."

"I do, but—"

He gave her a hard kiss. "That's all I need to hear, baby."

She was distracted by the endearment, which he'd uttered a handful of times. The first time she heard it was when he apologized for ruthlessly taking her virginity. She loved the soft, tender way he said it. Had he called all his girlfriends, baby? Even as she pondered this, Jesse knelt at her feet, pulled her dress up, and kissed her over her underwear. Her toes curled, and her blood thickened as desire snaked through her veins.

"You can't," she croaked.

"I can," he said simply, and with one tug had her underwear dropping to her ankle boots. "Hold this."

She obeyed automatically, holding her skirt out of his way before she belatedly tried to sidestep. "Mom and Dad…"

"Are occupied," he said as he draped one of her legs on his shoulder. "Like we're about to be."

Even as she braced herself against the vanity, she made one last token resistance. "Jesse, I don't think we should…"

"Shh, baby, we don't have much time."

Her lungs seized as his tongue slid through her folds. Two days ago, she wouldn't let him kiss her, and now she was letting him go down on her with their parents just a few rooms away. This wasn't right. It was disrespectful and immoral and wicked and… Her legs quivered as his tongue feathered over her clitoris. It was also mind-numbingly pleasurable and felt too good to stop.

"Ungh."

The garbled sound escaped as she rocked against his mouth. There was no self-consciousness. Not after what they'd done yesterday. Jesse made it clear that he loved her response and didn't want her to hold back. She couldn't if she wanted to. He fanned an inferno inside of her. Needs she didn't know she possessed and a soul deep hunger she worried would never be satisfied.

She looked down and saw Jesse watching her. The way he catalogued every hitch in her breath, every muscle twitch, unsettled her. Already, he knew so much more about her body than she did. What made her cave, what made her crazy, what made her sob. It still made her stomach dip when she locked eyes with him. Part of her still couldn't believe they were doing this. The other half wept with joy.

She ran her fingers through his hair and saw his eyelids droop in ecstasy. It amazed her how little it took for him. He was a natural sensualist. Uninhibited, unashamed, eager to please, and be pleased. It was a wonder he'd been single for four months. He was famished and she was reaping the rewards.

She clutched his hair and tipped her face up to the bright lights as she prepared to have her world blasted apart.

"Jesse!"

The sound of Dad's angry voice coming from Jesse's bedroom startled her so badly, she would have fallen if Jesse hadn't steadied her.

"Isaac, for God's sake," Lynne protested. "You're going to wake the whole neighborhood. Calm down. We don't know all the facts. Let's just see what they say."

"They haven't said anything," Dad retorted. "And I'm getting to the bottom of this right now."

She swung her leg off Jesse's shoulder and backed away, eyes wide with horror. Their parents couldn't know, could they? As Jesse got to his feet, wiping his mouth with the back of his sleeve, they heard her bedroom door being flung open.

"Violet!"

She jumped and hastily locked the bathroom door in case Dad tried to come in. He sounded pissed. What the hell happened?

"I'm in here, Dad." She looked around frantically for her underwear, snatched it off the floor, and pulled them on. "I'm getting dressed. What's going on?"

"Where's Jesse?"

She stared at him as she lied. "I think he went outside for something."

"I want to see you in the dining room. We need to talk."

She and Jesse stared at one another as the sound of their parent's voices faded.

"They know," Violet whispered and touched her throat, which felt like it was beginning to swell.

Jesse looked thoughtful. "I don't think so," he said, as he buckled his belt.

She couldn't believe his blasé attitude. "What else could they be talking about? I've never heard Dad yell like that in my life!"

Jesse clasped her face. "Whatever it is, we'll deal with it together. We're going to be okay, I promise."

His calm demeanor stopped her emotions from spiraling out of control. She hauled in a deep, steadying breath and tried to think rationally. If Dad had suspected they were intimate, he could have forced his way into the bathroom and caught them red-handed. He hadn't. Maybe Jesse was right, and it was something else. Clinging to that slim hope, she asked, "What do we do?"

"I'll go out your window and come around to the front door."

She pressed her ear to the door leading into her bedroom and walked in to make sure the coast was clear. Her heart was in her throat as Jesse quietly opened her window and climbed out. This was what their life had come to? She shook her head and started for the hallway when she heard Jesse say, "Morning, Mr. Davidson."

She wheeled around as their neighbor replied, "Jesse, what are you doing tending to the plants in your Sunday's best?"

What else could go wrong? She was tempted to linger to hear Jesse's reply, but the distant murmur of her parent's voices reminded her they were waiting for her. Hands trembling, she started down the hallway and prayed Jesse would hurry so whatever she was walking into, she wouldn't have to face alone.

The moment she entered the dining room; her parents fell silent. Dad's forbidding expression made her palms sweat. Mom looked troubled.

"What's going on?" Violet asked.

"That what I want to know. Is there something you want to tell us?" Dad asked.

It took everything she had not to wring her hands. Guilt and panic clouded her mind, making it hard to think. She couldn't hold Dad's intimidating stare, so she looked to Lynne for guidance. "I have no idea, what...?"

"We just received a call," Lynne said quietly. "Tucker's in the hospital, being treated for serious injuries we're told were caused by Jesse. Do you know anything about that?"

She mentally reeled. "Tucker's in the hospital?"

"Yes," Dad said tersely. "And I want to know why. The only reason Jesse would have given Tucker such a beating is because of you. So, Vi, what happened?"

Her rash behavior was coming back to haunt her. This was proof that no one got away with anything. Would she have to admit that she let Tucker touch her inappropriately and that's how Jesse found them? Knowing how upset and disappointed her parents would be made her eyes fill with tears.

"Oh, honey," Lynne said sympathetically and started toward Violet, but Dad held up a hand, stopping Lynne in her tracks.

"I need answers," Dad said curtly. "We've been lenient with you two because you've never given us any reason not to trust you, but I never thought I'd get a call saying Jesse put someone in the hospital. Do you know how serious this is? Tucker could press charges for assault!"

The blood drained from her face.

"Why did you break up with him?" Dad demanded. "Did he do something to you? Is that why Jesse attacked him?"

She opened her mouth, but nothing came out. She had no idea what to say. She willed Jesse to walk through the front door and jolted when Dad slammed his fist on the table, rattling their empty plates and cups.

"I knew I shouldn't have let you date that kid. He had trouble written all over him. I thought you had enough discernment to break it off. Now, I hear Jesse had to intervene on your behalf and beat him senseless. Do you have any idea how serious this is? What the hell happened that would make Jesse...?"

The front door opened. Jesse strolled in with his hands in pockets. She had no doubt he'd gotten out of that sticky situation with Mr. Davidson just fine. No one would suspect Jesse of doing anything immoral or unlawful, especially when he was dressed so impeccably. Jesse scanned the room with a benign expression, which vanished when his gaze landed on her distraught face.

"What's wrong?" he demanded.

"A lot at the moment," Dad said, crossing his arms over his chest. "You have a lot of explaining to do."

"Okay, about what?" Jesse asked, showing no sign of discomfort or guilt.

"About the call I just got saying you're responsible for putting Tucker in the hospital."

Jesse stared at him for a moment before he asked, "When did he go to the hospital?"

"Today."

"For what?"

"A skull fracture, a nasty concussion, and a few other presents you gave him."

"But that happened on Wednesday. If Tucker was hurt so badly, why wait so long to go to the hospital?"

"He thought the pain and dizziness would pass, but his parents finally forced him to get checked out."

"I-Is he going to be all right?" Violet asked, twisting her hands together.

"That hasn't been decided yet," Dad said testily. "And what I want to know from both of you is *why* he isn't all right." Dad focused on Jesse. "You want to explain yourself?"

There was a long silence before Jesse said, "I want to talk to you alone."

Violet took a step toward him, hand extended to stop him from saying anything.

"Stop right there," Dad ordered and shot her a hard look. "Start talking or go to your room." He raised a brow. "What's it going to be?"

She willed Jesse to look at her, to give her some clue about what he was about to tell them, but his gaze didn't waver from Dad. Why did he want to talk to their parents alone? He wouldn't make matters worse by talking about *them*, would he? It was bad enough that her recklessness led to Tucker being in the hospital. She didn't need Dad to know she'd also kissed Jesse, which led to her losing her virginity.

"Violet, go," Dad said.

She lingered a moment longer but had no choice but to retreat. She couldn't say anything without possibly contradicting whatever story, or truth, Jesse decided to tell. She walked to her bedroom, closed the door, and eyed the window. For the first time in her life, she considered running away, but that would be short-lived, embarrassing, and even more incriminating if Jesse didn't tell their parents everything.

She sank onto her bed and buried her face in her hands. Ten minutes ago, she felt worldly, mature, and powerful. Now, she was terrified of what repercussions lay in wait for her, Jesse, and Tucker.

What if Tucker sustained permanent brain damage? She had a flashback of his head slamming into concrete. Even though she witnessed firsthand the damage Jesse had inflicted, she hadn't even texted Tucker to make sure he was okay. Her only concern had been to break up with him once he returned to school. What was wrong with her? Technically, she was still his girlfriend, yet she hadn't checked on him and had moved on with another guy while he was recovering from his injuries.

Her only defense was that what happened between her and Jesse had been such a shocking turn of events that it eclipsed what happened with Tucker. So much so, she had completely dismissed him from her mind. From Tucker's point of view, Jesse had attacked him without provocation. She had been willing, and then her overprotective brother beat the crap out of him. If Tucker told his side of the story, Mom and Dad would hear about the compromising position Jesse found her in.

Her stomach lurched. She shot to her feet and put her ear to the bedroom door, but she couldn't hear anything. What was Jesse telling them? Why was it taking so long? Why was silence more ominous than shouting and glass breaking? Were their parents in shock? Is that why she couldn't hear their reaction?

Consumed by the need to do something, she started

organizing her backpack and was so deep in her head, she didn't hear the door open.

"Violet?"

She whirled to find Lynne peeking her head around the door.

"Are you ready for church?"

Lynne wasn't smiling, but there was no sign that she'd been crying. Lynne didn't look horrified, disappointed, or revolted, just weary. That was a good sign, wasn't it?

"Yes, I'm ready."

As Mom slipped back into the hallway, she dashed through the bathroom to Jesse's room, but he wasn't there. She hurried down the hallway only to find the living and dining room also empty. What the *heck*?

"They're waiting for us in the car," Mom said.

She opened her mouth to ask questions but thought better of it and stayed quiet. She had to talk to Jesse first. She flew down the steps and saw Dad behind the wheel of Mom's car. She slipped into the back seat and glanced at Jesse, but he was looking out the window, giving her no clue as to what just happened. She buckled her seat belt and twisted her hand in the folds of her dress as she waited for someone to announce her sentence.

They were several minutes away from church when Dad finally spoke.

"We got in touch with Tucker's parents, and thankfully it seems like there won't be any long-term damage. Jesse offered to go to the hospital to apologize, but they didn't want him there. They've decided not to press charges." Dad's hand cut through the air. "None of this is okay. Violence is never the answer and with something this serious, we should have been told instead of being blindsided with a call like that. I expected better from both of you. As punishment for his actions, Jesse's dropping out of football."

She audibly gasped. Football was Jesse's favorite sport, and he was one of the best players on the team. Last year, they made it to the national championship, and they were counting on Jesse to take them there again. Football was sacred in Texas and ranked just a few notches below church. She looked at Jesse for his reaction, but his face was still averted.

"Jesse claims that you weren't involved."

She looked in the rearview mirror. Although Dad wore sunglasses, she felt the impact of his stare.

"I don't believe that for a second. You're the common denominator here, and you break up with Tucker the day Jesse fights him?" Dad shook his head. "I'm revoking your dating privileges. You aren't allowed to date for the rest of the school year. You also aren't going out after school or on weekends for the foreseeable future."

Lynne reached across the console and gripped Dad's arm. "Isaac."

Dad smacked the steering wheel, clearly still aggravated. "No! I'm not going to be lenient with her. I've done that far too much already and look where that's got us. If Tucker's parents chose to press charges, Jesse could have destroyed his future, all because he felt the need to defend his sister from a guy I knew she shouldn't have been with! I'll be damned if Violet turns out like *her*."

Violet went rigid. He didn't say her name. In fact, he never had, but she knew exactly who he was referring to—the mother who left in the middle of the night when she was two. To suggest that she was anything like the selfish woman who had abandoned them hurt so badly, it stole her breath. She turned her face toward the window so Dad wouldn't see her face crumple.

"Violet made a mistake," Lynne said into the loaded silence. "And Jesse made a mistake. They'll be punished for keeping secrets, bad judgment, and they'll have to earn back our trust. It's a blessing that Tucker and his parents were so understanding. Let's leave it at that."

No one said another word as they pulled up to the church. Violet stepped out of the car and fussed with her dress to give herself time to get a hold on her volatile emotions. Lynne stood beside her and waited patiently. When she started toward the church, Lynne stroked her back. She didn't meet anyone's eyes as she walked up the steps and paused on the threshold, unsure if she should be allowed in the chapel after what she'd done this week. Several hundred years ago, she would have been stoned to death.

"Don't take what your dad said to heart," Lynne murmured as she put an arm around her waist. "He's upset, but he'll get past it. We all will."

She swallowed the lump in her throat. She didn't deserve Lynne's sympathy or faith in her. Tucker was just the tip of the iceberg. If Mom knew what she and Jesse had done... She raised her head and saw Dad standing beside a pew, watching her hover on the threshold, almost as if he knew... Abruptly, he turned away and took a seat, staring straight ahead at the empty stage.

"Have faith," Lynne encouraged as she started down the aisle to join Dad.

Someone came up behind her. Her heightened senses told her who it was, even though Jesse didn't speak. She had so many questions, but this was neither the time nor place. And did it really matter what tale Jesse told? Dad knew she was to blame, even though Jesse tried to keep her out of it. The worst part was, Dad was right. It was her fault. They would discuss this later. First, they had to smile and maintain their image as a loving, Christian family.

She moved through the crowd and entered the pew her parents were sitting in from the opposite end. Jesse settled beside her. She nodded to those who greeted her and couldn't avoid several hugs that made her feel even worse. They thought she was one of them. That she was still pure and good, and she wasn't. Not by a long shot. She felt sick to her stomach.

"This message has been on my mind all week," Pastor Sonny began, gravely eyeing the congregation. "How one sin can change the trajectory of your life. We assume one tiny sin won't hurt, that no one will find out about it, but no sin escapes God's notice."

Violet resisted the urge to slouch in her seat as Pastor Sonny made eye contact with her.

"We're going to examine the life of the great King David. He went from shepherd boy to king and was hailed as a mighty warrior, but one transgression robbed him of the blessing God had for him and caused the rest of his life to be plagued with pain and betrayal." Pastor Sonny paused for effect before he continued, "Of course, I'm referring to his affair with Bathsheba."

Violet knew the story of King David's infamous affair—how he spotted a beautiful woman bathing from the rooftop of his palace and summoned her to him. When Bathsheba became pregnant, King David had her husband killed in battle to claim her for himself.

"One sin," Pastor Sonny said thoughtfully as he strolled across the stage. "Adultery doesn't seem like such a big deal, but when a child is conceived, King David tries to pass the child off as the husband's and when that didn't work, he murdered his loyal soldier." Pastor Sonny shook his head. "People don't understand that one sin will always lead to another. Once you start on that path, you can't stop. Before you know it, you're trapped in a web of your own making. King David thought he got away with it, but God sees all, and the punishment was severe."

Pastor Sonny listed the many consequences of King David's sin, beginning with the death of the child that had been conceived during the affair. But it was the tragic story of the incestuous relationship between David's children, Amnon and his half-sister, Tamar, that made Violet's blood run cold. Amnon was so obsessed with his sister that he faked being ill to have his sister feed him and then raped her.

"It says here in verse fifteen that after Amnon had Tamar, he hated her more than he once loved her." Pastor Sonny paused so the congregation could take that in. "Can you imagine wanting someone so much that you risked everything to possess her, only to discover your all-consuming love was just fleeting lust? Amnon wanted her purely because he couldn't have her, and he paid for that sin with his life when his brother, Absalom, struck him down to avenge her."

Pastor Sonny held up a finger.

"King David passed his sins onto his sons, who mirrored and amplified them. We think one misstep won't hurt anyone and that if we're found out, we can handle the fallout, but we forget that it's not just us that's affected. It's our family, those we love most, who suffer the most for our choices. In King David's case, that generational curse was passed on. And it doesn't stop there. It trickles out to our friends and community. Everything you do matters. I think, if we keep that in mind, we could save ourselves and those we care about a lot of grief."

Convicted to her core, Violet closed her eyes. Discovering that she and Jesse engaged in a sexual relationship would devastate their parents on multiple levels. She and Jesse weren't blood siblings, but they had been raised as such and that's how their parents wanted them to view each other. Sex complicated things, which is why blended families discouraged it from happening in the first place. To make matters worse, their parents didn't believe in premarital sex.

If Dad grounded her for suspecting she had influenced the fight between Jesse and Tucker, what would he do if he found out she initiated a sexual relationship between her and Jesse? Jesse paid her midnight visits, but he'd never gone beyond that. She kissed him and then unwittingly taunted him by giving him the impression she was experienced, which made him lose control. She hadn't stopped Tucker or Jesse from putting their hands in her pants. She hadn't fought Jesse off when he put her on his bed. A part of her wanted to know and experience, and she had, without considering the aftermath or future complications. What if her carnal recklessness destroyed their family, as it had King David's? When she was younger, she'd been terrified Lynne and her dad would break up. What if she caused her worst fear to come true?

"In Luke 8:17, it says that all secrets will be brought to light and made known to all. If you think you're going to get away with your sin, believe me, you won't. It may take years, even decades, but your misdeeds will be exposed, and you will pay in one form or another. It's inevitable," Pastor Sonny said with such conviction that Violet wanted to drop to her knees and repent.

She didn't realize her hands were balled into fists until Jesse placed his on top of hers. She pulled away and would have scooted closer to Lynne, but she didn't want to bring unwanted attention to them. Jesse couldn't touch her like that anymore. They could never repeat what they'd done this week. For as long as she could remember, she longed for a family. God had answered her prayers and given her a mother and brother who gave her the love and affection she longed for. She couldn't lose them.

Right then and there, she began to pray. *Lord, punish me in whatever way You see fit, but please keep my family intact. My parents don't deserve to be hurt because of my choices. I swear I'll right my wrongs. I'll fix my relationship with Jesse. We'll never do anything immoral ever again. Please don't expose my weaknesses and faults. I'll do better. I'll do anything to make this right. Please have mercy on me.*

As if Jesse sensed her distress, he brushed the back of his hand against her thigh. This time, she moved away. Just as she predicted, Lynne glanced at her. Violet rested her head on her shoulder. Lynne didn't admonish her, but cupped her cheek, comforting her like she was a child. At that moment, she felt like one. Overwhelmed, ashamed, and wishing someone would clean up her mess.

"What some people try to do is turn their sin into something good, but nothing that begins in sin will be blessed by God. It will always fail," Pastor Sonny boomed.

She hadn't considered the long-term ramifications of sleeping with her stepbrother. She'd been caught up in sexual discovery, in fulfilling dark desires, and pleasure. How could she be so stupid?

Was it her imagination, or had Pastor Sonny looked directly at her several times? Did God give him the ability to single out which church members this message was for?

She'd been lambasted so severely, she could barely sit upright. Each point cut deep like a whip. Between finding out that Tucker was in the hospital and this message, it couldn't be clearer that God was giving her one last warning before she ruined her life.

Amnon's reaction after finally having his half-sister played over and over in her mind. *He hated her more than he once loved her.* It would kill her if one day Jesse despised her or looked through her as he did the other girls he'd dated. Before, she'd been his sister, which made her special, but by sleeping with him, she became like all the others. Easy, forgettable. There'd been no need to date and woo her—he went straight to sex. And she let him. What if, like Amnon, Jesse desired her because it was taboo and titillating and once he got his fill...?

Ice spread through her belly. It was better to end it now before anyone got hurt. Already, her feelings were engaged, while it could be just about sex for him. He was jacking off in her room even when he had girlfriends. They hadn't been enough for him. He was oversexed. Maybe any girl would do, and she was just... available?

"Let's pray," Pastor Sonny said.

Heart heavy, she closed her eyes. The tears that dropped to her lap went unnoticed as the pastor prayed over the congregation, hoping they could learn from King David's mistakes and do better in their own lives.

"Violet."

She swiveled on her chair to see Dad standing in her bedroom. They hadn't exchanged a word all day. During dinner, Lynne tried to lighten the mood by entertaining them with tales of her students. Violet hadn't been able to enjoy the food, company, or stories and had excused herself to take refuge in her room. Guilt lay on her shoulders like a heavy, suffocating winter coat. She hadn't been able to look Dad or Jesse in the eye. She wished she could reverse time and walk away from Tucker when he tried to pressure her to get in his car. So many red flags and missed opportunities to do the right thing. She could have saved them all a lot of grief is she'd stopped it from the beginning.

She spent her time cleaning the heck out of her room and purged all signs of debauchery. She washed her clothes and bedsheets, vacuumed, organized, and erased incriminating text messages. She also messaged Tucker, apologizing for what happened with Jesse, and asked if there was anything she could do. Her fervent, long-winded message received a one-word reply: *No.* Apparently, she didn't need to break up with him. It seemed the sentiment was mutual.

Dad advanced into her room and sat on the edge of her bed. "I was harsh with you today."

She lowered her gaze. "I deserved it."

"That phone call was a nasty shock. I'm glad Tucker's going to be all right and that Jesse got off with a tap on the wrist. It could have been a lot worse."

She nodded.

"I know Jesse didn't tell us everything and honestly, I don't think I could handle the truth. But I know one thing. Nothing could have caused such an extreme reaction from him except you. He'd do anything for you, even if it cost him everything. Do you understand that, Vi? Jesse came this close to having something on his record today that would never go away. Your actions have consequences now. Consequences that can mar your future."

"I know," she said shakily as her eyes filled with tears.

Dad let out a gusty sigh. "Just... be more mindful. Think before you leap. That's all I'm asking. Can you do that for me?"

She nodded and tried to give him a smile but failed.

Dad got to his feet and squeezed her shoulder. "Go to bed. It's been a long day."

Once he left her room, she walked into the bathroom and, for the first time ever, made sure to lock the door that led into Jesse's room. Jesse had approached her twice, but she shot him down. She didn't want to risk Mom or Dad hearing them talk and honestly, there was nothing to say. He'd been so sure no one would find out about Tucker, but like Pastor Sonny said, the truth would always reveal itself.

No one could ever find out about her and Jesse. If it got out, she knew beyond a shadow of a doubt that nothing would ever be the same. If Dad discovered they slept with one another, he wouldn't kill Jesse, but it could turn Dad and Lynne against one another if they defended their own child. Or maybe they would all realize she was the problem. Her nails sank into her palm. They had to end it now before anyone suspected. Perhaps they could work their way back to seeing each other as friends instead of lovers.

Tears slipped down her face as she brushed her teeth and readied herself for bed. When she walked back into her room, she paused. She had no doubt Jesse would come to her after their parents went to bed. She couldn't let that happen, even if it was just to talk.

Sniffling, she locked both doors that led into her room. Dad instructed them to leave their doors unlocked in case of an emergency. This was an emergency of a different sort. Boundaries that needed to be set.

She climbed into bed and willed herself to sleep, but Pastor Sonny's warnings made her toss and turn. It was just after eleven when the bathroom light came on. From the gap beneath the door, she saw a shadow approach and then the sharp snick of the doorknob as Jesse turned it back and forth. There was a pause and then a louder rattle as he used more force. She pulled the covers over her head as Jesse cursed.

"Vi!" he hissed.

She didn't move. Several minutes later, she lowered the comforter and saw the bathroom light was off. She blew out a breath, turned on her side, and prayed for wisdom and strength in getting them on the right path tomorrow.

CHAPTER 13
VIOLET

She was brushing her teeth the following morning when Jesse tentatively knocked on the bathroom door. When she didn't answer, he tried the locked door.

"Violet?"

When she didn't answer, she heard a thump. She wasn't sure whether it was his hand or forehead that hit the door.

"Violet."

The frustrated longing in his tone made her eyes water. She rinsed her mouth and quickly finished up her tasks in the bathroom. She unlocked his door before she double timed it to her bedroom and locked hers.

All night, she rehearsed what she would say to him. She had no idea how he would respond. He heard the same sermon at church yesterday. He had to see the parallels and recognize the risks they were taking—not just with their own relationship, but their family. After sleeping on it, she hoped he'd come to the same conclusion. Bottom line, he meant too much to her to risk losing him. He couldn't argue with that.

As she dated, she'd been pushing the limits with her

wardrobe, but today she wasn't trying to attract or please anyone. Not Jesse, Tucker, or any other guy. She pulled on jeans and a loose fitted top, put her hair in a ponytail, and put in gold heart earrings. Comfortable, simple, not sexy at all. She just wanted everything to go back to the way it had been before sex got in the way.

When she made her way into the dining room, she found Mom and Dad at the dining table doing devotions. This was usually something that happened on the weekend, not a weekday. Mom was typically in a hurry to get to school and on his days off, Dad was often working on a house project, fishing, or helping the church with something. Apparently, they were planning on being more present, which worked in her favor.

"Hey, honey," Mom greeted.

She was comforted by Dad's half smile. All was forgiven. Today was a new day and an opportunity to make good choices. She went into the kitchen to make herself oatmeal and stiffened when Jesse materialized at her side.

"Morning."

Her eyes flicked up, clashed with his stormy blue ones, and quickly looked away. "Morning. Do you want oatmeal for breakfast?"

"You left something on the bathroom counter."

"Sorry about that," she said lightly. "I'll grab it later."

"Jesse," Dad called. "You're going to talk to Coach Rick today about leaving the team?"

"Yeah," Jesse said curtly.

There was a startled pause and then Mom asked, "Do we need to talk more about this, son?"

"No," Jesse said and shocked them all by turning on his heel and walking out the front door.

Mom and Dad glanced at each other and then Violet as

she turned to watch his exit. Jesse had never talked back to their parents or showed any disrespect before. His terse tone and display of temper wasn't like him at all.

"Should I talk to him?" Dad murmured.

Lynne let out a long sigh and sat back in her seat. "Are we doing the right thing? This is his senior year. Making him quit football is a huge punishment."

Dad rapped his fingers on the table. "We can't let him get away with thinking what he did is okay."

"Of course not, but his team could make the national championships, and he's worked so hard."

"The only way for him to learn his lesson is to have him give up something he cares about. Anything else won't be a real punishment," Dad countered.

Through the living room window, Violet watched Jesse pick up the basketball and start dribbling on the driveway. She assumed he was upset about them when he probably wanted to talk to her about dropping out of football. It was a big deal. He was letting his whole team down. Everyone would want to know why he was quitting. What was he going to say? Her shoulders slumped. Another thing to add to the never-ending list of things that were her fault.

Glumly, she turned when the kettle screamed and poured hot water over the oats and added brown sugar and milk. She sat at the table, only half listening as her parents debated what was an appropriate punishment for Jesse. She secretly hoped they would come up with something else and couldn't conceal her dismay when Dad put his foot down.

"I didn't ban him from playing sports completely, which I could do. Giving up football will make him think twice before he acts in the future."

As Dad left the table, Mom focused on her. "Are you okay?"

"This is all my fault," Violet said and dropped her spoon, unable to take another bite.

Mom didn't deny it. "It's better for both of you to learn these lessons now rather than later." Mom chucked her under the chin. "This seems like a big deal now. It may seem like your world is ending, but one day you'll laugh over this." When Violet gave her an incredulous look, Lynne's lips quirked. "I swear you will. And as for your punishment, no going out with friends after school. Once Jesse talks to Coach Rick, you two come straight home."

"Yes, ma'am."

Violet lingered over her oatmeal until it was time to leave. When she walked out the front door, she saw Lynne talking to Jesse on the driveway. He had his head bent as he listened to his mother and nodded. As Violet approached, he unlocked the SUV so she could get in and went into the house to get his backpack while she fidgeted in the passenger seat. Lynne backed out of the driveway as Jesse got behind the wheel.

"We have to talk," he said as he fired up the engine.

Violet clasped her hands between her thighs. "I'm sorry that they're making you quit football. I know how much you love it. Maybe if you talk to Dad, you can convince him to—"

"I don't care about football. I care about us," he snapped.

Her heart skipped a beat. "We're fine."

"Are we?"

"Of course."

He braked a little too hard at a stop sign as he navigated through the neighborhood.

"Is that why you're locking me out of your room? Because we're fine?"

A hint of the aggression he displayed the day he beat Tucker's ass was coming back, making her anxiety skyrocket.

"I think," she began stiltedly as she plucked imaginary lint off her jeans, "considering what happened yesterday that you would agree that..." Why was she so nervous? This was Jesse. She could tell him anything. "That what we did..." she fumbled and burst out, "We can't do that anymore!"

The veins on his arms stood out as his hands flexed on the steering wheel. "No."

She forgot about her rehearsed speech. "What do you mean, *no*?"

He shot her a searing look out of narrow, glowing blue eyes. "You don't get to end us because you're scared or have a guilty conscience."

"I don't have a guilty conscience," she lied. "I just realized..." She dragged her hands down her face. "What were we thinking? You're my *brother*."

"We aren't blood related."

"But we were raised as siblings. I never saw you as anything else until..." She shook her head wildly and held both hands up like a traffic cop. "No. *No!* This ends now. We never should have let it get this far."

He reached over the console and gripped her thigh. "I'm not going to let you do this."

"Did you see Mom and Dad's faces when they found out about Tucker? Can you imagine how they'd react if they found out about us?" Her voice quavered as her mind conjured up all sorts of traumatic scenarios. "They don't even believe in sex before marriage and we..."

He squeezed her knee. "It's okay, Vi."

"No, it isn't! Nothing about this is okay. It's wrong and sinful, and we did it anyway! Mom and Dad would *die* if they knew!"

"We can't make decisions based on how Mom and Dad will feel," he said harshly. "We're old enough to make our own choices and accept the consequences, whatever they are."

"I-I'm not willing to accept the consequences for this," she stammered as she tried to brush his hand off her leg. "I'm not going to be the reason our family breaks apart. I've made a lot of stupid decisions, but I can fix this."

His grip tightened. "There's nothing to fix. You and I are supposed to be together."

"We will be! As siblings, as family, nothing more!" She smacked his hand. "You can't touch me like this! It's inappropriate!"

Her voice was rising. She was getting hysterical. Her emotions were a wild, feral thing clawing at her, making her lash out. She wanted this done, buried, over. Why was he arguing with her? Deep down, he knew this was the right thing to do, he just didn't want it to end *right now*. But it would have at some point, most likely when he'd gotten his fill. This was a novel experience for him—a girl ending things. He was just being stubborn.

"Stop pushing me away," he rapped out.

"I'm not pushing you away. I just don't want you to touch me."

"Yesterday I was licking your pussy, and today I can't touch you?"

His vulgar language was as shocking as a slap. She felt the blood drain from her face. "Don't talk to me like that."

"You really think we can go back to acting like siblings after I've been inside you? After everything we've done?"

"Yes!"

He shot her a look filled with incredulous fury. "Didn't the last few days mean anything to you?"

An invisible needle pierced her heart. Their day at the lake had been so special, almost dreamlike in its perfection. She would cherish that memory, especially since she knew they could never repeat it.

He squeezed her leg. "Vi."

She swallowed hard. "The past few days have been nice, but—"

"*Nice?*"

She flinched, partly because of his deafening shout and partly because, "You're hurting me."

He snatched his hand from her leg and ran his fingers through his hair. "I don't believe this."

"Isn't it bad enough that you have to give up football? That Tucker ended up in the hospital? How many signs do you need to convince you this isn't meant to be? Didn't you listen to Pastor Sonny's message yesterday?"

"I heard it."

"And?"

A muscle ticked in his jaw. "That has nothing to do with us."

Her mouth sagged. He was being deliberately obtuse. Pastor Sonny's message was a warning of how a seemingly harmless transgression could cause so much destruction. She wasn't willing to risk their family. Nothing was worth courting such an outcome. Couldn't he see that?

Was this proof that regularly indulging in sin changed a person, so they cared only about satisfying their cravings, regardless of anyone else's feelings? Was Jesse that far gone? Her resolve hardened. She vowed she would get them on the right path and that's what she would do, regardless of his bullheadedness.

"I want our relationship to go back to what it was," she said into the fraught silence.

"And if I don't agree?"

"You don't have a choice."

Out of the corner of her eye, she saw his head turn in her direction. He didn't say a word. He didn't have to. His gaze, sharp as the tip of a knife, slid over her. When she was on the verge of begging him to look back at the road, he did so.

"This wouldn't have happened if you hadn't caught me with Tucker. It started this domino effect that's led us here. I don't want anyone else to get hurt, and that's what would happen if we continued on this path. I don't want to disappoint Mom and Dad any more than I already have." She blinked rapidly as her eyes filled with tears. "And you mean too much to me to risk our friendship."

He said nothing.

"We won't talk about it. It'll be like it never happened," she said.

He didn't move a muscle, but the force of his anger was an invisible force that hammered at her, making it hard to breathe. She braced for an explosion that didn't come. Several minutes later, she slumped in her seat. His volatile temper unnerved her. He'd changed so much in so little time. She wanted her patient, considerate, affable brother back. This wasn't him.

She wanted everything to go back to the way it had been when she had nothing to hide, and she felt safe and clean and there was no threat of being exposed. He had to know this was destined to end badly. It was taboo, scandalous and if discovered, would haunt them for the rest of their lives. No one would support them exploring such a path. Even their friends would be horrified. Once Jesse had time to consider the long-term effects, he would agree with her. But until then, things between them would be strained. She hated being at odds with him, but it was necessary. He wasn't thinking clearly. It would take time to reprogram their minds, so they didn't see each other sexually. It was best to end it now before they hit the point of no return.

Although she knew she should leave him alone, she couldn't resist asking, "What did you tell Mom and Dad about the day you beat Tucker?"

"A complete fabrication."

She twisted her hands together in her lap. "Thank you for not telling them the truth." The silence that followed made her cringe. "I'm sorry. For everything."

"I'm not."

She wasn't sure what he meant by that, but didn't ask him to elaborate. It was a relief to reach school. Before he parked, she had her seat belt undone, and her backpack on her lap. When she hopped out, she expected him to say something in parting, but he didn't.

A group of their friends were several cars over. She approached Marissa, Brody, Anton and a few others with a big smile, determined for everything to go back to normal.

"Hey," she greeted.

"Where's Jesse going?" Anton asked.

She turned. She thought he'd be right behind her, but he was striding in the opposite direction, across the empty field. "No idea."

"SEE YOU TOMORROW," SHE TOLD MARIE BEFORE SHE HEADED toward the SUV. Jesse was already behind the wheel. She opened the passenger door and asked, "Did you talk to Coach Rick?"

"Yeah. Get in."

Apparently, his mood hadn't improved. The need to apologize rose again, but she knew it wouldn't do any good. She got in and fastened her seatbelt. "That didn't take long. I thought he'd try to talk you out of it."

"I talked to him at lunch."

Which explained why they were now creeping through traffic mere minutes after school ended. "Are you okay?"

"Does it matter?" he asked testily.

"Yes. If I hadn't let Tucker—"

"You saved his life. I wouldn't have stopped if you hadn't interfered."

That made her feel marginally better. "Have you told anyone besides Coach Rick that you're quitting?"

"No. Coach is going to break the news at practice."

"What reason did you give?"

He shrugged. "The truth. I made a mistake that made my parents pull me from the team. I deserve it."

She sat back and closed her eyes. Although Jesse didn't blame her, it didn't remove the crushing weight on her shoulders. She was grateful Jesse was speaking to her. She hadn't seen him all day and suspected he was avoiding her. Although she was secretly grateful he was making himself scarce, it made her feel even worse.

Although she did her best to act like everything was okay, she wasn't pulling it off well. Three of her friends asked if something was wrong. Georgia hadn't accepted her weak excuse and started interrogating her about the status of her relationship with Tucker. When she admitted that she and Tucker had broken up, her friends gave her hugs when she started to tear up. If they only knew the real reason she was crying.

Without conscious thought, she reached out to Jesse, seeking comfort, before she caught herself. She told him this morning that he couldn't touch her. That was a two-way street. Things were still too raw between them, even to hold his hand.

Her hand passed over her burning eyes. How had things gone off track so quickly? In a matter of days, it felt like she lost so much. Tucker, Jesse, her innocence, her parent's respect and trust. It had been a rollercoaster of highs and lows, and now she was at rock bottom with no idea where to go from here.

She hadn't expected this to be so excruciating. Why did doing the right thing feel like she was killing a part of herself? She felt drained, sad, and lonely.

She and Jesse were in the awkward, angry phase of a breakup. Even with her eyes closed, she sensed the battle going on inside of him. Whether that was because of her or the fact that his teammates and a good portion of the school would soon be speculating why he was quitting football, she wasn't sure.

When the SUV slowed, she opened her eyes and frowned as he turned into the same deserted park where he first kissed her.

"What are you doing? Mom wanted us to go straight home."

"She thought I'd talk to Coach after school, so we have time." He parked, undid his seatbelt, and turned toward her. "We need to talk."

Her heart skipped. "About what?"

His eyes narrowed. "About you and me."

"There's nothing to talk about."

He leaned forward, sky-blue eyes glittering as he stated, "You can't give me what you gave me and take it back, Vi."

"That was a mistake," she whispered.

"No, it wasn't," he clipped. "This..." He gestured between them. "Isn't a mistake. Can't you feel it?"

"Feel what?" she asked, feigning confusion.

He tensed. "Don't do that."

"Do what?"

"Act like you don't feel anything for me."

"I never said that. I love you. You're my brother."

He leaned in and growled, "We both know you haven't seen me as your brother for a while now."

It was the closest he'd come to acknowledging his late-night visits. The eruption of butterflies and heat in her belly horrified her. She thought declaring that their relationship was wrong would be enough to suppress her body's reaction to him. Not so. Her weak, susceptible flesh was eager to jump back into the fire, heedless of the consequences.

When she tried to turn away, Jesse clasped her face, forcing her to look at him.

"I've been in hell for so fucking long. I can't go back to that." He rested his forehead against hers. "You love me, and not just as a brother. Admit it."

Her heart slammed into her ribcage as her eyes flooded with the tears she'd been keeping at bay all day. "We can't."

"We can." His voice vibrated with implacable determination.

She wanted to leap into the deep end. To let him lead and take care of everything, but she knew he wasn't thinking it through. Indulging for the moment would only lead to more heartache. "Jesse."

"Do you honestly think how we feel about each other is going to go away? We didn't just kiss. I claimed every inch of you. You wanted it just as much as I did. You still do."

She flushed and braced her hand against his chest, pushing for breathing space. "It doesn't matter! This is wrong."

"Stop saying that. There's nothing wrong with this."

"If this is so *right,* then are you willing to tell Mom and Dad?" she challenged.

If he truly wanted her, he would be willing to tell their parents this wasn't a fling, but a genuine, loving relationship he wanted to pursue. No such words emerged from him. The long silence cut deep and confirmed everything she'd been thinking. He didn't care how conflicted she felt or that, if discovered, it would devastate their parents. Like Amnon, he was focused purely on sex and wouldn't stop until he quenched his needs. He also seemed fine with keeping their relationship a dirty secret. Why? So there would be minimal damage in the long run?

She wrenched away from him and ran her fingers through her hair as she tried to stuff down her feelings of being sullied and used. That's what she got for engaging in such a relationship. Regardless of how much her body enjoyed what Jesse did to her, it wouldn't last. She cattle prodded her hormones into submission and took a deep, calming breath. She promised God she would stop them from continuing down this slippery slope. Jesse was already too far gone, so she had to take a stand for both their sakes.

She stared through the windshield at the empty park as she said, "I've made so many mistakes. Mistakes with Tucker. Mistakes with you that have made things..." She swallowed hard. "Difficult. I'm sorry for that. I can't take it back, but I can do what's right, starting now. I just want to forget it ever happened."

Out of the corner of her eye, she saw he sat facing her, completely motionless.

"Please take me home," she said quietly.

"You think you can end it, just like that?"

Despite the way her heart banged around in her chest like a trapped bird, she turned her head to meet and hold his gaze. "Yes. Just like that."

Although his face remained blank, something shifted in his eyes that made the fine hairs on her nape stand up. Everything in her went on high alert. Obeying a gut instinct, she undid her seatbelt, yanked on the door handle, and tumbled out of the SUV all in one motion. She staggered before she caught her balance and stared at Jesse, who hadn't moved. Feeling frightened, foolish, and embarrassed at her overreaction, she glared at him.

"Get in the car, Vi," he said coldly.

She'd always trusted Jesse implicitly, but for the first time in her life, she hesitated. He seemed to be in control, but something told her if she got back in the car, he would cross every boundary she just set. She was ashamed that a part of her wanted him to. It would be so easy to get lost in him, but her fear of ending up alone was stronger than her sexual desires.

She slammed the door in his face and headed for the trail. They both needed to cool off. She'd go for a walk while he sat in the car and... She stiffened when she heard a door closing, the familiar beep of the SUV's alarm, and the sound of someone running toward her.

A hand wrapped around her upper arm. "Violet."

She pivoted to face him, squinting into the sun as she

went on tiptoes and enunciated through her teeth, "We're done talking. Nothing you say is going to make a difference. I've made up my mind. You have to accept it."

He searched her eyes. "That's your final word?"

"Yes!"

He nodded and glanced around. "You want to see the park?"

She blinked, taken aback by how quickly his mood had shifted. "I... I think I'll take a walk."

He gestured for her to precede him. She eyed him for a moment before she turned on her heel and strode off. She expected him to continue the argument, but he gave her space, staying a few paces behind her so she didn't feel crowded. After minutes passed without a word exchanged between them, her hunched shoulders dropped.

His forceful pushback unnerved her. He had grounds to be disgruntled, even angry, but she expected him to accept her decision with grace. He'd always been so easygoing, respectful, and willing to cede to her wishes and now... Now, she had no idea what was coming next.

She was seeing him in a new light. His broody edginess thrilled and alarmed her. She shouldn't be aroused by it, but there was no denying that she was. There was something wrong with her. There was no other explanation for why she'd gotten wet when he ordered her to get back in the car. This was *Jesse*, the brother who braided her hair, comforted her when Mom and Dad fought, and helped her with her homework. Why hadn't she ever picked up on the steel beneath his guileless smile? Why was she simultaneously attracted and repelled by it? This wouldn't do. She was supposed to be purifying her thoughts, but her mind was overwhelmed with graphic, inappropriate fantasies that she tried to smother without success.

Why had no one ever mentioned how addictive sin was? It was a drug one could get hooked on by partaking of the forbidden just once. Jesse was so consumed by it that he wasn't himself. He hadn't been for some time, though. Jesse had been sipping from the pool of debauchery far longer than she had. Who knew what he'd been doing with his exes, who were so eager to get back together with him? He hadn't been caught, which had emboldened him to this point. Being outed by Tucker should have been a wakeup call that he wasn't going to get away with everything. Why didn't Jesse get what he needed from another girl? Why put so much in jeopardy to sleep with his stepsister?

Her calves cramped as she went uphill. She slowed to catch her breath and made a mental note that she needed to exercise more. She was grateful when the path curved beneath some trees. As she paused to enjoy the shade, she cocked her head when she heard running water.

"There's a stream that runs parallel to the path. Want to see it?" Jesse asked.

When she nodded, he led the way through the trees. She perked up as she got a glimpse of blue up ahead. When they came to a small clearing, she put her hands on hips and surveyed the tranquil scene. Sunlight danced on the surface of the fast-moving water.

"I can see why you like coming here. It's beautiful," she said.

She closed her eyes for a moment, letting nature soothe her troubled thoughts. If only she could rewind the clock. She longed for a time when things were simple and inno-cent, but a part of her knew those days were gone. Like Eve, she'd taken a bite of the apple and now there was no going back to seeing the world in cute, pastel shades. Now, she could see every vivid shade of the rainbow and had firsthand knowledge of the temptations in the shadows. With adult decisions came severe punishments, complications, and impossible choices. But she was doing her part and keeping her promise to God. That's all that mattered.

A soft gust of air was her only warning. She opened her eyes to find Jesse in front of her. Her hand flew up in a protective gesture as she stumbled back.

"What are you...?"

"I can't go back to what we were."

His flat delivery made her freeze, but it was the strange, unholy gleam in his eyes that made her heart begin to beat like a drum.

"I-I want to go back to the trail."

Even she could hear the anxiety in her tone. Jesse's only response to this was to match her retreating steps. His eyes were fixed on her like she was prey. He wasn't even blinking.

In a distant part of her mind, she noted that he had pretended to accept her decision so she would let down her guard and bring her somewhere secluded where no one would interfere. They were a significant distance from the path without a soul in sight.

"Last week was a dream for me. Taking your virginity and then having you surrender so completely, giving me everything..." One hand balled into a fist at his side. "Now, you say you want to forget it ever happened, and I'm supposed to go back to treating you like a sister." He shook his head. "It doesn't work that way, baby."

"We have to get home. Mom and Dad..."

"Things were perfect until that call came in," Jesse cut in, ignoring her nervous chatter. "I don't care that I have to quit football. That's a small price to pay for giving him the beating he deserved."

"Tucker—"

He closed the distance between them with a speed that made her let out a startled yelp. He pinned her against a tree and gripped her face as he ducked down, so they were eye to eye.

"That's the last time you say his name," he said through clenched teeth. "I'm sick of hearing about him. I don't regret what I did. I'd do it all over again, except I wouldn't stop until I was sure the damage was permanent."

"You can't mean that!"

"I do." He trailed his knuckles down the sensitive line of her throat. "He had no right to touch you."

His pupils were so dilated, there was only a thin ring of blue. She should run, fight, or scream her head off, but she was locked in a strange paralysis that kept her pinned between Jesse and the massive tree at her back.

"You can't tell me you don't feel anything for me. I won't believe you."

His knuckles trailed down to her breasts. When he strummed her nipple, she jolted.

"You love what I do to you," he rasped as he cupped her breast and tightened his hold on her face, giving her no way to hide her reaction from him. "You want this so bad, you're shaking."

She was shaking. Whether it was from desire or terror, she wasn't sure. She wrapped both hands around his wrist and tugged. "Please don't do this."

"I've never felt like this about anyone," Jesse said almost to himself. "I thought I would be satisfied once I had you, once you gave yourself to me, but you're always trying to slip away." His expression hardened, and his fingers dug into her cheeks as he pressed his lips to hers. "But I have you now, Violet. And I'm not letting go."

He held her gaze as his hand left her breast and went to the button of her jeans. Her paralysis broke. She erupted into motion, but he was anticipating that and swept her legs out from under her.

She landed on her back without any idea how she'd gotten there. Winded and stunned, she lay there, staring at the underside of the tree's canopy until Jesse blotted out her view. He undid her jeans, yanked them to her knees, and slipped his fingers inside her. She sat up with an outraged shriek as he retracted his hand. Before she could defend herself, he shoved those same fingers into her mouth so deep that she gagged.

"Tell me again you don't want me," Jesse mocked.

Along with bile, she tasted her own honey. She wrenched her head to the side and coughed.

"We're not going backwards," Jesse declared with frightening calm as he positioned her on her hands and knees and knelt behind her. "Nothing's coming between us. No other guys, Mom and Dad, even God."

She reached back and pushed at him. "You can't do this!"

"I have to do this. For both of us." When she tried to scramble away, he pulled her back and smacked her butt hard enough to stun her into immobility. "You're scared of what people think and too ashamed to admit what you really want."

His fingers slipped inside her.

"Soaked, just like I knew you would be. Are you wet for your brother, Violet?"

"Stop!" she sobbed as she tore at the grass to get away.

He gripped her hips, hauling her backwards, and slammed in to the hilt. She screamed. The horrible sound bounced off the trees and ricocheted back to them. As she hung her head, panting, she waited for the distant shout of some Good Samaritan coming to the rescue, but there was nothing but the pleasant sound of the stream, which she now realized would drown out any call for help.

"I come here often because of how isolated it is," Jesse said as he blanketed her much smaller form. "Scream all you want. Nobody's going to hear you."

"This isn't you," she said, her voice thick with tears. "Something's wrong. Can't you see that?"

"You're what's wrong with me," he groaned into her hair. "I haven't been sane for over a year. You love toying with me and throwing obstacles in my path. I'd let you do whatever you want to me, but the moment things get rough, you want to run. I'm not going to let you do that anymore. You're sticking with me."

He began to move in shallow, hard thrusts that stabbed something inside her that made her keen and uproot the ground around her.

"How can anything that feels so fucking good be a sin, Violet?" he panted as his hand slipped under her blouse and stroked her stomach. "We were made for each other. Can't you feel it?"

She let out a choked sob as he planted himself deep. She couldn't believe this was happening—that he was so far gone that he would take her in a public place. He was ruthless, shameless, completely out of control. As he began to move more forcefully, her knees sank into the soft earth.

"We're supposed to be together. Everything in me says so. I know you feel it, too. I'd do anything for you, baby, anything."

She shook her head.

He slowed his pace and pressed his cheek against her clammy one. "What, baby?"

"You wouldn't do anything for me," she said raggedly.

"Of course I would," he whispered as he rocked his hips. "Tell me what you want, and I'll give it to you."

"I want you to stop."

He abruptly pushed on her shoulders, so her face was mashed in the grass and her butt was up in the air.

"You don't want me to stop, and I'm going to prove it."

CHAPTER 14

JESSE

Violet's upper body arched as she released a beautiful, muted scream before she went limp. As he lapped up what poured from her, she shuddered and tried to scoot away, but her body was weak and uncoordinated, and she was no match for him. Eventually, she gave up and let him have his way.

When he was content, he rested his cheek on her sticky inner thigh. He'd never been drunk or high, but he suspected it was similar to how he felt right now.

For a few hellish hours, he thought he may have lost her, but she was back where she belonged. He sated his demons and made sure he fed hers, too. He fucked her on her hands and knees before he went 69, straddling her face, forcing her to get him hard again while he made her come with his mouth. After that, he took her missionary with her ankles resting on his shoulders. That's when she began babbling about sin, Amnon and Tamar, and some deal she'd made with God. He didn't care about a fucked up, incestuous relationship that happened three thousand years ago or what she promised God. He had his own deal with God

—her. He lost his father so that God could bring Violet into his life. She was his destiny, his salvation, *his*. She belonged to him and he to her. Why couldn't she see that? What she labeled as sin felt like a spiritual cleansing to him. She was home to him, and he wouldn't let her destroy the ties he'd so carefully nurtured.

She climaxed when he did her missionary and then burst into tears. He'd never heard her cry like that before. She was distraught, inconsolable. Nothing he said would calm her, so he did the only thing he could think of—turn those pitiful cries into gasps of pleasure by burying his face in his favorite place. She fought him and called for help until she was hoarse, but God was on his side. No one interfered. He made her beg for release and wrung out two more orgasms from her before he was satisfied.

He kissed her mound before he got to his feet and sorted himself out. He absently brushed debris from his legs before pulling his jeans up. He was grateful he'd worn a black shirt instead of white. If not, it would have been covered in dirt and grass stains from all the rolling around on the ground they'd just done.

He surveyed Violet, who made a delectable picture. She was splayed on her back, blouse hiked up to expose her abdomen and bra, jeans caught on one ankle while her other leg was completely bare. Her pussy glistened from his ministrations, inner thighs red and swollen from the love bites he'd left behind. The urge to wring more affirmations from her was tempting, but they didn't have time.

He retrieved her torn underwear and pocketed them before he crouched beside her. "Vi."

Her only reaction to his voice was a tear that slipped from the corner of her closed eyelids.

"We have to go, baby," he said before he gripped her limp hands and pulled her up.

He wasn't surprised when she swayed on her feet. He'd been rough. Brutal, actually, but hearing her chalk up the best days of his life as "nice" and her dismissal of their relationship put him into a mindless state that didn't leave room for tenderness.

He steadied her before he unfolded her crumpled blouse and brushed grass, dirt, and leaves from her before he fed her leg into her pants and pulled them up. Both of their jeans were suspiciously dirty, but thankfully his dark shirt and her colorful top hid the worst of the stains.

"Can you walk?" he asked.

When she didn't acknowledge him, he inwardly shrugged and put her over his shoulder. She didn't fight or utter a sound. They were a ways from the parking lot, but now that he'd had her, he felt like he could climb Mount Everest.

He was grateful he didn't pass anyone on the path. He opened the SUV and settled her in the passenger seat. She finally opened her eyes, but didn't look at him. She stared straight ahead, expression blank.

He climbed in to fasten her seatbelt. She didn't react when he caressed her breasts or kissed her temple. She was acting like a lifeless doll. She was punishing herself for what they'd done, but he knew how to bring her back to life. When his mouth was between her legs, when he sucked on her nipples and played with her asshole, she went wild. Whatever was going on in her mind, he would overcome. He wouldn't allow her to withdraw, not when she was finally his. He would do whatever was necessary to keep her.

He retrieved his phone from his backpack before getting

into the driver's seat. He wasn't surprised to see thirty text messages and over a dozen calls from his teammates. He would deal with that later. The only missed call he cared about was Mom's. He called her back as he turned the key in the ignition.

"Are you home?" Mom asked.

"No, we're on our way. Violet wanted to take a walk at the park. We're leaving now."

He glanced at Violet as he reversed. She was doing a good job of imitating a mannequin.

"Coach Rick called Dad and I," Mom said.

"I'm not surprised."

"I'm sorry, Jesse, but Isaac feels that—"

"It's okay, Mom."

She sighed. "I'll see you two at home. Can you start dinner?"

"Sure."

"Thanks, son."

"No problem."

He hung up, tossed his phone in the cupholder, and rested his hand on Violet's thigh. She didn't push him away, which pleased him. What he felt when he pummeled Tucker was nothing compared to the red haze that engulfed him this morning when she tried to end them. The only reason he hadn't pulled over to deal with Violet was because he knew his parents would be expecting a call from Coach Rick after he quit the team. Once that was out of the way, he would deal with Violet. They wouldn't go home until things were set right between them.

He stroked her thigh. What he'd done was wrong, but it was hard to feel guilty when he'd come inside her, had her taste on his tongue, and she was sitting docilely beside him, letting him touch her. Right and wrong ceased to matter where she was concerned. His need to possess her trumped all else.

The days leading up to Sunday had been a dream. Violet surpassed every fantasy. He worried he would scare her with his intensity and need, but she not only matched him, at times it seemed her desires surpassed his. She eagerly jumped into every scenario he created. He couldn't believe she was finally his. Their bodies were made for each other. They were so in tune, words weren't necessary. Everything was perfect until that fucking phone call, which tore down the walls of the alternate reality he constructed around Violet to insulate her from the outside world.

The stark terror on her face when Isaac nearly discovered them in the bathroom told him she wasn't ready to come out to their parents. Between finding out that worthless bastard was in the hospital and Pastor Sonny's sermon, he knew the progress he made had taken a major hit. Sensing her mental anguish in church, he tried to comfort her, but she rejected him.

With their parents present, he'd been forced to give her space. Discovering she had barred him from her bedroom was a nasty shock. He hadn't slept and had no choice but to draw his own conclusions about what that meant, which she confirmed this morning on the ride to school.

A part of her was still that lonely girl, afraid of being abandoned if she let people down. Yesterday, she crumbled under the weight of their parent's disappointment. He had never viewed her need for love and acceptance as a defect until he realized she would never choose him over their parents. That wouldn't do.

If Mom and Dad found out, they wouldn't excuse such blatant immorality or allow it to flourish under their roof. He suspected their parents would go so far as to separate them. He was willing to face whatever consequences came from his actions, but he had to make sure Violet would stick by him, and she wasn't there. Not even close. She would rather break up than defy their parents.

He ignored the fire that heated his blood. They would get there. One day, Violet would love him with the same fervor that he did her. Until then, he intended to keep her as close to him as possible. He wasn't going to let Pastor's Sonny's lesson about King David's mistakes or their parent's disapproval keep him from her. He loved her. His life revolved around her. He wouldn't let anyone come between them.

When they pulled up to the house, he was relieved to see Dad's truck was gone. He slipped on his backpack before going around to Violet's door. She displayed no awareness of their surroundings or him. Her face was smudged with dirt, hair a tangled mess, and if either of their parents caught a glimpse of her, no explanation would get him out of this.

"We're home, baby," he said as he undid her seatbelt, shouldered her bag and tugged her into his arms.

He carried her to the house and hoped the neighbors were otherwise occupied. He headed straight for their bathroom and kicked both doors closed before he set her in the tub. He dropped their bags and caught her before she collapsed.

"We have to clean up." He flicked a ladybug out of her hair. "Do you want me to bathe you?"

She looked right through him with eyes the color of rich moss.

He cupped her cheek. "Violet?"

No response.

"I'll take care of you," he said and began to strip her.

Once her clothes were in a pile, he got naked and climbed in with her. He expected her to balk when he started positioning her so he could clean her thoroughly, but she remained strangely compliant throughout. He was grateful, since he didn't know how much time they had.

"I'm sorry I was so rough," he said as he ran the soapy washcloth over her skin. "Are you hurt?"

She didn't answer.

He had to shampoo her hair twice. He scrubbed every inch of her, including the bottom of her feet and between every toe. He wished he could linger. The fact that she was allowing him to care for her so intimately without shame pacified the entity inside him that had compelled him to take her so savagely. The need to reinforce their physical bonds consumed him. He planned to possess her as frequently as possible to maintain their connection, especially when her mind and body were at war with one another. Eventually, they would align once she stopped fighting what was between them.

Even though he'd had her multiple times, his body reacted to her nearness. He couldn't be around her and not want her. He thought once she belonged to him that his obsession would ease, but it was worse than ever.

She stood in the back of the shower, as animated as a statue, as he quickly cleaned himself. She didn't react to the water that dripped down her face or when he came to her. He couldn't resist giving her a gentle kiss she didn't return before he wrung out her hair, wrapped it in a towel, and hastily dried her.

His senses were on high alert as he dressed her in sweats. The only sign of the rough sex they had at the park was her swollen lips, but that could be excused in a dozen ways. He carried her into the living room, settled her on the couch, and put on her favorite show.

"I'm going to start dinner. Do you need anything?"

She didn't look at him or acknowledge his question. He kissed her forehead before he went into the kitchen. From the tortillas, beans, and vegetables Mom had on the counter, he deduced dinner was supposed to be tacos. Once the vegetables were cut and the hamburger was simmering on the stove, he fetched Violet's hairbrush.

He settled her on the floor between his legs and combed her hair. He'd always loved playing with her hair. So much so, Mom taught him how to braid it. He did so now before he placed her back on the couch and switched positions, so he was on his knees facing her.

Her eyes were more hazel than that startling green. His coddling was having the desired effect. Before Mom and Dad arrived, he needed her coherent. Violet had always worn her emotions on her sleeve. A lack of them would be more noticeable than anything else she could do.

"Violet."

No reaction.

He stroked the apple of her cheek. "What's between us isn't sinful."

Her eyes focused on him.

"People search all their lives for the connection we have between us. It's rare and special. It's worth fighting for."

Her gaze flicked away. The entity inside of him snarled at the rejection, but he had to be patient. He couldn't force her to catch up to his level of adoration and worship.

"Do you remember what you said after Mom and Dad left for their honeymoon?"

She didn't move, but he sensed her withdraw even

further. He ran his hands up and down her arms to stop her from tuning out and escaping in her mind.

"You said good things don't happen to you. You were terrified something would happen that would ruin everything."

When he clasped her face to force her to look at him, she closed her eyes in defense. She was trembling, which he took as a good sign. The ice was cracking. He nuzzled her, encouraging the breakdown.

"Those fears never went away. They're still here now, controlling you, trying to control me. This is a blessing, a fucking gift, and you're treating it like a curse." His lips captured the first tear that fell. "I'm not going to let you do it. I'm not going to let you destroy us. If you want to lie to Mom and Dad, to your friends, to God, I don't care, but you can't lie to me. I know you better than you know yourself." He kissed the shell of her ear and sighed in relief when she shivered. "Tell me you didn't like what I did to you. That you didn't feel painfully alive. You begged me for more."

She let out a choked sound.

"You want me, too," he whispered harshly. "I had to force you to suck me, but in the end, you wanted me to come down your throat."

When she punched his shoulder, he sat back and saw she was glaring at him through dripping eyes.

He softened and cupped her face. "Do you really think God is cruel enough to make us want each other if we weren't meant to be?"

"It's a test to resist temptation." Her voice was raspy from screaming.

"Or a test of our devotion to one another," he countered.

She shook her head.

"Don't compare what's happening between us to King David's affair with Bathsheba or those half siblings," he growled.

She pushed at his chest. "You're my brother."

"Not genetically."

"Legally, we have the same parents."

"Do the labels matter so much? What if I wasn't your stepbrother?"

"But you are! And anyway, it's still not okay! We're not supposed to have sex!"

"But getting married would make it right?"

Violet went ghost white.

"You..." she began in a strangled tone but was interrupted by the sound of the garage door opening.

Violet shoved him hard enough to make him rock back on his heels. She frantically wiped away her tears and then touched her hair and frowned as if she'd slept through him braiding it for her. He got to his feet but stole a kiss to put some color back in her face. He was on his way to the kitchen when Mom came through the door.

"Hey, kids."

"Hey, Mom."

When Jesse kissed her cheek, he caught the relief that passed through her eyes.

Mom clasped his face. "Are you okay?"

"Never better."

Mom blinked. "Really?"

"Going to the park put things into perspective and helped me clear my head."

He heard Violet's stifled gasp from the living room, but Mom didn't catch it. Mom followed him to the kitchen and perked up when she saw that everything was done.

"You're in pajamas already?" Mom asked, plucking at his sweatpants.

"We were sweaty and filthy, so we came home and washed up. Dinner should be ready in a few minutes. You can shower if you want. I got this."

Mom patted his chest. "Thanks, son. I think I will. Dad should be home soon."

THAT EVENING TURNED OUT TO BE BUSIER THAN ANY OF THEM anticipated. Coach Rick didn't give up. He called the landline to speak to his parents again, and several teammates stopped by to confirm what they'd heard and pleaded with Mom and Dad to change their minds. Jesse could see Isaac teetering on his punishment, but he didn't ask to be let off the hook.

When Isaac said he had to quit football, he'd been taken aback and initially pissed before he realized the time he would have spent at practice or at games could now be dedicated to Violet. If it came down to football or Violet, he would choose her in a heartbeat. Ultimately, he saw this as another reward for beating Tucker's ass.

It took two hours for his friends and teammates to accept defeat. He stood on the driveway as they let out dejected honks and drove away. Violet was beside him. She'd been drawn out of the house by the girls who'd come with their boyfriends or brothers. She was pale and subdued but functioning well enough that the only question her friends asked had been whether she was coming down with a cold.

Thanks to his behavior that morning and the parade of visitors, Mom and Dad were mainly focused on him at dinner. He thought no one noticed Violet's listlessness and the fact that she took just a few bites of the taco he made her until Mom rested her hand on Violet's arm.

"Honey, are you all right?"

As Violet visibly struggled to come up with a response, he asked, "I went too hard on you on the trail today, didn't I?"

Violet gave a little jerk and gaped at him.

"You're sore, aren't you?"

He was pleased by the flicker of rebellion in her eyes and charmed by the blush that hit her cheeks as she shook her head.

He sighed loudly. "Stubborn."

Violet yelped when he picked her up and snapped, "I'm *fine*! Put me down!"

"Don't be proud," he chided. "I'll go easier on you next time."

"You two," Mom chuckled as he carried Violet to her bedroom.

He closed the door behind him and made his way to her bed. He flicked back the covers before he set her down.

"Do you need Ibuprofen?"

"I said, I'm fine," she said sullenly and stared at the ceiling.

He glanced at the closed door before he decided to climb in beside her. Violet's eyes nearly bugged out of her head.

"Are you crazy?" she hissed.

As he stretched out, she rolled to the other side and would have escaped if he hadn't dragged her back where she belonged.

"Let me go!"

"Hush," he said as he gathered her against him and pressed her face against his throat.

"What are you doing?" she demanded, voice muffled.

"Giving both of us what we need."

"I don't want this," she said, wriggling, until he tightened his arms around her.

She let out an angry huff and muttered under her breath. The feel of her lips brushing against his skin made his blood sing. He ignored his body's reaction and focused on giving her the comfort that he hadn't been able to earlier in the day. He stroked her back, shoulders, and sides as he tried to soothe the physical trauma he wrought. For long minutes, she was completely rigid. Nearly fifteen minutes passed before she quivered and unwillingly collapsed against him.

"I didn't mean to hurt you," he murmured.

"But you did."

Her voice, thick with tears and tainted with fear, made him place kisses along her hairline.

"I'm sorry, baby."

"I've never seen that side of you before."

"Me either."

"You've changed."

"So have you."

She didn't deny it. More time passed before the last of her tension dissolved, leaving her boneless in his arms, just as he intended. He heard the distant clink of silverware and plates as Mom and Dad cleared the table, accurately deducing he wasn't coming back. He cuddled Violet against him, imagining a future where he could hold her like this without fear of being reprimanded for doing what felt like the most natural thing in the world to him. He thought she'd fallen asleep until her hand twisted in his shirt.

"I know this is special," she whispered.

His heart leapt at her acknowledgement.

She eased back so she could see his face. Her wide, beseeching gaze made his stomach twist.

"I don't want to ruin what we have with sex," she said in a rush.

He bit back a groan. "It won't," he began.

"*Please*, Jesse. Can we try to keep sex out of it and just see if...?"

Despite all he'd said, she was still in denial and trying to reverse the clock to a time they could never return to. She wanted to keep him at arm's length and was instinctively trying to loosen the bonds that sex fortified and strengthened every time he took her. He wouldn't allow it. He had every intention of exploiting their connection until they were so interlocked that she was a part of him.

As he tried to think of the easiest way to let her down, she cupped his cheek with a trembling hand.

Eyes sparkling with earnest tears, she said, "I don't want to lose you."

Nothing he said would reassure her that they were on the right path. She believed God would punish her for continuing their relationship by breaking them and the family apart. He had no intention of allowing either of those things to happen, but only time would prove him right.

"You'll never lose me," he promised.

"You'll try?" she pushed.

When he hesitated, her eyes welled with tears.

Pity made him say, "Yes."

Even as her face lit with relief, he knew he wouldn't keep his promise.

CHAPTER 15
VIOLET

2 MONTHS LATER

Violet lay on the couch in the living room with Mom and Dad, who sat in their individual recliners. Mom graded papers while Dad watched TV and switched from the news to sports and then an old, black and white sitcom.

"Isaac!" Mom said, exasperated. "Stop changing the channel. What about Violet?"

"It's okay. I'm used to it," Violet murmured.

And she wasn't watching anyway. When she was a child and had bad dreams or wasn't feeling good, she would sneak into Dad's bedroom and sleep on the floor. Just being near him banished the boogie man and made her feel better. At seventeen, she was hoping their presence would have the same magical effect, but the feeling of safety and comfort she was seeking eluded her.

She tensed when she heard a key turn in the front door.

"Hey," Jesse said as he entered with his backpack, gym bag, and a sweater slung over one shoulder.

"There he is!" Mom said fondly. "How was basketball practice, son?"

"Long." Jesse placed a kiss on top of Mom's head. "I'm starved."

"You should get cleaned up first. If you hurry, the food on the stove will still be hot."

Mom laughed as Jesse ran down the hallway to his room to shower.

"That saying about the way to a man's heart is through his stomach is true, isn't it, Isaac?"

"Yup," Dad said distractedly.

"What meal did I make that made you fall in love with me?" Mom asked.

"Hot honey chicken cutlets."

Mom grinned when she saw Violet watching her. "You're set, honey. You already know that recipe by heart."

"She isn't dating this year," Dad said as he changed the channel.

"I know, but that doesn't mean she can't keep an eye out for the one," Mom said with a wink.

Violet gave Lynne a weak smile before she returned her attention to the TV. She wasn't looking for the one and if she stumbled upon him, and he turned out to be as perfect as she'd always imagined, she'd tell him to find someone else. Someone who could give him what he was looking for. She had nothing to offer. The good qualities she'd once possessed had been wrecked beyond repair.

Her hand fisted under the pillow. Jesse hadn't kept his promise to keep sex out of their relationship. He hadn't even tried. Dad made her easy prey by not allowing her to attend after school programs, go out on weekends, and made Jesse her only option to commute to and from school. She was basically a prisoner, and Jesse took full advantage.

He was relentless in his demands, yet nauseatingly gentle as he pillaged and plundered. He took every opportunity to wring unwanted orgasms from her and comforted her when self-loathing got the best of her, and she burst into tears. Sometimes, when he felt a lick of remorse, he made promises that he couldn't keep for more than a few days. It was a hellish cycle of hope and then crushing disappointment.

His sheer brazenness astounded her. He ambushed her in the most unlikely places. School wasn't a safe zone. At any moment, she could be propelled into an empty computer lab or hustled under the bleachers so he could have his way with her. The only time she was truly out of his reach was in class, where she'd dozed off a few times. The stress was taking a toll on her. Her grades were starting a downward trajectory that she needed to get hold of before her parents saw her report card.

Jesse had easily worked his way back into their parents' good graces by utilizing the skills he picked up from the general contractor to fix things around the house. Little did Mom and Dad know, he was repairing the holes he'd made in his bedroom and covered everything up with a fresh coat of paint. Violet couldn't deny she'd been relieved when he got rid of the last reminder from the day he took her virginity.

She was so on hypervigilant, she sensed Jesse enter the room seconds before he spoke.

"Hey, Mom, how's Raiden doing?" Jesse called.

Violet tracked Jesse's voice into the kitchen, listened to the sound of him opening the cabinet to get a bowl, and heard the clink of the lid being set on the counter as he dug into the pot on the stove.

"He's doing a little better, but you can see how exhausted and confused he is," Mom said sadly.

Mom gave them frequent updates on Raiden, a student whose parents were in the midst of a nasty divorce, with the little boy caught in the middle. Raiden was so miserable, he begged to stay at school instead of going home.

"That's too bad," Jesse said. "I hoped after you talked to the mother, things would improve."

"No, she's too self-involved to see what she's doing to her son. Poor Raiden. He hugs me at least ten times a day. It breaks my heart."

"Maybe I can stop by and play basketball with him after school next week," Jesse offered.

Mom's face lit up. "That would mean the world to him."

Ambivalent emotions warred in Violet's chest. How could Jesse be the monster who had shoved her into the garage when she'd been stupid enough to get a drink of water after their parents had gone to bed to have his way with her, *and* the nice guy willing to take time out of his busy schedule to play basketball with a child going through a hard time?

Jesse appeared with a bowl cradled in his large hand. She stared at the TV, not acknowledging him or attempting to make space on the three-seater couch she sprawled on. She'd hoped he would eat at the table, go to his bedroom, or sit on the floor where he belonged. Instead, he stood there, waiting.

As the awkward moment stretched, Mom started to rise from her recliner.

"You can sit here, son."

"No need," Jesse said easily, and lifted Violet's legs before he sat and placed her feet on his lap.

Dad frowned at Violet, but she pretended not to notice.

She hated that Jesse had so easily outmaneuvered her. His poise under pressure astounded her. Jesse had put them in some risky, compromising situations, but his unruffled composure and well-mannered, caring facade immediately disarmed authority figures who would have otherwise known he was up to no good. Could she blame them for buying into his golden boy act? Even she, who had seen him at his worst, still wanted to believe that the sweet, supportive older brother she'd known and trusted was still in there somewhere, despite dozens of incidents that proved otherwise.

She crawled to the other end of the couch and braced her pillow against the couch arm before she resettled, tucking her legs up so she was no longer touching him. She didn't want to be near him, but she also didn't want to be alone with her gloomy thoughts. Since their parents were present, Jesse would be on his best behavior.

"Allison brought you home?" Jesse asked her, ignoring the fact that she had blatantly ignored him since he walked through the front door.

She inwardly bristled. It was none of his business who gave her a ride home, but knowing their parents were listening, she had no choice but to answer. "Yes."

Jesse hadn't been happy when Mom and Dad lifted the ban on after school activities and going out on weekends last week. She leapt on her reinstated freedom, hitching rides and hanging out with friends whenever possible. Jesse was further foiled by the start of the basketball season. He'd been strangely disinterested and reluctant to join, but Mom and Dad insisted, probably out of guilt for the horrible football season his team had.

When Jesse finished his food, he set his empty bowl aside and shuffled along the cushions. She tensed as he slipped beneath her oversized blanket. Debating whether she could tolerate him or bail and go to her room, it was a horrible shock when he grasped her foot and pulled it onto his lap. She raised her head to snap at him, but he and Dad were deep in discussion about the stats the sports announcer rattled off.

She tugged, but his iron grip wouldn't let her go. She couldn't believe his gall. He knew she didn't want him to touch her and did it anyway. He was constantly pushing her and took as many liberties as possible with others present because he knew she wouldn't cause a scene. He was such an asshole! She should jam her heel in his balls or crush his fingers with her toes, but it wasn't worth ruining the relaxed atmosphere.

She bared her teeth as his calloused thumbs ran along the bottom of her foot. She bit her lip to stop herself from moaning when he hit a tender spot. She hated how observant he was. When she stiffened, he lightened the pressure and when she wriggled her toes, sensing she liked what he was doing, he lingered. It was ironic that their silent communication was better than their non-existent verbal communication. She had nothing to say to him. He didn't care how she felt or what she wanted. She learned what he said meant nothing. How could he be so in tune with her in one area and completely deaf and dumb to her wants and needs in others?

"This is nice," Mom said, surveying them with a smile.

It was rare for all of them to be together on a Friday evening. The only reason she hadn't gone to the mall with Marie and Allison was because she thought Jesse was going out with Brody and Blaine after practice.

"We should start this weekend off right," Mom said excitedly. "Anyone up for a movie?"

Knowing Jesse had to be up bright and early to work with the general contractor, Violet assumed he would decline. She was annoyed when he said, "Sure. What should we watch?"

She didn't offer a suggestion, since she wouldn't be paying attention. They debated for a couple of minutes before settling on some action movie. As Mom turned off the lights and closed the blinds tight, so the only light came from the screen, Violet tried to remember the last movie night they had. She used to love huddling under the covers, eating popcorn mixed with assorted candies. The memories were tattered and slightly out of focus, like they belonged to someone else.

It was the same four people sitting in the same room in front of the TV, but the contentment and sense of security she used to feel when surrounded by family had been replaced with a feeling of stark alienation even though Mom and Dad were mere feet away. It was like sitting in front of a fire, but not feeling the warmth of the blaze...

A soft snore made Violet shift her head. She wasn't surprised to see Lynne had fallen asleep before the movie finished its opening credits.

"She always does that," Violet said with a shake of her head.

"She works hard. The moment she lets herself relax, she's dead to the world," Dad said. "Let her sleep."

Despite herself, Violet found herself drawn into the movie, which was non-stop action from the opening chase scene. She was so engrossed in the story that it took a while for her to realize that the massage had stopped, and she was lying there, relaxed and comfortable, with her feet propped on her tormentor's lap.

The moment she tried to pull away, Jesse gripped her

shin. He squeezed, telling her to stay as she was. How dare he? She tipped onto her back to kick him with her free foot and went rigid when his hand brushed over her bare thigh.

The TV screen went black as the main character dropped into a tunnel, plunging the living room into darkness at the same time that Jesse's hand slid into the leg of her pajama shorts and cupped her between her legs. She jerked as if she'd been electrocuted. Her confidence that he wouldn't make a move in front of their parents shattered into a million pieces. The sound of the character cursing and pounding the wall in frustration concealed Violet's uncoordinated, frantic bid to get away. She did an awkward backstroke like a swimmer as panic seared her insides.

An explosion on screen briefly illuminated the room. Her head snapped between both parents. Their recliners flanked the couch but were slightly in front of them and angled toward the TV. Mom's head was sharply tilted, indicating she was still asleep, while Dad perched on the edge of his seat, riveted by what was happening on screen. If Dad looked at them, the plush, oversized blanket draped over her body and Jesse's lap would conceal what he was doing, but... How could Jesse be touching her while they were in the room? Was he insane?

Jesse brought her attention back to him when his thumb slid inside her satin underwear. In the poor light, she saw Jesse's head turned toward her. He wasn't even trying to pretend he was interested in the movie. She strained to get away, but when he began to fondle her clit, she started fighting in earnest. When she savagely yanked on her captive leg, he flicked her underwear aside and sheathed his middle finger inside of her.

Her gasp was lost in a hail of deafening gunfire on

screen. Out of the corner of her eye, she saw Lynne sit up. Dad snagged the remote to turn down the volume.

"Too loud?" Dad asked.

"A bit, but that's why we have those speakers, right? To get the full effect?" Lynne yawned as she rose and stretched.

Violet clawed the back of Jesse's hand jammed between her legs. He made no move to withdraw, even as Lynne started toward them. Lightheaded with horror, Violet closed her eyes as Lynne kissed Jesse's cheek. As her body tightened in reaction to Mom's nearness, the tip of Jesse's finger curled, making her break out in goosebumps.

"Vi's asleep?" Mom murmured.

"Mm hmm," Jesse said distractedly, as if he was engrossed in the movie. "She fell asleep not long after you."

It took everything she had not to react as Mom leaned over her, so close to where her son's fingers were buried inside her. Biting panic engulfed her as Mom tenderly brushed back her hair.

"Sweet dreams, my sweet girl," Mom murmured before she moved away.

"My bed is calling me," Mom said around a jaw cracking yawn as she kissed Dad's cheek.

As Mom shuffled down the hallway, Jesse called, "Sleep tight," even as he withdrew his finger and smeared what it was coated with on her clit and rubbed.

A silent battle commenced with Jesse trying to conquer her body while she desperately tried to retreat. When his grip slipped on the leg keeping her captive, she lunged for the lamp on the side table and snapped it on. As light flooded the room, Dad turned his head and squinted at her.

"Is it okay if I leave the light on?" she panted as she

dragged herself to the opposite end of the couch, safely out of Jesse's reach.

Even though he clearly wished otherwise, Dad nodded and turned back to the movie. She buried her face on the arm rest for a moment, grappling for control over her body, before her eyes cut to Jesse. Her stomach flipped when he put his middle finger in his mouth. Damn him!

She shot to her feet and froze when Jesse began to rise as well. She had no doubt that he would follow her. He wouldn't have touched her with Mom and Dad present unless he was already past the point of no return. Knowing the movie would conceal the sounds of whatever he planned to do to her, she retook her seat. A muscle ticked in his jaw.

She adjusted her pants before she sat as far from him as possible and huddled in the circle of light to keep the wolf at bay. She ran shaking fingers through her hair and tried to ignore the telling movements under the blanket bunched on Jesse's lap. Was he actually going to...?

When Jesse shot to his feet, Dad's head whipped around.

"I have to be up early for work," Jesse stated.

Dad nodded. "I'm surprised you stayed up this long," he said with a glance at his watch.

Jesse grunted as Dad turned back to the screen. He stood there, staring at her for so long, that Dad turned around again.

"You need something, son?"

"No," Jesse said and stalked down the hallway to his bedroom.

She tucked her legs to the side and dragged the blanket around her once more, trembling. She couldn't believe he just did that. He pushed the boundaries, but he'd never gone *this* far. Did he have no shame or scruples? She clamped her thighs together and ignored the low throb between her legs. She hated the way he'd conditioned her body to respond to him, to yearn for him. A glance at Dad quelled the desire Jesse tried to ignite.

Would Dad believe her if she told him that the son he was so proud of was doing the unthinkable to her? Her chest tightened. Although Dad hadn't brought it up since it happened, she knew he still blamed her for Jesse putting Tucker in the hospital. Dad had absolved Jesse, but not her. There was something in his eyes when he looked at her that told her he suspected she was no longer innocent. If she got up the courage to tell him what Jesse was doing, and he didn't believe her or worse, accused her of being the problem, it would kill her. She turned off the light as her face crumpled.

"You turning in too, Vi?" Dad asked without turning to look at her.

"No. I'm staying."

Her shaky tone went unnoticed as the main character made an impossible, stylish leap from a helicopter.

How many times had she considered confiding in a friend, school counselor, youth pastor, or therapist who was sworn to secrecy? But who would believe her? Even she couldn't believe what was happening. The only person who would probably take her word for it was the one person who avoided her like the plague. Tucker had been on the receiving end of a temper that no one even knew Jesse possessed. Tucker had returned to school and explained his absence by spinning some tale about being approached by a record label. His return had briefly stirred up everyone's interest in her again, but this time, she didn't care. She had bigger problems to deal with—namely, her stepbrother, who everyone idolized and admired and thought wouldn't hurt a fly.

By the time the movie ended, she was once more stretched out on the couch with her head on the arm rest. Dad glanced at her and, when he saw she was still awake, flicked through a few channels before he settled on reruns of, *I Love Lucy*. When she was a kid, Dad only allowed her to watch old movies and shows so he wouldn't have to worry about anything explicit being shown.

They chuckled together as they watched Lucy's antics. When the episode ended, Dad got to his feet.

"You're going to stay up?" he asked.

"Yeah."

He came over and set the remote by the lamp so she could easily reach it.

"Night, kiddo."

"Night, Dad," she echoed.

She listened to him shuffle down the hallway as another episode began. She was tired but couldn't bring herself to go to her room. She turned off the lamp because the bright light was making her eyes water. She cocked her head when she heard footsteps making their way to the living room. Assuming Dad wanted a drink of water or had forgotten something, she looked up when a dark figure rounded the couch. When she realized it wasn't Dad, she opened her mouth to scream. Jesse lunged at her, clapping a hand over her lips before she could utter a sound.

He leaned down and rested his forehead against hers as he murmured, "I can't go another night without you."

Even as she prepared to bite his palm, he dragged her to the middle of the couch and flipped her onto her stomach. The blanket was tossed to the floor before her bottoms were yanked to her knees. Even as she turned her head to the side to catch her breath, Jesse was already sinking inside her. She clawed the cushions and kicked her feet as her body struggled to adjust.

"Shh," he soothed as he came down on top of her.

With her legs clamped together, he felt impossibly large, and though she was wet, it wasn't enough. The couch absorbed her groan as he withdrew and then pushed for more territory.

"Good girl. Almost there," he praised and ignored her furious hiss. "God, you feel so good, Vi. So perfect."

"What the hell are you *doing*? They could walk in any minute."

"I jacked off twice and still tossed and turned. My hand won't do. I need you. I need this. I'm going crazy. I can't escape even in sleep because I dream of you."

His hands skated down her arms until he reached her hands. Before she could pull away, he twined their fingers together.

"Do you know what it's like, never having a moment's peace? To want something so badly, you'll do anything to possess it?"

He shuddered and buried his face in her hair as he sheathed himself completely.

"Thank you," he said fervently.

"You're sick."

His tongue dipped into her ear before he breathed, "So are you. The difference between us is, I accept it."

She screwed her eyes shut as he began to thrust, stabbing deep, making her toes curl.

"This doesn't have to be sick. This doesn't have to be twisted. It can be beautiful if you'd let it. If you stopped fighting and let us be." His fingers tightened around hers. "I can feel you milking me and getting wetter. You love this."

She buried her face in the cushions as she tried to deny what he was saying, but her body wasn't under her command. It was under his, and it responded to him, bathing him in honey, welcoming him, while her mind did everything in its power to block out what was happening.

"You've been dodging me all week, denying me, denying yourself. Why do you do that? You want me to prove how much I want you? How I'm lost without you?"

Her stomach flipped as he released her hands and dropped off the side of the couch and pulled her bottom half with him. He positioned her so she was on her knees on the carpet with him behind her. Unfortunately, her face landed in the damp spot she'd just made on the cushions.

With a grimace, she straightened. Jesse immediately took advantage of the position to slide his hands beneath her top. He stroked her stomach and gripped her breasts as he gave her body time to adjust to him, to prepare for what was coming. One hand plucked her clit. To her disgust, she rested her head on his shoulder and spread her legs, giving him more access. He obliged while he sucked on her neck.

"Tell me you want this," he said darkly.

That cut through the sexual haze. Awareness crept back in. She yanked on his arm to get his hand off her breast, but all it got her was a nipple pinch that suffused her with more unwanted heat.

"Admit it. Just this once," he begged.

When she remained silent, his teeth sank into her shoulder.

"So stubborn," he growled and shoved her face into cushions that smelled of her weakness before his control disintegrated.

He blanketed her body with his as he began to move with hard, sure strokes. The only sound she could hear aside from Jesse's uneven breaths was Lucy wailing on the television. Between the hard, rhythmic smacking of their flesh and the TV, it was impossible to hear anyone approach. She prayed Mom and Dad were sound asleep as Jesse straightened and hauled her back with every thrust, so she took every inch, growling like an animal, desperately trying to meld them together.

Sensing he was close, she compounded her sins by touching herself to reach her own orgasm.

"Yeah, baby. Come with me," he said harshly as he picked up his pace.

When he climaxed, he folded over her, gasping her name. She ignored him as she chased her own orgasm, which was just out of reach. Jesse brushed her hand aside, strumming her clit, and encouraged her to impale herself on him until she shattered. He held her as she trembled, first with elation and, less than a minute later, with the familiar slap of shame and guilt. No matter what she did to foil him, they always ended here.

Jesse withdrew slowly. She pressed her thighs together and wasn't surprised when his hand slipped through his semen, pushing it back in before spreading it over her ass and lower back.

When he got to his feet, her mind urged her to get up, dress, and clean herself, but she couldn't move. She sensed Jesse leave the room and heard his bedroom door close seconds later. Even as the studio audience laughed, Violet wept.

CHAPTER 16
VIOLET

FOUR MONTHS LATER

Thumbs hooked under her backpack straps; Violet stood at the end of the driveway. Luck was on her side. Mom left early this morning to decorate her classroom for spring, allowing Violet to change up her commute without Mom asking questions.

As her neighbor passed with his dog, he nodded to Violet while also giving her a slightly puzzled look that made her blush. Embarrassed, but determined to follow through with her plan, she stared at the end of the street, willing her ride to appear and save her from going with...

"What are you doing?"

She stiffened, but didn't turn around to address the bane of her existence.

"I'm waiting," she said, stating the obvious.

"I see that. Waiting for what?"

"I'm catching the bus to school."

She was grateful they were in plain view of their neighbors who were heading to work or taking out the trash. It meant that she had countless witnesses if Jesse did something foul. He wouldn't, of course. He saved his reprehensible behavior for when they were behind closed doors. In public, his manners were impeccable.

"You're not catching the bus."

She tightened her grip on her straps. "Mom already left for work. She won't know we didn't ride together."

"But Dad will. He asked me what you're doing out here."

She whirled and spotted her father standing in the window with his coffee mug in hand. Damn. She hadn't thought to look in the garage to see if his truck was there. She assumed he was at work.

"You want to tell him what's going on or are you going to get in the car?"

Jesse's taunt made her vision bleed to red. He asked that question like he had nothing to hide, as if his future didn't depend on her keeping their secret. He should be kissing her ass, not provoking her. The fact that he was so certain she wouldn't tell anyone made her so angry, she couldn't speak. She wanted to. She *should*! But, as miserable as she was, she couldn't bring herself to get help.

On days like today, when Jesse pushed her to her breaking point, her mind played out every possible outcome. None of them ended well. If she released her pain, it would spread like a disease, infecting her family, rocking their church, and sending shockwaves through their tight-knit community. Nothing would ever be the same. Better to compartmentalize. To suppress her inner turmoil and believe that Jesse would come to his senses and stop. Also, confiding in someone meant explaining what was happening to her and... she just couldn't. That would make it all too real.

"Come on, Vi."

Jesse had the audacity to look exasperated with her, as if she had no grounds to be upset about what he did to her fifteen minutes ago.

"Violet?"

She broke eye contact with Jesse to see Dad standing on the front steps.

"Is something wrong?"

Bottled up emotions tore up her insides, making her eyes water.

Dad's expression darkened. "What is it?"

Her mouth worked before she finally got out, "Jesse pissed me off. I want to catch the bus instead of riding with him."

Dad blinked, clearly surprised. She and Jesse rarely quarreled. There had been no need to in the past.

"Jesse?" Dad prompted with a frown.

"I'll make it up to her."

Her skin prickled as Jesse gave that ominous promise.

"Avoiding your problems isn't going to solve anything," Dad admonished, shaking his head. "I taught you better than that. Settle it on the way to school. I'm sure Jesse didn't mean to upset you."

The pressure in her chest increased. A scream vibrated at the base of her throat.

Dad tossed Jesse a set of keys. "Take the truck. I need the SUV today." Dad gave her a level look. "Be good."

The subtle rebuke made it clear that he thought she was overreacting and being childish. Dad walked into the house. Several seconds later, the garage rolled up to reveal the truck that was almost as old as she was. It took a minute for her to have enough control to stalk to the truck instead of having a meltdown. Jessie didn't fetch his bag until she was settled in the passenger seat.

She buckled up and twisted her hand in the dark blue seat belt as the yellow school bus she'd been waiting for cruised past. All she wanted was a moment's respite from him, but it seemed like the world was conspiring against her.

Jesse didn't say a word as he started the truck and reversed out of the garage. Silence reined between them as they left their neighborhood. Her stomach was tight as a fist.

"Did I hurt you?"

He meant physically, but he didn't have to leave a bruise on her skin to hurt her. Marks made in passion would fade. It was the hundreds of invisible, razor-thin emotional cuts he inflicted that she knew would scar and haunt her for the rest of her life.

"Does it matter?"

He ran a hand through his hair. "I didn't mean to hurt you. That wasn't my intention."

"What *was* your intention?"

A muscle ticked in his jaw. "You know."

To scratch his itch before he started his day? She didn't fight back when he cornered her in the bathroom, ushered her into the tub, and pinned her against the tiles to ravage her. She didn't resist when he pushed her to her knees and fucked her mouth. It was only after he'd left her kneeling in the tub with her face dripping, and she heard Mom singing in the kitchen, that she snapped out of her daze and retched.

She wasn't sure why this morning was different from the others. He'd done far more demeaning things, but today it struck her how truly warped their relationship had become. The fact that they hadn't exchanged a word during that whole encounter, and he left the moment he achieved his goal, made her realize he'd truly turned into Amnon. He didn't loathe her, but he was addicted to using her to slake his lust and didn't care how that impacted her. Their relationship has turned into a sour, tangled, depraved mess.

Jesse had changed. He no longer cajoled. He no longer petted and stroked to prepare her for him. The affection she'd come to expect from him had vanished. She was just a body to him. No one seemed to notice that his smile wasn't the same, that he rarely laughed, and there was a hardness to him that hadn't been there before. When they were alone, and he wasn't wearing a mask, she was chilled by what she saw in his eyes. Her brother was gone and in his place was a stranger, one capable of anything.

When Jesse took the wrong exit, she gave him a sharp glance. "Where are we going?"

"For a drive."

Her blood turned to ice. "No!"

"We need to talk."

Talk? That was something they no longer did. Their commutes to and from school were done in complete silence. The only time they casually conversed was while hanging out with mutual friends or around their parents. If they were alone, Jesse was too focused on getting her on her back to ask about her day or hopes and dreams.

"We have nothing to talk about."

His hand flexed on the wheel. "We do."

She flung her hand in front of her. "So, talk! Why are we leaving Austin?"

"I don't want us to be interrupted, and I need to clear my head."

"We're going to be late for school."

"We'll make it back in time. We aren't going far."

She twisted her hand in the folds of her light sweater as they traded the congested, six lane freeways for a two-lane highway. At this hour, everyone was headed into the city for work and school, while she and Jesse sped in the opposite direction.

Despite Jesse's reassurance that they weren't going far, they were going further than she was comfortable with. She considered calling Mom and Dad to tell them Jesse had lost his mind, when he finally slowed and turned off the main highway onto an unmarked dirt road.

"Where are we?"

"We're almost there," he yelled as they rattled down the pitted road.

"Almost *where*?" she demanded, clutching the door handle.

"Here," he said as they rounded a bend.

Trees gave way to rolling flatlands covered in a blanket of bluebonnets that stretched as far as the eye could see. Taking photos amidst the wildflowers was a rite of passage for locals who flocked to every park, field, and even along the highway in hopes of getting the perfect shot.

As Jesse pulled off the road, she rolled down her window to admire the cerulean beauties. Until that moment, she hadn't realized what a gorgeous day it was. The morning chill was giving way to what promised to be a warm spring day. Birds chirped to one another. There was no sound of cars or people, just a lone farmhouse in the distance. The scene was so idyllic, it looked like a painting.

"Logan's aunt lives at the end of this lane," Jesse said. "I thought you'd enjoy seeing this."

"It's stunning," she murmured as she closed her eyes and tipped her face to the sun.

Her worries about getting to school on time and why they were here dissolved. Minutes passed in blessed silence. When she opened her eyes, she blinked back tears. She wasn't sure why. She braced her chin on her arms and stared at a sea of blue so dense, she imagined she could swim in it.

"Violet."

Her bubble of tranquility popped. Tension crept back in. Anxiety stole the sun's warmth from her face.

"What?" she said woodenly.

"I'm sorry if I went too far this morning."

The clean taste of toothpaste was canceled out by the aftertaste of betrayal, which tasted like bitter grapefruit. "But that isn't going to stop you from doing it again, is it?"

A pause and then, "No."

She swung around to face him as her chest quaked. "You have to stop! You can't do this anymore! Don't you see what it's doing to us?"

His expression was pained as he held his hands out to her in supplication. "I've tried, Vi. I—"

"Try harder!" she bellowed.

His Adam's apple bobbed as he swallowed. "I swear I am. But the more I resist, the more I try to push it down..." His hand balled into a fist. "The worse it is when I lose control."

"This isn't normal, Jesse. It's *wrong*!"

His expression hardened. "It could be right if you'd..." He looked away from her, down the empty road.

"If I what? Gave into you? Did whatever you wanted? Isn't that what I've been doing? What more do you want?"

"I want you to want me back!"

His bellow made her heart stop.

"You think it's enough to have your body?" he asked

harshly. "To have you give into me?" He shook his head. "I thought that would be enough, too, but it isn't. I hate the way you look at me. The way you stiffen up when I touch you when I know a part of you wants it." His hand slashed through the air. "Needs it just as much as I do. I want you to let yourself want me back, Vi, and stop punishing us."

"I don't want you." Her voice wasn't as adamant as she intended.

His eyes narrowed. "Don't lie. It isn't always force. Most of the time, you're wet before I even touch you. Three days ago, you were rocking back so hard on my dick, I had to brace myself. What—"

"That's my *body*, not *me*!" she shrieked.

"Your body," he repeated in a flat tone.

"Yes!"

He stared at her for a full minute before he said, "You're not going to give in, are you?"

"Did I fight you this morning?" she asked waspishly.

He dismissed that with a wave of his hand, as if it was of no consequence. Rage licked the walls of her mind.

"I mean, you're not going to admit what's between us," he clarified.

"What's between us is *gone*! *You* destroyed it!"

His hand, still on the steering wheel, went white as he gripped it, making the veins on the back of his hand stand out.

"I didn't destroy it," he said roughly. "I embraced it, surrendered to it. Your fear of change, of Mom and Dad and *God* made this into something bad, but it isn't. This is a goddamn gift."

His eyes gleamed with zeal, sending a trickle of alarm through her.

"Dad said what isn't meant to be, God won't allow. God

isn't stopping us from being together. He would have intervened in some fashion by now, don't you think? No matter what you do, God keeps pushing you toward me. He wouldn't even let you catch the bus! He brought us here so we could talk. Why can't you see that you're the only thing stopping us from being everything we're meant to be? Of being happy?"

"Don't you dare use God to justify your behavior. The only reason you've gotten away with it is because you're so good at fooling people, and I'm too weak to..." Her throat constricted as despair and rage warred within her. "You..." Eyes burning, she bowed her head as she desperately tried to regain control.

"It's not because you're weak. You haven't told anyone because you love me."

Her head jerked up. *"Love?"* She could barely get the word out. How dare he say that to her?

"You love me," he stated with such unshakeable confidence that she wanted to scratch his eyes out. "Deep down, you know we're supposed to be together. You wouldn't respond to anyone else the way you do to me."

"That's not true." The moment the words left her mouth, she regretted it.

"What's not true?"

His voice was calm, but she knew he was anything but.

She licked dry lips and couldn't resist casting a nervous glance around, but there wasn't a soul in sight. "I think we should go."

"What's not true?" he repeated.

When she didn't speak, he leaned toward her.

"It's not true that you only respond to me?"

She plucked at her jeans. He reached across the bench

seat and gripped her chin, eyes glittering with the threat of violence.

"If I find out you allowed anyone to touch you, I'd kill them."

"No one has!" She swatted at his hand, which only held her tighter. "I'm not allowed to date, and I don't want anyone, including you! In fact, I think *you* should start dating again."

"Date."

His voice was flat and emotionless.

"Yes, date. Have sex with other girls." She lifted her chin in challenge. "If I loved you, if I believed we were supposed to be together, would I push you toward someone—*anyone* else?"

The hand on her chin fell away. She was about to reach for her backpack to retrieve her phone when she saw his eyes glistening with tears. Her stomach flipped. She couldn't remember the last time she'd seen him cry. She was horrified by the overwhelming need to apologize and comfort him. What the hell was wrong with her? He'd hurt her immeasurably and broken promise after promise. Why the hell should she care that something she said had finally gotten through to him? She shouldn't care.

But she did.

"You hate me," he said quietly.

She swallowed hard.

"If you hate me, say it."

She opened her mouth, but nothing came out. Her voice deserted her when she needed it most.

His expression softened. "You want to hate me, but you can't."

"Stay back," she ordered as he reached for her.

"I'm not going to hurt you," he crooned and gripped her

leg and tugged, stretching her out on the bench seat with him hovering over her.

He ignored the hands that braced against his chest and rested his forehead against hers.

"You don't want me with someone else."

"Y-yes, I do!" she choked.

"Okay, baby," he said, clearly humoring her.

"I really do!" she insisted as he stroked her hair. "I'm serious. Get what you need from someone else. I'll interview them! I know what kinky shit you're into. I can find a skanky—"

His mouth covered hers. The kiss was hard and punishing, but when she stopped struggling, it immediately gentled. He began to kiss her tenderly, reverently, as he hadn't done for weeks. It was a shock, considering how he'd used her less than an hour ago. Her body quivered in delight, starved for affection and connection.

She tried to escape mentally, but Jesse wasn't rushing. He wasn't rushing to get off or worried about being discovered. His tongue tangled lazily with hers and enticed her to engage. She was drawn in by the taste of something sweet. What was that? Eager to erase the bitterness in her mouth, she allowed her tongue to dance with his and ignored his pleased hum. He'd eaten an apple for breakfast. Curiosity appeased, she tried to disengage, but Jesse didn't allow it.

He kept her mouth busy as he kissed her ten different ways—indulgent, deep, teasing, arousing. She couldn't keep up and was further distracted when his hand slipped beneath her sweater and covered her breast. By the time he raised his head and allowed her to catch her breath, her mind was spinning.

"You want me to kiss other girls like this?" he murmured as his lips drifted over her face.

She tried to gather her wits as he bunched her sweater under her chin. Even as she registered the cool chill on her bare skin, Jesse tucked the cup of her bra beneath her left breast. When he flicked her nipple with his tongue, she jerked like she'd been lashed with a whip.

"I love when your breasts get sensitive close to your period," he said before he latched onto her nipple.

He pinned her arms to the seat as she hissed and arched and bit back the urge to beg for mercy. It wouldn't make a difference to him. It never did. Despite his claims that God was on his side, she refused to believe it and prayed for divine intervention. Maybe the people in the farmhouse would get curious about why they were parked here and come investigate. Or perhaps a passerby would peek in, thinking they had car trouble or something had gone wrong. She strained to hear the rumble of a car, but all she could hear was the wet sounds of Jesse suckling and her own pathetic whimpering.

"You love this," he said raggedly, and turned his head from side to side, so her nipple dragged along his lips. "I could do this to you all day. You're so beautiful. A meadow of bluebonnets is nothing compared to you." He nuzzled her breast as he muttered, "I had girls offer me everything. I couldn't bring myself to take, even though I was desperate for relief. I'd rather be tortured in your presence and have you see me as a brother, then sink my dick into someone and try to picture your face while I'm with her. I need the real thing. I need you, Violet. No one else will do."

She tipped her head back to look out the open window and tried to follow the progress of slow-moving clouds as Jesse moved to her other breast. When she couldn't take anymore, she kicked her legs in frustration.

"Jesse!"

He eased the pressure and finally released her breast. He admired how puckered and swollen it was and peppered it with kisses before he buried his face between them.

"This has been hell."

His voice was muffled against her skin as he stroked her sides.

"I don't want it to be like this between us."

But it was, and there was no going back to the way it had been. Maybe in the beginning, they could have restored their relationship, but they'd gone too far. Their bond was so mangled, she couldn't imagine them having a relationship that was even remotely normal or healthy.

"I didn't intend to do this," he said, kissing the side of her breast. "I brought you here so we could talk about the future."

She stiffened. "What future?"

Jesse lifted his head and searched her face. "Ours."

She gaped at him.

"I'm going to graduate soon. I wanted to talk about what we should—"

"*We?*"

She shoved him hard enough to make him blink.

"Get off me!" she snapped.

He sighed. "Calm down."

"*You* calm down! Get the hell off me before I scream my head off."

It wasn't a huge threat, considering the isolated setting, but Jesse rose and sat behind the wheel as she shot up and hastily fixed her bra and yanked her sweater down.

"There's nothing to discuss with me. You're going to graduate and go off to college in another city or, better yet, out of state. I'll finish school and go my own way. Our futures aren't the same."

He stared at her, expression unreadable.

"There is no *we* or *our* or *us*. What we had, what we were, is gone. You..." She swallowed hard, eyes stinging with tears. "You hurt me more than anyone else. I trusted you. I never thought you of all people would ever..."

When he reached for her, she recoiled and wrapped her arms around herself.

"I want this to be over. I *need* it to be over." A tear slid down her cheek. "I need you gone."

"You don't mean that," he whispered.

He was clearly gutted. She ruthlessly stomped out the flurry of weak emotions that told her she'd gone far enough, that it wasn't the Christian way to repay evil with evil. She was supposed to overcome evil with good, but she didn't have that in her. All she had was anger. Lots of it. Months of suppressed rage and shame and helplessness erupted, spewing like hot lava. She had to get it out, to let him know how she saw him, and that there was no future where they were together.

"What's between us isn't a gift, it's poison," she said hoarsely. "It's corrupt and rotten, and nothing good has come from it. You think if it felt so good, if we were meant to be, that I would spend an hour scrubbing my body every time you touch me and still never feel clean?"

He went very still. She hardened her heart against the anguish creeping into his expression. This was her moment to end this once and for all, and she was going to see it through, even if it destroyed them both in the process.

"I hate that I can't look Dad in the eye. I hate that I have to watch every word I say because I'm terrified I'll let something slip. I hate that you were my first and that you conditioned my body to respond to you."

She trembled under the tremendous, crushing weight on her shoulders.

"You think what's stopping me from telling someone is love, but it isn't love for you. It's love for Lynne. Knowing what you are would destroy her."

"What am I?"

A tear slipped down her cheek as she said, "You're a monster."

His expression went blank, his vulnerability and agony vanishing so quickly, she wasn't sure it had been there at all. Silence reined. A bird swooped in front of the truck before it flapped away, chirping gaily. A breeze caused fine tendrils of hair to slide across her face.

"Say it, Vi."

She knew what he wanted to hear and finally had the strength to.

"You're right. I don't hate you." For just a moment, she saw hope flash in his eyes before she finished, "I feel nothing for you at all."

He didn't move a muscle, but the hairs on her arms stood up as something evil and inhuman stared out of Jesse's eyes. She got her first glimpse of the demon that lurked within him the day Jesse took her by the river. Recently, she'd begun to see him more frequently, as Jesse was ruled by his lustful appetites. The demon that used to possess him at night was now visible in broad daylight. He and Jesse were now one.

"I really tried, Violet," Jesse said ruefully, lips curved in a mocking smile as his eyes burned with wrath. "I tried for you, but I guess it wasn't good enough."

She clutched the door handle, heart pumping, as he cocked his head, examining her clinically.

"Telling a monster you feel nothing for him isn't very smart," he pointed out.

She stopped breathing.

"It gives him no incentive not to act like one."

Even as he reached for her, she shoved the door open and fell out of the truck. This was all horrifically familiar, but this time, she knew what he was capable of. Even as she scrambled to her feet and reached for her backpack to grab her cell phone, he slid across the seat after her.

For a split second, she considered trying to reason with him, but a glimpse of the bloodlust carved into his face convinced her fleeing was her only option. She plunged into the field of bluebonnets, her aim the lone farmhouse in the distance. She waved her hands, hoping someone was looking out of the window and would realize something was terribly wrong. She would have screamed in hopes that anyone within earshot would come to the rescue, but she didn't have time to haul in a breath when she could hear him gaining ground behind her. He was an athlete. Strong, fast. She would never make it.

Even as the thought crossed through her mind, Jesse tackled her from behind. The impact sent her sprawling in a patch of fluffy bluebonnets that cushioned her fall. She scrambled on her hands and feet, trying to get away. When Jesse hauled her back, Dad's training kicked in. She balled her fist and swung with all her might. Jesse dropped like a stone when she punched him in the ear.

Breath ragged, she continued on. As she stumbled through the wildflowers, she glanced back at the road. Her stomach lurched when she realized how far away she was. The farmhouse was her only hope. Out of the corner of her eye, she saw Jesse straighten. Panic gave her extra strength.

She ran full out, faster than she ever had. It was life or death. She could do this.

She was close enough now to make out more details of the house. The porch had a swing and pots of pink and yellow flowers. Whoever lived there was a good person. They would help her if they were home. *God, please help me,* she begged. *Prove Jesse wrong. Save me. If You do, I swear I'll...* she was struck down again before she could strike a bargain with God.

Jesse took the brunt of the fall and this time, kept his arms around her instead of knocking her off balance. They rolled. He pinned her clawed hand to the ground and leaned over her, gold cross swinging. His eyes were alight. She would never forget the strange formation of clouds dotting the sky, being hemmed in by cheery bluebonnets, and the look on Jesse's face as he looked down at her.

Time stopped.

"Jesse?" she panted.

He leaned down, kissed her forehead, and murmured, "Lord, forgive me for what I'm about to do."

Violet lay on a bed of crushed wildflowers. She was naked. She knew that should bother her, but she couldn't find the will to care. Nothing mattered. Not anymore.

A figure appeared in her line of sight. She didn't bother focusing on Jesse. Instead, she admired a cloud that resembled an elephant head. That was more interesting than anything Jesse had to say. She hadn't been honest when she said she didn't feel anything for him, but it had been a self-fulfilling prophecy because now she really didn't. He'd given her glimpses of the monster within, but he proved beyond a shadow of a doubt that her brother was truly gone. They could never go back to what they'd been. Ever.

Jesse pulled her into a sitting position so he could slip a shirt over her head. Gently, he pulled her to her feet. The shirt was so large, it covered her to mid-thigh. When he crouched to pick her up, she hung lifelessly over his shoulder and spotted her torn peach-colored sweater and stained jeans clutched in his hand. She closed her eyes as her stomach rocked.

Her head spun as he settled her in the passenger seat of the truck. Automatically, she pulled the seatbelt across her chest and clicked it in. She pressed her feet together, noting that she was missing a sock. She stared down the dirt road that hadn't brought one car across their path.

Jesse opened the glove box in front of her and pulled out one of Dad's red paisley bandanas. He splashed it with water before he began to clean her face. His hands were trembling, and although he was talking, it sounded like gibberish to her. She couldn't hear anything over the echoes of her piercing screams ricocheting around in her head, interspersed with static. If she had the will to speak, she would have asked him for water to rinse out the taste of blood, semen, and dirt in her mouth. Instead, she let him scrub her face until he gave up and rounded the truck to climb into the driver's seat.

The moment the truck began to move, she deflated, closing her eyes and slumping against the door. It seemed that she closed her eyes for a minute. When she opened them, Jesse was tugging her out of the truck, into a pit. She flailed before her eyes adjusted and she recognized their surroundings. They were in their garage with the door already down, which is why it was so dark. Her sluggish heart leapt.

"Dad's not home," Jesse murmured as he toted her into the house.

She had a feeling of déjà vu as he placed her in the tub. This time, she wasn't shellshocked and heartbroken. She was coherent and functional, but her emotions had been switched off. She was grateful.

In contrast, Jesse fluttered around her, his unshakeable poise, gone. His face was drawn and the glassy horror in his blue eyes warmed her because this time it was he who was rattled. He manically scrubbed her down and seemed obsessed with cleaning every nook and cranny, even cleaning inside her ears like she was a child.

When he tried to dress her in a nightgown, she reached for jeans and a top.

"Violet."

"I'm going to school."

He said nothing, just stood there in jeans and nothing else.

"You don't have to take me," she said.

He spun on his heel and disappeared into the bathroom. She hummed as she stared at her array of underwear. What color did she want to wear? She was still trying to decide when Jesse reappeared, clean and fully dressed. She frowned.

"It's been fifteen minutes," he said.

"Oh."

He swallowed. "I think you should stay here."

"No." She had to go to school where her friends were. Where she felt safe, even if it was just for a little while. She couldn't stay at home, in her bedroom. She would lose it.

Jesse didn't argue. He selected white underwear and held it out for her to step into. He pulled them up without copping a feel or doing anything else lecherous and dressed her in jeans and a gray hoodie.

She led the way back to the garage and climbed into the truck. Jesse stared at her through the windshield for what seemed to be forever before he got in. The garage door opened, flooding the space with light.

She had no idea what time it was, but traffic hour had passed. Even though there was a clock on the dashboard, she couldn't bring herself to look at it. Her surroundings seemed sharper, brighter, more vibrant.

"I'm sorry."

Jesse's croak made no impact on her.

"I swear, I—"

"Shut up."

Her voice sounded as empty and hollow as she felt.

"I don't know what's happening to me. Something in my head just snapped."

"You should seek help," she advised coolly.

Jesse turned into the school parking lot. There was no one around since everyone was in class. She reached for her backpack and ignored her filthy clothes on the floorboard.

"Violet."

She glanced at him. The monster was gone. In his place was a tormented teenager. If she didn't know any better, she would have thought he was the one who'd been attacked. He was pale, sweating, and looked devastated. He'd aged five years in a matter of hours.

"Report me," he ordered.

His words sliced through the blessed numbness and zapped some of her dead emotions back to life.

Jesse blinked rapidly as his eyes filled with tears. "You should get help. I've gone too far. I'll accept the consequences, whatever they are."

He leaned over, gripped her face between both hands, and kissed her. It was an apology, a goodbye.

He pulled back, whispered, "I love you," and gave her one last, hungry kiss before he hopped out of the truck and slammed the door behind him.

He stalked toward school without a backpack, hands in his pockets. She sat there for several seconds before she slipped out, shouldered her backpack, and headed in the opposite direction.

As she opened the door of a building, the bell rang. Students flooded the hallways. Everyone walked around her like she wasn't even there. No one called out her name or tried to stop her from reaching her destination. Her feet felt like they were in blocks of cement. The closer she got to the office, the more she felt like she couldn't breathe.

"Honey, can I help you?"

Violet stared at the smiling office clerk behind the desk. The woman had short, curly hair, and pink hibiscus earrings. The woman looked so cheerful and warm, like nothing bad had ever happened to her, while Violet felt like she had been hacked to pieces with a machete and was about to fall apart.

The woman's smile faded. "Honey, are you okay?"

Violet nodded, even as tears began to slip down her face. The woman rushed around the counter and rubbed her hands up and down Violet's arms.

"What's going on, dear? What's happened?"

"I..."

Violet gulped back tears. This was it. This was her moment. All she had to do was tell the nice lady what had happened to her—what had been happening to her for six months, and it would be over. She had proof—semen in her mouth, pussy, ass. She was raw, bruised, and had his DNA under her fingernails. Her scratches would be all over his body, and his tongue was still swollen from her biting it. This was the right thing to do—what he'd urged her to do for both their sakes.

But she couldn't do it.

"I think I have my period and stained my pants," she wailed.

The woman's face cleared. "Oh, honey, we've all been there. It's going to be okay. Come, let me help you."

Violet was curled up on the front seat of the truck when the driver's door opened. Jesse stared at her for a minute before he slid in and rested his hand on her head. She whimpered like a wounded animal as tears slipped out of raw, swollen eyes.

Once the sweet lady in the office gave her a tampon and reassured her that her pants weren't stained, she trudged back to the truck and collapsed on the seat. She lay there for hours, trying to gather the strength to go in and tell her story, but she couldn't move. She listened to the bells ring, knowing she was running out of time, and now it was over.

Jesse didn't tell her to sit up and put on her seatbelt as he started up the truck. As he drove, his hand sifted through her hair, stroked her cheek, and rubbed her quivering back while she sobbed.

Once Jesse parked the truck in the garage, he cradled her in his arms. She was too distraught to care if their parents were home but figured neither of them were when Jesse slid into bed with her.

He held her as she cried and beat her fists against his chest and screamed that she hated him. He didn't say a word. He let her rage and when it was over, he undressed her and tended to every mark he'd left behind.

It didn't surprise her when he eased himself inside of her. He didn't move, he just petted and nuzzled her. But she didn't want to be placated. She needed a release, an outlet for all the horrible things going on inside of her that were tearing her apart.

When she shoved him onto his back, he didn't resist. She rode him, setting a brutal pace that went on and on because her mind was too fucked up to let her climax. In the end, Jesse helped push her over the edge. When she collapsed on top of him, he held her until her breathing had evened out, and she was still and quiet. He didn't seek an orgasm for himself, but kissed her forehead, tucked the blankets around her, and left.

Violet turned on her side, stared at the far wall, and felt absolutely nothing.

CHAPTER 17
JESSE

3 WEEKS LATER

"I can't take it anymore. What's going on between you two?"

Jesse stopped in his tracks and turned to face Mom, who stood in the entrance of the kitchen, hands on hips.

"Vi," Mom said sharply as Violet tried to escape into the hallway.

Violet halted but kept her back to them.

Mom looked back and forth between them before she demanded, "What happened?"

Out of the corner of his eye, he saw Dad's head turn from the TV. Unease tripped down Jesse's spine, but he kept his face blank as Mom continued.

"From the moment you two came home from school until you went to sleep, you used to spend every moment together. I could hear you talking and laughing for hours, and now..." Mom swept her hands in the empty expanse between them. "You barely exchange a word. Isaac mentioned that disagreement you had a few weeks ago that made Violet so upset that she wanted to ride the bus?"

Mom shot Jesse a quizzical look, clearly expecting him to explain, but he remained silent.

"I thought you two worked it out, and we were all just busy—you, Jesse, with baseball, and Vi spending most of her time with Georgia and Allison because of that science project. But now, I *know* something's wrong."

Mom stopped, giving them the opportunity to confirm or deny her charge. Jesse slipped his hands into his pockets and gave Violet time to answer for both of them. He'd known this moment would come. It was only a matter of time before someone confronted Violet about her ghostlike appearance and the fact that she'd gone mute. Her fire, which had always been so much a part of her, had been extinguished.

Come on, baby. You can do it, he silently urged. He couldn't stand the suspense. Every day he wondered if it was going to be his last of freedom. Every time a stranger appeared in his classroom doorway or at practice, he wondered if Violet finally plucked up the courage to do the right thing, only for each instance to be a false alarm that left him drenched in cold sweat. The emotional roller coaster was exhausting. He wanted his fate decided. Waiting for the axe to fall was intolerable.

"Jesse?"

The uncertainty in Mom's tone sliced through his gut. Mom had always trusted him implicitly, but he glimpsed her bewilderment and a hint of apprehension. Had the incident with Tucker made Mom realize that she didn't know him as well as she thought, which meant he could be responsible for Violet's drastic personality change?

"Violet."

At Isaac's stern tone, Violet stirred. She turned, revealing a bloodless face and eyes so glassy and empty that Jesse looked away.

"Tell me this has nothing to do with Tucker," Dad ordered.

"This has nothing to do with Tucker," Violet parroted in a flat monotone.

Dad relaxed and glanced at Jesse. "You said you'd make it up to her."

He cleared his dry throat. "I tried."

Dad switched his gaze back to Violet. "That wasn't good enough?"

Jesse tensed. "It's not her fault. It's mine," he interjected swiftly.

Isaac's focus didn't waver from Violet. "I can't recall the last time I heard you two argue, much less fight. What could Jesse have done to make you hold such a grudge?"

Jesse felt like his heart was being squeezed in a vice. It took every ounce of self-control he possessed not to fidget as he waited for Violet to respond, but she said nothing.

"Ephesians 4:26 says not to let the sun go down on your anger. You've let this go on for weeks," Isaac said quietly. "The devil is always looking for an opportunity to come into a family and cause discord, to divide and conquer. There's nothing Jesse could have done that can't be forgiven."

"*Dad,*" Jesse stressed, but Isaac ignored him and continued his lecture.

"Matthew 6:14 says if you forgive others, God will also forgive you. No one is perfect. Give Jesse grace, Vi, so one day someone will do the same for you." Isaac paused a moment to let that sink in before he continued, "Jesse's running to the church to pick up supplies for the work we're doing on the McMillan's house tomorrow. Go with him. Talk. Bury this once and for all. If you can't resolve your issues, Mom and I will get involved, and we shouldn't have to. You two are adults now. Act like it." Isaac jerked his chin. "Go change, Vi. Jesse's leaving in five minutes."

When Violet didn't move to obey Isaac's order, the tension in the room thickened. Jesse sensed Violet wrestling with herself. His heart thudded in his ears as he waited for her to break her silence and condemn him. Isaac scooted to the edge of his seat, clearly ready to deal with this on his feet, but before he could, Violet abruptly turned on her heel and disappeared down the hallway.

As Mom watched her go with a concerned expression, Isaac's hard gaze cut to Jesse.

"You're always trying to protect her." Isaac held up a hand to stop his protest. "I know my daughter better than anyone. She's strong-willed, impulsive, and has a nose for trouble. Ever since Tucker, she's changed, and not for the better. She needs accountability. What's going to happen when you're not around to save her?"

He opened his mouth to crush Isaac's illusions about him and instead heard himself say, "I love her."

"I know you do." Isaac sighed as he leaned back in his recliner. "You'd do anything for her. She knows it and takes advantage."

Isaac was an honorable, hard-working, practical man, but when it came to matters of the heart, he was blind. Because he embodied everything Isaac had always wanted in a son, Isaac couldn't see his faults. On the flip side, when it came to Violet, Isaac discounted her good qualities and instead focused on the bad ones that reminded him of his first love that he'd never forgiven. How many times over the years had he defended Violet against a father, who was too hard on her and had never given her the grace he expected of her?

What would Isaac say if he confessed what he'd done? Isaac assumed because he loved Violet that he was incapable of truly harming her. He believed the same until she scorned his love and destroyed his illusions of a future together. He could set the record straight and clear her name. He steeled himself, but before he could speak, Violet reappeared.

She was dressed in black pants, a t-shirt, a light jacket, and a hat pulled low over her eyes. She didn't say a word as she crossed the living room to where he stood by the front door. He opened it for her. As Violet trotted down the steps, he looked back. Isaac had gone back to watching TV, but Mom's eyes were on him.

His mother was a glass half full, eternal optimist who believed that good would always prevail. She had a kind heart. He'd always thought of his mother as being somewhat naive, but as their eyes met, he realized the rose-colored glasses were missing and she looked... disturbed. Unlike Isaac, Mom wasn't blind. She may love him more than life itself, but she also loved Violet with the same ferocity and, unlike Isaac, she would believe Violet in a heartbeat. He flashed her what he hoped was a reassuring smile before he turned away, his stomach in knots.

It wasn't until he unlocked the truck that it struck him. He stared through the window at Violet, who stood on the opposite side. They hadn't ridden in this vehicle since that day. They couldn't switch to the SUV because he needed the truck bed for the paint cans and lumber he had to pick up. He blew out a breath before he pulled the door open. Automatically, his eyes scanned the interior, even though he'd thoroughly cleaned it. He turned the key in the ignition and waited.

It took Violet several minutes to open the door, and a few more before she actually got in. As she settled beside him, he sensed her reluctance, resentment, and the smallest trace of fear. He didn't blame her. He hadn't known he was capable of what he'd done in that field.

They rode in absolute silence. Despite Dad's decree that they sort this out, Violet didn't try. Both of them knew nothing could fix this.

He slumped in his seat and tilted his head back while keeping his eyes on the road. Violet was right beside him, but her presence was so faint, it was almost like she wasn't there at all. She'd become a wraith, drifting through life, lost in her head. Even though she loathed him, the urge to reach out and touch her, to bridge the distance between them, was a gnawing, dragging compulsion that made him tighten his hold on the steering wheel.

He hadn't touched her since the day they visited the blue-bonnet field. Not even a stray brush of his fingers while passing her a plate at dinner. He knew if he did, he wouldn't be able to stop himself from taking more, and he'd taken enough.

You think if it felt so good, if we were meant to be, that I would spend an hour scrubbing my body every time you touch me and still never feel clean?

The memory of her voice, filled with venom and revulsion, tore through him like shrapnel, reopening wounds that hadn't even begun to heal. He wholeheartedly believed Violet loved him and, at some point, would surrender to what was between them. It never occurred to him that their bond could fracture beyond repair or that, one day, she would look through him as if he wasn't there.

How had he misjudged her feelings for him so badly? Had he imagined her eyes following him months before she gave herself to him? Had he convinced himself she desired him when she didn't? He straightened and raked his hand through his hair as he shifted restlessly in his seat. No. It hadn't been all in his head. *She* kissed *him*, which tipped their relationship into the physical realm. And before the reality of their circumstances tainted what they had, Violet had given herself freely, eager to experience any and everything he could offer her. The memories of her initiation and the handful of days where they experimented to their heart's content reassured him that it wasn't all in his mind, even as it tormented him with what was forever out of his reach.

When their bodies writhed together and the crap from the outside world faded away, what bloomed between them was so special, he vowed he would do whatever it took to keep it. So, he'd ignored her struggles, denials, and breakdowns. Ignored her babbling about all the reasons why they couldn't be together. He tried to give her time and space to come to terms with what was between them, but the more he had of her, the more his appetite increased. The fact that her body wept for him, and she clung so tight in the throes, yet repeatedly rejected him, drove him insane. He assumed the constant imprinting on her body would overcome her reservations. He'd believed that in the end, love would conquer all.

How wrong he'd been.

I feel nothing for you at all.

Black spots marred his vision as rage engulfed him. He squinted at the road as he tried to think past the bloodlust. He lost his mind when she said that. When he realized she would never love him back. He built his life around her, and she wanted nothing to do with him.

She called him a monster, and he proved her right by giving his demon free rein. He punished her for not loving him back, for annihilating his dreams, and ruining the man he could have been. He mauled her like an animal, and she fought back with an aggression that, even now, made his dick hard. They had been stripped of all civilization, which resulted in a transcendent experience that unequivocally proved she was his equal. That field of wildflowers would always be his version of Eden and Violet, whether she wanted to be or not, was his wicked, savage temptress, Eve.

He glanced at her. She stared straight ahead, one hand loosely clutching the seatbelt resting on her chest. If she truly hated him, why hadn't she reported him? She'd been given many opportunities to expose him, but she hadn't. She claimed she didn't want to break Mom's heart, but Mom had nothing to do with how she let him tend to her when they came home that day or how she took what she needed from his body.

He took a deep breath and let it out slowly, ignoring the surge of adrenaline and the way his muscles flexed as his mind replayed her riding him. The only time Violet gave into their chemistry is when he roused her to a fever pitch, or she was too emotionally shattered to care about her scruples. Only then did she allow herself to indulge in their bond and allow it to soothe her.

The day after their violent clash, he visited the recruiter's office to complete the enlistment process to join the Air Force. He'd put off making a final decision in hopes that Violet would come to her senses, but he was running out of time. Mom and Dad assumed he was going to a local college. He stopped talking about the military because it had upset Mom so much, but he hadn't changed his mind. Joining the Air Force was a promise he made to his father that he always intended to keep. He had never second guessed his decision until Violet. If he went into the military, his life wouldn't be his own. He drove to that secluded location, intending to lay himself at her feet and have her decide his future, only to be told in no uncertain terms that she wanted nothing to do with him.

Any man who had been as brutally rejected as he had, should have been instantly cured of his infatuation. To have the love of his life encourage him to have sex with other females and to label their relationship as poisonous and rotten should have made moving on a piece of cake. He ran a hand down his face, disgusted with himself. If he believed in witchcraft, he may have believed she cast a spell on him because he still yearned for her. She was a part of him, imbedded bone deep. There was no getting her out. He'd tried. There were countless girls who would have him, but the one he'd kill for hated his guts. He still loved her and a part of him suspected that he always would. His life was a cruel joke.

He pulled into the empty church parking lot and reversed the truck to make it easier to load the supplies. He sorted through the keys Pastor Sonny had given him as he approached the chapel and lifted his head when he heard a door slam. He paused as Violet rounded the truck and passed him to jog up the steps. He couldn't resist staring at her ass and had a vivid image of her on all fours with the red outline of his hand on her right cheek along with a bite mark that had long since faded.

Need slammed into him with the force of a baseball bat. He'd taken great pains to steer clear of her. He'd been grateful that she caught rides with friends to and from school and had spent as much time as she could at their homes. It helped him wean himself off of her, to exercise self-control, but he was starkly aware that they were alone with no one around for miles on a late, quiet Friday afternoon.

His demon salivated and flashed erotic images in his mind, snapshots of their last, devastating encounter. Depraved desires snaked through his mind, edging out the pain of her rejection. He hesitated at the bottom of the steps. The reformed part of him wanted to order her to stay in the truck or, better yet, call their parents to pick her up. She wasn't safe with him.

But he didn't say a word. Instead, he made his way toward her, fingers tingling, heart racing. He knew what he was going to do. Maybe a part of him had known the moment she got in the truck with him. It was always going to end this way. If he was presented with the opportunity to have her, he didn't have the will to resist. Even if it jeopardized his freedom. Even if it wrecked their family. Nothing compared to the absolute bliss of possessing her. He would pay any price to have her. To be buried inside of her where he belonged.

It didn't matter if they ran the risk of being caught. He would take her anytime, anywhere. He didn't give a fuck if it was in God's house. If sex was all he could have of her, he would take as much as he could until she reported him, or someone put a bullet in his head. He was an addicted maniac. There was something terribly wrong with him for wanting someone who despised him. But he didn't care. He'd take her hatred and disdain. He'd take her fighting. He'd take whatever she gave him as long as he got *her*.

He kept his eyes downcast, maintaining the role of chastened stepbrother. If Violet looked into his eyes, she'd know what was coming. There was a fine tremor in the hand that inserted the key in the lock and turned it. He pushed open the door and Violet stepped through. He watched her walk down the aisle between the pews. Cast in the light that came through the massive stained-glass windows, she looked ethereal, untouchable. No matter how many times he claimed her, she remained maddeningly out of reach.

Hands on hips, Violet surveyed the empty stage. What was she thinking? He gave the church a cursory glance. This is where their parents married and where they'd come nearly every Sunday for four years. He spent countless hours here praying, worshipping, volunteering. He spent a significant portion of his summer renovating this church... For what? To have God laugh in his face and take from him the only thing he'd ever wanted?

Fury heated his blood. He'd been a good son, taking care of his mother when his father died. He studied diligently for good grades, worked hard to attain his skills as an athlete and earned his money through manual labor. He didn't cheat or steal. He had one dream. One weakness. One thing he desired above all else. He thought God placed Violet in his life because she was meant to be his, only for God to be one of the reasons Violet was convinced they couldn't be together.

Violet had quoted every scripture about how God judged the sexually immoral, and how sex outside of marriage went against God's design. He would have let Mom and Dad catch them in the act if he thought they'd force her to marry him. But he suspected their parent's remedy would be to bury their indiscretion instead of trying to rectify it. They would be relieved to ship him off to the military and ensure they had no future contact with each other, which left him with no leverage to bind Violet to him.

God and Violet had been major pillars in his life. They guided and shaped him. He gave them his all only to walk away empty-handed and heartbroken, with his best friend and soul mate lost to him for all time. God had played him for a fool, tormenting him with false visions and hopes that would never come true. Didn't God know what happened to faithful men who weren't rewarded? They stopped praying and took matters into their own hands. If being the good guy didn't get him what he wanted, what was the point of restraining himself?

He drew in a deep breath, taking in Violet's powdery scent mixing with the smell of old Bibles, furniture polish, and wood pews. He didn't have it in him to be gentle, loving, or patient any longer. He was desperate, deprived, and starving. With graduation just two months away and his ship date for the military pending, he had mere weeks left with her. He wasn't going to abstain. He was going to gorge, knowing, no matter how much he indulged, it would never be enough.

As if Violet caught the tail end of his thought, her head whipped around. The moment their eyes collided, hers flared in instant recognition.

"You promised."

Her voice was nearly soundless even in the hushed, quiet sanctuary.

"I've done my best." His voice was gruff with lust. "I've never been able to keep my promises where you're concerned. I can't be around you and not..." He swallowed hard and extended his hand, palm out. "It won't be like last time. I can be gentle."

When she recoiled, his hand balled into a fist and dropped to his side.

"Don't run," he ordered, knowing it would trigger primitive instincts that he was trying to stifle. She deserved gentle. She deserved sweet. If she came to him, if she allowed him to touch without fighting, he could control his rampaging demon, but if she... His control vanished as Violet bolted down the aisle.

If the back door had been unlocked, Violet would have escaped. Instead, she wasted precious seconds fumbling with the lock and had to dash away before he could get his hands on her.

She leapt up the stairs, intending to cross the stage, to reach a door on the other side of the sanctuary, but she didn't make it. He flattened her on the steps.

"You can't do this here!" she hissed fiercely.

He was pleased her warrior spirit was back. That meant he didn't have to rein himself in. He could indulge his demon's appetite and give them an experience that would be etched into their memories for all time.

"Why not here? God already knows what we've done," he said as he flipped her onto her back and unceremoniously yanked her pants down.

She engaged in a furious tug of war with him while simultaneously trying to keep an eye on multiple entrances. When he yanked hard enough to pull her down a step, she tried to kick him in the head, which allowed him to free one leg from her pants. That was all he needed. He ripped her maroon lace underwear off, forced her legs wide, and clamped his mouth on her pussy. Her breath whooshed out of her and her body went taut as a bow.

It had been weeks since he tasted her. Weeks since he'd

been inside her. The moment his tongue sank inside her, he knew he was lost. He'd gone back to taking her underwear to get him off, but that paled in comparison to this. To drinking from her. To feeling her thigh muscles quiver as she strained to get away. To the honey that spilled from her against her will. Those tormented, helpless sounds she made were music to his ears. His awareness of their surroundings vanished. He didn't care where they were or who tried to interrupt them. He wasn't stopping unless someone physically hauled him off her.

He slid his finger inside her to coax her to spill a little more for him.

"Please, stop," she begged as she hauled her quivering body up a step.

He followed, keeping his mouth on her while he felt around for her G-spot. He knew he found it when she let out a wanton moan that echoed around the sanctuary before she muffled it with her arm.

He lifted his head, eager for proof that she still needed this from him. She let out a stifled sob as he pushed her arm aside. She glared at him, eyes shining with self-loathing, lust, and hatred. She'd never looked more beautiful to him.

"You," she began gutturally, but her voice cut out when he cupped her.

Her thighs snapped together, trapping his hand, which he didn't mind in the least. As his fingers expertly stroked, her legs tossed back and forth.

"You've been missing me, Vi. Admit it," he rasped.

"You're a heartless..." She bared her teeth as she pulled herself up another step. "Evil."

She collapsed on the stage and turned on her side in the fetal position. Mouth watering at the feast before him, he took his hand from her to undo his jeans. Violet shot up and tried to make a break for it, but he was on her in a flash. She didn't gain more than three steps before he wrapped his arms around her and got her down on all fours. He put her in a chokehold as he blanketed her body with his.

"Nuh-uh, baby. You're not getting away. I've gone too long without you."

"Please don't do this," she pleaded.

"You want this so bad, you're soaking my jeans," he hissed as he rocked against her.

"We're in *church*!"

She sounded scandalized.

He pressed his cheek to hers as they stared at the rows of empty pews. "It doesn't matter where we are. I'll always want you."

He gripped her throat with one hand while the other undid his jeans and shoved them down.

"You know you want this," he panted as he dragged his dick up and down her weeping slit. "Your body still craves me. Still wants me to fuck you senseless." He nuzzled her as she let out a choked sob. "That's exactly what you want me to do, isn't it? Tell me that's what you want, Violet."

"You have no shame," she croaked.

"You have enough for the both of us," he mocked as he lapped up a stray tear. "How we feel about each other is nothing to be ashamed of. It's supposed to be something we rejoice in."

"The devil will say anything to make a sin seem like a gift," she said bitterly.

So now he was the devil on top of being a monster. All because he loved her and wasn't willing to lie about his feelings or hide how she made him feel.

"If the way of the righteous means I can't have this..."

He gently thrust. It was so quiet, they both heard the sloppy sounds her body made. She whimpered in shame and tried to hang her head, but he wouldn't let her, forcing her to face their invisible jury.

"Then I'll be a sinner," he said through clenched teeth and tried to hold back his beast, which wanted to slake his lust savagely, ensuring her submission and repentance. "I wish everyone could see you, dripping all over the stage, taking every inch of me. *Loving* every fucking moment of this. Whenever you come through those doors, and look at this stage, you're going to think of this, of us."

"No!"

She made a desperate lunge for the edge of the stage, but he held her in place. She wasn't going anywhere.

"Pray for divine intervention," he taunted as her vagina clutched at his invading cock. "If this is wrong, God will save you. He wouldn't let His faithful daughter be defiled in His own house, would he?"

She reached back and gripped his thigh, fingernails raking his skin. "Stop! You can't..."

He was so fucking tired of hearing her say that. He cut her off as he abruptly slammed himself inside of her, making her release a shrill scream that echoed around the chapel.

"I can't what?" he whispered, fingers tightening around her throat as his demon howled in triumph. "I can't fuck you in a church? I can't make you want me?"

"I hate you!"

Her words skewered his heart. Despair and lust tangled in a devastating mix that decimated his control and his desire to be gentle. He abruptly straightened and gripped her hips.

"You better hope someone walks through that door and saves you," he growled as he began to move in hard, brutal strokes that caused her whole body to jolt. "And puts us both out of our misery."

He took what he wanted, what he needed, or he'd go insane. He didn't hold back, couldn't. Not after being so long without her. He dared God to take her from him, to deny him this after everything he'd sacrificed. He made Violet beg, cry, scream, and moan. He was certain this form of worship had never been practiced here, but he ensured if God was watching, it was memorable.

He wasn't ready to come, but when she rippled around him, he almost went over the edge with her. He ground his teeth, fighting his response as she impaled herself on him, taking what she needed and shuddering in relief as he met her needs.

Unable to withstand another second, he flipped her on her back. He straddled her chest, knees pinning her arms on either side of her even though she was no longer fighting, but he wasn't taking any chances. He gripped her cheeks and forced her mouth open. His jubilant shout echoed through the church as he spilled, as he defiled a place he'd once considered sacred, and accepted the fact that he was going to hell.

Violet stared up at him with glazed eyes. Needing to prolong the moment, he slid his dick in her mouth and released her cheeks. He was tense, waiting for her to bite, but he relaxed and stroked her hair when she sucked and let her tongue feather over the sensitive head.

"Good girl," he husked.

That broke the spell. She went rigid beneath him and tipped her head to the side to expel his dick. She coughed and retched, but she'd already swallowed most of him, which is all he cared about. She began to buck and kick beneath him. He admired her for a few seconds before he rolled off her and collapsed behind Pastor Sonny's wood podium.

Violet stumbled to her feet and wove drunkenly toward her clothes strewn on the steps, swiping at her face as she hastily dressed. He listened to her run out of the church and the loud bang as the heavy door slammed shut behind her.

He waited to be clobbered by those incipient emotions that had dogged him since he jacked off at church camp—shame, guilt, regret, remorse, fear, disgust. All he felt was warm satisfaction. Anyone could have come in and discovered them, but God hadn't intervened. Maybe God hadn't abandoned him after all.

His climax left him drowsy, but he had work to do. He forced himself to his feet and dragged his jeans up and fastened them. He made his way to a closet with cleaning supplies and grabbed a spray bottle and washcloth. He wiped up all signs of debauchery before he began to execute the task Pastor Sonny had entrusted to him.

When he made his way out to the truck with four paint cans, he saw Violet huddled in the front seat. She hadn't been able to take off since he had the keys in his pocket and there was no one in the vicinity that she could ask for a ride. He propped the front door open as he loaded up lumber and the other building material they hadn't used during the renovation. Tomorrow, they would be working on the McMillan's house, members of the church who had a house in dire need of repair.

It took thirty minutes to load everything. By the time he joined Violet in the truck, the sun was beginning to set. He wasn't surprised when Violet angled her body away from him. If she had allowed it, he would have drawn her against his chest and held her. He wanted to tell her he loved her, that it didn't have to be this way, but he knew she wouldn't listen.

He knew she was hating herself, hating him. That was her default whenever they came together. It didn't matter how pleasurable and gratifying. She would always turn it into something amoral and twisted. She couldn't admit that a part of her reveled in what they'd done.

As they made their way home, he wondered what Violet would say to their parents. Had fucking in church pushed her over the edge? Was that the final straw? He felt a burble of unease, but it couldn't morph into true fear because of the overwhelming contentment that canceled out all else. His mind was empty, his inner turmoil gone. Possessing her in any capacity made him feel right, centered, whole. He refused to believe she didn't feel the same. It wasn't possible for such a connection to be one-sided. Their chemistry had been ordained by God. If she had loved him a fraction of how much he loved her, they could have conquered anything. Instead, she doomed them to lives where neither would ever be truly fulfilled.

When he pulled into the driveway, he glanced at Violet and waited to see if she had any last words for him before she decided his fate. She kept her face averted as she pushed open the door and hopped out. He ambled in her wake, hands in pockets.

As he expected, their parents hung around. Mom was still in the kitchen and Dad was in the living room. Both turned when they walked through the front door. Violet stopped in her tracks, clearly not anticipating this. He waited several seconds before he moved her inside so he could close the door.

"So?" Isaac prompted.

Mom came out of the kitchen, wiping her hands on a dish towel, her face still pinched with worry.

Violet was so rigid, she was trembling. He glanced down at her and saw her mouth open and eyes fill with tears.

"Violet?" Mom asked.

He curbed his arm around Violet's shoulders and turned her into him a second before she burst into tears. His hand sank into her hair and kept her face pressed to his chest as he said, "She forgave me, but she's still hurt and angry."

Violet's hand fisted in his shirt.

Mom's expression eased slightly. "Forgiveness doesn't take away the hurt, but it'll pass." Mom came up to them and rubbed Violet's back. "Are you okay, honey? Want to talk about it?"

His hand dropped to Violet's nape and squeezed. A second later, Violet shook her head.

"Violet helped me load up the truck. We're a little dirty," he said.

Mom nodded and stepped back. "Dinner will be ready in a half hour."

He glanced at Isaac and got a curt, approving nod. Isaac was satisfied with his explanation and wouldn't push Violet any further, for which he was grateful. He used his body to shield Violet from their scrutiny and ushered her down the hallway. He entered his bedroom since it was closer and directed her into the bathroom. Intending to get her in the shower, he started to lift her shirt without registering the fire in her eyes until it was too late. Her slap snapped his head to the side.

"You got what you wanted from me," she seethed. "Now, get out."

He ignored his throbbing face and reached for her. "It's not like that. I wanted…"

She wrenched away, grabbed her hairbrush, and held it like a knife. "I know what you wanted! It's the only thing you care about!"

"Vi."

"I swear to God," she choked. "If you touch me one more time, I'm going to lose it."

He held up his hands. "Okay, I'm going."

He backed into his bedroom. She closed the bathroom door and a second later, locked it. He stood there, face smarting, and heard the shower switch on to drown out the sound of her sobbing.

He leaned back against the door and closed his eyes. Those feelings he thought he bested came back with a vengeance, clobbering him over the head, drowning him in self-loathing. His chest swelled with the need to roar, but he swallowed it and staggered to his bed.

Even though he regretted the pain he caused, he knew that wouldn't stop him from partaking in the future. If he had a shred of decency, he would put Violet out of her misery and turn himself in, but he wasn't the self-sacrificing hero. Thanks to her, he'd finally embraced what he was. He wasn't the knight in shining armor. He was the villain. What self-respecting monster willingly walked into a cage? If Violet wanted him out of her life, she had to declare what he was to the world. Until then, he was going to take his fill.

At some point, she would find the strength to turn him in. He wasn't sure if that would be this evening over dinner or a month from now, but she would. If he wanted a chance at a future that wasn't behind bars, he had to get the hell away from her. Having the military dictate his life was the best thing for him since he had no control where she was concerned. It was best that he leave before they destroyed one another.

CHAPTER 18
VIOLET

1 MONTH LATER

"How was work, honey?" Mom asked as she set a pile of steaming bread rolls in the middle of the table.

"Funny you should ask," Dad drawled with a lopsided grin as he reached for one and broke it in half. "It was an eventful day."

Mom held up a hand. "You didn't deal with any dead bodies, did you?"

"Not today," Dad said as he bit into his roll.

Mom relaxed. "Okay. So, what happened?"

"The first call we got was from a woman who got her toe stuck in a faucet."

Violet came out of her reverie and frowned at her father. "What kind of faucet?"

"A tub faucet."

Violet's brows bunched together. "Why would she do that?"

"I stopped asking questions like that my first year on the job," Dad said as he forked up chicken and green beans.

"You didn't have to amputate anything, did you?" Mom asked.

"Ew, Mom!" Violet waved her hand to dissipate the images in her mind.

"No amputation necessary. Just some lubricant." Dad snickered. "She seemed thrilled to have an audience and carried on drinking her wine and eating chocolates long after the bubbles were gone." Dad bobbed his eyebrows at Mom, who gasped and smacked his arm. "I covered her in a bath towel, which she kept trying to take off while asking if any of us were single. She was entertaining, to say the least."

"Was she?" Mom said testily.

Violet's lips quirked. Automatically, her gaze flicked to Jesse to see his reaction to their parents' playful bickering. Her amusement faded. Jesse stared pensively down at his food, oblivious to their conversation. She noticed he'd been preoccupied lately. She could hear him pacing in his room in the wee hours of the morning. He'd also been coming home late from school, even when he didn't have practice.

Whatever was bothering him hadn't affected his sex drive, however. He was more ravenous than ever. Ever since they had sex at church, it was like he *wanted* to get caught. He was becoming alarmingly brazen. She didn't know who he was anymore. When he looked at her, she didn't see her brother at all, but a stranger.

At lunch today, Brody nudged her and jerked his chin across the cafeteria, where Jesse sat with an odd mix of people.

"What's going on there?" Brody asked.

"No idea," she'd said, but her gaze was on the stunning redhead who had her hand on Jesse's arm.

Georgia had pressed against her back to whisper excitedly, "Ooh. Are they dating?"

She'd turned away with a shrug while Brody said, "Jesse and Faye? He hasn't said anything about her, but it sure looks like she's willing."

While the guys joked around, Georgia said, "They make a striking couple. Jesse hasn't dated anyone this year, has he? What's the deal?"

When Violet bit into her sandwich to avoid answering, Georgia poked her in her side.

"You're his sister. You should be able to give us the inside scoop. I can't believe he doesn't tell you anything. You guys are always together."

"Jesse's a gentleman," Marie interjected. "He doesn't kiss and tell. He's the only guy I know who's stayed friends with all his exes. None of them has a bad thing to say about him, except for the fact that he broke up with them. He gave them princess treatment for a few weeks—opening their door, pulling out their chairs, buying them flowers, and then *bam*." Marie clapped her hands. "He says they're done. No warning, no explanation other than it wasn't working out. None of them can make sense of it. They'd take him back in a heartbeat if he asked."

"I think Madyson took it the hardest. I heard Trent broke up with her because Jesse's all she talked about." Georgia looked around before she added, "It's been, like, a year. You'd think she'd be over him by now."

"Can you really blame her? Jesse's everything any girl could want in a boyfriend."

Violet tuned out her friends and fantasized about her senior year when she wouldn't have to listen to her friends gush about what a gentleman Jesse was. If they only knew what he'd done to her on the way to school that morning...

Jesse's gaze abruptly rose and speared hers. Her stomach clenched. She switched her attention back to Dad and forced herself to eat, even though she wasn't hungry. She hoped Jesse dated Faye and transferred all his kinky, erotic fantasies to the gorgeous redhead instead of her. He was a sex fanatic. Perverted, twisted. He never missed an opportunity to have his way with her. The only time she was free of his advances was when she turned in for the night and locked the bedroom and bathroom door. The next day, the battle to avoid him began anew.

Jesse was still staring at her. She resolutely ignored him and focused on Dad, who laughed as he told a story about his coworker who had to defend himself against a guy wielding an umbrella like a sword while high on some psychedelic drug.

"And then, Derrick leaps at him and says…" Dad chortled.

"I joined the Air Force."

Jesse's statement was said so casually that Violet ignored it. It wasn't until silence fell, and she registered that Mom and Dad were both gawking at Jesse, that she processed what he said.

Shock made her fingers fumble her fork, which clattered loudly as it dropped on her plate. She assumed Jesse would go to college, but if he went into the military, that would be even better! Her lips curved in what felt like the first genuine smile she'd had all year.

"You did *what*?"

Lynne's hoarse voice snapped Violet out of her giddy delight. Registering the tension in the air, she bowed her head to hide her joy, but at Jesse's silence, she glanced at him and found him watching her through narrowed eyes.

"Jesse?"

Lynne's tone was part plea, part demand. Slowly, Jesse transferred his attention to his mother who sat across the table from him.

"I enlisted," Jesse said calmly.

"H-how? You didn't ask for my consent. I didn't sign anything allowing you to—"

"I'm eighteen, Mom."

Lynne's expression went from horror to outrage as she shouted, "You haven't talked about the military for years!"

Jesse didn't bat an eye at his mother's outburst. "Because it upset you, not because I changed my mind."

"You saw what losing your father did to me, and you're volunteering to put yourself in the same position?"

"I made a promise," Jesse said quietly.

Lynne slammed her fist on the table. "Do you think your father would ask you to honor that promise if he knew he would die at thirty?"

"He died with honor."

"He *died* instead of having a life with us. He *died* instead of getting out when I begged him to." Lynne's eyes glistened with tears. "Have you sworn in?" When Jesse hesitated, Lynne shot to her feet. "I forbid it, Jesse. Quit now before it's too late."

"Mom."

"I'm serious. I can't go through that again." Lynne ran her hands through her hair. "I can't believe you'd even consider..."

Violet jolted when Lynne abruptly turned on her.

"You didn't try to talk him out of it?"

Taken aback, Violet opened and closed her mouth, unsure what to say. She knew Lynne had a temper, but she had never been on the receiving end of it until now. Her glee vanished in the face of Lynne's wild despair.

"Violet didn't know. I did this on my own," Jesse interjected.

"Lynne," Dad said in a consoling tone. "Let's talk about this."

"Talk?" Lynne scoffed as she paced with her arms wrapped around herself. "Apparently, talking isn't something we do in this house anymore. People just make major life decisions without telling anyone."

"Mom, this is my dream."

Lynne planted her hands on the table and leaned toward her son. "You idolize your father, but his choices don't have to be yours. You don't have to walk the same path as him. There are better paths. You could be somebody, Jesse. You're talented in so many areas. Why let them decide what to do with your life? Why submit yourself to that harsh environment? You should enjoy your freedom." A tear slid down her cheek. "Why do you want to leave us?"

Jesse swallowed, displaying his first sign of discomfort.

"I don't want to leave you."

"So, don't! Don't go!"

Jesse lowered his gaze to his plate. "I have to do this."

"Why?" Lynne cried.

Violet's heart thudded in her ears as silence fell. Jesse was usually so careful and considerate of his mother. It was painful to see them at odds. Lynne looked distraught, but Jesse was standing his ground. Even though she'd initially been ecstatic at the news, Lynne's devastation was contagious and made her own eyes water.

A crack of thunder made her flinch as the heavens opened and rain began to lash the windows.

"Vi," Dad said quietly.

She was relieved to be excused from the table and the highly charged environment. No one said a word as she left her half-eaten dinner and made her way to her bedroom. She closed the door and winced when she heard Lynne explode. Her shouting was accompanied by another deafening boom of thunder that shook the house. She put on her headphones and let her punk rock music drown out the unexpected storms that had appeared out of nowhere.

Conflicting emotions sloshed around inside of her. On one hand, she was thrilled. If Jesse went into the Air Force, she'd be free. As Mom said, *they* would decide Jesse's life. He wouldn't be able to come home whenever he felt like it, like he would if he attended college and had holidays and school breaks. Once he signed, he had to fulfill his commitment, which was a minimum of four years for Active Duty.

It never crossed her mind that Jesse would join the military. Like Lynne, she used to get upset when he brought it up. That was when she actually cared about what he did with his life. Now, she wanted him gone. Out of her life, out of the state, out of the country, if possible. She bit her lip. She despised him, but she didn't want him dead. Lynne was acting like Jesse would be sent to the front lines. Surely, Mom was overreacting?

Is this what he wanted to talk about when he drove her out to see the bluebonnets? She assumed he wanted to talk about which college he should attend. He hadn't talked about the military in years. If Jesse had given her a choice of him going to college or the military, what would she have said? She tossed her hair, not willing to entertain such thoughts. Jesse's future wasn't her business. It was his, and he made the decision to enlist, which she was happy about —ecstatic, in fact.

Her life had become an endless tunnel with no light, no detours, no one to hold her hand. Jesse would jump her in the dark and corner and coerce her to get what he wanted before he disappeared, leaving her to piece herself back together and carry on, hand outstretched, as she tried to find her way in the pitch-black abyss. Sometimes, when she was too broken to walk, she crawled. She kept going, believing there had to be something up ahead. Jesse's announcement caused a pinprick of light to cut through the dark, giving her a vision of a near future where there would be no tunnel, no filth, no more structuring her life around ways to avoid him. There was an end to her misery and despite Lynne's fear, all Violet felt was overwhelming relief.

She tried to distract herself with homework, but her attention strayed. She tugged aside the headphones periodically to check if the coast was clear. The arguing went on for hours. Most of the time, it was Lynne who was shouting, but there was also the low murmur of Dad's voice in what sounded like a conciliatory tone.

She'd decided to turn in for the night and had just brushed her teeth and locked the bathroom door behind her when her bedroom door opened. When Mom poked her head in, Violet tugged off her headphones and held them in one hand as she took in Lynne's red, puffy eyes. Her anxiety spiked as she waited for the verdict. Had Mom talked Jesse out of joining the Air Force?

"Mom?"

When Lynne's face crumpled, she rushed forward, partly because it looked like Lynne was going to collapse and partly because she didn't want Lynne to see her jubilation. Comforting Lynne while she inwardly did cartwheels made her feel like a bad person, but she couldn't help it. No one knew who Jesse truly was. This was best for all of them, Lynne just didn't know it. As Lynne wept, that tiny bead of light in her tunnel began to expand and brighten, so she could practically feel its warmth.

Lynne pulled back and braced her hands on her shoulders. "Please talk to him. He hasn't sworn in. There's still a chance for him to get out of his commitment."

Alarm cut through Violet's contentment. "I... I don't think anything I say will make a difference. His mind is made up and..." She looked away from Lynne's heartbroken eyes. "He didn't tell me what he was going to do. It seems like he didn't want anyone to dissuade him."

Lynne squeezed her arms. "You're his best friend. You two are closer than blood siblings. If you tell him you want him to stay, that you need him here, he might do it for you."

Her throat began to close as anxiety ripped through her. "We've grown apart."

"You still mean the world to him. You can save him from making a huge mistake."

"I..."

"Just try. Please."

An invisible object obstructed her throat so she couldn't breathe, making her eyes tear. Lynne cupped her cheek, expression softening, assuming they were on the same wavelength when nothing could be further from the truth.

Lynne kissed her cheek. "Sleep. Hopefully, we'll wake up and this will all just be a horrible dream."

After Mom left, she waited a few minutes to see if Dad was going to pop in. When he didn't, she locked that door, too, and climbed into bed. She stared at the ceiling as she listened to the rain hammer down on the roof. A tree branch Dad had been meaning to cut scraped the side of the house as the wind picked up.

Is that what Jesse had been doing after school? Getting his paperwork and tests done to qualify and enlist? Even though Jesse hadn't sworn in (whatever that meant), hopefully he was too far along in the process to back out without consequences. She would do almost anything for Lynne, but begging Jesse to stay wasn't one of them. She pounded her pillow as she turned on her side. Jesse would be fine in the military. There was no need for Lynne to worry about him. This was a dream come true.

SHE WOKE WHEN A HAND CLAMPED OVER HER MOUTH. HER EYES flew open as a man sat on top of her. She panicked and thrashed as his weight sank her into the mattress. She let out a scream that was significantly muffled by his hand and the storm, which was still raging.

A head ducked down, and a nose brushed against hers before she heard, "Happy I'm joining the military, baby?"

Her heart stuttered at Jesse's furious hiss.

"If I hadn't promised my dad I would follow in his footsteps, I wouldn't be going anywhere," he growled as he took his hand away.

Fear made her strike out. She heard a satisfying crack as her palm hit his cheek. He cursed and a second later, his mouth landed on hers. The taste of spearmint mouthwash overwhelmed her as his tongue invaded. She raked her nails over him and realized he was naked. He hissed, back arching as she tried to draw blood. His mouth left hers and coasted down to where her neck flowed into her shoulder. He sank his teeth into her as he grabbed her wrists and pinned them to the mattress. She kicked her feet as he bit to punish. When she whimpered, he eased the pressure and then kissed her throbbing flesh as if he hadn't used brute force to make her submit like they were part of the animal kingdom.

"You want to fight, baby? I'm in an obliging mood," he

said against her skin. "Mom used everything she could to make me quit." His tongue slid over her racing pulse. "I assume she asked you to beg me to stay?"

She clenched her teeth.

He nipped her jaw. "Answer me."

"Yes," she said sullenly.

He lifted his head to look down at her. With her night-light at the foot of her bed, his face was in shadow, but she still felt the intensity of his stare.

"So? What are you going to do, Violet?" He pressed his lips to hers. "What are you willing to sacrifice to make Mom happy?"

"I love her."

He stilled.

"But not enough to ask you to stay."

He was silent for a beat before he said, "So be it."

He parted her legs with his knee and nestled his erection between her legs. Her flimsy pajama shorts were poor protection from his scorching heat and his hard dick, which she knew would be inside of her very soon. She yanked at her imprisoned wrists, which only made him tighten his grip. She wished she had the balls to scream her head off and have Mom and Dad catch him in the act. But she would rather endure whatever Jesse had planned than witness the look on Dad's face when he discovered she was no longer pure.

"You can't do this here!" she said desperately. "Mom and Dad are right down the hall!"

"Then we better be quiet."

As he brushed kisses over her face, she considered head-butting him. What was with this affectionate bull-shit? They rarely kissed. All he usually cared about was getting off. Foreplay was minimal. That's how she preferred it. She just wanted to get this over with. Why...? She stiffened as it finally hit her.

"How did you get in here? I locked both doors!"

"I broke the lock on the bathroom door."

"You—"

"Ask Dad to repair it, I'll break it again."

He slid off her onto his side and hauled her up in bed, so she was propped on her pillows. Before she could roll away, he yanked her camisole down and latched onto her breast while his hand slid into her pants.

"You want me out of your life, fine, but that means I get full access," he growled as he parted her.

His middle finger slid in with embarrassing ease.

Ashamed by her body's response, she snapped, "Can't you get this from Faye instead of me?"

"Faye?" he muttered around her nipple.

She gritted her teeth. "Yes, the redhead hanging on your arm at lunch."

His dick jerked against her thigh. "Jealous?"

She smacked his shoulder as his thumb began to tease her clit. "No! I want you to find someone else to fulfill your sick fantasies instead of me!"

"There's little chance of that happening," he said distractedly as he worked her. "Faye's brother just joined the Air Force, so I've been talking to him about his experience and what to expect. I've been connecting with others who are joining other branches, and Faye decided to tag along. She's nice, but..."

He rubbed himself against her.

"She isn't you." He kissed the base of her throat. "Touch me, Vi."

Her hand balled into a fist. Quick as lightning, the hand in her pants disappeared, and his wet finger was shoved into her mouth. She gripped his wrist with both hands to stop him from shoving his finger down her throat.

"I swear to God if you don't put your hand on me, I'll…" He let out a breath when her hand closed around him. "Good. Now, stroke me the way I taught you."

She obeyed, simultaneously sucking on the finger he hadn't withdrawn from her mouth. He hissed through his teeth and arched into her touch.

"Slow down," he ground out.

Fuck you, she thought, tightening her grip to make him blow.

She sensed his control snap a second before he yanked her hand off him.

"I warned you I wasn't in the mood," he hissed.

When he sat up and reached for her, she lost her temper. Screw him! She didn't care about his mood or what he wanted. He wasn't supposed to do this kind of shit when Mom and Dad were present. What the hell was wrong with him?

They tussled. Her stuffed animals and pillows went flying. Jesse leapt off the bed, yanked her onto her back and dragged her, so her head was hanging off the mattress. Before she could figure out why he'd positioned her so bizarrely, Jesse cupped her jaw, forcing her head back. She had a split second of warning before his dick slid into her mouth and Jesse planted himself in her throat.

She panicked, hands and legs wheeling through the air as she choked. Jesse withdrew enough for her to breathe. She coughed and tried to turn her head aside, but he collared her throat and ordered, "Be still."

She moaned in protest and pushed at him, but she was trapped by his iron thighs and the rock-hard dick impaling her mouth. In this position, she was completely helpless and at his mercy.

"You didn't listen to me, so now we're going to do this my way." He let his hand wander from her throat to her breasts. "You're gonna suck me until I tell you to stop. You fight me and try to make me come before I'm ready, you'll regret it."

Slowly, he pushed forward. She screwed her eyes shut and made a concentrated effort not to fight him and control her gag reflex. She heard him expel his breath and knew he was pleased when he gripped her breast.

"Yes, just like that," he groaned.

She gripped the backs of his corded thighs and obeyed every husky command. She was rewarded for her good behavior when he yanked off her bottoms, spread her thighs, and put his mouth between her legs. As all the blood rushed to her head, she felt a euphoric rush. Jesse knew her body well and used everything in his arsenal to rouse her to a fever pitch. She got so lost in what they were doing that she grabbed his ass to yank him toward her so she could take every inch of him.

She felt more than heard his guttural groan before he yanked out of her mouth as if it were an electrical socket. As she lay there, panting, he cupped the back of her head and lifted it to give her a deep, wet, upside-down kiss.

"That's my girl," he husked before he pulled her into a sitting position.

She didn't have time to get her bearings because he pulled her off the bed and promptly bent her over it. She buried her face in her tangled sheets, which was convenient because a second later, she screamed when he slammed inside of her. He froze with his body blanketing hers, but she was too far gone to care. She bounced under him and wrapped her hand around the back of his neck, urging him on. He dropped his head on her shoulder, panting as he grappled for control.

"You're killing me, Vi."

"Hurry," she whispered.

Outside, the storm seemed to be picking up, thunder crashing like cymbals, gearing up so they could have this moment.

He nuzzled her cheek. "Tell me you want me."

She bared her teeth. He wasn't satisfied that he controlled her body, he always pushed for more. He was such an asshole.

"Vi, you need this, same as me. You can't deny it." When she didn't answer, his hand fisted in her hair. "Why can't you admit it?"

Because she would rather die than give in completely. He may rule her in these moments, but there was still a part of her he hadn't conquered. Would *never* conquer. It was what gave her the strength to resist and soldier through every day, even though sometimes she considered giving up. She would never surrender that piece of her identity to him. If she did, she would be lost.

He capitulated with a ragged, "Fuck," before he began to move.

With nature colluding with them to disguise their forbidden tryst, she let herself go. She let herself enjoy the pleasures of the flesh she normally denied herself in the light of day and made demands he gave into, leading to an orgasm that made her gnaw her sheets.

"Tell me," Jesse pleaded. "Just this one time. Please."

She ignored him and lay like a limp, wrecked doll. She knew what to expect and wasn't disappointed when he went berserk. Jesse took his frustrations out on her body.

When she began to make too much noise, he clapped a hand over her mouth. When that didn't work, he shoved her face in the mattress and put a pillow over her head. He ended up using it himself when he came, folding over her and shouting her name into the stuffing.

Even as he spilled inside of her, he shoved the pillow away and hissed, "Deny all you want, but we both know the truth. You love what's between us, you're just too much of a coward to admit it."

He pulled out of her, spilling down the back of her thighs. By the time her quivering legs collapsed, and she landed on her knees beside the bed, he was already gone.

CHAPTER 19
VIOLET

2 MONTHS LATER

Despite the warm July evening, there was a healthy fire crackling in the fire pit. The backyard, house, and garage were filled to capacity for Jesse's farewell party. Firefighters mingled with Jesse's coaches, teammates, and their church friends. It seemed that half the neighborhood had decided to attend. Mom's friends, mostly teachers, went around patting cheeks and catching up with students they hadn't seen since elementary school.

Violet couldn't believe this day had finally come. Jesse was leaving tomorrow. A part of her kept expecting something to go wrong—for his paperwork to fall through or there to be some mix up that would eject him from the military before he could be shipped off, but everything had gone smoothly. Mom tried to talk Jesse out of his decision until he swore in, and there was no turning back. This week had been rough on Mom. She'd excused herself multiple times from the party to have a crying session.

A commotion in the house caught Violet's attention.

She started forward as Dad emerged, carrying a massive cake. People clapped Jesse on the back and ushered him toward the table where Dad set it down. The cake had a pair of combat boots, a fighter jet, and the Air Force logo with, "We will miss you, Jesse," written on it.

At everyone's urgings, Jesse posed with his cake. Violet felt obliged to take pictures. Not for herself, but for Lynne. Even with everyone calling out for Jesse to look in their direction, he looked directly at her. She hastily took the photo and then fiddled with her phone until Dad began to address the crowd with his hand on Jesse's shoulder.

"I'm happy you all could join us to celebrate Jesse before he sets out on his journey," Dad said in a voice that carried clearly across the backyard. "I couldn't ask for a better son. Lynne and I are so proud of you. We know you're going to do great things in the world."

Everyone whistled and cheered as Dad and Jesse gave each other manly claps on the back. Lynne walked up to Jesse, dabbing her eyes with her handkerchief. Clearly too emotional to speak, Lynne kissed Jesse on the cheek and gave him a hug.

As people turned to Violet with expectant faces, she felt a flash of panic. No one told her she'd have to say a few words and give Jesse a public farewell.

"Come, Vi," Dad said, beckoning to her. "Let's take a family photo before we cut the cake."

She pasted a smile on her face as she made her way over. She and Lynne stood side by side, while Dad and Jesse stood behind them. As everyone playfully jostled for the best position to take their photo, pride swelled in her chest. She knew what the photos would capture. Dad and Jesse with their impressive, fit figures towering over her and Mom, who wore matching floral dresses, hers in pink and

Mom's in yellow. Dad and Jesse wore matching white button up shirts for precisely this reason. Mom had known there would be a ton of photos taken and wanted them to be ready. Their family had its issues, but at that moment, Violet didn't want to be anywhere else. This is where she belonged.

Blinding flashes came from every direction. Their heads whipped back and forth, trying to give everyone the opportunity to get the perfect shot, but it was so chaotic that everyone began to laugh. Grinning, Violet stepped forward, only to be stopped by a pair of arms that pulled her back against a toned frame. Jesse wrapped his arms around her, pressed his cheek to hers, and rocked her from side to side. A series of "aww's" came from the women who thought Jesse's gesture was sweet. She kept her lips curved as her nails sank warningly into the back of his hand.

"Violet! Jesse! Look here!"

She looked in the direction of the voice and saw her friend Allison holding up her phone to take their photo. She endured Jesse's touch for a few more seconds before she tried to move away. Jesse hesitated for a split second before he released her.

"This cake is something else," Violet said enthusiastically as she stepped up to Mom's side.

"And it's supposed to taste even better than it looks," Mom said as she handed Jesse the first slice, which was a shocking bright blue.

"It's blueberry?" Jesse asked, eyeing the cake warily.

Mom laughed. "No, that's just dye. It's chocolate."

Everyone laughed at Jesse's obvious relief. As Dad went to fetch ice cream, Violet arranged slices of cake on a tray and began to circulate through the crowd.

She was waylaid often. It had been a while since she'd

seen her uncles—a mix of firefighters, paramedics, and police officers who had known her since she was born. They wanted to know if she was going to follow in Dad's footsteps, as she'd said she would when she was five. They guffawed when she gave an adamant, "Nope!"

After a series of hugs, she moved on and found herself face to face with Pastor Sonny. "Hey!"

"Hey, yourself," he said and eyed the last plate on her tray. "Is that spoken for?"

"No! It's all yours."

She handed it to him and prepared to run when he tapped her shoulder.

"I've been meaning to talk to you, Violet."

Her heart dropped to her toes as she turned back to him. "You have?"

She avoided him just as much as Jesse, if not more so. If anyone could discern what was happening, it would be Pastor Sonny. He was a kind man, but his gaze was piercing and stern, and she felt like he could see straight through people to their rotten core. She dreaded going to church. It seemed his sermons were tailor-made to rip her conscience to shreds every week.

"Yes. I was wondering if you were interested in becoming a mentor for the youth."

"Mentor?" She cleared her throat. "That's... wow."

His eyes tracked over her face and fractionally narrowed. "You're not interested."

It wasn't a question.

She tucked the empty tray under her arm and glanced around the room instead of meeting his eyes. "I've never considered being a mentor."

"That's why I think you should do it. I notice you prefer being in the background, assisting rather than taking a leadership role, but I think you have a lot to offer. I've known you since you were a little girl. You have wisdom to share with the young ones who need guidance for this next stage in life."

As she struggled to think of something to say, he lightly touched her arm.

"Think about it and let me know."

She watched him walk away before she gave herself a shake and hurried out to the backyard to do exactly what he said she liked to do—assist. Assisting meant she didn't have to take the fall if something went awry. Assisting meant there was always work to be done. Keeping busy kept her from pondering too much. He thought she had wisdom to share? She was the last person anyone should come to for advice. She'd made a mess of her life.

When she tried to load her tray again, Mom gave her a little push.

"You've been on your feet all day. If people want cake, they'll come looking. Enjoy the party. Go hang out with Jesse and your friends."

Mom jerked her chin at the fire pit where most of the teenagers had congregated. She didn't want to talk to anybody, but she could see Mom wasn't going to let her continue to bustle around.

She accepted the cake slice Mom placed in her hands and wandered over to her peers. Allison hopped up from the lounge chair where she and her boyfriend, Jesse's class-mate, Blaine, were relaxing.

"This picture of you and Jesse is so *cute*," Allison exclaimed as she tapped her phone screen. "I already posted it and everyone is dying."

Allison held up her phone, so Violet could see the photo of her and Jesse. She wasn't expecting much, considering how far away Allison had been, but the edited results were devastating. She and Jesse beamed at the camera, faces pressed together, his arms wrapped around her. There was no trace of unease, anger, or bitterness on her face. She looked like she didn't want to be anywhere else but in his arms. They looked happy. How the hell was that possible?

"Violet?" Allison lowered the phone and steadied her plate, which was shaking. "Are you okay?"

She pulled herself together. "Yes, of course."

Allison rubbed her arm. "I can't imagine how you feel. You two are inseparable. It's going to be so weird seeing you without him."

"He's following his dream."

Allison nodded. "I had no idea he wanted to go into the military. Most thought he would go into the NFL. I heard some scouts were interested in him, and that's why Coach Rick was so upset when he quit football."

Violet's stomach flipped. "I never heard that."

Allison gestured to her boyfriend. "That's what Blaine said."

"And what's Blaine's plans now that he's graduated?" Violet asked, blatantly changing the subject.

Allison lit up. "He's staying here."

"That's great. But didn't he get into Dartmouth?"

Allison looked over her shoulder at Blaine before she turned back and whispered, "He decided to stay for me. He was worried we wouldn't be able to do long distance, so he'll wait another year before we decide where we want to go."

"Aww, you guys are so in *love*," Violet teased.

Allison practically glowed. "Yes, we are. I think he's it for me." Allison gripped her arm and whispered, "He proposed."

"What?"

"He didn't get me a ring yet, but we've talked about getting married after I graduate next year." Allison gave a little squeal. "Can you imagine me married exactly a year from now?"

"No."

"Well, if we do, just know you're going to be a bridesmaid." Allison giggled when Violet made a face. "Come on. Who doesn't love a wedding? Is it crazy that I want to be the first friend to get married and have kids?"

"Yes," Violet said emphatically.

Allison pouted. "Can't you be happy for me? Isn't he a great guy?"

Violet swallowed hard. "He's the best."

"How lucky am I to have found *the one* in high school? What are the chances?"

Their mindsets couldn't be more different. Allison was thinking of settling down and getting married and having kids, while Violet felt like her life hadn't begun. She wanted freedom and to get away from everyone and everything she'd ever known. Commitment was the last thing on her mind.

Instead of voicing her negative, cynical thoughts, Violet smiled and offered Allison a piece of her cake.

Two hours later, the crowd had significantly thinned as people began to take their leave. The mood had shifted as well, becoming more somber as people said their official goodbyes. Everyone kept giving her sympathetic pats or squeezes, assuming she was taking Jesse's departure as bad as Lynne when she felt nothing at all. Her stoic demeanor had been getting her some odd, sidelong looks. Shouldn't people be happy she wasn't imitating a human water faucet?

She escaped down the hallway for a break from the intense scrutiny and entered Jesse's bedroom. His door had been left ajar, so guests could use their bathroom if the other was in use. She was relieved to discover it empty. She turned to close the door, which abruptly began to swing open again.

"Oh, I'm sorry," she began with a laugh, intending to say the bathroom was occupied, but her voice died when Jesse pushed his way in. "What are you...?"

She didn't get to finish her question because his head swooped down, and his mouth settled on hers. He clasped her face and kissed her like the world was about to end. She was momentarily stunned, but the sound of someone cheering in the distance reminded her that they had a house full of guests. What the hell was he *doing*?

She wrenched her mouth away. "Have you lost your mind?"

"This should be the happiest night of my life," he said gruffly. "Everyone I care about is gathered in one place to see me off. I'm about to set out on my lifelong dream and make my father proud. I should be over the fucking moon, so why do I feel so miserable?"

Had one of his friends slipped him alcohol, even with cops and a pastor present? Sucking in an annoyed breath, she looked up, intending to snap him back to reality, but the sight of his spiky lashes and blue eyes shimmering with tears made her mind go blank.

"How did I fuck this up so badly?" he said thickly.

She averted her gaze. "Everyone will be looking for you. You should go back to the party."

"I can't leave tomorrow with things like this between us," he said, resting his forehead against hers. "Tell me there's a chance we can still be together in the future."

"This isn't the time for this!" Her voice was terse with stress.

"We're out of time, Violet. This is it." He massaged her nape to encourage her to look at him. "Tell me I didn't lose the most important person in the world to me."

She braced her hand on his chest and strained away from him. "The door isn't locked. Anyone could come in. All these people are here for you. You should be focused on them, not—"

"Look at me!"

His raised voice made her stiffen in alarm.

"Are you crazy? What the hell are you trying to do?" she hissed.

His face flushed with anger as he gripped her shoulders and gave her a shake. "I'm trying to get through to you. I need you to stop looking through me and actually hear what I'm saying."

Of course, he was forcing this confrontation the night before he left, when everyone they'd ever known was just a few rooms away.

She jutted out her chin. "What *are* you saying?"

His hands flexed on her shoulders. "I'm saying that I know what I did was wrong, and you have every right to hate me. I promised to protect you and couldn't protect you from myself."

His expression was a mix of frustration and desperation.

"I know I need to work on myself and that it's best for both of us if I leave. I told myself I wouldn't pressure you, but I need to know." He brushed her hair back with trembling fingers. "Give me some hope. Tell me there's a part of you that still feels something for me."

She held his gaze and deliberately let seconds that felt

like hours tick by. She felt no remorse as his face contorted with pain.

He swallowed hard, making his Adam's apple bob. "Can you forgive me?"

Months ago, she forgave him without thinking, naively believing what Dad said—that no act was unforgivable. But what Jesse had done to her, what he stole over and over again... it wasn't forgivable. As if he heard her thoughts, a tear slid down his cheek.

"Vi," he whispered, but whatever he was going to say was interrupted by someone calling his name.

Fear gave her the strength to shove him hard enough that he rocked back.

"They need you. Go!" she ordered.

His anguish was plain to see. Hopefully, everyone would attribute his distress to nerves over leaving home for the great unknown.

"Violet."

"Go, now!" she said harshly.

He swiped his sleeve over his dripping eyes before he turned and walked out of the bathroom. She stood there for a minute, staring at the place where he'd been standing, before she glanced in the mirror and saw her pale, blank face. Abruptly, she pushed on the door that led to her bedroom. The drawers she'd pushed in front of it, so no guests would wander into her bedroom by accident, gave way. Once she was in, she repositioned her makeshift barricade and locked her other door as well. She sent a quick text to Mom, letting her know she had a migraine and needed to lay down, and got a heart emoji in response.

She kicked off her shoes and, without bothering to change, lay on the bed in her dress. She stared at the ceiling with her hands folded neatly over her middle and tried to relax. Jesse's behavior and mood swings over the last few weeks had swung from one extreme to the next. Some days he was cold and remote. On others, he was cruel. The worst days were when he was affectionate and kind. She didn't know which Jesse she would get day to day, so she kept her guard up and didn't trust any version of him she encountered.

Including this one.

Can you forgive me?

Her hands balled into fists. How dare he ask her that after everything he put her through? He'd hijacked not just her junior year, which was one big blur, he'd taken over her *life*. He segregated her from everyone, making her an outcast not just amongst their friends, but in their family as well. Because no one believed he was capable of such dastardly deeds, she had no one to confide in or turn to.

To have her brother, who she trusted implicitly, turn into her worst enemy was a betrayal of such epic proportions that she still couldn't wrap her mind around it. She hadn't just lost her sense of self—she lost her best friend and confidant. The person she used to run to for comfort, advice, and support disappeared. In his place was a monster who looked like him and sounded like him but did the most horrific things to her. He weaponized all her faults and weaknesses against her.

Jesse stopped seeing her as a person. She became an obsession, an object to be conquered and claimed. Sex whittled their relationship down to nothing. Their verbal communication and emotional connection ceased to exist, leaving them with no foundation to rebuild upon. He irreparably damaged her trust, not just in him, but herself. How could she trust her judgment when she'd been so easily duped by his sincere, good brother act? How could she not have sensed the evil lurking behind his guileless smile? Her confidence and self-esteem had taken so many blows, she didn't feel like a whole person anymore. She no longer knew how to make a simple decision without examining it from every angle and listing every possible repercussion and consequence.

Lately, Jesse's fixation had gone into overdrive. It was like he was trying to fuse them together. He was insatiable, possessed. To preserve her sanity against his brutal onslaught, she wrapped herself in a cocoon that insulated her from his destructive wrath. The more erratic and out of control Jesse became, the calmer and more detached she was. She could see that infuriated him, but she didn't care. Self-preservation was all that mattered. All she had to do was hang on just a little longer.

She'd been counting down the months, weeks, and now, hours. She glanced at the clock and felt her heart soar. Twelve hours until he was gone. Until she got her freedom back. Until everything went back to normal. All she had to do was close her eyes. When she woke, they would have a few hours together, and then she could close the book on this chapter of her life and move on.

CHAPTER 20
VIOLET

Violet lurched up in bed before her eyes were fully open. Sunlight filtered through her blinds. She sprang up, energized, even though she'd only gotten a few hours of sleep. She tossed and turned past midnight, listening to the constant hum of voices drift down the hallway. She worried that she may have to deal with Jesse on his final night, but thankfully, he'd been otherwise occupied.

She muscled aside the drawers to gain access to the bathroom and hastily locked the door that led to Jesse's bedroom before she washed her face and brushed her teeth. There was no sound coming from Jesse's bedroom. Either he'd gotten even less sleep than her and was already up, or he was sleeping soundly. She hoped it was the latter so she wouldn't have to deal with him until he was ready to leave.

As she pulled her hair into a ponytail, she met her eyes in the mirror. Although her body buzzed with excitement, it didn't reflect in her dull eyes or stony expression. Keeping their secret had taken its toll.

Once Jesse was gone, she could actually sleep through the night—what a concept! She could enjoy life again. This was her last full summer in Texas. She should enjoy it because after she graduated, she was going to get as far from here as Mom and Dad would allow. Jesse hadn't even left yet, and she was already dreading him coming home for a visit. She needed a place where she felt safe. As long as he was allowed to walk through the front door, that would never be here. She wanted to forget everything that had happened between them and bury the sinful desires he provoked within her.

Tell me I didn't lose the most important person in the world to me.

If that were true, he would have respected her boundaries. He wouldn't have gone as far as he had. He had moments of remorse that never lasted long. Several times, he had the gall to suggest the things he did were an act of love. He was so manipulative and controlling. He would say anything to justify his behavior. His acting skills would serve him well in the future. It had gotten him this far without being caught.

She unlocked Jesse's door before she escaped back into her bedroom and hastily changed out of her pajamas. She walked down the hallway to the dining room but paused when she heard Mom sniffling and Dad's consoling tone.

"I don't want him to go," Lynne cried.

"You knew this day would come. Jesse's smart and strong. He's going to do well in the military. It's what he's always wanted," Dad said.

"He's just liked his father. He's too willing to lay his life on the line and too loyal to let anyone down. He'll give his life to them when there are so many opportunities outside of the military. He could have done anything! I was hoping he would change his mind and take after you."

There was a pause before Dad said, "It's not like my job doesn't come without risks."

"But at least we get to see you throughout the week. I can't believe he didn't stay for Violet. They were so close. What happened between them?"

Violet retreated to her bedroom. Mom had been convinced she could make Jesse change his mind and had badgered her more than Jesse. Every day, she had to lie through her teeth about pleading with Jesse to stay and being repeatedly turned down. Lynne's disappointment made her feel awful. Trying to act as if she were upset about Jesse's choice when it couldn't be further from the truth drained her. She couldn't wait for him to leave. The strain of keeping up this act was killing her. Once he left, Mom would learn how to cope without Jesse being within arm's reach, and they could build a new life without him.

She pushed her bedroom door open and stopped on the threshold when she saw Jesse standing beside her bed.

"Morning," he said.

"Morning," she echoed and stayed where she was.

He wore shorts and a white tee with his gold cross on display. His eyes were bloodshot and puffy from lack of sleep. She hoped, for his sake, his training didn't begin the moment he stepped foot on base. Actually, on second thought, she hoped there was a drill sergeant ready to stomp his ass the moment he arrived.

"You look..."

He ran his hand through his hair. "I didn't sleep."

"What time did everyone leave?"

"Brody left an hour ago." He rubbed the back of his neck. "I can't believe I'm leaving today."

"I think it's best."

He winced but nodded. An awkward silence fell.

"You should rest while you can," she said.

"No. I can always catch up on sleep. I don't want to waste the time I have left."

His eyes moved over her with such naked hunger that she tensed.

"Vi..."

"Mom's crying," she interrupted. "You should go to her."

"She has Dad."

"But she wants you."

"She's going to have to get used to me not being around." He extended his hand, palm up. "Please."

She hastily drew back. *"No."*

"Not that. I just want to hold you, I swear. I..." His expression morphed into one of abject torment. "I need you, Violet."

Ignoring his beseeching tone, she turned on her heel and marched down the hallway. When she entered the dining room, she was grateful to see Mom's episode had passed, and she was cooking in the kitchen while Dad sat at the table, drinking coffee and reading his Bible.

"You're up early, Vi," Dad observed.

"Couldn't sleep," she said and tried to look sad. She must have done a good job because Dad held out his arm. Since he wasn't one to offer hugs, she seized the opportunity and let him wrap her up tight. A second later, his hold loosened.

"Jesse," Dad greeted, ruining their moment.

She didn't turn to look at him but walked away to help Mom. She took over cooking, so Mom could sit with Jesse. Pastor Sonny's words slipped through her mind as she served breakfast and hopped up every time someone needed something. For some reason, she couldn't stay still.

Her hands fidgeted on her lap as Dad shared the passage he'd been reading in his Bible and wove the scriptures into Jesse's new beginning. Mom and Dad said fervent prayers over Jesse to protect and guide him. When silence fell, an opening for her to add her two cents, she was saved by a knock at the door. The general contractor Jesse had been working with hadn't been able to make it to the party last night, so he stopped by to see Jesse before he left. Even as Jesse stepped outside to chat with him, several cars pulled up.

Grateful for the interruption, Violet began to tidy up. She paced around the backyard, picking up stray napkins and plastic utensils that didn't make it into the trash, before she attacked the pile of dishes. Her gaze kept flicking to the large clock on the wall. Why were these last hours dragging? When the dish rack was full, she moved onto the half bath their guests had used and gave it a thorough scrub down.

When she emerged, yanking off her rubber gloves, she saw Dad's perplexed expression. She raised her brows in inquiry.

"Are you okay?" he asked.

"Yes. Why?"

"Don't you think you should be...?" He held up a hand. "Never mind."

She jutted out her hip. "What?"

"Nothing," he muttered. "Just thought you'd rather be doing something other than cleaning toilets right now."

She supposed he thought she would be clinging to Jesse's side to soak up every last second with him. A glance out the front window showed that even more people had come to say last-minute farewells. Jesse was surrounded by a small crowd. There was no need for her to fawn over him. He had enough admirers.

As she plugged in the vacuum, she saw Mom and Dad exchange concerned looks. They seemed unnerved by her calm, practical demeanor. She almost wished she could give them the over-the-top emotional reaction they expected so they would stop looking at her like she was a freak. She was *fine*. A little anxious because she hated good-byes in general. She had no idea how she was going to handle Jesse's farewell with their parent's present, but she would deal with it when the time came.

She'd vacuumed all the bedrooms and hallway and had made her way to the living room when Dad strode to the front door with Jesse's duffel. Her head whipped toward the clock. Jesse had to leave in less than fifteen minutes. The blast of excitement was so potent that she went light-headed and dropped to her hands and knees. She was so happy, her eyes welled up. He was really leaving. The vacuum roared beside her, concealing the sound of her weak giggling, which escalated into joyous laughter. She wasn't sure how long she stayed that way, but she snapped out of her delirium when the vacuum switched off.

"Violet?"

Mom's hand smoothed over her hair before it rested between her shoulder blades.

"Did you fall? Are you okay?"

She nodded and opened her mouth to reassure Mom that she was fine, but there was an invisible obstruction in her throat.

Mom rubbed her back in a circle. "Honey, what's wrong?"

Lynne's concerned tone punctured a hole in Violet's cocoon. The rush of euphoria was overpowered by a vicious flood of emotion that grabbed her by the throat, strangling her so she couldn't breathe.

"Isaac, come! Something's wrong with Violet. She's shaking like she's having a seizure or something. I—"

A horrible sound ripped through the room. It was the bone-chilling, tortured scream of a wounded animal. It went on and on. Violet tried to raise her head to see what was going on, but for some reason, she couldn't move. Why wasn't anyone helping the poor thing? It sounded like it was being gutted. Someone had to make it stop.

There was a flurry of activity around her, and then she was lifted into the air. Strong arms wrapped around her and her face was pressed against an all too familiar chest. In a distant part of her mind, she realized the awful sound had stopped. She didn't want Jesse touching her, but she wasn't in control of her faculties. She was trembling, covered in cold sweat and... sobbing? When had that happened?

"Oh, Vi," Mom choked. "What should we...?"

"Give us a moment," Jesse rasped.

He moved swiftly. Violet's ponytail swished from side to side as he carried her somewhere. He cupped the back of her head as he spoke to her, but she couldn't hear a word when she was drowning in a churning sea of emotions she'd suppressed for far too long. They were back with a vengeance, ambushing her at the worst possible moment.

Her wailing had turned into pitiful whimpering by the time a door closed.

"Thank you, God," Jesse murmured fervently as he lowered her onto something soft.

Mortification, confusion, and despair sloshed around inside of her as she tried to wipe her eyes, which was difficult since Jesse was trying to cover every inch of her face in kisses. She realized they were in her bedroom, and he'd settled her on the edge of her bed.

"I... I don't know what's wrong with me," she said raggedly.

"Say it," he pleaded. "I need to hear you admit it just once."

"Say what?" she said fretfully as she swiped at her dripping nose.

"Tell me you love me."

"What?"

She jerked back and raised her hand to slap him, but he anticipated that and seized her wrist.

"Don't fight. We don't have time," he said urgently.

"How dare you say that to me?"

Even in the midst of her fury, she kept her voice down, aware Mom and Dad were probably hovering at the end of the hallway.

"You're crying for me," he pointed out, staring at the tears that continued to trickle down her cheeks.

"I'm crying *because* of you, not *for* you, jackass."

His fingers flexed around her wrist. "You screamed like someone plunged a dagger in your heart, Vi."

A part of her had suspected that she was responsible for that bloodcurdling, banshee shriek, but she hadn't wanted to admit it to herself. She scraped her mind for a plausible explanation for her breakdown. Ten minutes ago, she could have gone jogging and now, she felt like she had the flu. She was feverish, shaky, nauseated, and her body ached like she'd been beaten with a bat.

Jesse cupped her clammy cheek. "You care for me, Violet. As much as you want to deny it, as much as you wish you didn't, you do."

Her free hand twisted in his damp shirt as she bared her

teeth at him. "How could I possibly love someone who's hurt me as much as you have?"

His mouth twisted in a bittersweet smile. "Because when you love, you do it with your whole heart. You give so completely, there's no taking it back."

Even as his words speared her heart, she held his gaze as she enunciated in a voice that trembled, "I do *not* love you."

"Okay," he said gently.

"I hate you," she spat.

His fingers brushed through her waterfall of tears. "I know."

She desperately tried to get a hold of herself as her emotions ravaged her insides. "I need you to go."

"Is that what you really want?"

"Yes!"

He looked down at the hand she didn't realize was still twisted in his shirt. She was horrified to see that, contrary to what her mouth was saying, she was tugging him toward her. She released him as if he burned her and shot to her feet. She snatched tissues from her nightstand and frantically mopped up her face. What the hell was wrong with her? Why couldn't she stop crying?

"Violet."

She whirled with a snarl. "Why are you still here? Go! *Leave!*"

His eyes were a little wild as he stared at her. "I would have stayed if you asked me to, but it's too late."

Her heart skipped. "I didn't ask you to." That fiery volcano inside of her spewing lava added, "Why would I ask you to stay? I'm thrilled you're leaving! This is a dream come true. I've been counting down the days!"

"You're going to deny it to the bitter end," he said with a shake of his head.

"There's nothing to deny! I hate your guts!"

His eyes narrowed a second before he lunged at her. He clapped a hand over her mouth before she could utter a sound and drove her backward into the wall.

"You don't know when to quit," he bit out through clenched teeth. "If I had more time, I'd prove what a fucking lie that is."

He buried his face in her hair, inhaled, and groaned before he slumped against her.

"How am I going to live without you? I miss you already, and you're right here." His hand fisted in her hair. "I'm going for both our sakes, to give us time and space to regain some sanity."

He tugged on her hair, forcing her head back to look at him. His shadowed gaze, full of aggravated yearning, moved over her face.

"Hopefully, while I'm gone, you'll come to your senses."

She yanked his hand off her mouth to hiss, "I have come to my senses! I never want to see you again!"

A muscle ticked in his jaw. "You're so fucking stubborn."

She pushed at his chest. "You have to go."

"Kiss me goodbye."

She went rigid. "No!"

"Please. Just this once," he said raggedly and brushed his lips back and forth across hers, tempting her to engage. "One last kiss."

Why did her heart feel like it was breaking? Why was her entire body trembling with grief and sorrow? This is what she wanted. What she'd prayed for. She reached the end of the tunnel but hadn't stepped into the sunshine. For some reason, she hesitated in the shadows and wasn't making a break for freedom. What the hell was wrong with her? Why had one of her hands twisted in his shirt, once again holding him to her, instead of shoving him away as he deserved?

As if he knew her tumultuous thoughts, his mouth curved in a shaky, agonizing smile. His bloodshot eyes were suspiciously bright.

"You're beautiful on the inside and out, pitying a monster, even though you try not to. I can see you're fighting it, but God did say to love your enemy."

Even as she hauled in a breath to verbally rip him to shreds, he disarmed her when he brushed the tip of his nose against hers, a gesture of affection he hadn't done since they were kids. Her mind flooded with memories of a happier time. A time she hadn't allowed herself to think about because it hurt too much to remember how much they'd lost. How had this all gone so wrong? Her mouth trembled as a tear slipped down her face.

"I'm sorry, Violet. For everything. If you can't forgive me, have mercy on me."

She wasn't sure why that plea made her stomach drop but combined with the sound of an invisible clock ticking, she felt a mounting sense of dread and urgency. This was it. He wasn't going away for a weekend or even a week or two like he did when he went to sports camps. He was *leaving*. They didn't know when they would see each other again. His life wouldn't be his own once he walked out the door. The military would dictate everything from here on out. She despised him, but if something happened to him, and she denied him this, could she ever forgive herself?

Shutting down all rational thought, she clasped the back of his neck and set her mouth on his. Anger was her driving emotion. She funneled the tornado of her destructive emotions into him. She was the aggressor, the one who nipped and bit and wanted him to hurt. He let her do what she wanted to him and when she gave him an opening, he returned her aggression with tenderness. He kissed her in a way that left her feeling raw, shaken, and heartbroken.

When her legs gave out, he held her in the crook of one arm and cradled her face as he cherished her and repented for all the wrong he'd done. Attuned to him as she was, she sensed his desire, but it was tainted by the sharp tang of fear. Realizing he wasn't as confident as he appeared, she couldn't stop herself from trying to console him. Her fingers bunched in his hair as she kissed him back, comforting and reassuring him in the only form of communicating they had left.

"Jesse?"

Mom's call seemed to come from a million miles away.

Jesse reluctantly disengaged and cleared his throat before he called out, "I'll be out in a minute."

Eyes awash with regret moved over Violet's face as if he were trying to memorize it.

"Thank you," he said gruffly, and tried to ease away from her, but her arms locked around him. "Violet?"

She was struck with sudden terror over a future without him in it. He had been the only constant in her life for almost five years. He was her tormentor, but also her protector. A part of her knew he would always have her back, and now she would have no one. She was going to be alone again.

"Vi, I have to go."

"Jesse."

She heard the inadvertent plea in her voice. Pain ripped

across his features as he closed his eyes, shedding a tear that he transferred to her when he gave her a hard kiss.

"I'll come back," he said fiercely, before he ripped himself away from her.

She took a step after him, hand outstretched to grab hold of him, but he was too quick. He didn't look back as he strode out of her bedroom. She listened to his swift, heavy footfalls go down the hall.

"Is Violet okay?" Mom asked.

"No," Jesse said curtly. "She isn't going to see me off. We have to get going."

There was a flurry of movement and then the sound of the front door closing, the rev of an engine, and then silence.

Violet dropped to the carpet and finally let loose the scream that had been bottled up inside of her. Now that she was alone, everything she had crammed down for over nine months spilled out. She raged, pounding the carpet with her fists until they were numb. She cried until she retched and, when she collapsed on the bathroom floor, wondered why she felt like she'd just lost her best friend.

<hr>

Violet tossed and turned. She moved around so much, her fitted sheet came undone, forcing her to remake her bed.

By the time Mom and Dad had returned home, she was semi-presentable, though her eyes that were nearly swollen shut let them know what she'd done in the interim. Strangely, her volatile emotional state seemed to have cured Lynne of hers. Mom spent the rest of the day treating her like she was sick—swaddling her with blankets even though it was hot as hell outside, making her soup, and coddling her.

Violet pummeled her pillow before she flopped on her side and stared at the bathroom door that she'd closed out of habit. Now, she could leave it open if she wanted to. She had to remember to ask Dad to fix the lock. She was so tired, she felt ill, but she couldn't sleep. She should be dead to the world, getting the best sleep of her life. Instead, she was staring at the door, willing it to open.

With a low growl, she rolled out of bed, yanked the door open and marched into Jesse's bedroom. She surveyed his tidy, empty room, illuminated by streetlights, with bitter, glistening eyes.

She ruined the taut sheets when she crawled over it. She breathed deep. The scent of his musk imbedded in the sheets comforted, even as it infuriated her.

She rolled onto her back and, under the gaze of his favorite football player, sank her hand into her pajama bottoms. She was soaking wet. Depraved memories played through her mind, making her writhe and pant and when she came, she hated that she moaned his name.

She stared at the ceiling as she came down from her high. She thought she was reclaiming her sexuality by masturbating in his room, the place where he initiated and corrupted her. She should have felt victorious, but as always, she felt empty. She couldn't believe he was really gone.

She turned onto her belly and, in the darkness, sobbed her heart out.

"Violet?"

She opened her eyes and was confused by the orientation of the room until she realized she was in Jesse's. Mom stood in the doorway with bleary eyes and messy hair.

She opened her mouth to say something, but before she could, the tears started again. Mom's expression softened as she came forward. Violet held up a hand, not wanting to be touched, but Mom ignored that and hauled her into her arms.

"I know, honey. I miss him too," Mom murmured.

Violet fisted her hand in Mom's robe. Her body still yearned for him and her emotions were still entangled, despite her best efforts to block him out. It would take time to break the ties between them, but once she did, she would never let him back in.

CHAPTER 21
VIOLET

2 MONTHS LATER

"HAPPY BIRTHDAY TO YOU. HAPPY BIRTHDAY TO YOU. HAPPY birthday, dear Violet," Mom and Dad sang. "Happy birthday to you!"

Violet couldn't help but laugh as Lynne clapped, hopped, and sang at the top of her voice. The kindergarten teacher in her had never been more evident than at this moment.

"Now close your eyes and make a wish!" Lynne encouraged and held up a finger. "And know that all your dreams are within reach!"

Violet dutifully closed her eyes for show and waited an appropriate amount of time before she blew out the candles.

"Woo-hoo!" Lynne cheered and turned on the dining room lights to reveal the smoking candles. "Eighteen," Lynne marveled and wrapped her arms around Violet. "I can't believe it. You're all grown up."

Violet allowed herself to lean into Lynne. Dad watched them with a fond smile.

Lynne kissed the top of her head. "You're the best daughter. We're so happy to have you here with us."

Violet lowered her gaze and ignored the sudden lump in her throat. Lynne gave her a squeeze and went into the kitchen to fetch bowls and ice cream.

"Did you have a good day at school?" Dad asked.

Violet nodded and, to avoid eye contact, reached out to stroke the velvet petals of a rose in a vase in the middle of the table. "Everyone remembers my birthday since it's back-to-back with us starting school. My friends got me enough balloons to make my backpack float," she joked.

"Are you sure you don't want a party? This is the first time you haven't had one, and eighteen's such a special year," Lynne said as she cut into the strawberry cake.

"I don't need a party. I'm happy with this," Violet said, gesturing between the three of them. "And you paid for us to go to that concert. We'll celebrate then."

"Here you go." Mom placed a generous slice of strawberry cake and two scoops of ice cream in front of her. "For the sweetest birthday girl."

They had followed the same ritual for her birthday that Lynne established five years ago. She woke to one dozen pink roses and red velvet pancakes for breakfast, followed by her favorite meal for dinner and now strawberry cake and ice cream. Usually, she had a party on the weekend after her birthday, but this year she asked to skip it. The concert tickets Mom and Dad had bought for her and her friends were more than enough. Everything was as it should be. Better, actually. So, why wasn't she happy? Why didn't she feel anything?

She refused to look to her left, where Jesse used to sit.

Even though he wasn't there, she felt the heaviness of his presence. He was everywhere and yet, nowhere. It had been almost two months since he left. She assumed once he was gone that she would magically revert to who she'd been, only to realize that part of her was gone forever.

Her grand plans of enjoying the rest of her summer never came to fruition. After Jesse left, she shut down. She had a hard time getting out of bed and struggled to do basic daily functions. The thing that snapped her out of her zombie state was Mom suggesting she speak to Pastor Sonny or one of the other church leaders. Fear of being questioned galvanized her into action.

She thought she would no longer have to act, but she was putting on the performance of her life. All eyes had always been on Jesse. Without him to deflect everyone's attention from her, she now had to work three times as hard to appear normal. She did what was required of her. She did her chores, went to church, and had recently returned to school for her senior year. She responded when spoken to and smiled on command, but she felt absolutely nothing. When she was alone and no longer had to pretend that she was like everyone else, she plummeted into a mental space so bleak that she worried about her sanity.

Although she'd been half expecting it, her heart stopped when Mom's phone rang. Mom dropped her bowl with a clatter and sprinted to the counter, where the phone was charging. From her delighted expression, Violet knew who the caller was before Mom announced, "It's Jesse!"

As her body went numb, she asked Dad, "How's Uncle Perry?"

Dad took his gaze from Mom and focused on her. "He's still in the hospital." Dad shook his head. "He dropped two stories with that toddler in his arms. The kid didn't have a scratch. Perry's lucky he just broke his leg and not his—"

"Violet?"

She turned her head and saw Mom holding out her cell phone.

"Jesse wants to wish you a happy birthday."

Even as dread weighted down her limbs, making her stumble as she rose from her chair, Violet tried to look eager rather than sick to her stomach.

Mom gave her a puzzled look as she handed over the phone. "Jesse said he's been trying to get in touch with you all day."

Violet pressed the mute button before she said, "Really? Huh. I don't know why I didn't see his messages." She put the phone to her ear and said a bright, "Hello?"

"Violet?"

The sound of Jesse's voice unleashed a torrent of emotion that made her knees buckle. She braced her hand on the table as she bowed her head and closed her eyes to get a handle on herself.

"Thank you," she said, as if Jesse had wished her a happy birthday and tried to inject some warmth and enthusiasm into her voice as she asked, "How are you doing?"

She hadn't heard his voice since the day he left. She blocked his number so he wouldn't be able to contact her, and managed to avoid speaking to him whenever he called their parents by making herself scarce or saying she would call him back on her phone and never doing so. She considered having a party just to have more people around so she would have an excuse to skirt this phone call. Stupidly, she'd hoped Jesse would forget or be too busy to call. Now she had no choice but to carry on a fake conversation in front of her parents. She would leave it up to Jesse to explain why he was unable to hear anything on his end. He was good at making up lies.

"I'm sorry, I didn't get your messages. Maybe I need to get my phone checked out," she said.

"Mom, are you there?" Jesse asked impatiently.

Her nails sank into her palms. Memories swarmed over her, reviving needs she was desperately trying to forget. She opened her eyes and saw Mom watching her intently. Violet flashed a megawatt smile as she said, "We just finished dinner. We're eating cake and ice cream." She let out a false laugh and said, "No. Not German chocolate cake, but we did have buttermilk pie recently. Dad got two pies all to himself."

"That's what you get when you go to the military! No home cooked meals!" Dad said loudly and took a swat on the arm from Mom before he carried his bowl into the living room to finish eating in front of the TV.

"Mom? Violet?" Jesse called.

Violet moved into the kitchen as Mom began to clear the table and asked, "What have you been up to? Are they treating you good?"

"Mom," Jesse bit out.

Violet's stomach churned. He sounded different. Harder, colder. Even his voice had deepened.

"Mom? What the hell?" Jesse snapped and hung up.

Violet blew out a breath. "Uh-huh," she said, nodding. "That doesn't sound too bad." She wiped down the counters as she chattered for show. "School's been good. At first, I loved driving myself everywhere, but now I miss being a passenger princess. Can you believe that? Oh my gosh. You know who I saw recently? I..."

She yanked the phone away from her ear when it began

to ring loudly. Why hadn't she thought to turn off the volume? Damn! When Mom frowned, Violet widened her eyes. "I didn't even know we got disconnected."

She answered the phone and immediately pressed the mute button again.

"How long was I talking to myself?" Violet asked ruefully.

"Mom?" Jesse called in a clipped tone.

"That long?" Violet chuckled before she flicked her hand. "I was just talking about school and wishing you could chauffeur me around like the good old days."

When Mom turned away with a smile and went to join Dad in the living room, Violet's tense shoulders dropped.

Jesse's voice abruptly hardened. "Damn it, Vi. I know you're there. Answer me."

Her hand tightened on the phone. "You're almost done with basic training, right?"

"It's been two months," he rasped. "Let me hear your voice."

Fuck him. She wouldn't give him anything he wanted ever again, even if it was just the sound of her voice.

"Oh, really?" she asked, trying to sound interested.

"If you don't talk to me, I'm going to tell Mom," Jesse said.

Outrage seared her throat. She should be the one threatening him, not the other way around! She wanted to slam the phone on the counter until it came apart in pieces. Instead, she held her smile, though it was now more of a sneer as she unmuted the call. Thankfully, Mom and Dad were watching the news and not paying attention to her.

"You're an asshole," she said quietly.

He exhaled before he said grimly, "This is the only way I can get you to talk to me since you blocked me."

"You're blocked for a reason."

He ignored that and asked, "How... how have you been?"

He sounded nervous and awkward.

She glanced at Mom and Dad before she hurried down the hallway to her bedroom. If she had to speak to him, she wanted privacy to say what she needed to.

"I was okay until I had to talk to you," she retorted as she closed her bedroom door and punched one of the balloons a friend had given her.

"I wanted to tell you happy birthday."

"Thank you," she said ungraciously. "Is that it?"

"No, I..."

"You what?" she demanded. "What do you want from me?"

She hated the warble in her voice. She'd hoped the next time they interacted that she would be stone-cold, but clearly, not enough time had passed. His voice whipped her emotions into a frenzy. She hated that he had such power over her, but she hated even more her body's response. The neglected space between her legs throbbed, begging to be possessed. What the hell was wrong with her? What kind of sicko missed the fucked-up things he used to do to her?

A filthy slut, that's who, her inner critic jeered. She bit her lip hard enough to make it bleed to disrupt the scathing litany and focused in time to hear Jesse say, "I want what I've always wanted. You."

Her hand whistled as it slashed through the air. "You can't have me! You'll never have me. I want nothing to do with you. Why can't you understand that?"

"I didn't call to upset you," he said wearily

"Then you should have left me alone! You know I don't want to talk to you. Why force me?"

His voice shredded as he said with a little heat of his own, "Because I miss you! Not seeing you, not being able to talk to you has been hell. We've never been apart this long. I'm going crazy. Don't you miss me at all?"

She swallowed the lump in her throat. The worst part was, she did miss him, and she hated herself for it.

Her prolonged silence made him sigh. She couldn't see him, but she imagined him running his hands through his hair.

"I thought..." He hesitated and then said in a rush, "The day I left, you held on to me. You didn't want me to go. Damn it, you kissed me back, Vi!"

She flinched as her stomach churned, threatening to expel her favorite cake. That day haunted her because it demonstrated how weak she was when it came to him. It didn't matter what he did to her. Her defenses would never be as strong as they needed to be where he was concerned. She had to keep him at a distance, which was possible now that he was in the military. She thought she'd built up some resistance to him, but this phone call proved her shields were as sturdy as wet napkins.

"You can't hold what I did that day against me. I didn't know what I was doing! I was messed up—I'm *still* messed up because of you. I don't know if I'll ever be..."

She pressed the back of her hand to her mouth to smother a rogue sob without success. She shut her eyes, utterly humiliated. She hadn't even been talking to him for two minutes, and she was spiraling out of control.

"Don't cry," he said gruffly. "Or so help me God, I'm going to show up."

"I'm not crying," she lied defiantly. "And you can't 'show up'. They decide what you do now."

"That's why I wanted to talk to you. I'm almost done

with basic training, and I have the opportunity to come home before I—"

"*What?*" she quietly shrieked.

"I may be able to stay for a week or two before I ship off to Alaska."

"D-did you mention this to M-mom or Dad?" She was so rattled, her words tripped over one another.

"No. I wanted to talk to you first. It was supposed to be a surprise for your birthday."

"*No!*"

"I need to see you," he said desperately. "I'm dying without you."

"You can't shove me back into your twisted game again! I can't do it!"

"I won't," he began earnestly, but she cut him off.

"Don't make promises we both know you can't keep!"

The thought of seeing him again threw her into a panic. She thought she would have six months or more to prepare before facing him. The thought of seeing him any sooner was horrifying.

"You don't know what you did to me," she said in a strangled voice. "I am not okay. I'm just starting to feel human again, and you want to come back and break me all over again."

"I don't—"

"You've done it countless times! That's all you know how to do! I don't know how you can live with yourself when I don't want to live with myself. How do you do it?"

"*Violet.*"

His voice cracked like a whip, but she didn't want to hear what he had to say. He had to stay away. Her sanity depended on it. She was barely hanging on. If he came back, it would destroy her. She couldn't take another round of him, not when she had finally adjusted to his absence. In the past, she did her best to keep him from seeing how much damage he inflicted, but she would reveal all if it would keep him at bay.

"I thought once you were gone, I would feel better, but..." She shuddered as the ever-present shame rose up to choke her. "Every time I get in the car, I think of all the things you've done to me in it. I go to church, and I think of what you did to me on that stage. I go to school, and I think of all the places you took me, the things you forced me to do..." Her hands brushed at the invisible sludge she could feel on her body, but could never remove, no matter how hard she scrubbed.

"Baby."

She stomped her foot. "Don't call me that! Don't call me anything. Don't talk to me!" she said wildly as she mentally unraveled.

"Violet."

"Do you know what I did today?" She clutched the phone in a death grip as her eyes filled with tears. "My friends wanted to treat me to lunch, but instead of going with them, I drove to that park where you broke me the first time. The place where you showed me the real you. I sat there and thought about ending it all."

There was no sound on the other end of the line. She wasn't sure if the call dropped, but she kept talking. Now that she'd confessed the dark path her mind had taken to the one person who would understand why, she couldn't stop.

"I am barely hanging on," she said hoarsely as tears poured down her face. "All the secrets and lies... I can't do it anymore. I can't live like this."

As the pain mounted to an unbearable degree, her eyes

flicked around the room for something to inflict damage on her person before she closed her eyes, willing away the violent, compulsive urges brought on by the self-loathing she couldn't shirk.

"If you ever felt anything for me, you'd stay away."

Silence.

"I'll never ask anything of you ever again," she pleaded. "Just don't come home, at least while I'm here. After I graduate, you can see Mom and Dad whenever you want."

"Is that what you really want?" he asked in a stifled tone.

"Yes."

There was a brief pause and then, "If that's what you need."

Relief made her legs weak. She collapsed on the edge of her bed and dropped her face in her hand. "Thank you."

"Violet, I... I never meant to hurt you."

She knew he heard her whimpering because his voice broke.

"I swear I can fix this if you give me a chance."

"You can't f-fix something that's shattered into a m-million pieces," she said raggedly.

"I'll spend the rest of my life finding every piece and putting it back where it belongs," he said fervently.

"I used to think you were heaven sent," she said in a hollow voice. "I loved you more than I loved myself. I made so many excuses for you because I didn't want to believe the truth." Her breath hitched before she finished, "You're the worst thing that ever happened to me. I don't ever want to see you again."

The call ended. She wasn't sure if they got disconnected or if he hung up. Either way, she was grateful because she reached the end of her rope. The phone tumbled across the carpet after it fell from her nerveless fingers.

She had officially severed their bond. She felt the disconnect as acutely as if she severed a limb. Internally, she was screaming that same bloodcurdling cry she had the day he left. It was the grief-stricken wail of a woman who had lost someone she didn't think she could live without, but she had no choice. Cutting him out of her life was the only way she could cope. She had the misfortune to give her heart to a monster who damaged her so severely, she would never be the same. It was the right thing to do, so why did she feel like she was back in that dark tunnel without light or hope?

She wrapped her arms around herself and folded at the waist. Fat, salty tears rained down on her pink heart socks. Her agony was so profound she couldn't make a sound.

She lost countless battles, but she just won the war. Jesse would honor his promise. She would never see him again. She should have been elated and relieved. Instead, she mourned. Jesse was right. When she loved, she did it completely, which meant she would never be whole again.

AUTHOR'S NOTE

I hope you enjoyed this installment of Jesse and Violet's story. This prequel was written almost 6 years after I wrote Corrupt Idol. I never intended to write a prequel, but when I read Corrupt Idol during a break from another series, my brain started turning over some ideas.

Piecing their history together through details I carelessly dropped in Corrupt Idol was an interesting challenge. I hadn't planned for this book to be dual POV, but was pleasantly surprised when Jesse stepped up to the plate in chapter 1. I don't know if any book has surprised me as much as this one has. I felt like every chapter held a twist or revelation I was clueless about until Jesse or Violet decided to share it. This book was an emotional rollercoaster that challenged me personally and professionally. I stepped back and let the characters tell the story at their pace. I think the results are heartbreakingly, uniquely theirs.

I do plan to write a sequel to Corrupt Idol, but I have contracts and other projects I need to fulfill as dark romance writer, Mia Knight. I will post an update when I am back in Violet and Jesse's world! If you'd like to read the raw draft of Corrupt Obsession or deleted scenes, you can join Ream.

Thank you for coming on this journey with me. If you have a chance, please leave a review and recommend my books to other readers. This helps me out so much, especially since my stories are banned from most retailers.

Thank you for your support. I couldn't do this without you.

Sincerely,
  Dinah

BOOKS BY DINAH HARPER

Possessing Violet Series:

Corrupt Obsession

Corrupt Idol

About the Author

Dinah Harper will have you squirming in your seat and looking around to make sure no one can see what you're reading. The *Possessing Violet Series* is the first of many erotic novels she has planned.

Please be patient. She is currently under contract for several projects as dark romance author, Mia Knight. When she resumes her work as Dinah Harper, she will update her blog and social media. Sign up to her newsletter (https://www.subscribepage.com/DinahHarperNews) to stay informed about future releases!

Website: https://dinahharper.com

instagram.com/authordinahharper

bookbub.com/authors/dinah-harper

goodreads.com/dinahharper

reamstories.com/miaknightwrites

Acknowledgments

I wanted to thank all of my supporters on Patreon & Ream! I wouldn't be able to do this without you. Your support grants me the time needed to bring this story to life and I'm so incredibly grateful for each and every one of you!

Special thanks to my amazing Super Patrons/Baddies:

- A. Jay
- Alexandria
- Bibiana
- Carrie Cross
- Pooja
- Sam Sodi
- Sami Bullock

www.ingramcontent.com/pod-product-compliance
Lightning Source LLC
Chambersburg PA
CBHW030754310726
48969CB00005B/1403